The
Dog I Loved

The
Dog I Loved

SUSAN WILSON

ST. MARTIN'S PRESS ❧ NEW YORK

First published in the United States by St. Martin's Press, an imprint of St. Martin's Publishing Group

THE DOG I LOVED. Copyright © 2019 by Susan Wilson. All rights reserved. Printed in the United States of America. For information, address St. Martin's Publishing Group, 120 Broadway, New York, NY 10271.

www.stmartins.com

Designed by Omar Chapa

Library of Congress Cataloging-in-Publication Data

Names: Wilson, Susan, 1951– author.
Title: The dog I loved / Susan Wilson.
Description: First edition. | New York: St. Martin's Press, 2019.
Identifiers: LCCN 2019019290| ISBN 9781250078148 (hardcover) |
    ISBN 9781466890473 (ebook)
Classification: LCC PS3573.I47533 D63 2019 | DDC 813/.54—dc23
LC record available at https://lccn.loc.gov/2019019290

Our books may be purchased in bulk for promotional, educational, or business use. Please contact your local bookseller or the Macmillan Corporate and Premium Sales Department at 1-800-221-7945, extension 5442, or by email at MacmillanSpecialMarkets@macmillan.com.

First Edition: November 2019

10 9 8 7 6 5 4 3 2 1

To my grandchildren, Claire, Will, and Rocco.

And in memory of three dogs we loved, Bonnie, Hunter, and

Moshup.

Author's Note

Earliest in its settlement, the area now known as Dogtown was once the Commons and populated by settlers on Cape Ann who preferred the relative safety of the boulder-strewn highlands to the coast and its vulnerability to pirates and weather. By the Revolution, most of those who could had migrated to the coast, where the sea provided a better living than the difficult terrain best left to sheep. The land was deforested, Gloucester had become a renowned port, and the small village was left to those who were on the fringes of society, mainly women. Independent, doing whatever needed to be done to keep body and soul together, it was inevitable that the women, many of whom were widows of soldiers who had fought in both the Revolution and the War of 1812, came to be regarded as mad, cunning, harlots, and, of course, witches. The dying village became pejoratively known as Dogtown, as the widows were known for keeping dogs. No one has kept a record of what these dogs looked like or were called, only that they were the widows' protectors and companions—their familiars.

Prologue

Ours have been watchers for generations. We are the guards and keep our charges safe. We never forget our purpose, our contract. They need us, my kind, as they did in the ancient dark days. They still do. They are the lost, the friendless, the grieving. You've seen us, huddled beside the homeless, giving comfort to the unnerved, the ill. We have done so for centuries. Where we once guarded against predators, we now guard against loneliness.

We keep to the shadows until we are needed.

Part One

Rosie

The judge gaveled her verdict and gray flooded my vision, as if a Technicolor world had reversed itself into black and white. The gray shrouded me as I was led from the courtroom into a holding cell. I don't remember anything beyond being in that cell until the van that took me to Mid-State Women's Correctional Facility drove through the high gates that would be my perimeter for however many years I would be incarcerated. I had been sentenced to twenty years. At my age, having then just turned twenty-five, it might as well have been life. The grayness that encompassed my vision was abetted by the gray scale of my environment, walls, floors, bars, even the stainless-steel tables and chairs in the dining hall; the bland food. The high windows, crosshatched with wire, showed only the hazy dirty white of sky. The only dash of color that broke through my clouded vision that first day was the bright red tie that Warden Hinckley wore against a dingy white shirt.

I was marched, hands and feet shackled—as if I were a danger to anyone—into the building, processed in every way

as humiliatingly as possible, and then I meekly followed my
inmate guide to the cinder-block-and-steel space that would be
my new home. A set of bunk beds, a seatless toilet/sink combination. Two tiny three-drawer bureaus. My cellmate—sorry,
roommate, as in some arcane nod to civility our cells were always referred to as our *rooms*—wasn't there, but evidence of
her presence was dense in that tiny space. Crayon drawings
taped to the walls, a single photograph of a curly-haired child.
A pervasive odor. I sat on the edge of the lower bunk and
waited.

If my vision had become monochromatic, my hearing had
gone dull. The silence of submersion. That's what it felt like,
being underwater. This time, my submersion might have been
giving in to drowning.

The gray cloud that enveloped me darkened perceptibly.
My roommate had arrived. Treena Bellaqua was a big woman,
tattooed like a Fiji fisherman, and fifteen years my senior. "Don't
talk to me, don't look at me, and don't put your stuff anywhere
near mine and we'll get along." I'd had bad roommates before,
and I should have tried to muster some spine in order to claim
what should have been mine, but that might have proved to
be futile and, frankly, dangerous. Instinctively, I didn't look her
in the eyes. I presented no challenge. The fact was, I wasn't up
to any sort of challenge, I could hardly breathe, much less go
toe-to-toe with Treena. All I wanted was the quiet oblivion of
elusive sleep.

"Get offa my bed. You got the top."

"I'm sorry. I didn't know."

"That's your one—and I repeat, one—pass. Next time, I
won't be so nice."

Self-preservation is involuntary, even in one so distraught
by circumstances that the only imaginable release is self-

destruction. I meekly climbed up onto what would be my only oasis in a metal and cement jungle.

It wasn't a predestined trajectory. I was the good girl, the smart one, the hope of my parents, the only girl and the youngest of six. I had the exquisite Communion dress, the tap-dance lessons, the pink, pink, pink of my tiny bedroom, my bike, my dresses. My mother indulged herself in creating out of my rough clay the girl child beloved of big Irish families. Innocent. Devoted. Loyal.

No, I wasn't the Collins destined for a life of crime. Bobby was the one in our family voted most likely to end up in Walpole. He, too, bucked our expectations and thumbed his nose at his past. Instead of ending up behind bars, he ended up with an MBA. I started off with a Seven Sisters education, and found myself on this very gray day being escorted into Mid-State Women's Correctional Facility, convicted of murdering my fiancé—well, technically I was convicted of *voluntary manslaughter*, but when you're sentenced to twenty years, why quibble about legal nomenclature? I was behind bars.

Charles Montgomery Foster came into my life in a somewhat old-fashioned way, given the ubiquitous online dating scene that most of my friends liked. I was a recent college graduate marking time before my first "real" job with a minimumwage gig as a barista. Charles was one of the Hugo Boss–suited people who descended from the glass towers of their downtown Boston office buildings to grab a macchiato—no froth, soy milk, caramel drizzle. He looked like he might have been in finance, or a lawyer; there is no distinction in the uniform of suit jackets and slightly loosened Vineyard Vines ties. What Charles looked like to me was the kind of man who might be interested in hiring a very well educated, unskilled but enthusiastic-to-learn young woman desirous of a high-income career path. He looked, in other words, like someone *with* a high income. My Bunker Hill slice of Charlestown might not have been considered a sophisticated neighborhood, more Dennis Lehane's mean streets than Charlestown Navy Yard penthouses overlooking Boston Harbor, but I knew good threads when I saw them, and good manners. And a really nice haircut. Charles was in real estate development, which I soon learned meant being among those whose main interest in the poor side of town was to gentrify it through urban renewal until the locals were forced out.

I never intended to fall in love with Charles. I only wanted a job, a good one. One that would help me keep up with the student loans that sucked my barista paycheck dry and left me living back with my parents and my paraplegic brother, Teddy. Teddy was thirteen years old when he got in the way of a bullet meant for someone else. I was eleven and suffered a quick demotion from highly favored child to appendix. The rest of his brothers treated him like he was not just handicapped but also emotionally fragile. While they would beat on one another and say truly horrible things, with Teddy they were reserved. Not so much me. And Teddy loved me for it. For treating him like he was just like the others, rude, smelly, dirty-mouthed, and bossy. Teddy hated Charles on sight.

Charles—never Charlie, or Chuck, or Chick, as anyone named Charles would have been called in my neighborhood—hadn't actually become a Hugo Boss–wearing corporate type through hard work and an upward trajectory. He was a lifelong rich kid. When they speak of being born with a silver spoon in your mouth, Charles was just such a one. It's a pretty common story. The inherited wealth coming down through generations of really smart money-manager types, the original wad having been earned on the exploitation of workers. In

Charles's case, his family wealth came from oil. Not crude, but whale oil. His whale ship-owning ancestor was smart enough to get out of the business before it became last century's technology, moving right along to textiles, and then, when that industry began to fail, the early-twentieth-century version of Charles Montgomery Foster turned to armaments. Given the never-ending need for the materiel of war, the family has been capitalizing on the world's propensity for conflict ever since. Of course, Charles never spoke of it, preferring to let most people believe his money came from the more pacific growth industry of real estate development.

Throughout that summer, I began to anticipate Charles's daily arrival, to notice that he was beginning to flirt back, our banter becoming a well-practiced foreplay to a better acquaintance. I started keeping a second white shirt just in case the first became stained. Even early on, I recognized a fastidiousness in Charles, who always accepted his frothy drink with a napkin in his hand. Coming from a big, messy family, I thought him ever so sophisticated. *Refined.* That was the word.

If I thought that being in prison was going to be a little bit like being in a women's college, I wasn't entirely wrong. Estrogen-stoked drama. The sameness was a cadre of women all vying for sink time. Getting our periods simultaneously. Mooning over the pretty boy—or girl—celebrity of the moment.

In college, there were LUGs—lesbians until graduation. I quickly discovered that in prison there are LURs—lesbians until release. There were some real love affairs going on, and if one partner was released, there was real heartbreak. The divide between the incarcerated and the free is of Grand Canyon proportions. The released did not come back to visit the left behind; they were not allowed to come back—even if they had wanted to.

Another key difference was the range of ages among the incarcerated. Where college had at best a prodigy of fifteen and a thirty-year-old mom attending on a special returned-to-college scholarship, here my peers ranged from nineteen to seventy-five. Pubescence to senility, and every life stage in between.

The differences showed in other ways. Where my classmates in college demonstrated their superiority to my origins in fashion and in high culture–referenced witticisms, my fellow inmates at Mid-State flaunted their badassness in demonstrations of power. Influence. Intimidation. I thought I was as unlike them as I had been unlike my classmates. But in college, all I wanted was to be *like* my classmates, to blend in.

In college, I was Target to their Bergdorf. In prison, I was Target to their St. Vincent de Paul charity shops. In college, I was a quick study, and by my second year no one would ever have known that I hadn't actually skied in Aspen. I presented myself as just as sophisticated as they were by wearing thrift store chic. I started a trend. In prison, we all wore cheap jeans and Keds.

I thought that as I had acquired the right table manners and used impeccable grammar, I would easily fit into Charles's world. I had moved beyond my respectable, if rough-around-the-edges, upbringing. If my neutral accent slipped now and again into East Boston, Charles would let me know. I thought I was passing. Except that Charles's mother, Cecily Foster, sniffed out my humble beginnings like a bloodhound sniffs out a fugitive. More than a misplaced *r*, it was my name. Mary Rose Collins. Rosie. The Mary is after my maternal grandmother, herself named in honor of the Virgin. The Rose is after my dad's eccentric aunt Rosalie, who left home to pursue stardom and ended up portraying an Irish maid on a radio soap opera before she tragically died. Mrs. Foster, née Burgess, was one generation from English aristocracy, or so she would have you believe, and we all know how the mid-century English viewed the Irish. Good for servants, not so much for family.

In prison, I was once again the odd one out. I hadn't been raped by an "uncle" or been a drug mule for a boyfriend. Or impregnated at fourteen. I wasn't there because of strict mandatory sentencing for possessing a few too many ounces of pot. My blue-collar origins stood me in no good stead in this mix of rural poor, urban poor, underserved, undereducated, and overwhelmed women. And my venture into the upper-class world, however horribly it had turned out, only made me less adaptable. Besides, I was only one of maybe seven white women in the prison. I stood out. If you were white, you had to have done something truly heinous to get put in this maximum-security penitentiary; white women with slightly lesser crimes were sent elsewhere to serve out their terms. The fact that I had killed my fiancé didn't even give me enough cred to get a little bit of respect among women who had tortured rivals, shot or stabbed boyfriends. Women whose craving for drugs was ceaseless and their moods volatile.

Oh yes. Cecily Foster had made damned sure that I was thoroughly punished. I was never offered a plea bargain, which at worst might have put me in a minimum-security correctional facility; at Mid-State there were no white-collar criminals, no accidental felons.

Money and influence. Cecily Foster wielded them as if they were tools of some craft known only to the upper reaches of society. Charles was her only child. Even before the accident, Cecily hated me, the cheap harpy who'd dragged her boy down into associating with the common.

I, of course, had neither money nor influence. The valuables I might have hocked to afford a real attorney—including my massive engagement ring—were declared not my property at all; the heirloom ring and everything else of Charles's estate went to his only living relative, his mother. Every avenue toward relief was blocked to me by Cecily's seemingly limitless reach into the bastions of law and society.

I picture her still, sitting in her Long Island living room overlooking the sea while I sat in a cheap motel room and stared at a cheesy seascape. Her manicured fingers working the phone, making a call or two, a plaintive injured tone; a promise of support for a judge's favorite charity—anonymous, of course.

I was poorly defended, and that failure led to the worst of the charges that might have been brought against me, voluntary manslaughter, a crime of passion. In all of this, I have never denied that I caused the fatal accident, but I have never said that I wanted it to happen. It was an *involuntary* act. An accident. I should never have stood trial. I should never have been defended by a public defender stooped under a case overload exacerbated by her screwed-up personal life. But my almost mother-in-law was the one who really managed my conviction. What public defender, even one without the challenges Wendy Delorusso had, could stand up under the assault of one of Connecticut's best prosecuting attorneys? Cecily Foster made damned sure that I was punished for the death of her only child, her son, Charles. As if having caused his death wasn't punishment enough. As much as I truly hated him, truly felt so aggrieved at what he had done, I was sorry about what had happened. Even if I had been exonerated instead of incarcerated, I would still have had to live with the knowledge that I had killed someone.

One Saturday afternoon in the late fall, Charles Foster arrived at my coffee bar dressed down—no suit, just a pair of Diesel jeans and a North Face jacket zipped up. He was wearing boots, those good heavy Timberlands. Without a tie, and with a woolen cap pulled on over his expensive haircut, Charles looked years younger, less unobtainable.

For years now, I have looked back at that day, playing the game where you say to yourself, If only . . . If only I hadn't agreed to fill in for a coworker—this wasn't my regular shift; I was never at the coffee bar on Saturdays. If only I hadn't taken that not-quite-earned break. If only I hadn't worked up the nerve to stand beside Charles, intent on his BlackBerry, and set the last chocolate chip cookie in the case down in front of him. "On the house."

Given the months of banter, the flirtation, even at this point a few inside jokes, I was emboldened to push past the barista/customer definition of our association. I sat down opposite him. "Would you ever want to go get a drink?"

Charles pulled his attention away from his BlackBerry. His eyes were an oceanic gray, surrounded by spiky dark lashes. He paused long enough for me to worry I'd overstepped myself. Then he said, "Yeah. I would."

If only Charles Montgomery Foster hadn't decided to grab a hot drink before driving to New Hampshire to ski, he might still be alive.

When you are in prison, all you want is for time to pass quickly. You want the hours to fly by, the days, weeks, and months to slip away. Every day passing is a day closer to release. Of course, they don't fly by. Boredom lengthens the days; you live with a routine that seems designed to slow time down. When you are a child, days are elongated. School lasts forever; Christmas will never come. Everyone knows that as you grow up, those days shorten. Weeks are fleeting; one season falls into the next with astounding rapidity. Try living in a prison. If you want to slow time down, that's your place. I had my jobs, six months in the prison laundry, a stint as a janitor, another in the kitchen, serving up heavy, starchy meals. I had a place at the white women's table three meals a day. I stood in lines. I circled the exercise yard, working off those meals. I flattened myself to the ground during lockdown. In the outside world, you know what day of the week it is by your "To Do" list or your agenda or your favorite television programs. In prison, it didn't really matter what day of the week it was. Or month. Or year.

Time was measured out in paroles and release dates. My first cellmate, Treena, fulfilled her sentence and vanished. A new inmate replaced her, and I claimed the lower bunk and warned her off trespassing into my territory. A week later, she managed to hang herself in the shower room. The next inmate to bunk with me was a repeat offender, and I was scared back onto the top bunk.

The one day that had some variation in it for me was Sunday. Out of a deep-seated need to feel normal, I attended the nondenominational service in the chapel. And then I stood in line for a turn at the rank of phones. Even though I knew that it was no longer true, I pictured my mother, still in her church dress, apron tied over it, getting Sunday dinner into the oven. I pictured her in our kitchen, an imagined summer sun warming the pale yellow linoleum, even if it was actually snowing outside, the wet snow against the windows further obscuring any natural light where I stood in my fluorescent world. I just wanted to hear her voice, to ask after everyone. And, every Sunday, the phone went unanswered.

Meghan

In the service they had called her—ostensibly behind her back—"Captain Buster." Meaning ballbuster. Meaning she was as hard on them as she was on herself. It was a sweet play on her actual name, Custer, and far better than the comparison to her unrelated namesake, George, of Little Bighorn fame. Capt. Meghan Custer had no particular ambition to become a general, and certainly not to annihilate Native Americans. Her main desire was to keep her soldiers out of harm's way, conduct whatever mission they had been assigned, and get them all back home safely. Home being an FOB, forward operating base, nestled in some godforsaken chunk of Iraq or Afghanistan. Three tours, and she was only thirty-five. No boyfriend back home, certainly not children. She bled for those women in her unit who kept up brave faces as they Skyped with their children, blew kisses to their babies. She understood the keen desire to have family back home praying for you every day, someone whose image you kept in mind as you "fought for freedom," but in some ways she saw it as indulgent selfishness.

Besides her parents, she had left no one behind except a couple of cousins and a jingoistic uncle whose pickup truck sported a pair of snapping flags, Old Glory and the black MIA/POW flag. He was her father's older brother, and his war, like her dad's, had been Vietnam. Where her dad's experience had led to a fifteen-year career in the army after the war's end, an honorable discharge, and putting it all behind him, her uncle's war had ended in alcoholism and a constant need to keep that war's failure front and center in his politics. When Meghan sat with him in his double-wide trailer, he told her that he was proud of her. And, especially, that her dad was proud that she was picking up his sword; the tacit suggestion that it was her late brother, Mark, who had been expected to carry on the military tradition in the Custer family, but she would do. Meghan didn't quite agree. She knew that neither one of her parents was particularly pleased with her having chosen to follow in her father's footsteps.

Now she leaves only tread marks in the dirt. No footsteps ever again.

The only thing that helped was a little pill, slightly ovoid in shape, a miracle of science in the battle against chronic pain. In another century, Meghan imagined, she would have had to find a Chinese opium parlor in order to find relief from the tidal pain in her back, rising and falling almost as if it were directed by the moon. She wondered if opium parlors ever had handicap-accessible entries. She wished that the permanent numbness of the scars on her face would migrate to the division in her spine where pain sat upon the blank space where her legs felt nothing at all. She could stick a pin in her thigh and feel nothing; she could pinch her face where the grafts were shiny with a combination of man-made material and human-grown skin and feel only the pressure.

The VA doc was certainly willing to prescribe the little pills, with a mild and perfunctory caution not to abuse them. His smile, knowing. Knowing that her self-control was blown away as much as her usefulness to the army. Honorable discharge. Purple Heart. Big deal. Done and sprung. She far more valued the tiny lapel pin depicting the emblem of the Cavalry, her division, that her father had pinned to her collar that overcast summer day when she'd reported for basic training. It was his. And having it meant the world. Having it meant that her father, although initially opposed to the idea of his daughter becoming a career soldier, was proud of her choice. Not once did he mention that he'd always expected to pin this on Mark's uniform.

Meghan pushed her chair away from the dorm-size refrigerator, where a bottle of water cooled. Everything in this halfway house of a rehabilitation center was set low for people like her. She knew that outside, where she was supposed to be after today, she would be reaching and looking up like a five-year-old in a grown-up's world for the rest of her life. Everyone in her life would have to bend down to look her in the eye.

"You're ready, Meghan," the occupational therapist had assured her, pleased with how skillfully Meghan used her modified utensils. Pleased with the way she could maneuver from wheelchair to desk chair, to toilet, to bed using the slant board. How clever she'd become in protecting nerveless feet from banging against doorjambs.

Tomorrow she would be released to move back in with her parents. Thirty-five years old, consigned to being dependent upon two late-middle-aged people working through their own miseries. Her mother suffered from arthritis. Her dad had high blood pressure. How was it fair to thrust a *disabled* daughter back into their lives? She should be taking care of *them*. Hadn't they suffered enough? First, her older brother, Mark, pride of

the Custers, hope of the family, the one actually meant to follow in Dad's footsteps, was killed by a teenaged drunk driver
in a car wreck the day before his high school graduation. Now
she was wrecked. Her mother put on this sad, brave face every
time she came to visit, as if she didn't dare let her guard down
and remind Meghan of what had happened, as if smiling and
gossiping about neighbors would override the fact that they
were in a hospital, not a city park. Her dad ran around making sure that everyone was taking better care of her than of
anyone else in this godforsaken museum of wounded warriors;
asserting his paternal powers, believing that a captaincy now
thirty years out-of-date gave him the authority. How was she
going to live with this day after day?

The pill went down. Meghan pushed herself away from the
fridge, covered her lap with the handmade lap rug that her
mother's next-door neighbor had crocheted. It was an ugly
thing, pink and green, in some homage to Lilly Pulitzer. Floppy
crocheted blooms stuck out of it, catching on everything. But
she could hide her damaged hand under it. Meghan waited for
the pill to take effect. They'd be here soon.

"We got it for a steal." Meghan's dad stood beside the white
conversion van, holding out his arms as if he were some kind
of American Dad car salesman. Meghan half-listened to him
crowing about features and accessories, all of which seemed
more designed for adventurous campers than a chick in a
wheelchair who couldn't get into the driver's seat. The point
of the van wasn't her freedom; it was their ability to transport
her. It was a glorified ambulance. The good news? The windows were tinted, so no one would be able to see her face.

Dad pressed a button and a flat ramp lowered itself to the
ground. Mom literally applauded the moment it was level with

the sidewalk cut. Meghan felt her mother grasp the chair handles. "No. I'll do it." She hadn't yet "graduated" to a motorized wheelchair, so pushing the chair was all manual effort. Meghan's physical therapist had spent months working on Meghan's upper body, promising that she'd come out of the rehab hospital able to get herself around. The day before, the therapist had given Meghan a pair of fingerless gloves like the kind weight lifters used. "To prevent blisters. Pavement is a lot harder to travel on than linoleum."

"Too late." Meghan had held up her scarred hand. "I don't even feel them. But thanks. This will keep them from scaring any little kids. Unlike my face."

This grievance was not a new one to the therapist. It had become a daily complaint and one that the physical therapist had learned to ignore rather than encourage. "I'll see you next week," she'd said, referring to a house-call appointment. She hadn't even waited till Meghan worked her way out of the room, new gloves still sitting on her lap, before turning her attention to a incoming patient.

Once Meghan was in the van, her chair tethered down, her dad suggested a celebratory lunch out. It had been more than two years from the incident in Afghanistan to a hospital in Germany and then a series of facilities until her transfer back here to her parents' home in Florida. In all that time, Meghan had scarcely breathed fresh air, only when transported from one VA hospital to another; then to this rehab hospital where she'd lived, yes, lived, for five months. The brief time on the sidewalk before being lifted into the van was as close as she'd come to being outside, and now the van was filled with the air conditioner pumping out against the summer heat. Not air, some false equivalent to air. She shivered. "I'd rather just go home." She imagined that she could get to the deck, get through

the slider, sit in the sun, flaunt the advice against direct sunlight on her scars and hope that the heat would remind her of
in-country, of being with her troops. Of being a soldier.

The wheelchair wouldn't fit through the sliding door to the
lanai. It was the one door in their tiny house that they hadn't
thought to enlarge. "You know, we've been talking about putting in a French door there," her dad said, and she shook her
head, saying, "Don't worry about it." Meghan could see the
scars of unpainted Sheetrock revealing where the opening to
her bedroom, once the guest room, had been made larger, and
where the doorway to the downstairs bathroom had been retrofitted. Both doors had paddle handles—no need for turning
a knob. Except that she couldn't close the door behind her.
"Mom! Can you close the door?"

"Do you want some help, honey?"

"I can manage." First thing they'd taught her in rehab: how
to lift herself from chair to toilet. Unfortunately, in this house,
the toilet wasn't situated in a convenient way and the effort
ended up humiliating her.

That evening, they sat out on the lanai, watching a light-
ning storm approach. Her dad had lifted her out of her chair
and her mother had folded it so that they could get her and
her chair out here. Meghan could feel how the strain of lifting
her hurt her father, who'd had a bad back for years. He certainly couldn't do that on a regular basis. No one spoke, and
the weight of failure bore down on all three.

Rosie

LaShonda Greene, tiny, pretty, hard-wired to be belligerent. Incredibly smart. In another life, under wildly different circumstances, she would have been valedictorian at my college. She would have become a world leader. Instead, she was serving eighteen to twenty-five years for using that intelligence to rob a bank. Unfortunately, as she told me, despite meticulous planning, a guard was shot dead and that was a game changer. "He shouldn't have gotten all hero on us. Shouldn't have thought he was some kind of Lone Ranger. Poor fella. What did he care if we took that money? They weren't gonna pay him no prize money for stoppin' us." LaShonda's eyes were a preternatural green, more big cat than human. Like a cat's eyes, they glittered in the gray light of the overhead fluorescents, giving her a sparkle better suited to a fly girl than a felon. "Waste of life."

"Do you regret it? That he died?" I meant was she sorry that she and her boyfriend *caused* his death. There had been no intention of killing the man; it was just an unfortunate outcome. Like my killing Charles.

LaShonda shrugged. "It was his own fault, you know. I mean, I didn't pull the trigger, but I might've if Deon had given me the gun like I told him to. So, I guess I'm lucky. Accessory, not killer. But, yeah, maybe I do feel a little bad about how things turned out. He was one of those old guys, probably happy to have this shit job standin' on his feet all day, nobody talkin' to him. Too poor to retire."

LaShonda and I worked together in the prison laundry and had struck up a casual friendship folding sheets together. As prison jobs go, it wasn't the worst. At least at the end of the shift you had something to show for the time spent. And it smelled good. I think my pay was maybe ten cents an hour, and it went toward my commissary account, so that I could buy the little things that make prison life livable: a candy bar now and then, ramen noodles, prison-approved dental floss. Nasty old-fashioned sanitary pads that made me feel like I was back in diapers. Real luxuries. Unlike some of my compatriots, I didn't receive funds from anyone on the outside to supplement my commissary account. No one even sent a letter.

"What about you?" LaShonda snapped a towel; it crackled with static. "You care that he died, or you care more you got caught?"

"It was an accident. I shouldn't be in here."

LaShonda laughed, yanked another hot towel out of the massive dryer, and folded it. "That's what we all say."

"But it's true. I didn't see him." Blinded by angry tears, I didn't see him. "I wasn't used to the car."

"Then why you here? Sounds like a *tragic accident*."

"His mother hates me."

"Man, if my man's mother hated me that much, I'da been in here a lot sooner."

"She's got powerful friends."

"Couldn't you get a better lawyer?"

"I got a public defender."

LaShonda laid the folded towel on the pile and gave me a look of absolute skepticism. "No way. You don't look like the type that goes through the system. No offense."

"None taken. I *am* the type that goes through the system. I haven't got any money. My family hasn't got any money." I didn't add that I was alienated from my family. The Collins family doesn't take disloyalty well. We call it "burning bridges."

"So your PD was as good as mine?"

"Probably worse. She'd been a PD most of her career, so she no longer cared; she was too jaded to feel like she could make a difference anymore. She was lazy. More than once I was pretty sure she was high."

"Yeah, sounds like mine." LaShonda giggled. "You're better off with some fresh-out-of-law-school kid, stars in her eyes, wavin' her Mount Blank pen like a sword, defendin' the rights of the innocent. Thinkin' she's makin' a difference."

I smiled at LaShonda's Montblanc reference. My father would have liked her. He liked the unpretentious of the world.

Putting on airs is how my mother saw it. My new habits. Like preferring Starbucks to Dunkin' Donuts. Buying wine by vintner instead of the two-for-ten kind at the local bottle shop. Disdaining chuck roast and choosing to have barely singed sirloin. I'd come home from my Seven Sisters college ready to go back to my plebeian life. Indeed, I had fitted right back in, leaving the thrift store chic in my closet and going back to Target and Old Navy for my clothes. I worked at that fancy-schmancy coffee bar and dreamed of finding a job that would put me on the path to getting my own place, but I imagined it somewhere in the old neighborhood, or maybe Somerville, where all the other recent college grads and twentysomethings were making their way in the world. I fell in with my old friends, and we haunted the karaoke bars and flirted with boys who could pass for my brothers. I made sure that Teddy had company in that long hour before my mother came home from work to start dinner and my father banged through the front door after a "pop" with the boys. We'd play endless games of Scrabble, with me placing his tiles on the board where he directed me. Teddy had a good vocabulary, reading being one of the things he could do independently with what motion he had in his left hand. Thank goodness for e-readers.

And then Charles came into my life, and, like Henry Higgins, he looked at me as his Eliza Doolittle. I was his project.

It wasn't a whirlwind romance, although spring did seem to come earlier that year. Charles inched his way into my life, almost teasingly. A call, a text. Silence. A midwinter ski trip. Two weeks of "too busy to get together." A late-winter weekend in Saint Thomas. First-class flight and accommodations; inseparable for three whole days and then he was off to some business meeting in Chicago and I didn't hear anything. It was all right. I wasn't losing my heart to him. At least I didn't think so. Nonetheless, by May I began to think that maybe he ought to meet my parents. His mother lived in New York, and we hadn't yet reached the stage of making a special trip to meet her, at least that's what he implied when I asked, but my family was within a few miles of where we met. A zip over the Zakim Bridge, turn right off the Somerville exit, and there we were.

As I had learned to do in college, I always referred to my neighborhood by its proper name, Charlestown, because that had more cachet. So when I finally confessed to Charles that I was from the poor side of town, he was mildly appalled. After that, the closest Charles came to my neighborhood was when he sent an Uber to collect me for a Friday-night date. A fact duly noted by my mother, who wondered aloud why if he was such a gentleman he wouldn't collect me himself, not send a taxi.

"He's downtown already, so why would he come here to go back there? And it's an Uber."

"He's paid someone to pick you up. It's a taxi."

Teddy came into the dining room in his clunky wheelchair. "Ma, give Rosie a break. At least he's not making her pay for it." He docked his chair at his place at the dining room table. Mom set down a plate of pasta in front of him.

"I'd like to meet this young man. Mr. Uber."

And that's when I thought that maybe it *was* time. I was beginning to think, maybe even hope, that maybe Charles and I were a couple. The stop/start of his early courtship had settled into a rhythm of daily contact. We'd slept together. I hadn't left a toothbrush at his place in the South End, but I had one in my purse.

Just after the server had removed the dinner plates and set the dessert menu in front of us, I asked the question: "Would you like to come to my parents' house on Sunday for dinner?" I tossed this out casually, as if it had just occurred to me. "They'd like to meet you."

Charles had his wineglass lifted to his lips. A very expensive merlot, as I recall. His face was unreadable behind the balloon glass. He didn't answer right away, and I took that as a negative and then instantly worried that I'd pushed some off button on the relationship by being presumptuous. "At their home?"

"Yes. My parents' house." Perhaps he thought Sunday dinners were restaurant meals.

"Aren't they on the Somerville line?"

"Close." Weird questioning, but I was just happy that he hadn't rejected the idea out of hand. "East of the community college." Where I might have gone had I not been encouraged by my favorite teacher to expand my horizons.

And then he set his glass on the fine white tablecloth and smiled. "That would be very nice."

I was as nervous as a squirrel in a roomful of hounds that first meeting—one of only three—between Charles and my parents. I was afraid that my father would make some inappropriate remark that normally we'd just laugh off, something racist, off-color, or, worse, some crack about rich Republicans. He did.

I worried that my mother would make a big deal out of Charles's hostess gift of a bottle of expensive, to her, wine. I knew my mother. She was certain to say something about saving it for later. She did.

I was hyperaware of all the flaws in my family's grammar and table manners and the way the crucified Christ hung on our living room wall. The minute we walked into the house where I had grown up, with its threadbare rug and Bob's Discount Furniture living room set, I was convinced that this was the baddest idea in a world of bad ideas. All the sophisticated veneer I had developed in college was exposed as a façade by my beloved family. I just knew that Charles would bolt.

He didn't.

It was sometime after that first visit when Charles began making plans for us every weekend. He started bringing me silly little things, like a new lipstick he said would be a better color for me, and a tight little bolero sweater he said would make me look even more slender. Why didn't I consider a new hairstylist? I kidded him about being such a metrosexual and he only smiled, his eyes brighter than usual, as if I'd touched a pleasant nerve. He made an appointment for me at a place on Newbury Street, where a simple haircut could run into the hundreds. "My treat," he said. "My treat." He advised the stylist, and I came out of the shop looking like the million bucks Charles said I was worth. I worried out loud that I would never be able to keep up with the style, bluntly letting him know that I could never afford a Newbury Street look on my own. Again, his eyes brightened and he smiled. "You won't have to."

I look back on this and I wonder at my naïveté, or maybe it's the 20/20 hindsight of finally recognizing what a subtle monster control is. What can look like kindness and affection is far more sinister. The kindness and affection weren't meant for me; they were meant for this figment, a miniature living golem. Charles wanted to mold what he saw as raw material into something of his own creation. It just took me a long time to figure out what he was doing. Who doesn't like being treated to spa days and facials? Who wouldn't want to be escorted to invitation-only trunk shows and be handed a credit card? I began to amass a closet full of clothes worth more than my college tuition—a loan I was no closer to paying off than I had been when I first met Charles.

On one of my increasingly rare nights out without Charles, my high school bestie, Brenda Brathwaite, patiently listened as I extolled the generosity of my new boyfriend, doing a little humble bragging about the trouble I was having finding room in my closet.

"How come you never post anything about him on Facebook?"

"He's very private. He told me right from the start that he didn't want to be on my page or anyone else's."

"Does he have one?"

"No. Just the page for his company. All very professional."

Brenda ran a finger along the rim of her margarita glass. We were in a little Downtown Crossing Mexican place. "Have you met his parents yet?"

"Not yet. Charles says that he's really too busy right now;

he wants to make it an occasion. And it's just his mother. She's very busy in New York with her charity work. We'll probably meet over the holidays." Holidays that were months away.

Brenda has known me all my life and so she has no filter when it comes to saying what's on her mind when it pertains to me. "Sounds like you're the 'other' woman."

"What do you mean?"

"Come on, Rosie. He spoils you with stuff, but he never takes you home to Mom. He comes and goes in your life according to his schedule. He claims there's no position open in his firm. I took a look. There're a couple of entry-level marketing positions open in Wright, Melrose & Foster that'd be just perfect for someone like you."

"You're full of it. He's being sensitive about nepotism."

"You're not related."

I waggled my eyebrows to suggest that there was a *yet*.

"He's probably worried about having you around when he decides to go back to his wife, or breaks it off out of guilt."

"Brenda, he's not married. I would know."

"Googled him?"

Now it was my turn to smile. "Yes. Of course. One broken engagement, but never married."

"Okay, my bad. You just keep having fun, and feel free to give me your select hand-me-downs when you're closet is too full."

"Look, you're being kind of unfair to Charles. Let's go out on a double date, you and Leon, and me and Charles. You'll get to know Charles and he'll see that my friends are the best."

"You're on."

Except that Charles hated the idea. His capacity for finding reasons not to double-date with my friends was limitless. Neither did we ever go out with his friends. The closest we came was bumping into one of the principals in the firm, Laurence

Wright, and his wife at Rialto, in the Charles Hotel. Although Mr. Wright politely suggested we join them, Charles declined and we took the table for two he'd reserved. It wasn't until later that night, as we snuggled under the covers in our "weekend away" room at the hotel, that I realized Charles had never introduced me by name to Mr. and Mrs. Wright. An unusual lapse of manners, for which I chided him, but he only laughed and told me I was being a child. Of course he'd introduced me. But he hadn't.

I was sorry that Charles died, of course. Before the trial, I grieved for him in a way, and flashes of his easier side would come to me, forcing on me a heavy guilt; but the truth was, I was relieved to be free of him. Of his oppressive nature. After the trial, I realized that his style of oppression had only been transferred to the more overt oppression of prison. If he'd kept me imprisoned by his jealous, controlling nature, now I was in a real prison, and no guard here cared the least for my emotional state. They weren't guarding *me* jealously; they were guarding the world *from* me.

By my second year at Mid-State, I had "adjusted" to my circumstances, meaning that I went about my day no longer crying. I'd found the limited library. I went to my laundry job. I ate and walked the yard and didn't cry. I listened to my mother's unanswered phone and didn't cry. I got used to my fellow inmates, even growing to like some of them, especially LaShonda. Once I had a dream that she and I were sitting opposite each other in a restaurant. She wore a fascinator and I wore a hijab. The waiter came to take our orders, and it was Charles. In the dream, LaShonda looked at me and said, "He's nothing." I woke up in a sweat.

By my fourth year of incarceration, I was in the law library,

trying to fathom some legal precedent that would free me. I
had stopped calling home. Like a rising senior, I had learned
the ropes and I handled the four-times-a-day head count. I
passed down the corridor with very little interference from inmates or guards.

Nearly four years in and I no longer felt like the fearful
young woman, innocent of the crime and innocent of the ways
of the gray world of prison. I saw them arrive, those youthful
ghosts of me. Trembling, weeping, calling for their mothers. I
felt for them, but I wasn't kind to them. Kindness slows the
hardening of the carapace you need in prison. Now I felt fully
armored by my certainty that my life was fixed in the amber
of prison rules, mores, and constant sense of threat—from fellow inmates, from randy guards. Some inmates got through by
talking about what they would do when they got out, who they
would see, what foods they would enjoy. Not me. By my fourth
year, I had accepted this joyless, soul-dead life.

Meghan

Meghan Custer tipped the vial of pills into her hand. Only three left; no matter how many times she checked the bottle, there were always only three magic bullets. She didn't miss the fact that she thought of them as magic *bullets*. Over the past few weeks, as she entered her third year of this version of herself, the *crippled* version, the idea of a real bullet had begun to have some traction. She knew where her father kept his guns. She certainly knew how to use one. Idly, she wondered if it was possible to miss the weight of a rifle, its doglike constant companionship and protection. Meghan had been very good with her service weapon. When that politician did the blindfold assembly of his rifle as some kind of political statement, she'd laughed out loud. Easy peasy. Who couldn't do that? What did that prove except that the United States military schooled its soldiers very, very well?

Only three pills left in a prescription that was supposed to last until the end of next week. If she'd had any independence at all, she would have found another doctor to write her another script. Too bad docs no longer made house calls. The bigger problem was that her mother wasn't blind to Meghan's opioid use. The scourge of mankind, according to the press. It seemed sometimes that the opioid epidemic had come along at exactly the wrong time for Meghan. A few years ago, the physicians would have been more than happy to keep her supplied, but now, not so much. They suggested alternative therapies, like yoga, for God's sake. Meghan clutched the three little pills in her fist, then placed them, one by one, back in the vial.

"Mom!" Meghan took a little satisfaction in the sound of the dishwasher being slammed maybe a titch more energetically than it needed. Her mother was a saint. Everyone said so. Forced back into motherhood, the physically demanding motherhood of dressing her daughter; the emotionally challenging one of having a thirty-six-year-old daughter with the mood swings of an adolescent, the unkindness of a teenager, the self-pitying funk of a preteen. Meghan wasn't unaware of having become a difficult person, but she couldn't find a way out of it. "Mom!"

"What is it, honey?" Her mother leaned into the bedroom doorway. She didn't look like someone whose every activity was vulnerable to interruption. She looked, as always, ready to help. It pissed Meghan off no end, this eternal patience.

"I dropped my phone."

Evelyn Custer knelt to retrieve the wayward phone from under the bed, where it had bounced. She handed the phone to Meghan and then straightened the unkempt bed. The bed, a high-tech multiposition one, wasn't supposed to be called a hospital bed, but, for all intents and purposes, it was, and it was hard to keep it neat. "Would you like to have grilled cheese for lunch?"

"Yeah, sure. Fine." Meghan opened Facebook and scrolled down, looking for something interesting.

"Whenever you're ready."

"This is getting old, isn't it?"

"I don't know what you mean."

"Me. This." Meghan swept her hand across her lap.

"Of course not."

"Don't be a martyr." Meghan didn't look up to see if her rottenness had had any effect. It was as if she was trying to be a bitch. And her mother just kept turning that other cheek.

"Meghan?"

"What?"

"Yeah, I am. Tired of it. Tired of being the mom with the wounded warrior feeling sorry for herself."

Meghan kept her face away from her mother. She never cried, not once, except for the men who were lost that day. Not once for herself. Now the tears that stung still weren't for herself, but for her mother. She withheld the tears that just might be in regret for the bitch she knew that she'd become.

"But, Meghan, I don't consider it martyrdom. It's a challenge, yes. Pleasant? Not so much. But I love you and I'm so grateful that you are a grump instead of a memory."

"Sorry. I don't know what gets into me." She maneuvered her chair to face her mother.

"You need a break."

"We both do."

Later, Meghan found her mother in the laundry room, folding a basketful of towels. She grabbed a lapful and got busy. As simple a task as folding still-warm towels from the dryer made her feel a little more useful. A little less of a child. Less of a burden. Her mother had been right; she needed a break. A break from being dependent. As well-meaning as her parents, especially her mother, were, in some ways Meghan felt as though they were contributing to her dependency on them. It wasn't being ungrateful, no. It was a growing suspicion that she was being coddled. She, who had endured the untold discomfort of boot camp, who had once been able to carry more than half her weight in body armor and equipment, now had a parent practically wiping her bum for her. She desperately wished that they all could take a break from this.

A flicker of memory teased at her, a vague taste of an old desire. She suddenly remembered how it felt in those long-ago days when she was aching to leave the family home and strike out into her adult life. It felt like this, like this *stage* of her life must soon come to an end. In high school, she could see the way out each time she filled out a college application. There was no such scripted way out of this stage unless she could regain her independence.

Meghan handed her mother the short pile of folded towels and reversed her chair out of the laundry room.

Rosie

Far too early in my twenty-year sentence to apply for parole, I'd just been denied a retrial, which was, in my view, my only way out before menopause. Even though I hadn't honestly expected the courts to take my request seriously, I was bitterly disappointed. One thing that you have plenty of time to do in prison is reflect on the past. The endless "time-out." *Just sit there, young lady, and think about what you've done.* So I was trying to figure out where my life had so egregiously gone off the rails, when the prison counselor suggested that I start writing my life down, like a memoir. "Sometimes seeing the words written down inspires an understanding of events." She was full of wisdom, that one. So, I did. I was so bored, mostly spending my free time lying on my bunk and picking at my cuticles until my fingers bled. Otherwise, I wandered through the days in a funk, a cloud of despair the size of an island surrounding me. The writing may have used up some time, but it did nothing to dispel that funk; on the contrary, the more I examined my life, the deeper the funk became. It was hard some days to tell if it was fear, or grief, or anger, or regret that ruled my outlook. Some blend of each, I suppose. A perfect fusion of the dark emotions. And I was one of the lucky ones. Too many of my comrades were suffering from not just the loss of their freedom, whether through drugs or crime or bad boyfriends, but the wrenching loss of their children. When I first arrived, I dwelled upon the rift that had separated me from my family; but, almost four years in, I had come to understand that the separation from one's child was far worse. They suddenly had no control over where their kids were, or with whom. The visiting hours were fraught with tears and acting out. Or silence as a child who has never lived with his mother treats her as a stranger.

My sixth roommate, Darla, was typical of the women I knew. Convicted of a nonviolent drug crime. In her case, as she put it, convicted of stupidity. She'd opened her home up to a brother who was a drug dealer. Of course, she told me, she had no idea he was a dealer, although she did know he was a user. When the police came and raided her house, she was swept up into the bust. Her children, a baby boy and a two-year-old girl, were absorbed into the foster-care system and she had been fighting to get them back ever since. Mandatory sentencing meant that she would not have her own children back until they were in middle school, and only then if the authorities released them to her—and there were no guarantees of that.

Some of the mommies were luckier, and their mothers or their aunts had their kids. Darla had no one and so hadn't seen her babies since the day the Child Protective Services people wrested them from her arms.

Darla's nocturnal weeping had kept me awake all night, so I was in a particularly black humor at work in the laundry. I was in no mood to chat, to laugh at the jokes that the other inmates got from their Wednesday afternoon visitors. To hear the gossip about the creepy guard who liked to do pat-downs, who also traded bubble gum for hand jobs during count.

"You see this?" LaShonda handed me a flyer with its photo of a happy, panting Labrador retriever and bold lettering: **Be a part of a new program. Learn how to train therapy dogs while serving your time.**

"No. Where'd you get it?"

"That new counselor has 'em in her office. She thought I might like to try."

The flyer gave very few details, only that candidates must have an impeccable record for two consecutive years to be considered. Well, I had that. In spades. In the forty-two months that I had been inside, I had accrued not one demerit. Never sent to segregation. Not one hair-pulling, screaming fight. Part of that was because I kept my head down and my mouth shut. The other was that I had no ambition. I stood my ground, but I didn't challenge anyone's authority, guard or inmate.

"Let's do it." LaShonda didn't usually express excitement; she was more of a low-key kind of person.

"Me?"

"Yeah, you."

Except for the occasional dog sent in for drug searches, I hadn't seen a dog in years. I certainly hadn't touched one. Not since Tilley. And the memory of her limp crushed body in my arms sent a jolt through me. I handed the flyer back to LaShonda. "I don't think so."

I lived "inside," but not in a bubble. I'd heard about this kind of program before, one with male inmates and farm animals. The idea being that animals have a salutary effect on the hardened humans. I was not thoroughly hardened, but I had lost my ability to care. I was sad. I was lonely, LaShonda notwithstanding, and we really were together only during work hours. The unspoken inmate protocol was that like gathered with like, so I wasn't invited to sit at her table in the dining room, and I would never presume. You learn the subtle signals in prison or you don't survive. *Your kind isn't welcome here.*

"It'll be fun, Rosie. Come on."

"I can't."

"Don't you like dogs?"

"I do." Suddenly I felt tears forming. I sniffed them back. What had happened to my little Tilley had everything to do with why I was here at Mid-State.

My Newbury Street haircuts were now a regular appointment, and afterward Charles always pulled me into one of the high-end clothiers that lined the street, so now my workout clothes were Lululemon and my shoes came from Italy or England. Even the most fashion-forward of my college friends would have been hard put to develop a collection like the one that Charles's munificence afforded me. It helped, he said, that I seemed to be built to wear these expensive clothes and that dressing in down-market rags was such a crime. His words. I turned in my beloved Levi's for True Religion.

Speaking of religion, that was another quirk of mine that Charles preferred I let go. He grew demonstrably uncomfortable whenever I mentioned that I'd gone to Mass with my mother. He texted me during Christmas Eve service, although he knew that I would be in church at that time. A sexy text. Like the rest of my generation, I couldn't not look at it, even as the priest glanced my way. The Fosters and their forebears were nominally Protestant, and paid a little lip service to the notion. They could recite the Lord's Prayer, knew a few hymns, and could follow the Book of Common Prayer through important funerals without getting lost. I thought that as long as they lived by the idea of doing right, being kind, that was okay. It wasn't as important to go to church as to live the ideals. Which, of course, they didn't.

The point is, I was getting a taste of the good life. And I liked it. But that taste came with a price. One that my mother noted.

"That another new coat?" My mother was peeling potatoes over the kitchen sink. She wore her usual at-home uniform, a pair of Wrangler jeans saggy in the bottom, and a short-sleeved cotton shirt that had seen better days. If she left the house, she'd swap out this outfit for a venerable pair of black pull-on pants and a blue blouse complete with a bow. And, always, on her feet a pair of black Naturalizers. She was a fashion plate, that's for sure. Teddy was there, working slowly on a jigsaw puzzle that I believed had been on the edge of the kitchen table for two years. It took him as much effort to place a piece in that puzzle as it might have taken someone else to sink a basket from mid-court.

"Yes, it is. Do you like it?" Charles had given me a trench-style coat, perfect for mid-spring in New England. The material, a heavy silk cotton, felt lovely between the fingers. The color was khaki, a nod to the military antecedents of the style. I spun like some girlie-girl to show how the skirt of the coat flared.

"Don't care much for the color, but it suits you." She set the peeler down and wiped her hands on a paper towel. "Do you know anything about this?" She handed me an envelope, the top of it destroyed by someone's careless opening of it.

I looked at it, noted the letterhead with an impulsive smile, and pulled the letter out, completely bewildered at why my boyfriend's firm would be writing to my mother and father. I won't lie; it crossed my mind in that split second before unfolding the letter that Charles was asking for my hand in a most formal manner, a very Jane Austen moment quickly blasted by the real purpose of the letter. An offer on their house. A lowball offer. It seemed as though Wright, Melrose & Foster, Charles's firm, had designs on this down-at-the-heels section of Bunker Hill, this last bastion of the struggling classes.

My parents' house wasn't one of those granite and brick antique town houses that appear to have grown out of the ancient pavement rather than having been built. There was no charm to it, a simple two-story frame house fighting for balance at the midpoint of the hill on which it stood, flanked on either side by a house just like it. Brown-with-tan trim. Flaking paint. Semidetached gutters. The three houses faced their future across the narrow street. On the other side of the street, where three houses built in the same era and the same style as my parents' house had been, now stood an architect-designed apartment building with a façade that mimicked the granite and style of the antique and well-preserved town houses. This building towered over the cowering houses across from them, their penthouse dwellers forced to suffer the view. I was at college when those houses were bought and cleared away. Over the course of the four years I was in school, the six-story building grew up, casting its shadow into my childhood bedroom.

My mother had served corned beef and cabbage for Charles's first, and only, meal chez Collins. It was so trite. If I had been home when she began to cook, I would have convinced her to make something less stereotypical. Plus, it made the house smell like a nineteenth-century tenement. It did occur to me that she was doing up the Irish for Charles's benefit. Not to impress, but to remind him of my origins. In her own way, my mother could be as much of a snob as Cecily Foster.

We pulled up in an Uber. Parking on our street being as difficult as it was, Charles could hardly be expected to shim his

mint 1968 Chevy Camaro into a tight space. To say nothing—
and, to his credit, he didn't—about the vulnerability of a vintage car. Just the curiosity factor alone would have been a
problem.

Charles was still dressed in his workaday clothes, which
is to say, a fashionably tailored charcoal gray suit, a crisp white
shirt that looked like he'd just put it on, and a tasteful tie. The
only suggestion that he wasn't going into a board meeting was
that he'd loosened the tie. I was, on the other hand, just off
shift, still in my black jeans and white work blouse, still smell-
ing of expensive coffee. I scampered up the steps to the front
door and waited as Charles remained on the sidewalk. He was
looking at the house, and I had that elevator-drop feeling.
Maybe he was going to cut and run. He didn't. He came up the
steps, keeping his hands at his sides, not touching the flaking
wrought-iron railing.

In the inimitable Collins family way, every single one of
my brothers had shown up to meet "the new guy." I was screwed.
There was the array, all five of them managing to be in the
living room at the same time, looking like the Patriots had
fielded half the offensive line. To cap it off, the patriarch himself, Bert Collins.

If Charles felt like he'd walked into a scrum, he didn't show
it. There is something to be said for good manners, and my
boyfriend quickly put out a hand to my father and gave him a
good manly shake. "Pleased to meet you, Mr. Collins." Charles
was a veteran of high-powered meetings and he didn't underestimate this one. He looked my dad in the eye.

"Call me Bert."

For one exceedingly brief moment, I thought we'd be okay.

Any other boy I'd brought home was treated as if already
part of the family. Teased and fed. Invited to sit on the couch
and watch the game. Threatened with gelding if he should go

too far with me. Charles was so very different from my other boyfriends. The boys from my teenage crushes were just like my family; they came from people like us. And they were exactly that, boys.

Within fifteen minutes, the common language of men petered out. Charles's interest in sports was limited to lacrosse and sailing. He was not conversant with mechanics. He knew the stats on his car, but not the workings. Politics, well, we just skipped that topic altogether.

However, as Mom served up the corned beef—Charles declined the cabbage—the talk turned to real estate. Paulie was finally at the point where he was hoping to buy a house and bemoaning the lack of affordable housing stock.

"Hey, Charles, you're in real estate. Got any advice?"

"I'm not in sales. I'm in property development."

"So, you build?"

Charles took a small bite of meat. "Our firm handles large-scale corporate projects."

"So, no dumpy little houses?" This from Paulie.

"No. Sorry." Charles neatly laid his knife and fork across his half-full plate. A man with no appetite, another black mark. "We deal in the millions."

"So, who's for dessert?" I stood to clear the plates. "Mom's made her famous Jell-O cake."

As soon as I helped Mom clear up, moving as fast as I could so as not to leave Charles alone with the brothers too long, we got ready to leave. Dad was in the bathroom, I remember, and we could hear him coughing. He'd been doing this for so long that it had become part of the sound track of our lives, but I could see Charles wince at the gross noise. It was pretty ugly, and just how ugly, we would find out soon enough.

Charles did not put out his hand to say good-bye to my father. I noticed that Dad didn't put out his, either.

"Thank you for a lovely meal, Mrs. Collins."

"Wish you'd enjoyed it more." Mom didn't mince words.

Dad opened the door. Stood there like a sentry, waiting to
see the back of this high-flown suitor. I could hear the television in the background, the brothers hunkered down to watch
a game.

"It was lovely. I'm a man of small appetite."

Mom harrumphed and left us at the door. To leave food on
one's plate in our household was an insult. I knew that Charles
was going to be a hard sell from now on.

"Oh, Mr. Collins?"

"Yeah?"

"Just curious. How much did you pay for this house?"

Dad shut the door behind us.

Charles took my hand as we waited outside for the Uber. "I
want to show you something." He walked me across the steep,
narrow street. "See that?" He pointed to a plaque, fixed by brass
bolts into the granite beside the Federal-style front doors of the
new apartment building, WRIGHT, MELROSE & FOSTER DEVELOPMENT
COMPANY. "That's ours." He sounded so proud, as if he were
showing me something very personal, an accomplishment.

"No. I'm sure it's nothing he knows about." How easily I could
fool myself. The trench coat was so very warm in this steamy
kitchen, and I took it off, revealing my workaday barista uniform. "I mean, sure, he has to know about the idea, but not
that they've sent this letter. I'll bet he'll be mad." I grasped for
reason, for sense. If Charles and/or his company were scout-
ing our area for such a project, wouldn't he have at least mentioned it to me? It would seem not. So I decided that this was
just some upstart in his company firing off letters without his
knowledge. But even as I thought that, I knew that there was
nothing that Charles didn't know about in his real estate world.

He fielded phone calls at all hours and no matter what we were doing. Terse with underlings, fearless with senior partners.

"Call him, Rosie. Ask him what's going on." Teddy pushed away from the table. "I don't want to move."

"Nobody's moving, Teddy. I promise." The first of oh so many unkeepable promises. "This is just somebody's fishing expedition. Besides, there's no law against saying thanks but no thanks." Was there? Who says no to progress? To Charles?

My phone was in the pocket of my nice new trench coat from Donna Karan.

Charles almost never answered during the day, but this time he did. Almost as if he knew I'd be calling once I got home. "Hey, babe." His voice did not sound like that of a man determined to make his girlfriend's parents homeless.

"My mom got a letter from Wright, Melrose & Foster."

"Really?"

"Something about buying up all the houses on this street. Their house."

"We want to complete our multiphase project."

"So you do know something about this letter? Did you send it?"

"No."

"Is this cast in stone, this project?"

"Not stone, exactly. There are any number of players in the mix. Any number of variables. First steps."

"Okay. So, what should they do with this letter?"

A pause while I could hear Charles speak to someone in the office. "Just have them toss it."

"Thanks."

"For now."

It happened during count, when every inmate must go to her "room" and wait to be enumerated by one of the cadre of guards who perform this task. It could be a dangerous time for us, depending on the guard, depending on his mood. I was alone in my room, Darla having been sent to the infirmary with a bad cold. He stood there, staring in at me framed by the open cell door. A big guy. Officer Tierney. Either he was lazy or he thought a scruff was attractive. He stared at me and smiled. "What if I leave this door unlocked and you come on down to the closet?" The closet was a utility closet, where I knew that certain assignations took place. I shook my head no. "I got something you might want, you know, in exchange for a little favor." He pulled a tampon out of his pants pocket. "Whole box where this came from." He put the tampon back in his pocket, then slowly unzipped his fly. "Ten minutes in the closet with your mouth and I'll give you two. Ten minutes with your pants down and you'll get the whole box."

None of my choices were good. If I rejected him, he could send me down to seg on some trumped-up charge; if I accepted, he'd expect more favors. Either way, I had to live with myself. I looked like everyone else in the place—that is, faded, sloppy, and desperate—and I don't know why he thought I was a good target that day, except that Darla wasn't there. Maybe he thought I was lonely; after all, I never had visitors. Maybe it was the Irish thing, him a boyo and me a lass. The idea of this great ugly man touching me made my skin crawl, and I declined as casually as I could. "Thanks, but I'm going to have to say 'No thank you.'" I waited. I pulled a *People* magazine off Darla's shelf. I began to flip pages, as if he weren't standing there, my door unlocked, the rest of the guards busy with count.

"I'm gonna leave the door as is. Think about it." He moved away, but his eyes were still on me.

Our guards, not all, but enough of them, were effectively predators in a buffet of small mammals—small, deprived, and extremely vulnerable mammals. As I sat there, shaking, I saw

the long corridor of my bleak future, fending off this kind of
threat. Maybe not being able to fend it off with a guard a little
more determined. I was lucky, I suppose, that this was the first
time I'd been propositioned, and I knew that that mercy had
more to do with my race than with my lack of allure. Most of
the guards were white and they mostly preyed on the black
girls.

I lay awake that night, not just because Darla was back
from the infirmary and still coughing her lungs out. Every
sound from the corridor twanged against my nerves. How was
I ever going to get through sixteen more years of this? The
sameness, the fear, the boredom, the hopelessness. The physical deterioration and intellectual stunting. What evil would
Tierney visit upon me for my rejection of him?

When I did finally fall asleep, I dreamed of a dog. A large
shape, shaggy fur, kind eyes. In my dream, the dog stood over
me as I lay on a wide, soft bed. In my dream, I felt safe.

I walked over to the table where LaShonda and her girls were
having breakfast. "Let's go talk to the warden."

Warden Don Hinckley always reminded me of Tom Hanks's
soccer ball companion, "Wilson," in that movie about being
stranded on a desert island. Like the ball, Warden Hinckley
was a little deflated, smooth-cheeked, and always had the same
expression on his face—something between meditative and explosive. When he pulled his heavy black-framed glasses off
his face, he wanted you to know that he was paying attention
to you, sometimes not in a good way. This time, he snapped
them off and nodded. "Okay, I'll put your names in for the program."

"And then what happens?" LaShonda stood like a good soldier standing at ease, hands behind her back, chin up.

Hinckley slid his glasses back on. "I guess they'll interview you. If you appeal to them, you'll get dogs. Puppies. I really don't know that much about it; not really sure I'm okay with it, but, hey, if it rehabilitates inmates, I'm not going to stand in your way. As long as they don't crap all over the place." He waved us off, smoothing his ubiquitous red tie. When I first arrived at Mid-State, I thought he was making a political statement; later, I realized that the warden was as color-deprived as the rest of us.

We walked out of his office, suppressing girlish giggles. "You ready for some rehabilitation?" I shouldered LaShonda; she bumped me back.

"You ready to be pickin' up dog crap?"

In college, the first three years flew by and I was suddenly a senior. In prison, not so much. There aren't any benchmarks. No freshman, sophomore, junior designations that mark off the years toward the accomplishment of graduation. You don't graduate from prison. If you're lucky, you get paroled. The seasons lumber by, marked only by the heat or the cold, the sad, limited decorations for the holidays; the arrival of new fresh-faced guards and the departure of the hardened, cynical old-timers taking early retirement.

So now, at the end of my fourth year of incarceration, I might finally have something to look forward to every day. A real purpose to fill my endless empty days.

Rosie

I was as excited as a giddy teenager about to meet a pop star that day the puppies were brought in. LaShonda and I waited together in the activities room. Although ultimately there would be four of us in the program, this day it was just the two of us. We kept giggling. For two women who were serving time for felonies, we were being pretty silly. "I almost didn't get here today."

"Why?"

"Almost got into it last night. Denise stole my 'phones. Said they were hers."

"What'd she want them for?"

"Guess hers are broke. She wanted 'em to go to the movie."

"What'd you do?"

"Well, I was kinda in a hard place. If I *gave* 'em to her, that'd mean I agreed they were hers, and I'd never get 'em back. If I didn't, she'd force me to fight her for them."

"So, what happened?"

"I was gettin' kind of angry, could feel my blood pressure goin' up. Then I remembered that today was goin' to be the day to get the puppy. If I smacked her, I might keep my headphones, but I'd lose my opportunity. So in the end, I said, 'Denise, you want to *borrow* these?' She say, 'Yeah. That'd be dope.'"

I laughed. "You did the right thing."

LaShonda nodded. "This puppy better be worth it. I might have lost a little status on my unit with bein' nice to Denise."

Status. Cred. Power. Loyalty and honor. *Omertà* by any other name. Some days you couldn't tell whose star had risen and who was in disgrace, so it was better not to speak to anyone. Some of these women knew one another from shared history; there were unresolved boyfriend disputes, ongoing street rivalries. More than a few were related, so old family issues popped up now and again. LaShonda had put much of that behind her because of this program, wanting something better.

The far door opened, and even before we saw the puppies, we heard them. Toenails on linoleum as the pair of Labrador retrievers scrambled to rush into the activity room without a clue as to why they were there. It was enough for the exuberant pair to be in a new place; that was excitement enough to get them dancing and peeing.

The director of the program, Edith Moore, held two leashes, against which strained the puppies. One was black and the other, Shark, was that wonderful shade of near-edible brown.

I put out a hand and Edith Moore put a leash in it—the one attached to Shark.

I could feel the presence of the guard behind us, how alert he was to our movements. I quickly stepped back from Ms. Moore. The puppy was very interested in the exchange of his leash from his known person to this stranger, and he fixed his brown eyes on me. I knelt and let him kiss me. His soft pink tongue tasted my cheek right at the corner of my mouth. It was the first kiss I'd had in years. It was the first affection I'd had, and I misted up. The puppy's tongue found the moisture and erased it. Even now, after so much time, I can conjure the emotion that gripped me in those first few minutes of my acquaintance with Shark. The immediacy of my love for him. A *coup de foudre* of emotion I had not been expecting; tainted, however, by the fact that I only had him to give him up; I would prepare him for leaving me. Ten minutes into our association and I couldn't fathom how I was going to do that. I prayed that Edith Moore didn't see the love on my face. If she had, she might have intervened and seen that she'd made a mistake about me and taken him away right then.

As with anything in the prison, it had taken months before LaShonda and I, plus two other inmates, were accepted into the program, and then, finally, introduced to our puppies. Five days a week, our job was to housebreak them, and give the dogs basic training, like sit, stay, heel, and down. On the weekends, volunteers took our dogs to give them "real world" training, like riding in cars and being social with people who weren't incarcerated. These dogs, mostly Labs, were meant as assistance dogs, dogs that would accompany their ultimate owners everywhere, doing everything from emotional therapy to flipping on light switches.

Every Saturday morning, we trainers watched as our trainees got to do what none of us ever got to do: walk free. We would hand the leashes over to the volunteers, remind ourselves that before long these pups would be on their way out for good, paroled, as it were. They would have become productive canine citizens, their prison months behind them, their future bright. It never failed to amaze me, though, that each time a dog was led out of the activity room by his volunteer, he would always look back at his inmate, as if worried he might not see her again; or, maybe sorry that she wasn't going with him. When one of our fellow inmates was released, I don't recall seeing that woman ever look back.

The puppies' Sunday-night returns to prison were moments of high excitement, tails wagging and tongues lolling, just plain happy to be home, even if home was a prison. They had no idea, of course, and so their innocent happiness was infectious. How can you be sad when a half-grown pup is romping around, hoping you'll play tug-of-war? The sound of toenails on the linoleum was the best sound in the world. I dreaded that inevitable day when my puppy would leave me behind forever.

Shark looked like his namesake whenever he flipped over onto his back and let his jaw hang open, tongue draped over his perfect white teeth, kept polished by Milk-Bone biscuits and my diligent brushing. He was a chocolate Lab, his coat just the color of a Milky Way bar. He came into my life when he was twelve weeks old and stayed there until just before his first birthday. It was always there, the fact that he would leave me. It was one of the things discussed when I was interviewed for the program: Could I handle saying good-bye? Of course I said yes. I wasn't going to lose this opportunity by being honest. If I excelled at this program, then I would have another puppy to work with, and I believed that would be consolation enough.

Knowing that our partnership was limited, and that he had a future beyond these bars even if I didn't, informed every day with my dog. Even if I got to train a hundred other puppies, he would always hold a special place in my heart; Shark would always be my first.

Charles and I had been dating almost a year when he suddenly decided that it was time that I met his mother. "She's heard all

about you, Rose, and would love to have you be her guest for
a weekend in the Hamptons."

"I don't know if I can get the time off."

"Of course you can. We'll fly down on Saturday morning."

The letter from Wright, Melrose & Foster had been ripped
into tiny pieces and tossed before my father got home that
night. I'd assured my mother that Charles wasn't about to steal
their house. Our house. I'd heard of eminent domain, but I
didn't think it applied to this. I really didn't know, and I didn't
mention it to my mother.

Teddy pressed another puzzle piece into the eternally unfinished puzzle. "You know, there's something I just don't like
about that guy."

"Teddy, he's my boyfriend."

"Maybe he just likes you for your house."

I responded with something crass and got a withering look
from my mother.

I was cowardly around Charles. After that impulsive call,
I never again brought up the subject of the letter to him. I never
pressed to ask if his firm really was intent on buying out those
last three homes on our street. I didn't want to know. I didn't
want to be lied to.

"Mary Rose. You must be Irish." Cecily Foster sipped a delicate
taste of the "very dry" martini that Charles had made for her.
We were seated in the great room of her Hamptons "cottage."
The panoramic view of Long Island Sound was breathtaking
even for a girl who was no stranger to the water. Boston Harbor
and its islands maybe aren't breathtaking, but it's a pretty scene.

"I am. Mostly." I have plenty of Irish pride; I come from a
part of America that is renowned for its Irish ethnicity. Some
of my antecedents had been here since the Revolution. Others

had arrived in the mid-nineteenth century, hungry and in dire straits. I smiled at her, my Irish pride showing.

"And Collins. Any relation to the poet Billy Collins?"

"I wish."

"Catholic, then, I presume?"

I was so awestruck by my surroundings that I didn't hear the bigotry in that offhanded remark. Who in this century was biased against a mainstream religion? It wasn't like I even had a crucifix around my neck. Much later, I would understand how my fellow inmates who were of Muslim origin felt at the sidelong glances, the hostile looks at their hijabs.

I should have known then that I was in trouble. Cecily Foster had only the bluest of blood flowing in her veins and she'd married a man equally patrician. In their insular world, blacks were politely tolerated, Hispanics were staff, and folks like me, of blue-collar origin, were to be avoided.

"Mother, you and Rose have something in common."

"What's that?"

"You have the same alma mater."

Cecily raised one eyebrow. "How interesting. I was a legacy student. Were you?"

"No. I was a scholarship girl." Best to get that right on the table. I tried not to see Charles's reaction. He'd been so sweet to try to prove my worth to his mother through our common alma mater, and I'd tossed the goodwill away with the mention of receiving need-based help from a scholarship association that sought to diversify the student population, which trended toward being upper-middle-class and beyond. I could hardly add that the scholarship covered only my first year; thus, I was one of the legion of debt-burdened graduates.

Cecily Foster was a lot like some of the girls I'd met my first year. I'd encountered her type before, that saccharine niceness obscuring their fear and hostility toward someone who is otherwise *not our kind.*

"Rose graduated summa."

"Well, of course, I married at the end of my junior year." Somehow, Cecily made that sound like an accomplishment far greater than my exemplary grades. It probably was. She was sitting in the great room of a palatial summer house overlooking Long Island Sound, tastefully dressed in Lilly Pulitzer and pearls. I was living at home with my parents and shilling coffee for a living.

A black woman in a pink uniform came into the room to announce that luncheon—the last three letters stood out to me—was ready. We picked up our drinks and drifted out onto the terrace. Charles took his mother's arm in a display of filial grace. Later, I would figure out that he was just making sure she got to the table without spilling a drop.

When I sat down for my first prison meal, also lunch—without the last three letters—I was asked how long I was in for. In the same mildly curious tone of voice, Mrs. Foster asked me what I did. I had prepared for this, practicing acceptable variations on selling fancy coffee. But before I could answer, something along the lines of "finding myself before I launch out into the world by working behind the counter of a specialty coffee shop and learning some of life's hard lessons," Charles sprang a surprise on me. "Rose will be coming to work for Wright, Melrose & Foster."

"Charles?" The tomato on the end of my fork dropped to my plate.

"And moving in with me."

How like Charles never to have mentioned this to me.

Cecily's reaction was marvelous. "Are you to be engaged, then?" The Botox prevented her from frowning, but her eyes glittered with terror.

"Not quite." Charles went back to eating his lunch, as if he hadn't just dropped a bomb on both of us.

"Oh, I see. It's an *arrangement*. Of course." The terror modified into relief. Boys must sow their wild oats.

I was a communications major, I knew code for *whore*. "Charles, we really should talk about this."

Charles fixed his gray eyes on me, lifted his square chin, and smiled. "Louisa, would you please bring us a bottle of that Dom Pérignon I know Mother has tucked away? I think we should celebrate."

The one thing that I was sure Cecily Foster and my mother would have in common was their distaste for this new *arrangement*.

Along with our dogs, we were introduced to our trainer, a nervous youngish man, Jack Dunham. At first, I thought the nerves were because of us, of being in the same room with inmates, but I soon figured out that he was just one of those fidgety kind of guys. The only time he was relaxed was when he was focused on demonstrating the commands: sit, stay, heel, down, the four elements that comprised the basic training of these puppies. Once those commands were perfected, we would take on the work of teaching the puppies how to be helpful to their ultimate handlers. Two were destined to become bomb-sniffing dogs working for the TSA. Others, like my Shark, were earmarked for service- or assistance-dog work: flipping light switches and picking up dropped objects; standing still to support someone's rise out of a chair; standing close to absorb fear, nerves, panic. I knew right away that Shark would be perfect at the latter. A lot of my own darkness of spirit had been dissipated simply by his presence in my life.

Now every day was different; routines were new. I even spent more time in the prison yard, rehearsing Shark on his commands, with the distraction of other inmates and the fresh air. And playing fetch with him. The greatest privilege was the evening last call, when we were allowed to go into the exercise yard with our dogs just before lights-out. The first time we were let out, I looked up and saw stars. I hadn't seen a night sky in all its glory in years. Despite the overwhelming presence of the prison lights, there, in the middle, was a patch of dark sky, pale stars pinned to it.

Shark

He's happy to meet this new person. In his short life, he's been cosseted and played with and cuddled and asked to learn certain manners. He's getting better about most of them. This new person has a different scent than the ones he's known since he left his dam's side. Where all the others carry the scent of the outdoors, this one does not. Her scent is that of inside. But as he investigates her more thoroughly, even going so far as to taste her skin, he understands that she is going to need his fun sense more than any of the other people in his short life. So he flops onto his back and pretends to bite her foot. He is instantly rewarded with that altogether marvelous sound of human laughter.

Meghan

"You should talk to that fella." Meghan's mother glanced toward a young man sitting opposite them in the physical therapist's waiting area. He wasn't any more remarkable than any of those who did their obligatory hours with weights and stretching and balance work. Scruffy, vacant-eyed; a cane across his lap and the prosthetic legs showing beneath his cargo shorts. The only distinguishing thing about him was the presence of a dog.

Meghan stubbornly refused to follow her mother's glance, instead scowling at the suggestion she go make small talk with another client in this place just because they had one common trait, military service. Okay, two things in common, serious and obvious wounds.

"Ask about the dog," Evelyn whispered.

Meghan pursed her lips in annoyance, but her mother wasn't taking the hint.

"Okay. I'll ask him. Sir, we were noticing your dog. Is he a service dog?"

"Mom, for God's sake, it's got a vest on; of course it's a service dog."

The young man's face went from glum to bright. "Yes. She. She's a trained service dog. My lifesaver, to tell you the truth."

Evelyn got up from her seat beside Meghan and went to sit with the young man. "What does she do for you?"

As he talked, he stroked the dog's head. The dog, a golden retriever, had her eyes riveted to the man's face. Her soft muzzle was open, showing a row of perfect white teeth and a pink tongue.

Meghan feigned a deep interest in a *Women's Health* magazine showing fit young bodies, which only reminded her of what she'd lost. But, out of the corner of her eye, she watched, half-listening as her mother interrogated the wounded warrior. "Where did you get her?" Evelyn sat on the right side of the young man and spoke close to his ear, as if she assumed that he, like Meghan, was hard of hearing.

"My buddy heard of this program and called me. Best thing I ever did."

Meghan dropped the magazine and it flopped to the tile floor with a slap. The dog broke from her study of the young man to look at Meghan, the half-open mouth now closed, ears on alert for threat. "Oh, Mom, sorry . . ." She breezily gestured toward the dropped magazine.

Evelyn ignored Meghan and continued her conversation with the veteran.

Then one of the physical therapists came to the door. "Mr. Silensky."

The young man got himself to his feet, the dog beside him. "Her name's Ivy. Thank you for not trying to pet her. She's working."

"I knew better than to do that. Good luck." Evelyn gave

the veteran one of her most winning smiles, reminding Meghan of the way she'd smile at the gang of boys who used to come to their house after school, Mark's friends. Offer up a welcoming smile and a plate of brownies.

Evelyn returned to her seat beside Meghan, picked up the fallen magazine, and put it back on the pile of reading materials. "Next time, you should talk to him."

"Why? I'm not interested in getting a pet."

"You know as well as I do, they aren't pets. They're service animals."

"What I see is one more creature for you to take care of. Remember why we didn't have pets when I was a kid? Too much work, you said."

"We moved too much, Meghan, and besides, I'm just suggesting that you might be interested."

"Again, to what end?"

The effort to change position made it a nightly exercise in how long she could tolerate being in the position she was in before she extended the effort to roll to her other side. In those long hours, she rehearsed the names and ranks and smiles of those she'd been close to in-country. She didn't want to forget them. She didn't want them to forget her. The air-conditioning in her room was set too high. Her arms were freezing; the thin Florida-weight blanket did nothing to warm her. I'm a creature of heat, she thought, of hot, dry living, with the taste of fine windblown grit flavoring everything. She licked her lips. She should call out, demand that the air-conditioning be shut off, but she knew that the heat that would then envelop her would be of a thick, viscous, humid variety and as unlike Iraqi heat as mud is from sand. She pushed the button that would elevate her. She had finally convinced her mother that she didn't need bed rails, reasoning that as she couldn't turn over, how was she going to fall out of bed? Sitting, she could reach the trapeze that dangled over her bed.

That embarrassing moment in the waiting room with her mother making nice with that dog-assisted vet had gotten Meghan thinking about the military working dogs that she had known. Real service dogs. Bomb sniffers. Security guards. Keeping watch with their handlers. Carrying their own burden of gear and never complaining. Never counting the days until the end of deployment, just doing their best. One dog in particular came to mind, an explosive-detection dog. Not one of the aloof Belgian Malinois, but a spaniel. He looked more suited to a snuggle on a couch than poking his nose in and around vehicles stopped at checkpoints, sussing out with his remarkable nose the hint of explosive material. All for a chance to play with his tug-of-war toy. Sidney, his name was. And his handler turned a blind eye when one of the newer soldiers, sitting po-faced in the convoy, pale and swallowing hard against fear, reached out to the soft-coated dog, running a trembling hand along the dog's spine, stroking his ears with nicotine-stained fingers. Okay, maybe once or twice she'd given in to the temptation to touch the dog, to feel the strange comfort of his pink tongue touching her hand.

Meghan looked down at her hand, the soft fabric of the lightweight blanket clutched between her fingers.

Although she professed to hate it, Meghan, by necessity, spent a lot of time watching television. Her day had become a routine of morning news shows, afternoon movie picks, and evening sitcoms. Her mother had finally given up trying to convince her that she wasn't purposeless. Right now, Meghan felt that her purpose in life was to blot out thinking with mindless television. The opiate of the masses, hadn't someone said that? How apt. Once she got comfortable, she could focus on whatever nonsense was in front of her instead of the nagging pain, raise the volume to drown out the incessant desire to relieve that pain with an oxycodone pill.

Tonight, she'd accidentally tuned in to a documentary about therapy dogs, and as the remote had slipped out of her hand to the floor, she was helpless to flip the channel. With both of her parents out of the house for an hour, there was no yelling for help. She really had no interest in watching this "heartwarming" documentary that would make her angry. Angry because of the exploitative nature of pity. In her opinion, the documentarian would milk the pity scene, the struggles, the self-consciousness of the tragically handicapped, either from birth or some terrible accident of fate; and then, the glorious moment—and who was to say it wasn't scripted?—of success when the dog would bring the veteran some out-of-reach object, like a phone or a freakin' remote. Oh, no, *let's hear it for the dog.* Life will be wonderful now.

And yet, there was something poignant about the autistic kid and the dog who made it possible for him to manage in school.

One section of the program, maybe a quarter of the broadcast, talked about dogs being trained to work with wounded warriors. She thought that she recognized the inside of Walter Reed. Then again, maybe all VA hospitals looked alike. They interviewed a guy with raging PTSD and another like the guy she'd seen at therapy, a double amputee.

She hadn't seen him lately. The last time she'd seen him leave the building, the dog was at his side and he was laughing at something. The big window of the waiting room looked out over the parking lot, and Meghan couldn't help but notice that he was being picked up by a young woman in a top-down

Mini Cooper. She didn't jump out of the car to help him. She
kissed him. The dog leaped into the backseat.

The PTSD sufferer looked into the camera and acknowl-
edged that he might not still be alive if it weren't for his dog.

The documentary broke for a PBS fund-raising segment.

"Meghan, do you want a drink?" asked Evelyn, back from
her single hour of respite.

"Mom, come in and watch this."

The fund-raising segment over, the documentary had
moved on to who trained these dogs. Various organizations
were mentioned, but only one was featured. On-screen, an
African-American woman dressed in plain blue jeans and a
T-shirt talked about how her dog, a Labrador, was almost
ready to take on his mission, to be the constant companion
of a returning veteran suffering from multiple injuries. "I've
worked with him for almost a year and I can tell you that this
dog knows his job." What was remarkable about the woman
was that she was identified as an inmate of a correctional facility in New York. The look on the prisoner's face was joyful,
and a little sad. The expression on the soldier's face was
clearly one of hope.

And there it was, the money shot, a former U.S. Navy SEAL
with tears in his eyes.

"I could find out where Ken Sllensky got his dog."

"Don't."

"Why not?"

"If I do it, and I'm not saying I will, I would want to go
through the prison program."

Evelyn smiled, putting her hands on her daughter's shoulders. "Whenever you're ready. We can make room for a dog."

"No. Don't you see? The whole point of getting a service
dog is so that I can leave."

Meghan felt the loosening of her mother's hands on her shoulders. "Okay."

There was no local program where they lived in Florida. There was a program in New York, and another in Connecticut. "Mom, why don't you call your cousin Carol. Doesn't she live in Fairfield?"

"We haven't had any contact with the New England cousins in years."

The glue holding the relatives together all those years ago had been Evelyn's grandmother, Henrietta Baxter, matriarch over all. Once Gramma had passed, and as Meghan's dad had gone from posting to posting, her mother let the connection to her living cousins thin out. They'd all last seen one another when Mark died. A Christmas card now and then. Evelyn was clearly squeamish about imposing on a long-lost relative, but Meghan was not. Once you've been blown up by an IED, there's little to be squeamish about. "Never mind, I'll call her. Hand me my iPad. Nothing more fun than looking up long-lost relatives online. I'll see if I can track her down on Facebook."

By the end of the day, Meghan and her first cousin once removed, Carol Baxter-Flint, had friended each other. By the end of the month, Meghan's parents had put her on a plane headed for Bradley International Airport, where Carol and Don Flint would meet her plane.

Rosie

Shark and I made great progress in our basic training, the stuff of sit, stay, down. Heel was coming along, and of the four dogs in the program, I can say without exaggeration that he was the cleverest. LaShonda's Mimi was a cute pup, but stubborn. Zella and her Lab struggled, and I think it was because she didn't have quite enough patience to stick to it. She got frustrated, and I wasn't surprised when she dropped out of the program. Next thing I heard, Zella was sent down to seg. I was sorry to hear that; after all, you had to be clean of infractions for two years before even being considered for the program. LaShonda told me later that Zella had gotten word that her teenage son had been killed on the street. Her only child, a boy she had barely had a chance to raise. So when Edith came to help us work on specialized training, I took her aside.

"Zella really needs another chance." I told her what I'd heard. "She needs this. She may not realize it, but I think it would help a lot more than getting into trouble and being segregated." Shark was sitting on my feet, as he liked to do, and the weight of him doing that reminded me of being held. Not held by a boyfriend, but by a parent or dear friend. Maybe he reminded me most of Teddy, who would roll up next to me and wrap his arms around my waist and press his head against me and tell me that I was the best sister he had. Our joke. Of everyone I had lost, I missed him the most.

"I wish it was up to me, Rosie. But it's not." Edith had been disappointed by Zella's failure, and by the fact that no one else stepped up to take her place. The dog had been moved to the New York facility. We missed her, the only yellow Lab in the group, a portly little dog who would do anything for a chance to chase the ball.

The remaining dog was another black Lab, Scooter, who was handled by a tough lesbian whose insecurities manifested themselves in her being equally silent and combative. But with her dog, Pilar was all mushy-squishy, lovey-dovey. Because we were often in the activity room together, and all working toward the same goal, Pilar eventually showed us a certain wry charm. But we kept it to ourselves rather than jeopardize her reputation as a hard-ass among the rest of the prison population.

So, there we were, three women of varying backgrounds, crimes, and sentences. Eventually, I knew, these others would be paroled. With success in this program, they might even earn their way out via time off for good behavior. Their remaining sentences combined were half a decade less than the sixteen years I still had left unless God was good and the elusive parole I hankered after was granted. Every time I was eligible to ask, I was bluntly denied parole. Cecily Foster's reach was long and her anger undiminished. That sounds paranoid and like something out of a bad novel, but it was true.

The other loss that was inevitable was, of course, that these first dogs would graduate from our care and go into the hands of those for whom we'd trained them. It was hard enough on weekends to watch our dogs happily join up with the volunteers who socialized them on the outside. If we were successful, we knew that soon enough we'd have another puppy to work with, and that was some comfort. In our own lives, we'd each suffered catastrophic losses, and so losing a puppy to a PTSD sufferer or a paraplegic was not a loss, I told myself; it was a sign of success.

Not long after I got Shark, I got in line at the bank of telephones. I leaned against the wall, moving up slowly and taking the long wait to school my puppy on sit and stay, but mostly I spent the hour introducing him to the ladies who gathered around, each one profoundly desiring to touch this dog. They oooed and aahed and one or two even embarrassedly wiped away a tear. When Teddy was in the rehabilitation hospital after one of his surgeries, volunteers would bring in pets for the patients to cuddle. It was pretty much like that with Shark, who became this emissary from the life outside, an emissary of normal, and one happy to lick noses. I wiped up his excitement-caused piddle, and when it was finally my turn at the phone, I wasn't nervous anymore about dialing my mother's number.

On the rare Sunday when she would answer the phone, the minute my mother heard the prison operator's voice asking if she'd accept a call from Mid-State Women's Correctional Facility, she would hang up. This time, she didn't. I considered that progress, and maybe it was the surprise of getting a call on a Wednesday instead of a Sunday that kept her from hanging up. Maybe she was alone in the house. At any rate, she said yes.

My mother listened without comment to my nattering on about getting into the dog-training program. I gushed about having this wonderful, smart, active puppy and how he distinguished me from most of the other inmates—although I referred to them as ladies, not inmates. It was a bit like not mentioning the recently deceased to the chief mourner, in the vain belief that by keeping mum you wouldn't remind her of her loss. An impossibility. Nonetheless, I tried hard to pretend as if I were in a new women's college, never using the words *prison, inmates, guards,* in the naïve hope that my mother wouldn't remember that she was on the phone with her convict daughter. To hear me talk, I was just away, not incarcerated.

"He's so darn smart. You should see him. His little face gets all scrunchy, just like he's trying to figure out a puzzle. He'll do anything for a game of fetch." We trained with toys as rewards, not treats. Shark lived for his tennis ball, and Mimi would do anything for her squeaky. Scooter loved tug-of-war.

Even as I pontificated on the various training methods we were employing, I knew that my mother was struggling to stay on the phone with me, and I talked faster and faster, as if my dime was going to run out. She had never once come to Connecticut to see me and she had forbidden my brothers to make the trip. Ever the obedient sons, even well into their thirties, they complied. She avoided most of my calls, and I don't know if she ever even opened up my letters. I certainly never got one back from her. It wasn't what put me in there that alienated us; it was what had happened long before. In my mother's view, I had abandoned the family, turned my back on them in their critical moment, and I was dead to them. Do you remember that scene in *Fiddler on the Roof* when Tevye, pushed to accept two daughters' independent choices for marriage, cannot and will not accept his last daughter's choice of the Russian soldier? That's kind of what it was like. I had gone a treasonable step too far.

My brother Patrick had sat in front of me, cradling a cup of hot coffee between his big hands. He had that Collins skin and hair, both tending toward red, especially in circumstances like the one he found himself in on this winter afternoon. Like the rest of us, he had blue eyes framed by sandy lashes. My third-eldest brother, he was always the spokesman for the family. Unlike the rest of us, he didn't have a diminutive added to his name—Paulie, Frankie, Bobby, Teddy, and Rosie. He was Patrick or Pat. Maybe that's why he always seemed more mature. He was the only one with a proper adult name. No wonder, now that I think of it, I always called Shark "Sharkey."

"Out with it, man. What brings you to the posh side of town?" We were in a coffee shop near to my South End apartment—the one I now shared with Charles. I had been shocked to get Patrick's call, his dour request that I meet him that day.

"It's Dad."

"Bronchitis again?" I was mildly ashamed at my cringing at the sound of Dad's wet cough and the fact that I had been embarrassed by it in front of Charles at that dinner with my folks.

Pat unclenched his coffee cup and reached for my hand. "Cancer."

Such an awful word. Followed by the particular variety our father had, mesothelioma, a word like a curse. All the years he'd spent in construction, ripping out insulation from old buildings, tearing down ceilings, he was breathing in the asbestos that filled the air. We all knew about asbestos; of course we did. Nowadays, workers wore proper protection. But our father had begun working when he was fifteen years old, long before anyone knew how deadly it could be.

"How? He's been a supervisor for as long as I can remember. He doesn't do the grunt work anymore."

"Rosie, it doesn't work that way. He was exposed twenty-some years ago. He's been living with a time bomb."

"Oh my God." I blew my nose into a paper napkin. "I've got to go home."

"Yes." Patrick removed his hand from mine. "You need to be there." It had been some months since I'd last been home. *Home.* Why did I, a grown woman living in a large, well-equipped apartment with a man who gave her everything, still think of her parents' cramped house as home?

"Pat?" I couldn't quite bring the words to my mouth. Asking how long he had seemed like an inconsiderate question. One that would suggest I had other things on my plate. Other concerns.

"I don't know. We don't know."

So I told Charles that I would need to spend more time with my family. He kept an arm around my shoulders as I weepily described to him the bare facts that my brother had described to me. No, we didn't know how long, but that I needed to be there with them.

"Of course," he said. "You can see him after work as often as you want."

"I think I need to do more than that."

"Like what?"

"I don't know. Be there for my mother."

Charles smiled at me, revealing perfect teeth but no humor. "But what about me? I need you, too."

"I know you do."

Having grown up in a large family, even though the only girl, my share of parental attention was parceled out in small dribs of necessity. Always there was someone else's needs, a permission-slip crisis while I was trying to get my mother to notice my crayon drawing; if my mother was overseeing homework at the kitchen table, it was one of my less achieving brothers who got the lion's share of attention. And then there was Teddy. After his injury, I was simply grateful to have my father's nod of approval as I sashayed around the living room in my prom dress. I loved my brother, and told myself that it was everyone's job now to make him comfortable. So when Charles told me so often that he *needed* me, I mistook that for filling a gap in my emotional life. I mistook it for fulfilling *my* needs.

The rift was exacerbated when I announced that I was moving in with Charles.

I had been living back in my parents' house for well over a year when Charles and I met, and almost a year later, I informed them that I would be moving. In. With. Charles.

"I'm over twenty-one." I didn't even try to keep my powder dry.

"You won't be happy with him." My mother folded her arms across her midsection, lifted her chin, and then pointed at me. It was as if she was placing a curse on me. I could almost hear the bones rattle, smell the brimstone.

Of course, that letter from Wright, Melrose & Foster did nothing to further relations. Not the first one, and certainly not the several others that followed.

"I have to go." The only four words my mother had spoken through this lopsided conversation.

"Okay. Are you okay? How's everyone? The kids must be getting big." I had a bunch of nieces now. The younger ones were kids I'd seen only in the family Christmas photo that my third-eldest brother, Patrick, sent every year, probably against Mom's wishes. In some cosmic irony, my brothers had produced only female children. Paulie's eldest was a freshman in high school and Frankie's wife had just had a baby girl.

I might have been talking to a garden statue for all the response I got.

"Okay, then. I love you."

Nothing.

"Everything okay?" LaShonda took the dead phone from my hand.

"Yeah. Everything's fine." Just then I felt a nudging against my leg, Shark pressing himself against me, and I realized that he'd been leaning against me for the past few minutes. I bent and stroked his smooth head. "Everything's fine."

Shark

This inside woman fairly quivers with agitation. She holds that thing against her head and he can smell the odor of unhappiness exude from her pores. He breathes it in and pushes himself against her as hard as he can in order to make it stop. She presses the thing against her chest and then slams it down. He jumps up, barks, and then sits on her feet. He knows that it is his job to make her be happy again. It's his work and he is proud to do it. *Please smile at me.*

Meghan

Meghan hadn't been expecting that she'd have to undergo a lengthy application process just to get in line to take advantage of the puppy-and-prisoner program. Somehow she had imagined that it would be more like jumping onto a moving train, that the process was more or less ongoing. Handicapped—no pun intended—by the fact she had to utilize the Connecticut program because the only way she could do this was by imposing on her near-stranger cousin Carol cut her chances of getting in by half. There were only four dogs being trained in Connecticut, and over fifty hopeful candidates for placement. The odds seemed terribly stacked against her. Meghan ticked off the boxes for why she felt a dog would help. Physical limitations, check. Seizure disorder, no. Anxiety disorders, check. Independence issues? Check, check, check.

Carol was being a good sport about having a special-needs relative descend upon her just as she was done launching her children, was settling into a contented empty-nest situation, and was getting back to focusing on her pet projects. Meghan's arrival had effectively thrown her back into a caretaking role. Accommodations had been made. A temporary ramp was attached to the front door, marring the lovely curb appeal of their gambrel roof mid-century Colonial-style house on a cul-de sac in Fairfield. It stuck out like a derisive tongue.

"Once I have an interview, I'll fly home. It's going to be a longer process than I ever thought. I can't impose on you. . . ."

"Nonsense. We love having you." When she said this, Meghan could see a flash of her mother in Carol's face, a trick of genetics that cast a kindly expression into a distinctive trait shared by two people who barely knew each other. Meghan wondered if she sometimes had that expression and decided that she probably didn't. She more resembled her father's side of the family; plus, she never was very kind, or selfless. Not anymore.

"Look. Let's be honest with each other. You didn't bargain for this, and I'm very, very grateful, but I won't be a burden longer than necessary."

"Meghan, you're family and you've had a long, tough journey. We're thrilled to be able to see you through another part of it. A good part."

Meghan nodded, not trusting herself to speak. She reached out to touch Carol's hand. "Mom said you were the best of the cousins. She was right."

Carol and her husband both worked in the city, commuting in on Metro North, leaving the house before seven in the morning and sometimes not returning until after nine at night. "Once the kids were gone, we didn't have to rush back, so now we indulge ourselves in staying later, grabbing dinner and then getting a later, less crowded train back. Will you be all right?"

"Yes, of course. I can fend for myself."

"You might be bored."

"Maybe. But that's kind of how my life is."

It was Carol's turn to take Meghan's hand, the unscarred one. "You'll get a dog, Meghan. And then you'll get back to your life."

"I hope so." Back to what? For so many years, her life had been that of a soldier, then a patient. She wasn't going to return to either of those pursuits. If indeed she successfully acquired a dog, what then? When she mentioned this, Don Flint, her cousin by marriage, suggested that, with her undergraduate degree in history, she might pursue the law or teaching.

Late at night in her soft yellow bedroom in the guest wing of the Flints' house, Meghan wondered if she'd gone off the deep end, thinking that having a service dog would really move her forward. She half-decided to call it quits. If she didn't hear from the organization tomorrow, she'd pull the plug on this quixotic quest after elusive independence. Chalk it up to a pipe dream.

After a restless night, Meghan was late getting up in the morning. When she rolled in from her bedroom, Carol was dressed for work and sitting at the island counter, a coffee mug in her hand. She was smiling, and, once again, Meghan saw her mother in Carol's face. "You look pleased with yourself this morning." She grabbed the mug that Carol had left on the counter for her. Poured herself coffee.

"FedEx was here."

The application was complete, the interview scheduled. For the first time in, well, maybe forever, Meghan fussed about what to wear. Uniforms had one singular advantage: You never had to worry about what to wear. The military told you what to wear for what occasion. Fatigues or formal wear, khaki or dress uniform. Living as she did in sweatpants and sweatshirts, Meghan was left to decide which set to wear, the navy blue or the more cheerful cherry red. Carol just shook her head. "No. We can do better than that."

The next evening, Carol came home with a bag from Athletica. "Not exactly formal wear, but I think that a change of fabric will cheer you up." Carol pulled a set of technical-fabric snap-side warm-up pants and a nylon shell windbreaker out of the bag. "And the pièce de résistance, tada! A pair of crisp New Balance trainers."

Meghan cradled the sneakers in her lap. "Carol, I can't . . ."

"Of course you can. I've missed a lot of your birthdays, so happy birthday."

"It's not till . . ." Meghan began to laugh. "You're too much."

"My pleasure."

It wasn't as easy for Carol to get Meghan into and out of her sedan as it was for Meghan's dad to do it with the fancy van, but they managed. The interview wasn't at the prison, contrary to what Meghan had expected, but in an office building in Danbury.

Edith Moore greeted Meghan in the foyer of the building. Carol bent and gave Meghan a kiss on the cheek and walked away. The elevator doors opened and Meghan wheeled herself in, Edith behind her. What was it they said? If you could pitch your sale in the time it took the elevator to arrive at your floor, you had a better chance of making the sale.

"My company had an MWD, military working dog, a bomb sniffer, who three times saved my platoon. I know how valuable a dog can be. I really believe that having a dog will—"

"Captain Custer, Meghan, hang on. Let's do this right."

The elevator doors opened. Edith waited until Meghan

eased herself over the slightly out-of-alignment edge. She didn't offer to help, made no move to push the chair.

The office was clearly arranged with people like Meghan in mind. No desk, but a broad conference table high enough that she could slip her chair in close. Edith sat at one end, Meghan along the long side, facing a bank of windows. A sweating water carafe and a stack of plastic cups were on the table, placed conveniently to Meghan's position. Meghan resolved not to reach for it, betray no weakness. But wasn't that the point? She needed a dog, a service dog. She needed help.

Edith opened a manila file folder and looked at the contents, her mouth pursed a little. Meghan wondered if that meant she was worried, or was it just a habit? So many others had studied file folders with her name on them—medical files, performance files, military files. What would this particular file reveal? What in it pointed to Meghan's being deserving of a service dog, of help?

"Shall we get started?" Edith's pursed mouth gave nothing away.

"When will I know? About being accepted into the program?"

Edith closed the manila folder with Meghan's name on the tab, closed her eyes for a moment, and sighed. "Very soon. We've got three more candidates to interview for this round. Two of them have been on the list for half a year."

"Is that your way of letting me down easy?"

"No. It's just the truth. From what I can gather, you prefer the truth over obfuscation."

"Yes." In the field, in-country, it never paid to understate a situation. A soldier who wasn't perfectly blunt with news or information wasted valuable time.

"Then I'll be honest."

Meghan felt a surge of the same kind of jitters as she'd once felt walking into an Afghani building. Not enough to be compromised, to be a danger to herself and others, just enough nerves to be alert.

"You have as much chance as anyone."

Carol Baxter-Flint considered her cousin Meghan to be a hero. Anyone who joined the service and went not once, not twice, but three times overseas into, as the expression went, harm's way had to be a hero. Captain's bars. Responsibility for the enlisted. Uncomplaining deprivation. That was hero stuff for sure.

"I hate it when people say I'm a hero. I didn't do anything particularly heroic, except do my job." They were sitting in Carol's kitchen, a glass of wine in front of each of them. It was that quiet hour before dinner preparations. A full week had gone by since Meghan's interview and Meghan had just announced that she would be making a plane reservation home if she hadn't heard anything by midweek, at the day-ten mark. Every day that went by seemed as though it was a prelude to disappointment. And that amazed her, because she hadn't been so keen on the idea of a service dog six months ago, and now she was bucking herself up for disappointment.

"I think that you're being modest."

Meghan wanted to change the subject. "You and Mom used to go to Gramma Baxter's for the summer?"

"We did, and all the others, too. It was a grand place, full of life. Just like Gramma."

"I wish I'd known her. Gramma Baxter."

On the wall in the hallway that led from the kitchen to the bedrooms, there was a line of family photographs, all of them black-and-white. Meghan rolled past them on her way to her room without too much attention, as they were all above her head. Carol went to fetch one of them. "This is Gramma

Baxter. Your great-grandmother." She handed the framed five-by-eight photo to Meghan.

Meghan studied the face in the picture. The stern-faced woman, perhaps in her late fifties, early sixties—it was hard to tell with that generation—was wearing a flowered dress with a white collar and was seated in an overstuffed chair, a big dog by her side. Her hand was on the dog's head, and the flashbulb had given the animal a peculiar light in its eyes.

Behind her in the photograph was a lineup of the third generation; Meghan recognized Carol, and her own mother, Evelyn, who looked to be about six, but the others were strangers. Carol introduced Meghan to the Baxter cousins, three boys and the eldest girl, Donna, who had the sad distinction of being the first of that generation to pass away.

"And the dog?" Maybe it's just that dogs had been on her mind, but she was pleased to see that, at least in the past, her family had been dog people.

"Boy." Carol said. "One of several mutts of unknown origin who showed up on the doorstep. She never looked for them; they found her."

Meghan handed the photo back to Carol.

"You and your mom should be getting the family newsletter. This bunch is just the tip of the Baxter iceberg."

"Do you all still go there?"

"No, but the house is still in the family. Once Gramma died and the cousins were raising their own families, it got harder to get together."

Carol went to rehang the photograph and Meghan rooted around the drawers for a potato peeler. Wineglasses were refilled as the two women got to work. As they did, the conversation turned to the second interview. "I feel like I'm getting closer, but I'm scared to get my hopes up too much."

"There are other programs, Meghan. We can find another one if this doesn't work out."

"I know. I've done some research and that's a possibility. But there's something about the prison program that appeals to me The idea of rehabilitation on several levels."

"Yours and some inmate's?"

Meghan nodded as she picked up another potato. "Some thing like that."

Carol looked at her watch. "Don will be home in a few."

"He's a good guy."

"Yeah, I know. It's why I have to forgive the fact he can't get his dirty clothes into the hamper. Harvard Law and no common sense, I always say."

Just as she picked up the last potato, Meghan's phone rang. A Connecticut area code. Meghan felt her heart bang against her chest and she was certain that her voice shook as she said hello.

Suddenly, Carol was there, her hands on Meghan's shoulders.

Rosie

All of a sudden, it had been ten months, the longest period of time I'd had since my sentencing where I didn't hate every minute of the day. My days started with a wet nose pressed into the warm skin of my neck. A quick dash outside to the exercise area, and then I fed Sharkey his breakfast, put him back in his crate, and went to get my own. By now, LaShonda, Pilar, and I sat together in the dining room, wanting nothing more than to talk about our dogs, to see how the other dogs were doing versus our own. Of course, we all believed we had the best of the best, but the truth is, *we* were all doing remarkably well in the training of our dogs. Our *dogs* were doing remarkably well, considering none of us had ever trained a dog before. We were well past the basics and were into our specialty training now. The dogs had passed from gawky puppyhood to the punk stage to being almost fully grown. They were ready to take on their assignments.

The other inmates gave us our space and, except for the

very first time we'd sat together to eat, made no comment about it. There we were, white, black, Hispanic, hetero and gay, laughing, sharing training tips, making up our own little clique. We had the dogs and their training, and that gave us common ground. That gave us the roots of friendship. We called ourselves the "Sisterhood of the Dogs."

One Wednesday, I was called down to the warden's office, where Hinckley announced that Edith Moore, the director of the program, was in the visitors' room and I should go meet with her. My heart flipped over. I knew that this could only be about Shark's going to his new partner. I walked out of his office, Sharkey at my side.

Pilar and Scooter were coming down the hall.

"Edith is here. She wants to see me." I was fighting to keep control over my voice, my hands, my heart.

Pilar patted my shoulder. "*Sé valiente. Todo está bien.*"

I didn't think it could ever be all right.

Edith Moore wasn't an attractive woman, but she always dressed beautifully in skirts and blouses that I knew were from good stores. A cashmere cardigan or velvet bolero jacket made the conventional and completely understated outfit stylish. I wanted to touch the cashmere, see if my fingers remembered the lovely softness of that yarn. I wondered if the velvet would feel like Shark's coat. Charles had dressed me in cashmere and velvet, leather and suede. It's funny, the kinds of things you long for when you're separated from luxury. I missed scented soap. I longed for the feel of something other than denim against my skin. I even missed polar fleece. I guess it wasn't luxury that I missed; it was softness.

"Miss Collins, thanks for seeing me." As if choice was an option for someone like me.

"I'm glad to see you. Do you have news for me? About a . . ." I wasn't sure what word to use. I was afraid that my emotions would reveal how not fine with this I was.

"A trainee. Yes. I think we have the perfect match for Shark."

"Good." I didn't sit down, and I knew that made the guard a little nervous, but he kept still. "When do I get to meet him?"

"Her. Next week. She's a wounded warrior. Paraplegic with a compromised left hand, some hearing loss. Burns."

"I'm so sorry." I sat down in the chair opposite Edith. I could feel the guard's relief.

"That's why you're here to help. You and Shark. You and she will work together with him for two weeks, every day, three hours a day. Shark won't be going out again for training weekends. Rosie, it's your job to teach her the commands." I nodded.

"And his job is to learn to take them from her," Edith said.

"He'll do it. He's really quick. He loves to perform."

"And you need to transfer his attachment to you to her."

Again, I could only nod.

"Okay, then." Edith got up to leave. "See you next week."

"Edith. Did you know that my brother was a paraplegic?"

Edith stood in the doorway to the hall that would take her back to the outside world. A guard held it open for her. "Yes, I did. You mentioned it in your first interview. It's one of the reasons you were chosen to be a trainer."

When my father got sick, I tried to divide my time between Charles and my family. When Dad was hospitalized, as he often was, I stayed home with Teddy. His jigsaw puzzles had been moved to the dining room and so we worked on the puzzles on the table that now was rarely cleared for family meals. I would return to the apartment I shared with Charles,

weary and sad. Charles would greet me as if I'd been off gal-
livanting with girlfriends, a little coldly; only later, after I had
cajoled him with sex would he think to ask how my father was.
And he never asked if there was anything he could do. I chose
to think of Charles as my oasis in the desert of my father's prolonged illness—an illness we all knew he wasn't going to recover from. I chose not to think Charles had an empathy
problem, but, rather, that as an only child he had had no experience with a family like mine. How could he?

My new job with Wright, Melrose & Foster was in the marketing department, where our job was to develop a steady
stream of positive outreach to potential clients. Social media,
newsletters both online and in print, a glossy brochure with
WM&F properties, some actual, some still imagined, complete
with the smiling faces of employed people enjoying an archi-
tecturally impressive building situated on a block where once
only trees—or run-down homes—had stood, as depicted in the
"before and after" renderings. The focus was to match properties with clients and then with architects. In effect, WM&F was
a matchmaker.

My job was an entry-level one. About as entry as you can
get. I filed, tallied clicks, and, yes, fetched coffee—a job for
which I demonstrated a remarkable proficiency. A proficiency
that might mean I'd never get promoted out of this modern-
day steno pool.

I was so excited on my first day. I had moved into Charles's
South End condo over the weekend and the flush of this new
step in our lives had me singing a cracked-voice version of Be-
yoncé's "Put a Ring on It." I wasn't being ironic; I was being
silly. Charles frowned, and reminded me of a very important
rule. No one at work was to know that we were a couple. "It
wouldn't look right. It would look like . . ."

"Nepotism?" I laughed.

He didn't answer.

"Where am I supposed to say I live?"

"At a nice address. We might be neighbors."

"Hellooo, neighbor." I sashayed up to him, did a little Marilyn Monroe shimmy.

"Hello yourself. New to this neighborhood?" Whatever else he would turn out to be, Charles was a pretty good lover.

It was getting late, and Charles, a clock watcher, grabbed the keys to his Camaro, which he had garaged half a block away. I slipped on my nice new Kate Spade heels, my lovely trench coat, and grabbed my bag. "I'm ready."

"Rose, you take the T. Or a cab." He shoved a few twenties into my hand. "We can't get out of the same car."

"I thought we were neighbors. Wouldn't you offer me a ride?"

"Don't be late to work on your first day, Rose."

I pulled off the heels and put on my Nikes to make the run to the T stop. I was probably going to be late my first day at Wright, Melrose & Foster.

And then one day, he called me into his office, something that he'd never done before. As far as anyone knew, we were strangers. My job did not take me into his circle.

He was beaming. That's the only word for it, like someone had turned on an inner light I'd never seen in him before. "Rosie. Pack your bags; we're moving to New York."

"I can't move now." I said it and immediately regretted it. The look on Charles's face spoke volumes, as they say. Clearly, he was surprised at my refusal. I didn't know if it was the fact that I so quickly stuck a pin in his excitement, or that he had truly not given my situation any thought at all.

"I'm only going to ask you once, Rose. This is your moment to decide if what we have is what you want."

"I do. It's just that this is such a bad time for me to leave."

"It's been a 'bad time' for you for the last six months. Are you telling me that you're going to put your life on hold, our life on hold, for however long your father survives?"

"No, of course not." But, of course, that was exactly what I had been doing. Over the past few weeks, Charles had convinced me that I didn't need to go see my father every evening when he wasn't in the hospital, but at home. When Dad was hospitalized, Charles was a bit more understanding, particularly as the hospital was closer and I could sneak over there on my lunch hour. And visiting hours had an end. I was often home just as Charles got home. He seemed to work later and later, and I assumed it was because I was otherwise occupied with my dying father. As it turned out, what Charles was doing was setting his company's new venture into motion. A New York City branch, of which he would be the top dog. This wasn't simply moving up in the company; it was the equivalent of becoming a founder. This wasn't a choice; this was destiny, according to Charles. He was taking his grandfather's success and building on it. Plus, he was going home to New York, where his mother had already offered us—him—her rarely used apartment overlooking Central Park.

At this point, Dad was back at home, where a hospital bed had been set up; the dining room table, incomplete puzzle still on it, was pushed to the back wall. A curtain on a tension rod hung in the doorway, affording him some privacy. The television—my family had only the one—had been moved into the dining room, as well, so he was rarely alone, especially during playoff season. My mother could cook and keep an eye on him. My job was to be the entertainment. Sometimes that was telling him stories about my day at work. Sometimes it was just flipping the channels until we found something that he could doze off to. I found it hard to leave after those visits, and despite the alternative arrangement of my childhood home, it still felt like I belonged there. It was comfortable, even with the weight of my father's disease changing the tenor of our family conversations from gruff to mild.

It took me a week before I announced that I would be moving with Charles to New York. It took that long for me to formulate my story. In my family, it was always family first. Charles wasn't family. Charles wasn't even close. My parents had received another letter, this one with a slightly higher offer in it. I had promised to look into the matter, but I never did. I wasn't in any position to go about questioning the decisions of senior management. I knew, even if my parents didn't, that I was still a flunky at Wright, Melrose & Foster.

What my parents also didn't know was that Charles had dangled the most tempting of fruits before me as an incentive toward making the decision he wanted me to make—we would announce our engagement to the world, which included WM&F. I was to be made public. So, in one way, this big move to New York was what made possible my being outed as Charles's girlfriend. Otherwise, I would continue to be the shadow girlfriend. I was withholding that bit of information because it just seemed wrong to find happiness while my parents' lives were being torn apart.

I left Edith in the visiting room and went back to my cell, where I lay on my bed and broke the rules by letting my dog climb up with me. I knew in my heart that whoever she was, this Meghan Custer, she would probably let Sharkey climb into her bed, too. Who wouldn't? He was dependably comforting. I whispered into his ear, breathing in his doggy scent. "Are you ready to complete your mission? Are you ready to leave me?"

Shark

There it is again, that sadness, but this time it is tempered with something else, an excitement that has his inside person working him twice as hard as she has done before—making sure he has his commands down, making sure he gets tons of playtime as a reward for simply doing what she asks. Even the dog knows that something special is coming.

A new word keeps being said: *Meghan*. It doesn't seem to be a command, and there is no action that is required after it is said, but he knows that there is significance in it. And, soon enough, he realizes that this is a name, like his own, something that identifies a particular human. And there she is.

Meghan

It was strange, but the prison didn't seem so foreign to Meghan as she might have thought. So many years of being a part of a large military-industrial complex had softened her attitude toward gunmetal gray and razor wire, uniforms. The first guard to greet her thanked her for her service, as did the second. The third, who opened the door to allow her to wheel into the visitors' room, bent down and whispered, "Two tours."

"Where?"

"Helmand Province."

Meghan touched his hand with her scarred one. "Good man."

"Where were you?"

Meghan shook her head. She was here to get better, not to have an informal reunion. "I'm here now."

Edith Moore had arrived ahead of Meghan and was sitting at a table in the visitors' room. Each rectangular table had four orange chairs fixed two to a side. Meghan rolled up to the empty end, keeping Edith to her right, where she could hear

her better. The high windows, crosshatched with wire, allowed
in enough light to reveal the sad, utilitarian nature of the room,
the mottled beige linoleum, the grimy tables, the ugly plastic
chairs. There was no one else in there, but the place still held
the odor of bodies, of the women and their families who filled
this place on Sunday and Wednesday afternoons. She couldn't
imagine children being brought in here to visit mothers.
Mothers should be associated with kitchens, with playgrounds
and baths at night.

"So, when do I get to meet her?" Her mouth was dry and
she wished she'd brought a bottle of water. "It's been almost
an hour."

"Soon. We're on their schedule, not ours." Edith, dressed
for the occasion in an A-line wool skirt and white blouse with
a floppy bow set both her palms on the surface of the slightly
sticky table. "This inmate has been working with her dog for
ten months. She's never done this before, so I don't know how
she'll react to actually giving him up. They all go into it knowing that the training is a temporary thing, but emotions aren't
always predictable."

"But she has to give him up."

"Yes, and I think she'll be okay, but just be prepared."

Meghan glanced at her phone, another minute went by,
then another. She thought about making a joke—"It's just like
the Army, hurry up and wait"—but didn't. A starling flitted
by the high windows, a dark etch against the blue sky. "What
did she do? To be put in here?"

"She's doing her time. What she did to be here has no rel
evance as to how well she'll train you to work with the dog.
We don't reveal that information; that's up to the inmate to
volunteer. And don't expect her to."

Another minute. Meghan was beginning to wish she'd taken
a pill. Something to take the edge off. She was uncomfortable,

but not in pain, and that had become her rule: She had to be in pain to take a pill. Knowing that she was going to have to be completely functional to take on the training of the dog had been a great incentive toward keeping the little white pills in their vial.

Finally, a door opened. Edith and Meghan looked up from their contemplation of their own hands to see a young woman come into the room accompanied by a uniformed guard. Her strawberry-blond hair was bundled into a loose bun, a few tendrils framing her face. She wasn't wearing a prison jumpsuit as Meghan had pictured, but generic blue jeans and a white T-shirt, plain white sneakers on her feet. *So, this is an inmate in its natural habitat.* But, she's smiling and there is something so very ordinary about her. Like Meghan, she's a little nervous. "Hey there, I'm Rosie."

They met for the first time without the dog. Meghan was surprised to be as nervous as she was, a feeling more appropriate to a first date. If you'd asked her what she was expecting, she would have said, "Not Rosie Collins." Not someone so, okay, say it, *normal.* No tattoos, no horns, no gum chewing, no foul-mouthedness. Meghan could see that Rosie was as nervous as she was. Maybe she wasn't expecting someone quite like *her.* Quite as wounded. And then Rosie said something that floored Meghan. "What kind of ride is that?" Meaning her wheelchair.

"It's not my regular one. I've got a motorized one back home."

"My brother coveted a motorized chair, but could never afford one."

"Wounded military?" She was ready to suggest a phone number for help.

"No. Homegrown wounding. He was a victim of gun violence. A paraplegic."

"I'm so sorry."

"We all were. It was a long time ago."

Meghan most often encountered people who tried hard to ignore the fact that she was in a wheelchair. They either didn't speak to her or spoke loudly, as if she were deaf. Which she kind of was, but still. Or they crouched down, so that she felt like a child being addressed by an adult. Rosie's quick acknowledgment of the chair made Meghan feel, in a very odd way, almost normal. The elephant wasn't allowed into the room.

Later, Meghan thought that if she and Rosie had met in a spin class or at a party, they would have hit it off and probably met up for drinks some Friday night. If they had been normal, they would have fallen into a friendship like two regular girls with similar interests. For Meghan, female friendships were few and far between, juxtaposed as they were by frequent deployments. Her female friends were also soldiers. They had one another's backs; they shared cookies from home; they wept privately together. These were intense relationships that were different from having a civilian friend. A civilian friend made sure your bra straps weren't showing; a soldier made sure your body armor was in place. They had a deep connection while in the field, but so often that connection was gone as soon as someone was sent home or reassigned.

"So, Rosie, what got you interested in this program?"

"Anything to change things up. It's pretty boring in here."

"I'll bet it is." Oddly, there were parts of this place that reminded Meghan of hospitals. Maybe it was the institutional vibe. Excluding the razor wire, of course.

"And why do you think a dog will help you?"

It was, of course, the first question in the first interview Meghan had endured while applying for the program. Her answer hadn't changed. "I need my independence back."

"Okay. Shark will help you with that."

"That's his name, Shark?"

"Yes." For the first time, Rosie looked unhappy. "I call him Sharkey. He's a Labrador, really sweet . . ." And then she stopped talking, turned her face away from Meghan.

Meghan glanced at the guard stationed in the corner. Edith Moore was talking with the other training pair meeting for the first time. She cautiously reached across the tabletop with her damaged left hand. "I'll make you proud of him. I promise he'll be as happy with me as he must be with you."

Rosie's blue eyes were moist, but she blinked hard and a toughness bloomed. "I know. I couldn't do this unless I believed that he's going to be doing a very important job."

"When I was in Afghanistan, we had military working dogs, bomb sniffers. Those dogs had critical jobs, and we know that they saved our asses so many times. I envied the attachment those dogs had with their handlers. And, you know what? Sometimes those handlers went home and the dogs were assigned to new handlers. And they did their jobs with the same zeal as they had with their original handlers." Meghan saw the guard notice the verboten touch. "The thing is, those dogs never forgot their first handlers."

"How do you know that?"

"I just do."

Rosie laughed. The toughness faded and a set of tiny dimples appeared.

Carol was waiting for Meghan at Edith's office building, where the van with the other candidates for service dogs had just arrived back from the prison.

Meghan pushed herself off the lowered ramp and over to Carol's car.

It was a physical negotiation to get Meghan out of the chair and into the front seat, but somehow they managed it. Carol slid into the driver's seat. "How did the meeting go?"

"I think it went really well."

"What's the dog like?"

"I meet him tomorrow. Today was a meet and greet with the . . ." She hesitated, wanting another word besides *inmate*. "Trainer."

"What's she like?"

"I think we're going to get on just fine."

"Your mom called me."

"How is she?"

"Concerned that you haven't called her, given her an update."

"There wasn't much to tell her."

"There is now."

Meghan rested her head against the seat, closed her eyes, suddenly exhausted. Tomorrow everything would begin to be different. Tomorrow she'd start her canine education, learn how to command the dog to pick up what had been dropped, to flip wall switches she couldn't reach. To find her missing socks. To help her when she felt the black cloud of despair looming. Tomorrow she would learn independence once more—an independence that precluded going back to Florida to live in her parents' house ever again.

There he was. At last. Shining coat, white teeth, kind eyes. Shark. Sharkey. No, for her, he would be *Shark*. Meghan rolled into the activity room, paused ten feet from where Rosie stood with the dog sitting at her heel, the leash in her hands. This is the moment when everything will change, Meghan thought. In a dream last night, she'd been running; a dog, more shadow than actual, ran beside her. In some kind of magical thinking, Meghan had been imagining that Shark would bring her back to her feet. She pictured looking down on him from above, not practically eye-to-eye, as he was now. Rosie had brought

him over to her for their official, program-sanctioned, introduction.

"Shark, sit."

The dog, the color of a Dove Bar, sat in front of her. Like a
gentleman, he didn't push himself on her, but his head bobbed
and his open, laughing mouth confessed his impatience to be
touched. She wanted to lay her head against his. Instead,
Meghan, doing as she was instructed, put out one hand for him
to sniff, then touched his head. The skull was hard beneath
amazingly soft skin. His small brown eyes were outlined in
faint pink, and he studied her without blinking. "Shark. Are
you ready to help me?" He hun-hunned a response, and his
thick rudder of a tail whipped back and forth as he stood and
told her, *I will.*

"I think he likes me." Meghan looked up from the dog and
saw Rosie's crumpled face, and her heart broke for the inmate.

"He does. He's going to love you." Rosie wiped away the
tears, and Meghan watched her make the transition from emotionally overcome to being a good soldier. This was what she
had been working for; this was what she would do. "Let's go
over some of his basic stuff today."

Shark

He is used to being handed over to the person who takes him outside to ride in a car; to meet other people, other dogs. To be mindful of sitting quietly and not barking when it's not appropriate. He likes the person who takes him out, but he likes his person inside better. And now, there is another person, another woman, one who doesn't squat to greet him, but requires him to go to her. She never gets up, but rolls around, and he has begun to adapt his repertoire of tasks to meet her commands. She is so good with the tug-of-war toy. Really spot-on. Shark finds himself sorry when she rolls out of the room at the end of the session. And he is banging his tail against walls and furniture at the start of the day when he thinks that she might be coming to play with him. He recognizes that new word *Meghan* as identifying this person, and whenever his inside woman says it, he gets a tail-thumping thrill. He loves Rosie, but he connects to Meghan in a way that he doesn't understand but accepts as correct.

Meghan

They were allotted three hours per day to work together. Two weeks, fourteen days only. It was assumed that by the time their sessions were complete, the dog and Meghan would have perfected their partnership. By the end of week one, it already looked that way, but neither Meghan nor Rosie suggested that the mission had been accomplished. They were both enjoying the process too much. Shark enjoyed the process too much. Even though the focus was on the dog's training, conversation had begun to flow between the two women, and within three sessions, Meghan felt as if Rosie completely understood her. She didn't lavish sympathy on her; she pushed Meghan to work harder. Maybe it was having been raised with a handicapped brother, or maybe it was just her nature, but Rosie didn't give Meghan any passes; if she said, "Don't praise him until he's done the job," Meghan obeyed. In return, Meghan didn't shy from asking Rosie—quite against the rules—what had put an intelligent woman like her in a place like this. So Rosie told her.

It occured to Meghan that she had very few female friendships. Good female friendships. Maybe none. With all the moving around she'd done as a kid, she'd learned early on not to
form attachments. Some pals were better correspondents than
others, but even the good ones tended to peter out; or maybe
it was that she let go, more so than that they were spun out of
her orbit. Her military friendships were deep, but equally temporary. And her wounding had further separated her. She was
on one side of a divide from those who had never lost their
purpose. Or had it taken away from them. Maybe that was why
she felt such kinship with Rosie. She, too, was looking out over
a chasm.

"And you?" Rosie asked after telling her story. "What happened?"

Even Meghan's parents hadn't heard that story. They knew
what had happened, but not how. They knew, approximately,
where, but not the details of the blinding, choking, terrifying
helplessness. The losses. The way Meghan had been rendered
null and void.

Shark rested his chin in Meghan's lap, then shifted to
Rosie's, back and forth as he tried mightily to be of comfort to
a pair of women who exuded equal amounts of anguish. At
first, he thought that they were hurting each other, and he
whimpered. But then he began to understand. As a mother dog
will sacrifice her food for her pups, these beloved humans were
gifting each other with their hearts.

At home at Carol's, one day away from finally leaving Mid-State
Women's Correctional Facility with the dog, Meghan and Carol
talked about Rosie's situation. "She's really a victim of abuse,"
Meghan said.

"Don't you think that maybe that's what they all say?"

"No. She never actually called it that. Just told me about

how controlling her boyfriend was, how he separated her from her family when they needed her."

"Was that enough for her to kill him?"

Meghan can feel herself getting mad. "First of all, it was an accident."

"Again, isn't that what they all say?"

"Carol, are you playing devil's advocate, or do you really think I'm that poor a judge of character that I could be taken in?"

"A little of both."

Meghan took a breath, sipped her predinner glass of wine. "I haven't told you what he did, what she found out he did. It's pretty heinous."

Meghan was no stranger to awful things done to living creatures, human or otherwise—IEDs, missile attacks, car bombs that killed women and children, the killing fields of war. But for a grown man to be so cruel as to snuff out the life of a small dog hit her hard. Rosie had knelt beside her, and it seemed to Meghan that she was telling this story for the first time. She kept her eyes on the ugly tile floor, only raising them to Meghan at the very end. Meghan could see that the image of that little dog's body had never faded for Rosie.

They had one more day together. Tomorrow she'd bring Shark home. And within a few weeks, Meghan, with Shark's help, would launch herself back into the world. She had a plan. And she would never forget what Mary Rose Collins had done for her.

Rosie

The day that Shark and Meghan "graduated," I was a wreck. Even LaShonda, whose dog, Mimi, had graduated the day before, was beginning to lose patience with me. On that day, I'd handed her a coveted roll of toilet paper to stanch her tears, but the next day, she'd gotten word that a new puppy was coming her way, so she had something to look forward to, and her tolerance of my weepiness was growing thin. "Come on, girl. Be proud. You and me been together now a long time and this is the first time I seen you cry."

"First time I've wanted to."

LaShonda leaned down to get in my face. "Be freakin' proud of what you've done. This is a good thing. Don't make what's her name, Meghan, sad on this day."

I *was* proud of myself, of Shark, and of Meghan. I wouldn't spoil the day for her. "You're right. I'll behave."

I got one of LaShonda's extremely rare smiles.

As Shark and I walked into that activity room for the last

time together, Meghan was there, and she looked as nervous
as I felt. Then I got it. I wasn't just saying good-bye to Shark. I
was saying good-bye to the only person who actually could be
called a friend, making Shark's loss doubly grievous.

In the outside world, people lose touch all the time, but
usually there is a grace period, a few years when communication is strong, then grows weaker, then is done. It wasn't that
I didn't hear from my old high school friend Brenda Brathwaite, but the contact had devolved to a card at Christmas.
Thinking of you. But she wasn't on my approved call list.

It is said that as long as one person remembers you, you're
never entirely dead. Right then, my one person was Meghan.
And she was being exuberantly licked in the face by Shark.
How long before he forgot me? A day? A week? As I had so often observed, the greatest divide is between prisoner and free.

Edith Moore, impeccably dressed as always, put her hands
on the handles of Meghan's wheelchair. "Time to go, Captain."
And Meghan Custer and my first dog, Shark, left me behind.
As they rolled out of the activity room on this ordinary Thursday afternoon, it was over. No grace period.

Shark

The air in the room was heavy with human distress. He couldn't
quite get a read on it. There was that exclusively human sound
of laughing. He wagged his tail at that. But then there was this
undercurrent of sighing, shallow breaths that suggested something being held back. And then his inside person handed his
leash to the person who never stood up. Alert to every nuance
of human body language, he still couldn't quite parse what was
happening. And then he understood. His inside person, *Rosie*,
was commending him to the sitting person, *Meghan*. His loy-
alties were being reassigned. He knew that he had achieved
some benchmark of behavior, because everyone was happy
with him. He was told repeatedly what a good boy he was.

And what a good boy he needed to be.

Part Two

Rosie

The clang of a closing prison door sounds exactly the same whether you are entering or leaving. When I entered Mid-State Women's Correctional Facility, it was that sound that I could not get out of my ears. The aural representation of utter loss of control, of the complete subsuming of my free will. It sounded my punishment. Today, that clang should represent the return of my independence, my life. But instead, when the bolt strikes the plate, I am as afraid as I was on the very first day of incarceration six years ago.

I stand in a long corridor. At the end of it is a door that I may push open. I have been handed the things that I came in with and I am dressed in a rumpled skirt and blouse that barely fit, as if I had never chosen them once for their flattering style. I have no pantyhose so my flats stick to heels that have worn only sneakers and white socks. I feel exposed. Is this how a slug feels, its rock being lifted away? Dirty and vulnerable and unprepared.

I was in an empty room working with my latest dog, Lulu,

when I heard "Inmate Collins, report to the warden's office."
Because the training classroom was quiet, the announcement
was distinct. It is never a good thing when an inmate is sin-
gled out by name; like when you're kid, it is never a good thing
to be called to the office. I thought that maybe Edith Moore
was there, although Lulu was nowhere near ready to be paired
with a trainee. I leashed Lulu and we set off together.

Warden Hinckley's door was open, and the guard nearest
to the office put out his hand to take my dog. This was unusual.
Generally, the dogs were with us no matter where we went. I
would have refused, but I had learned over the years that
resistance is always punished. I didn't want to lose the privilege of being one of the three women in this place allowed to
be a part of the puppy program by being shortsighted or stubborn. The guard could hold the leash for the ten minutes I
might be in with Warden Hinckley.

You can imagine my surprise when the warden stood up,
as if this were a social call and he a gentlemen. He gestured to
the hard chair that served as a guest chair, not that anyone who
ever sat in it was a *guest,* a word freighted with the concept of
free will. I sat. Then he sat down in his chair and smiled at
me. Only one thing crossed my mind at his odd behavior: He
was going to tell me that my time with puppy program was
over. I was so certain that I could feel the anticipatory tears of
heartbreak burn behind my eyes even before he spoke. I was
doing so well with Lulu; within the next couple of months she
would, like my first dog, Shark, and my second dog, Harry, be
ready to fulfill her potential as an assistance dog. I couldn't
imagine what I'd done that would merit losing this one thing
that made getting up in the morning worthwhile. Except, of
course, my continued rebuffing of Officer Tierney's advances.
Had he decided to make trouble for me after all?

"Mary Rose Collins, you're being released today."

By this time, my pulse was beating a tattoo inside my ears, and when he said, "You're free," I didn't hear him.

"I'm sorry?" I must have looked like a dolt. Charles had always hated it when I didn't understand something he was telling me. He'd accuse me of not paying attention, or, worse, not being interested in what he had to say.

"Rosie, your conviction has been vacated." He didn't add "congratulations," but I thought that he meant that. This was the outcome I had longed for but, after six years, no longer expected.

"How?" The word sticks, I could barely manage to get it out. "Who?" I couldn't form complete thoughts.

"You've been advocated for."

I wasn't sure this was a real word, and the grammar was suspect, but I took his meaning. Someone had come to my rescue.

"By whom?"

"The Advocacy for Justice."

"What's that?" I'd heard of the Innocence Project and the recent success of the podcast investigations, but this wasn't familiar. More important, I had to ask, "How, why, did they choose me?" And why hadn't anyone told me? The questions just kept piling up, and I could barely get them out. The warden stroked his red tie and shrugged his round shoulders in a classic gesture of indifference. If Warden Hinckley knew anything about this miraculous turn of events, he wasn't saying so. "Look, Rosie, just be happy and get the heck out of here."

I stood up and found myself having to touch the edge of his desk to keep my balance. "What do I do now? How long do I have before I leave?" My practical side edged its way into my thinking. I had to arrange things. I had to make plans. I had to finish Lulu's training. I couldn't just, oh my God, just leave, could I?

"You can take half an hour to pack your stuff and reclaim your personal property from storage. There's some paperwork. But then, Rosie, you're free to go."

When I walked out of the warden's office the guard was gone. And so was Lulu. I ran down the corridor, into the day-room, but she wasn't there. I saw the guard, back in his glass-fronted office. "Where's my dog?"

He just kept his eyes down and had a smirk on his fat face. He pretended he couldn't hear me. I started banging on the plate glass. "Where is my dog!"

"Rosie, what's goin' on?" LaShonda and her latest dog, Emmy, stood there. LaShonda looked at me like I'd lost my mind.

"He's taken Lulu." My hands dropped to my sides. Is it possible that some good news is too powerful to absorb all at once? That the fact of my release was buried beneath concern over Lulu seems to me now to have been a coping mechanism, a way for my mind to catch up with my new reality. Some people might have passed out from the shock; I freaked out about my missing dog. "Oh, my God, LaShonda, they're letting me go."

So now I stand outside the clanging gate. And I have no idea what to do.

The sun is blinding, and I wonder if my sunglasses are still in the purse that has been sitting in some basement locker for years. No. They're gone. An expensive pair of Maui Jim shades evidently too tempting to resist "confiscating." I have what money they handed me, plus the twenty-dollar bill in my wallet that I put in there the last day of my other life, a symbol of blind hope that I would need a cab to get home because I wouldn't be convicted. An expired driver's license is the only other thing in my wallet. Idly, I wonder if I can get it renewed, and just the idea of going to the DMV gives me the willies. I don't think that I can be comfortable in any sort of institutional setting just yet.

Needless to say, there is no one to meet me, not that I was expecting anyone. Who would come? As far as I know, no one even knows that I've been released. Did anyone reach out to my family? Wouldn't they be here, waiting for me, if someone had? I'd watched out the window when my fellow inmates were set free. I'd witnessed the moment when they were once again embraced by someone who loved them. Sometimes it was a boyfriend, or a husband. Most times, I'd seen mothers and sisters come to collect the prodigal child. Most heartbreaking were the children who wouldn't come. They'd hold back, shy in front of this person they hadn't had in their lives for who knew how long. Their mother would open her arms, and there'd be this aching pause before the children fitted themselves back into her life. Would any of my brothers, silent these six years, come fetch me home? The bigger question is, Where is *home* for me? Certainly not New York. I was never at home there. I was a barely tolerated foreigner in that world. Likewise, if I never see Connecticut again, I will be quite happy. Home, to me, must be Boston, must be my ragged, beloved chunk of Charlestown. But how will I get there? Who will welcome me back?

I glance back at the big stairway window that looks out over this area. There is no one standing there watching me leave. Oh, wait. Yes there is. LaShonda and Pilar are standing on the stairwell, and they both wave to me. LaShonda lifts Emmy and makes the dog wave, too. I feel a wash of emotion rise from my gut to my eyes. I will never see them again. I am just like all the other parolees. I don't want to look back. I will never look back. But, I do wave and blow a kiss before I turn away.

The prison isn't within walking distance of anywhere, but I have to start. Once I reach the end of the long prison drive, I will have to decide which way to turn. I have no idea where I am, deposited in this strange land as I have been, blind to the surroundings of my incarceration. Before I reach the pavement, a long, green, old-fashioned car pulls up to the curb. I recognize it as a vintage Oldsmobile. All fins and chrome. The driver leaps out. "Miss Collins?" He's a tiny man, and he looks like a little kid driving his old man's car.

Instinctively, I step back, look to see if any of the guards are watching. Of course they aren't. I am no longer their concern.

"Yes."

"I'm your lawyer." He comes toward me; one hand barely bigger than my own is already poised for a handshake. I step back, catch my heel against the curb. Quick as anything, he grabs my hand and pulls me back into balance. He might be a small man, but he looks me right in the eye. "Pete Bannerman. We've got a lot to talk about."

He opens the door of the grand old car and I sit, click the old-fashioned lap belt into place. And I am launched into my new life.

"Tell me again how this happened?" I am in Bannerman's office, seated on a plump couch the color of a bruise. He's kindly offered me coffee, and I have been momentarily distracted by this taste of heaven.

"You were—how should I put this diplomatically? Screwed over by your"—he pauses, fingers the air, looking for the right words—"public defender."

"I am aware." I take another sip of coffee. "I had no choice, Mr. Bannerman. I have no assets."

"Yes, but you deserved better than . . . I'm sorry. That's

hardly professional. Let's just say that a review of your case disclosed a number of mistakes."

"Well, yes. But, Mr. Bannerman . . ."

"Pete, please."

"Pete. What led you to reexamine the case? I've been trying for years to get someone to pay attention, with no success. Frankly, Cecily Foster has done everything in her power to make sure that didn't happen."

"First of all, I wasn't in on the investigation; that was the Advocacy for Justice. Why they settled on you, I have no idea. The only thing I'm involved in is this." He gets up and goes to his desk. I wonder if he buys his suits in the boys' department of Brooks Brothers. He comes back with a letter that bears no letterhead, no return address, and no signature. Buried deep within the legalese it is, essentially, a job offer.

I hand it back, realizing that this isn't an original letter, that it is a transcription. "Who is it?"

"Ever read *Great Expectations*?"

"Of course. Ninth-grade English." I pick up the china cup with the last of the good coffee in it. "So this is some Magwitch? Someone for whom I've done a good deed in my childhood?"

"Not entirely, but you do have expectations."

"Pete. You are being far too mysterious."

"So's your benefactor. I will tell you what I am allowed to tell you. There is a family foundation involved. The Homestead Trust. They have a property in Gloucester and they need a project manager. I can't tell you if this family foundation is responsible for getting the attention of the AFJ on your behalf or if they simply make a habit out of hiring . . ."

"Ex-cons?"

"I don't know if that's the word for it."

"I will always have been a prisoner. No amount of reframing my past is going to remedy that fact."

"Rosie. Just be happy."

If I thought that Pete would make things clear by his explanation, I was wrong. I still feel so out of body that it is easy to think that I'm actually in some kind of dream state, that maybe I hit my head and have awakened in an alternate universe where I am no longer in prison, handling wonderful dogs, but down some rabbit hole, having coffee with a diminutive Mad Hatter. As I recall, that tea party was interrupted by the Red Queen calling for Alice's head. Cecily Foster's perfect avatar.

The offer is that I take charge of a property in Gloucester, Massachusetts, commit to living in it for possibly a year while overseeing its rehabilitation. Housing with a modest paycheck.

"I have no experience rehabbing houses."

"They've hired a general contractor to do the work. Your job will be to administrate the project, basically oversee the work and spend the money."

"I don't know what to say." This is an understatement. I'm flummoxed, afraid. I have no home. I have no job—unless I take this mysterious offer and head off to a place I've been maybe twice in my life. But it isn't far from Boston; it isn't far at all.

Pete sits patiently waiting for me to come to the only conclusion I can.

"All right. I'll take the offer."

Pete Bannerman, my new best friend, hands me a cell phone, a really nice one, so many generations from my last that I hardly recognize what it is. He gives me a quick tutorial on its functions and then quietly leaves the room. I stare at the keypad. I sneak a look at the contacts, predictably empty. If I was hoping that all the numbers I needed would be handily logged, I was wrong. I have two numbers committed to memory. There are two people I need to tell my good news to. Well, three if you count Edith Moore, who will need to know from me that Lulu is currently trainerless.

I am suddenly shy. What if my great news is just news to them? I have a rush of self-consciousness, of fearing that I am mistaken if I think that anyone cares that I am free, that my status in the eyes of the world has been upgraded. Pete won't stay out of the room indefinitely, so I'd better get over myself.

My first call is to Meghan. It is Meghan Custer who has remained a steadfast friend long past the time when she and Shark were my trainees. She never avoids my calls. She sends care packages and, until she moved to New York, she managed, with Shark, to visit me. My only visitor. Unless you have been separated from all whom you love, there can be no understanding of how beautiful a smiling visitor can be. The first time, a complete surprise, I wept from the kindness of it. So it is no surprise that my first free-from-prison-operator phone call isn't to my mother, but to my friend.

Meghan is wildly excited and makes me feel like this strange turn of events isn't going to disappear in a puff of smoke. I won't wake up tomorrow back on my bunk. "I couldn't be happier for you, Rosie." Shark barks in the background and I get really excited thinking that I will be able to see them again. On my own terms. I can hug Meghan. I can drop to my knees and hug Shark.

"I guess I still don't understand how this all happened, or why. Six hours ago, less, I was an inmate. Now, I'm . . ." My words trail off. I have no word for what I am now.

"You're a free woman, Rose Collins."

If I thought that being exonerated would bridge the chasm between myself and my family, I was quite wrong. My next call is to my mother. It is the first time in a very long time that I don't have a prison operator asking if the recipient will accept a call from an inmate of Mid-State Women's Correctional Facility. With no buffer between us, my mother has only the choice of speaking to me or hanging up on me. "Mom, it's me. I'm free. My conviction was vacated."

"Rose?"

I bite back the pithy remark: "Do you have another daughter in prison?" Instead, I burble on about having been released, how I can't wait to see her.

Dead silence.

My unforgiveable sin wasn't killing Charles (conviction vacated or not, I did cause his death) or even turning my back on my family in favor of living with Charles, of moving to New York when my family needed me the most. My filial disloyalty wasn't just in not being there when they needed me, of not being there physically when my father finally succumbed to the preventable plague of asbestos particulate–caused cancer. It was in not defending the family home from the rapacious machinations of Charles's company, Wright, Melrose & Foster. I don't think they ever understood that I had no power, no sway, no voice in the matter. My mother has chosen to believe that it was my fault. I should have never brought him to the house and I should never have made the devil's bargain with him that I did. Unforgivable.

So today, my mother keeps silent on the phone, but I can hear her breathing, and as long as I can, I keep talking. "I'm heading to Cape Ann, to work as a project manager for a family trust. They're fixing up their old house and it's a good job. Temporary, though. I'm not sure how much I know about being a project manager, but I'll figure it out."

"Who did you say got you out?"

Just having her break into my soliloquy gives me hope. "I don't know who they are. Advocacy for Justice. I don't know how they knew about me, and I really don't know how they got past Cecily Foster's reach, but here I am."

"And where are you?"

"I'm in New Haven for a couple of days. The Trust is putting me up in a hotel until I can get my driver's license and, well, some clothes." Here goes nothing. "Mom, I'd like to come see you, and the boys, and everyone before I drive up to Cape Ann. You're on my way." I'm attempting to get in every word before she hangs up on me.

"I don't think that would be a good idea."

"Why not?" I feel the burn of tears. Why won't she let me back into the family? It wasn't my fault.

"This has been really hard on your brother." When my mother said "your brother," she only ever meant Teddy. Whereas everyone else had grown up, Teddy would always be there, always need her, infantilized by his injuries. There had been a time, when I was a little girl, that I was jealous. Teddy got the lion's share of Mom's attention. Here I was, the longed-for girl child, and suddenly I was just another kid in the house, Teddy sucked up all of her time and most of her available emotions. By the time I was a young adult, I understood it, but I still chafed on occasion. And that was what my mother accused me of that day she'd called to ask that I come home for the duration. "You are too old to still be jealous of Teddy. He needs so much help and I can't be in two places at once."

"I'll see what I can do."

"I'm begging you, Rosie. Quit your job. You can get another one. We'll pay your bills. I'll pay your bills."

I didn't tell her that I had no bills to speak of. Charles

covered everything. Everything. I had no job. The position Charles implied I would take in the New York offices of WM&F failed to materialize.

"Rosie, come home."

I told Charles that I was going to visit my parents for the weekend. This time, he was unnervingly supportive of my "quick" visit to my family. "I'll run out to the Hamptons for the weekend. Have a family visit of my own." What neither one of us said was that Cecily Foster would be ever so pleased to have Charles to herself. My presence in her house was never comfortable for either of us. Despite my every effort to be a good potential daughter-in-law, Mrs. Foster viewed me as, at best, a guest in her home. Both of them. Technically, she'd moved full-time to the house in the Hamptons, giving us her Central Park apartment. On the afternoons she came into the city for luncheon or a committee meeting, she might simply drop in, so I dared not move so much as a bibelot to make the apartment my own; I never knew when she might just show up in the foyer, bringing in the cold air with her. I tried it once, moving a Meissen vase from one side of the mantel to the other so that I could set a family picture where the light from the windows wouldn't obscure it. Without a word, Mrs. Foster removed the picture, handed it to me, and put the vase back where it had been. "Why don't you put that in your room?" I might have stuck a bobblehead souvenir from a pie-eating contest on the mantel by the way she handled my family photo with such disdain.

I was throwing a few things into my overnight bag when Charles came into our bedroom. He put his hands on my shoulders and gave me a squeeze that suggested I should take the later train to Boston. He nuzzled my neck, did that thing that always gave me a frisson of desire. "Why don't you drop by the hairdresser while you're in Boston. I still think she gives you the best version of your style."

"If I can get an appointment. I'll only be there a day or so."

"Stay longer. Have a really good visit."

I was a little surprised by his sudden generosity of spirit. Usually, he sulked when I went away, and, at times, I thought he was perhaps jealous of my relationship with my family. A relationship that had, admittedly, begun to fray. "Won't you miss me too much?"

"Oh, I will. But . . ." And Charles took my face in his hands. "I need you to do a little work for WM&F."

"Go on." A giddy little imp of excitement at being offered a role in his company percolated in my chest, nearly deafening me to Charles's next words.

"I imagine that your father's medical bills are substantially more than his insurance will cover."

"I don't know. Probably. I haven't discussed it with them." Immediately, I knew that I should have been less head-in-the-sand about my parents' finances. About how they were paying for all these treatments.

"Let them know that Wright, Melrose & Foster will cover his out-of-pocket costs."

"Oh my God, Charles, that's so generous. I can't thank you enough." There was a less-than-three-second interval when I thought that Charles Foster was a kind man. That he was capable of generosity toward my family even though I knew he wasn't ever going to love them.

"In exchange for a purchase and sales agreement on the house."

The hope of Charles's selflessness flattened out into a wash of sick feeling. "My parents would never sell. Where would they go?" Bunker Hill was their neighborhood, their identity. I couldn't imagine them anywhere else. I couldn't imagine them ever agreeing to sell the house that they had worked so hard to own. Even as I thought that, I knew that the houses on either side of theirs had been sold. And I knew, without a shadow of a doubt, who the buyer was.

Charles gave me a shrug. "If WM&F doesn't buy it, someone else will, and I doubt they'll get the kind of money we're offering. It's inevitable. They'll have to divest of their only asset to keep up with those bills." *Divest. Asset.* My childhood home reduced to currency.

"How much? How much are you offering?" I deliberately used the pronoun *you.*

He shrugged again, a gesture not of uncertainty, but of reluctance. "You know that's WM&F's business, not yours."

"What do you mean? How is it *not* my business? They're my parents."

"I can only say that your father's medical bills will be somewhat less burdensome."

Somehow, Charles's munificent declaration that WM&F would cover all out-of-pocket medical costs had shrunk to *somewhat less burdensome.*

"I won't do it." I turned my back on him, began stuffing things willy-nilly into my suitcase.

I felt his hands upon my shoulders, his fingers digging deep, finding that spot in front of my collarbone, the spot where it can feel so good, and then hurt. "Don't be a child. Don't be sentimental. Do you want your mother to be a poor widow, or one with a few dollars left?"

"Where will they go? Where will Teddy go?" I heard a subtle acquiescence in my use of the future tense.

"You can help them, Rose. Help them have some control over their future." His breath was soft against the skin of my

neck. He'd had mussels for dinner and I could smell a faint lin
gering garlic. "Being a good daughter may not be easy, but, in
the end, they'll thank you."

How wrong he was.

Meghan

The dog sits in front of her, panting and hun-hunning, his amber eyes locked on hers. He is fairly vibrating with excitement. It's hard not to catch some of that primal enjoyment, to laugh out loud at the expression on his face. Who would have thought that a dog's face could have so much character? Meghan is even getting so she can read his thoughts. Right now, his only thought is for her to toss the ball. He's performed the task she's given him, to flip on the light switch that sits just above her head, and so he's entitled to his reward, a tossed tennis ball. He'll retrieve it, drop it into her lap, and then hope for another task. Her pitching arm is getting stronger. The ball flies out of her office and she can hear it bounce down the hallway. Shark scampers after it and she hopes that he won't plow down any unsuspecting visitor. The rest of the staff at Don Flint's law office are used to the disruption.

Two years ago, Meghan couldn't have imagined herself being a functional adult ever again, and here she is, in New York City, with a job, an apartment, an improved relationship with her parents, who still want her to come home but have accepted that while she's never going to be the daughter who left for Iraq, she's on her way toward normalizing her life, and that means not living in their Florida home. The law offices of Don Flint and Associates rarely calls upon the skill set she learned as a captain in the army —for instance, the effective use of night-vision goggles—but her leadership skills have come in handy. Her official title is special projects manager, and her job is to oversee the nonlegal elements of complicated situations. She is unafraid of pressing down hard to get facts, arranging for meetings between players who might not want to meet, and proud to have earned the sobriquet "Sarge" from the rest of the office staff. "Actually, it's Captain," she'll say when someone playfully mocks her sometimes intense style. The fact that the others are willing to tease her makes Meghan's reach toward a normal life that much closer.

And she owes it all to Shark. No, not just to Shark but also, of course, to Rosie.

The day that their training ended and she left the prison dayroom with Shark by her side, Meghan was silent, holding back the bolus of emotion that she had never expected to feel. Maybe it was the fact that she and Rosie weren't allowed that all too human expression of affection, a departing hug, that she felt like her business with Rosie was unfinished. Maybe it was that she felt like she was, in some way, abandoning Rosie; worse, taking the inmate's only joy away from her: Shark. Meghan wasn't blind to the way Rosie loved that dog. Another woman might even have been jealous and sure to establish her own rights to the dog's heart. But that wasn't how she felt. "Edith, what are the rules about coming back here and visiting?"

Edith, just ahead of Meghan, turned and shook her head. "It's never come up before."

"I want to."

"It may not be wise."

"Why?"

"Shark needs to be devoted to you. That's the contract. Rosie has done her job and she'll have another dog soon."

"Edith, I'm not talking about Shark. I'm talking about Rosie. I'm talking about me."

Meghan tilts a photograph on her desk so that the late-afternoon light doesn't obscure the image. Most of the other staff around here have pictures of their kids or their fiancés on their credenzas. She has a photograph of Shark, a beautiful head study that almost looks contrived, like one of those pictures of beautiful people they put in frames as an enticement to purchase that particular frame. The real deal is flopped down beside her, the tennis ball firmly clutched in his predator teeth; his eyes are blissed out, his tail thumps, and he clearly is hoping that she'll find something else for him to do. She gives him the command to shut the light off.

Shark takes Meghan's motorized wheelchair as a reason to go for long walks. He is no longer satisfied with a spin around the block, avoiding the steeper inclines. Now he trots along, leading her farther and farther afield from their apartment. There is an enclosed dog park a block or so away, and if they don't find themselves there, he sulks. Meghan has one of those ball-tossing devices, and it's a good way to retain her upper-body strength, flinging a tennis ball as far as she can. The long summer twilights have been a blessing, as she's spending so much time in the office.

Her cell phone rings with the ringtone she's assigned Rosie, the theme from *Born Free*. Meghan isn't above a little irony.

"Hey, how's it going?"

"Great. Just packing up for the trip to Gloucester."

"How are you getting there?"

"The Trust's lawyer, Pete Bannerman, helped me get my license renewed, and, can you believe it, I've got a car!"

They chat, almost like ordinary friends, about the newish Forester that Pete has secured for her, about Meghan's new motorized wheels. Meghan finds that she can't picture Rosie anywhere but in the prison dayroom, and she has to keep reminding herself that her friend is not standing at a rank of pay phones, but ensconced on a hotel bed, or standing at a wide window overlooking a parking lot instead of a prison yard. "You okay to do this?"

"I am. I won't lie; I'm pretty nervous, but it's okay."

"You'll be fine."

"I keep thinking that if I get pulled over, I won't know how to explain myself."

"First of all, you won't. Second of all, don't go down that path."

Rosie blurts, "I wish you were coming with me. At least for a bit."

Meghan has no answer for this except to reiterate that Rosie will be fine. "You're a strong woman; you've endured so much. You can do this." Shark drops the moist tennis ball into Meghan's lap. She fingers his ears. "I should go."

"Just tell me how Sharkey is doing."

"So perfect. Everyone at the office loves him. He's getting so spoiled."

"No treats."

"No treats. I'm a stickler about that."

"It's good to hear your voice," Rosie says.

"Yours, too. Be well."

"I'll send pictures of the place so you can see what I'm up against."

"I'd like that."

Meghan signs off, sets the phone down in her lap. The first time Rosie called her was the day she was released. The shock of her sudden change of fortune had been obvious. She'd struggled with telling the story, trying to cope with a narrative that made no sense. Going from no hope of parole to exonerated, from lockdown to a hotel room with room service all in the same day. She wept. "Oh Meghan, I don't know how to feel."

Meghan had counseled a long hot shower and to use all of the hotel-supplied toiletries. That got Rosie laughing.

Shark is back and again drops the yellow ball in Meghan's lap. She fixes it into the flinger, heaves it with all her might. The dog is a ballistic missile after a target. Boom!

"Too bad he doesn't like fetch." An African-American man with a curly-haired mixed breed is standing beside her.

"He actually prefers tug-of-war, but this is his second favorite."

The man, fortyish, balding, unclips the leash from his dog and sends her on the same trajectory as Shark has gone. The two dogs meet, greet, and run back to their owners. Meghan notices that his dog wears a harness similar to Shark's, the badge of service dog prominent on both dogs' backs.

As the dogs burn off energy, their owners, like parents on a playground, fill in all kinds of details about the dogs, but nothing about themselves. Still, as Meghan motors home, she feels like she's getting to know her neighborhood better, one dog owner at a time.

Shark

This is the best. So much of his short life beyond his few weeks with his littermates has been in the exclusive company of human beings. This place, what Meghan calls the *dog park* is redolent of the marks of others, better, there are actual dogs to play with. The rough and tumble and the delicate all convene to chase balls, sticks, and one another. Some are more friendly than others, and he's learned to be conservative in his approach, but, for the most part, everyone has the same goal; mark territory and run free.

And now there is this other dog who has the same job, comfort and aide to her human. Shark likes this new dog, *Spike.*

Rosie

It took me five minutes to get the courage to turn the ignition on. It took me six to swallow the bile that accompanied having to back out of the driveway at Pete's office. I knew he was looking at me through the curtain, wondering if I had the guts to put my innocence to the test. By the third red light, I had stopped shaking.

On Google maps, it looks like a straight shot through central Connecticut to Cape Ann, an optimistic three-hour journey from hell to my new adventure. Interstate 84 to the Mass Pike, then swing onto I-95 to its 128 terminus, and Bob's your uncle. Except that I've chosen to begin the journey to the next place in my life during rush hour. I'm slowed way down through Hartford, but once past East Hartford, it's open road to the state line. I'm sailing along by that time, cheerfully confident I'm making good time, when I get to the unpredictable Mass Pike, where I-84 débouchés onto it and all these lanes of traffic compete with the speeding vehicles already on the

Pike that want to move over to the Sturbridge service plaza. Worse, there's been a car fire on the right shoulder a mile down, and that's the real holdup.

Creep, stop. Creep a bit more, get excited. Stop. I'm supposed to meet the contractor at eleven. It's ten-thirty now. Ignoring the lighted signage along the turnpike that reminds me that texting and driving is illegal, I text Tucker Bellingham, the project's general manager, to let him know I'll be late. Great way to make an impression as the new project manager. I'm no traffic virgin; I know this east-west route very well.

I crank up the radio in a vain attempt to muffle the persistent thoughts that have engaged the worst parts of my brain since the moment Warden Hinckley set me free. *Why me? Why not me?* It's an interesting dichotomy. My case is hardly sexy: White woman runs over heinous but rich boyfriend, revenge or accident? If I knew who had recommended me to the Advocacy for Justice, maybe I could better understand why I was chosen to be advocated for. I think back to my erstwhile fellow inmates, and there isn't one who might not have benefited from the attention of a nonprofit group bent on getting justice served where justice had been thwarted. Certainly LaShonda deserved a second chance. She, too, had been victimized by a boyfriend, and the system. I'd said as much to Meghan, and all she said was that it had been my turn—my turn for something good to happen.

LaShonda had said about the same. If there was resentment or jealousy in those green eyes, she kept it from me. "Hey," she said, "life sometimes gives you a break. Take it and run."

Surrounding the topography of my thoughts is the extreme pleasure of changing radio stations. I dabble in oldies, news, classical, and rap. I have a choice!

And then, as these things do, the road opens up, we pick

up speed, and I am over the bridge spanning the Annisquam River and around the two rotaries into Gloucester by one o'clock. It takes a little more time to find the Homestead, mostly because I drive by it, convinced the my nav app is wrong. I leave the well-kept county road, turning onto a narrow lane. This can't be the place. This looks like it's ready to fall down. It's dressed in clapboards so old that they appear soft, with tinges of green at the edges and no obvious paint. Despite my lofty title, I'm no expert on construction, but the roofline seems to sag; no, it does sag, like a inverted bow. There is a four-square chimney in the center of it, and the roof shingles that should surround it are missing; tar paper flaps in the light breeze. Blind windows flank either side of the black front door, two on one side, one on the other, giving the house a lopsided face.

The yard, such as it is, is a wonderful example of the term *benign neglect*. Weeds flourish in the uncut grass, itself a stalky brush of more gold than green. I realize that I've stopped dead in the road, so I follow a two-track dent in the grass that leads to a barnlike structure appended to the house by a breezeway, or what must have been a woodshed back in the olden days. I shut the car off, grab my phone, and text Mr. Tucker Bellingham, principal of Dogtown Construction Company, to say that I have arrived. In a moment, I get a text back; we'll meet here at two o'clock.

That's fine. I'm starving.

The coffee shop is so busy that I have to sit at the endmost counter stool. I'm facing myself in a mirror. I try not to look at the face reflected back at me, because she looks like someone I used to know, but I can't recall her name. I haven't had a proper haircut in a very long time, all those expensive layers have grown out, along with my highlights, replaced by premature gray, and I have gotten into the habit of tying it back, a look that narrows my face, a face that is the very definition of prison pallor. It's not that I hadn't spent time outside. With the dogs, I'd had the one privilege of access to the prison yard whenever I needed it. But the yard is walled, and the sun is a reluctant visitor, and the very climate within the prison steals the color from your cheeks. There are no beautiful women in prison. Any beauty a woman walks in with is quickly taken from her. The stress of communal living, the poor-quality food, the constant tension, the loss of privacy, all suck the beauty from her face and her soul. I look at myself in the mirror across from me and see a pinched and faded remnant of who I was. My nose looks more prominent. My brows are shaggy and I should put on lipstick. I should find a CVS and buy some.

The other reason I don't want to keep looking in that unforgiving mirror is that I am aware of the proximity of men in this narrow place as reflected in that mirror. Workingmen, come to grab a cup of coffee between jobs; retired men, killing time before having to go home. Men in the fluorescent yellow vests of construction jobs; men in blue jeans and flannel shirts. Heavy leather work boots. Thick white or black rubber boots, suggesting a maritime profession. Big men, most of them. Bearded or not, balding; potbellied or slender. Put a gray guard's uniform on any of them, switch out the hammers hanging from their utility belts for truncheons, and they could have been the same men I encountered every day in prison. In a world of women, it was the men who controlled the universe. Warden Hinckley, Officer Tierney, and the rest of the sundry poorly trained guards who either bullied or flirted, or worse. In my experience, men are not to be trusted.

"Can I have this wrapped, please?" I ask the woman behind the counter. She plops my half-eaten egg-salad sandwich into a Styrofoam container far too big for it. I order a coffee to go. I drag a few dollars out of my jeans pocket and hope that it's enough. I remember to take in a deep breath, to let it out slowly. The passage between the counter and the booths is narrow, and I have to wait for a guy standing at the register to move enough that I can squeeze by and get out the door. He doesn't notice me standing there, take-out container held at chest level, coffee seeping its heat into my hand. I need to make him move; I need to get out of here.

I am attempting a clumsy dance step to sidle out behind him when he suddenly turns and, sure enough, bumps the coffee in my hand. The lid pops off, but, miraculously, the spillage hits neither of us, only the floor. I feel the scarlet of anxiety hit my face.

You are so clumsy, what is wrong with you? Charles's voice is always in my head at times like these.

"Oh, ma'am, I'm so sorry." The guy quickly grabs a handful of inadequate paper napkins out of a dispenser and starts sweeping away the mess. "Marcy, can I get this lady a new coffee?" He rises to his full height and I am put in mind of a bear on its hind legs. He's one of the flannel shirt guys I've been trying not to look at.

"It's fine. No, please. I don't need another. There's plenty left." I bolt out the door, dropping the remains of the coffee and the sandwich into a trash can. I lock the doors of the Forester. Officer Tierney liked nothing better than bumping into you, making sure he led with his crotch, knocking the food tray out of your hands. Standing there watching with his serpent's eyes as you bent to pick up the mess. Especially after I had declined his offer of sex in exchange for feminine products.

Back at the Homestead, as my benefactors call it, I get out of the car. I pull the key that Pete Bannerman gave me out of my jeans pocket and realize that I don't know if it's the key to the back or the front door. I try the front door first. It sports a very tarnished door knocker in the shape of a fish. Just out of curiosity, I lift it by the tail and drop it to see if it still works. It does, although the hinge squeaks. I bet some 3-in-One oil would fix that. There are cracked panes in the flanking windows, and I wonder if the windows will have to be replaced. Modern energy-efficient windows would certainly help with what must be enormous heating costs for a leaky old house like this. Well done, me, a very pertinent observation with its companion suggestion. I try the key, but it doesn't fit. So around to the back I go.

Approaching the back of the house, I think that it looks as bad as it did from the front. Maybe worse, because, at some point in the house's life, a clumsy addition was tacked on, aluminum-sided, sporting those crank-out windows, completely at odds with the rest of the house. A vent pipe sticks up through the roof, and I figure this must be for the bathroom. There is a slouching screen door, sans screen, its cranky hinges protesting as I pull it away from the back door. I try the key, but it doesn't fit this lock, either. Guess I'll have to wait for Bellingham. Maybe he's got the right key. Unless there's a door I haven't spotted.

In the meantime, I'll explore the yard. The day is just lovely and having the freedom to stroll around and, literally, sniff the flowers is a delight. My circumnavigation around the house and property takes me to a stone wall. There are gaps in it, places where the drystone construction has given up, gravity has won, and the stones, many of them dressed granite, have fallen off, seeking a return to the earth. I notice one rock with something painted on it. I brush the lichen from its surface and read *Boy*. It gives me a little shiver. Is some poor nameless child buried here, all by himself? And then I think, No, this is a pet. A dog, maybe. I look around for other markers. Have I come across a pet cemetery and should I be prepared for a Stephen Kingesque haunting? But there don't seem to be any others, at least none marked by hand-painted stones.

I spot a tangle of undergrowth and skinny trees on the other side of the tumbled rock wall. If I was a country girl, I might be able to name the trees and bushes that fill in the space beyond the wall. I know oak; at least I think I do. Maybe beech? That white-and-black tree must be white birch. Isn't that what the Native Americans used for canoes? I'll have to ask someone. I don't know who. I don't know anybody. Oh wait! I have a smartphone, so I guess I can look it up for myself.

Here's something I can identify, blueberries! Or are they huckleberries? I can't tell the difference, but they are sweet, and I pluck a handful to make up for the lost half of that pretty good egg-salad sandwich. When I was a kid, we used to go blueberry picking at those U-Pick-Em places up Route 1. I have a flash of memory, of Teddy, on his feet, dropping berries into my pint basket. I grab another handful of berries. After so many years of fruit privation, the sweet tang of ripe berries is beyond luscious. I feel a ripple of excitement in my gut, I can go to the supermarket and freakin' *buy* fresh food! My circumstances have changed so rapidly I haven't had time to process the magnitude of it. Little realizations keep popping up, and I add them to the string of happiness beads that each moment away from Mid-State accretes. I pop another handful of berries into my mouth. Blueberry juice stains my fingers and I lick them.

A massive silver pickup truck pulls up beside my red Forester. DOGTOWN CONSTRUCTION COMPANY is professionally lettered on its side in gold and blue. Tucker Bellingham has arrived.

As I approach, the driver climbs out of the truck. It is my dance partner from the diner.

"Tucker Bellingham?"

"Yes. I'm sorry, are you with the clerk?" He does that man

thing, looking around for the man who should be standing here instead of this woman.

"I am the clerk. Mary Rose Collins."

There is this little flush of embarrassment that hits his cheeks above the gray-shot black goatee he sports, "Oh. Okay. Of course. M. R. Collins. I thought it was Mr. Autocorrect."

"Not what you were expecting?" I'm not going to think about why Pete managed to keep my gender out of the conversation. I'm just hopeful he kept the really important things about me out of the conversation, too. "Mary Rose—M.R. Mostly known as Rosie."

Bellingham shrugs off his faux pas. "We've kind of met, haven't we?"

"We have. The incident at the coffee shop."

"Righto. Sorry about that."

"Ah, I can't seem to make this key work." Better a non sequitur than an explanation.

Tucker takes the key and leads me into the woodshed and then to a side door, unlocks it, and gives it a shove with his shoulder. "After you."

Now is my moment of reckoning. I go in.

The woodshed door leads directly into the kitchen. The only thing that suggests the twentieth century, much less the twenty-first, is the combination gas stove, which is white, with a fringe of hardened grease. The sink is black soapstone, with a brass faucet and a sloping enamel drain board. A china cup is on the drainboard, a remnant of the last occupant, maybe her last cup of tea. No saucer. A woodstove protrudes from the mouth of a fireplace, and there is a rag rug centered in front of it on the warped brown-painted floorboards. Whatever colors the braided rug might have once been, it is now a uniform gray color, and even as I step on it, a plume of dust rises from it. I feel like I'm treading into a crypt, a burial place.

"Stove works. And I had a gas delivery made. Oh, and the water is on."

"Is there hot water?"

"Looks like the water heater died a long time ago. We'll get a new one in soon."

Tucker is clearly familiar with this place, and he leads me around, enumerating the ideas he has for its restoration. They all sound expensive, and I figure that my first responsibility to the Homestead Trust will be to make sure he's working off its page. Except that I have no specifics. No budget. No idea.

How am I ever going to stay here? We haven't even gone upstairs yet and I'm ready to bolt. "I'm not sure how I'm even going to stay in this house; there's no heat, no hot water. It's pretty . . ."

"Primitive?"

"Yeah." I don't add that this place makes prison look positively luxurious.

"You won't need heat just yet, and I'll show you how to use the woodstove. You can boil water on the gas stove. If you think the beds aren't usable, I'd suggest that you head down to Cabella's and pick up a good cot and sleeping bag. It's roughing it, yeah, but, hey, the Trust obviously thinks you're up for it."

I have to ask, "Who are they, the Trust people?"

"Damned if I know. I just talk to that Pete Bannerman guy."

Thus goes any fleeting hope that I'll find out who my benefactor is.

"And why do you think they hired me?" Clearly, he doesn't know the actual arrangement; that this is some kind of bizarre test of my spirit by an unknown benefactor.

"I don't know. Probably the same reason why they hired me. I'm the best. You're probably good at what you do, too."

· I wonder what it is he thinks I'm good at. I haven't been good at anything in a very long time.

I follow Tucker back out into the warmth of the summer day. He's given me a rough idea of the work he's already got lined up. As early as tomorrow, I can expect workmen. I wonder if I can find someplace to hang out while they're here. The idea of being in the presence of men is still uncomfortable, and I wonder if I'll ever get over that.

Tucker yanks his truck door open, climbs in. "So, tomorrow, then. Welcome to Dogtown."

"I thought this was Gloucester."

"It is." He pulls away, leaving me standing in the unkempt yard.

I watch him drive away, and fight the urge to call Meghan right this minute. I need the voice of someone who will tell me that everything will be all right.

I've made camp in my new digs, racking up a few bucks on the "business" credit card that Pete handed me. A decent folding cot, which I've set up in the kitchen with a Coleman sleeping bag; a composting toilet because, despite what Tucker said, there is no dependable plumbing in this house—one flush and the ancient commode blew a gasket. He told me that the last tenant—Henrietta Baxter, he said her name was—didn't seem to mind the lack of hot water or other modern amenities, such as a shower. I can't complain. Which is to say, I shouldn't complain. I don't have to share that fly-specked mirror over the nonfunctioning sink with anyone else. I have a giant economy-size box of tampons, and being able to reach in and get one whenever I need it is priceless. I don't have a supply of ramen noodles hidden away, I have actual cans of Campbell's soup, six varieties, sitting openly on the shelf in the pantry. My first trip to the grocery store took two hours, my eyes dazzled by choice.

I have silence.

I am not used to silence. I lived in an unquiet house, then a noisy dorm. Not to speak of life in prison with the bells and sirens and loudspeaker announcements day and night; the perpetual sound of someone yelling or crying or cursing God. Even living with Charles wasn't quiet, not living as we did in the city. Here I don't even have the soft hiss of car tires on the macadam in front of this house, situated ever so close to the road. After seven o'clock, there is scarcely a car going by. I wonder who would call should this place go up in smoke? Who would notice? The most reliable noise is that of crickets, knelling the end of the day. At dawn, the birds twitter and cheep and caw and rasp, and the fact that I can hear them so distinctly only reminds me that I am alone. I have never really been alone. I longed for the concept while incarcerated; a moment's privacy seemed attainable only through breaking rules and being sent down. But now, now that I have hours alone either before the various crews join me for the day or after they go home, I realize that I have never been prepared for solitude. I come from a full house. I don't think that there were more than a handful of times when I had more than an hour by myself there, and those times only when my mother had Teddy out for his therapy or for a checkup.

I find myself lying awake tonight, plucking at the slippery surface of the sleeping bag in an attempt to get it smoothed out over and under me. Other than my own grumbling about the uncooperativeness of the sleeping bag, there is complete silence inside, not even a ticking clock to keep me company. The single brass faucet doesn't even drip, no relentless hypnotic rhythm to fix upon. I think I hear an owl outside. Certainly crickets. Needless to say, I quickly give in to a little

wholesome wild imagining. A creaking sound from upstairs—
is that the house settling, or someone there? Old house noises,
not quite inside, not quite out. Something hits the roof. Acorn
or intruder? This place is ancient; surely one or two of its former inhabitants must be lingering. A scratching in the walls,
and I draw the sleeping bag over my ears.

Earlier, I'd called Meghan and she'd patiently listened to
the odyssey of my travels and the oddness of my accommodations. Her only advice: "Hang in there. It'll get better."

A while later, in a doze, not truly asleep, I startled. Is there
movement outside? A rustle in the long grass? Is someone moving out there? Someone who might think this abandoned-
looking house is a good place to seek shelter? I sit up, yanking
the bottom of the sleeping bag, which had slumped to the floor,
back onto the cot. The slick material hisses as it moves against
the mattress. Of course, it was just the sound of the bag slipping, not some creature—or worse, human—slinking around
the back door. Still, I get up and turn on the one working lamp in
the house. It was never dark in prison, so having a lamp on in
the bedroom-cum-kitchen is no problem for me.

When I was with Charles in New York, I thought that I was
lonely. What I was, it seems to me now, was simply being
bored. Now I am actually alone, and I suffer a different kind
of loneliness, not one of being left to my own devices all day,
but as one who has been alienated from those I love, those who
used to love me. At first, this estrangement from my family felt
temporary, forgivable. I had this childish belief that families
had to take you back, that they had to love you. My transgres-
sion was in making the choice I had, and it was only after
Charles's death, and the upending of my life, that I realized
that that choice had cut so deep that I would never be welcomed home.

I am more persistent now that the wheel of fortune has turned for me once again. I call my mother every day. I leave voice messages for her and, as an unreformed pesky little sister, I group text my brothers. I see the lengthening one-sided thread, as if I'm casting my line into an empty sea.

It rained last night, and the tall grass of the backyard is glittering with droplets in the early sun. I've become an early riser. As soon as the sun breaks cover, I wake up, surprised every morning that I am awakened by the sun and not fluorescent lights. I make my coffee in an old-fashioned percolator on the stove. It's taken a few tries, but now I have the timing down perfectly. Cup in hand, I go out through the path that I've trampled in the unkempt yard—Tucker has promised a mow crew will show up by the end of the week. It rained hard enough that the path is muddy, and I regret wearing my new Nikes outside. There's a stone bench, or maybe it's just a big rock no one could move, so it's become a bench, but it's situated perfectly to sit and enjoy coffee and nature and make a plan for the day. The bench is nearby Boy's stone, and I feel like I'm communing with his (presumably) canine spirit as I sip my wickedly strong java. It makes me feel less alone, which makes me wish that I was comfortable around the workmen. But I think that may take some time. It has been a while since I was in the company of a nice guy. A trustworthy guy. Someone who didn't want something from me. Or who made me into a target. These guys are too much like the men I spent the last few years staying away from. Not that they aren't polite, quiet, and honed in on their tasks, not on me. But some habits of fear are hard to put aside when circumstances change.

I hear Tucker's truck horn. I'm sure he's afraid of catching me in dishabille. He has no idea that I've grown quite used to strange men seeing me in my nightclothes. Or even wrapped in a raggedy towel on those occasions when a sudden lock-down resulted in my being forced to the floor as I was coming out of the shower. He certainly can't imagine the squat-and-cough routine. He doesn't know that I have no modesty.

As I push myself off the rock, I glance down and see a paw print. It's huge, too big for a dog, I think, and then I wonder if there are wolves in this area. Maybe coyote feet are bigger than I thought. I'll ask Tucker if I should be nervous. I'm a city girl, after all. Now that I've noticed them, I follow the paw prints as they appear here and there in the exposed muddy patches in the tamped-down grass. Here's one, there's another, and then I'm standing in the barn. Not exactly in the barn proper, but in that connector that Tucker calls the dogtrot, the covered space between the house and the barn. Ancient splits of firewood are stacked in it, and I imagine the former residents were happy to have a dry cover for their heating source, and a way to fetch it without having to go outside. The paw prints—and by now I'm convinced these are a wolf's—lead into and out of the dogtrot and away, as if the beast took himself across the road.

"Good morning." Tucker has found me standing in the dogtrot. I point out the paw prints. I assume that anyone built like he is, outdoorsy, would know what these prints signify. "Look at this. Can you tell me if this is a wolf print?"

Evidently, Tucker was raised right, and he doesn't make fun of me. At least not immediately. "Uh, no. I don't think we have wolves out here, at least not anymore. I'll check with the fish and game people if you'd like."

"How about a coyote?"

"That's more likely." Like a good Boy Scout, Tucker examines the set of prints, and he admits that they are unusually large. "Be careful about leaving trash around."

"I'm composting."

"Keep it in a container. You don't want to attract skunks and raccoons; they're coyote food."

Maybe I should get a dog. A random thought that sends a little thrill through me. I could do that. I have the freedom. No one's permission to ask, no application to fill out, no waiting period. Nothing so small it could be killed by a man's hands. Something big, with a big bark. I picture it exactly. Almost like I've seen it before. Something assertive, but not aggressive— unless I require it. Loyal to me. Mine alone, never to be handed over to anyone else.

Shadow of a Dog

The woman moves, as they often do, in slow perambulations around the property, reaching out to touch the reedy stem of tall grasses, placing a soft palm against the flaking wood of the barn. She goes into the barn, and he watches, hidden behind the rotting stack of cordwood that has been in this place since beyond time. He takes a deep breath, reading the air as it moves ahead of her. Reading the trail of scent she leaves behind. They are always the same. Alone. Like with this woman, the aura of darkness emanates from within them.

He will watch. He will wait. She's not ready yet, but he is confident that she will be ready soon to accept his help.

Meghan

He was there again, the balding black guy with the curly-coated dog, a mixed breed named Spike, despite her being a girl. Their after-work schedules seem to bring them to the dog park at the same time every weekday afternoon. Five-thirty. She goes right after work, and he works at home and is ready to stop for the day by that time. After a few weeks, they finally got around to introducing themselves.

"Marley, yeah, that Marley."

"Rasta parents?"

"Something like that."

"Meghan Custer. No, not that Custer."

He squatted down so that she could see his face. "Iraq or Afghanistan?"

"Both."

"Me, too." He stood up. "Spike's my service dog. PTSD."

"Shark's mine. For obvious reasons."

After that, it got easier. After that, it seemed like a cup of coffee would be nice. Soon enough, that after-work dog park meeting took on certain aspects of friendship. They rarely mentioned their military experiences, but it was nice to have someone around who didn't treat her like some kind of exotic creature. Not just the wounds but the whole experience of being in a war, being in the military, tends to be beyond the scope of most of the very nice but somewhat clueless people Meghan spends her days with. Marley is more like the guys she lived, ate, and survived with, sometimes a little jokey, sometimes very, very quiet.

"Hey, Rosie."

"Meghan, you wouldn't believe this place." Rosie doesn't sound thrilled, that's for sure, as she enumerates the flaws in the old house. No hot water! No shower! Sleeping on an army cot because the beds are beyond gross.

Meghan listens patiently, her fingers hovering over her keyboard, as she was composing an email when she answered Rosie's call. "That's nice. Sorry, that's not nice."

"You okay?"

"Just working, babe."

"Oh, man, I am so sorry."

"Not to worry. Hey, just think, you can make a phone call anytime you want. You can go to Target."

"Yes, Meghan, I am free to poke around mindlessly."

"How quickly we adjust."

"Sorry. I'm just frustrated. And this Bellingham guy is a pain."

"Who's he?"

"The contractor. Excuse me, the *general* contractor. He wants everything done authentically, so there's no ripping up, knocking down, and the freakin' paint has to be analyzed for original color, and now he's waiting for some special kind of recycled floorboards from a teardown in New Hampshire, so there's this gap in the front room's floor that I'm afraid I'll fall into should I take up sleepwalking. You'd think he was making it into a museum instead of a family retreat."

"Sounds expensive." Meghan opens a new blank email. TO: don@donflintlaw.com

"I guess so. Guess the Homestead Trust has the dough. They must want it done properly."

Meghan lets Rosie rattle on for a bit longer before signing off. Maybe she should have interrupted her unintended soliloquy, spoken of Marley and his dog, Spike, but Meghan is of a cautious nature; she's not quite ready to mention Marley to Rosie. She's not quite ready at all.

Now that she no longer lives with them, Carol and Don Flint are frequent visitors to Meghan's fifth-floor apartment. They pop in for a drink before heading to the train, or bring takeout and the three of them spread it on the small kitchen table, an indoor picnic. Without his tie and with his suit jacket flung on the back of the couch, Don stops being the principal partner of the law firm and goes back to being her cousin's soft-spoken husband. The gentle soul who believes that everyone deserves a fair trial and a fair shake at life. Second chances, he says, are his favorite kind.

Meghan has, oh so casually, mentioned her "friend" Marley Tallman to her cousins, in the context of someone who has also enjoyed a second chance.

"Where did he acquire his dog?" Carol is clearly keeping a poker face. If it had been her mother, Meghan would have been subjected to the third degree. "Not a prison program?"

"No, another program altogether. One that matches rescue dogs with veterans."

"I'm glad that there are other programs out there, and it

makes me think that you would have gotten a dog even if you hadn't been accepted into the prison program."

"But I wouldn't have Shark. That's like saying if you married a different man, you'd have had different children, but they wouldn't have been the ones you did get."

"And I wouldn't have known the difference."

"I suppose. You can't know what you've missed by chance. Still, I'm really happy that I got into that program. That I got to know Rosie."

"Tell me how she's doing." Carol holds her plate up to Don, who slips another piece of chicken onto it.

"She's—I don't know the best word. I guess *confused* captures it. The effect of having been abruptly released and then finding herself in charge of a crazy project is really disconcerting, but she's coping. Mostly by kvetching."

"You should go see her."

"Not yet. It's too soon."

"Why?"

"I might confuse things for her."

"So, will you ever tell her?" Don sits down opposite Meghan. "We can only go so far with this."

Shark

Shark is sitting in his special corner, but his eyes are on the people. He likes it when these two come to their place. He likes the atmosphere of human kin. Of calmness. So when a flicker of tension arises in Meghan, he leaves his corner and touches her elbow with his nose.

She rewards him with a pat, and a tiny piece of chicken. Life is good.

Meghan

Meghan's wardrobe has evolved to include an array of brightly colored skirts and capri pants, expensive, but made especially for ladies like her—that is, adaptive, comfortable, and paired with a growing collection of blouses and T-shirts that emphasize the toning in her arms. So when Marley suggested an away-from-the-dog-park outing, she finally didn't have to worry about what to wear. "What do you think, Shark? The plum-colored pants with the white blouse?" There is no one in her apartment to witness her treating this dog like he's an arbiter of fashion. She doesn't even feel like she is joking. Shark, ever alert to her needs, sniffs each piece of clothing. "Or is the lilac blouse a better choice?" He gave the white blouse a second sniff. Sat in front of Meghan. Huffed.

"The white one it is." So far, the dog hasn't let her down sartorially.

As Meghan tilts her makeup mirror to apply scar-masking foundation, she gives herself a smile. A year ago, less, she wouldn't have been doing this, this primping. One of the unexpected benefits of having Shark, of having his nonjudgmental presence in her life, has been a lessening of self-judgment, that need to measure her every action against the old Meghan, the soldier Meghan. The old Meghan would have viewed a casual suggestion to see the new exhibit at the Metropolitan Museum of Art as a day of challenges, from dressing to transportation to being hampered at every turn. She would have viewed it like a military exercise, preparedness, moving from point A to point B, analyzing the components and thus building up a tension that would have quickly squashed any potential pleasure in what is, really, a simple idea. With Shark by her side, exuding his doggie Zen vibes, she looks at new ideas as opportunities to show him off.

Today, she uncaps a new red lipstick and admires the way the bright color drains the emphasis away from the glistening scar where her ear used to be, a vacancy now well hidden behind a fall of russet hair allowed to wave naturally to her shoulders, freed from the military dictum of a low, tight bun.

"This isn't a date." She caps the lipstick and looks into her mirror at the dog's face poised behind her, his muzzle resting on the back of her chair. "It's just a nice idea." She hears the thump of tail on tile. Marley Tallman is a nice guy, a friend. A friend with whom she has a lot in common. Not just the service but also the fact that, although Marley came back from his last deployment physically unharmed, his dog, Spike, is as much a necessity to his well-being as Shark is to hers. Spike may not have to flip light switches, but she presses herself close to Marley, nuzzling his palm whenever the crowd gets a little too big, or when there is a faint metallic scent in the air. It was the first thing Meghan noticed: The dog's attention to the man, far and away more concerned with her person than with the rubber ball, was, to Meghan, a dead giveaway that this was a partnership out of the same mold as her partnership with Shark.

Meghan's intercom bleats.

Marley's voice sounds rusty over the box. "It's me."

She buzzes the outside door open and swings the apartment door wide, backs herself up to leave room for her guests. Shark sits patiently beside her. He's wearing his service dog vest. The minute she puts it on him, he changes. He transforms from goofball to all business.

Spike, tall, lanky, and blond, like a canine Marilyn Monroe, is wearing her version of the service dog vest. She, too, observes a professional aloofness, although her tail hasn't gotten the message.

"It's okay. Go say hi." Marley fills the doorway. His last name is Tallman and it is exceptionally apropos. Outside, even standing beside her, he hadn't seemed that large. In her tiny, uncluttered space, he looms. And he is suddenly awkward.

"Sit, please." Meghan has two chairs, an expensive leather power recliner that her parents gave her as a housewarming gift, and a floral overstuffed chair only a grandmother could love. Meghan makes no excuse for it. It came from Carol, by way of her mother, and therefore is something of a family heirloom. Both chairs face the wall with the television and are separated by an occasional table at exactly the right height for Meghan's use. There's a yellow tennis ball balanced on it and a rope toy, a lamp that only requires a tap to turn on.

Marley removes his newsboy hat and lowers himself into the floral chair. "I've got an Uber outside."

"Can he handle my chair?" This is better; she can meet his eye.

"Yes. I made sure." Inside, he looks older, and she can see a hint of gray in his close-clipped hair. It isn't the old of aging, but of being old before your time. It's why she's taken to bright colors, to red lipstick.

"Then I say, let's go."

The Uber is a Honda Odyssey, and the driver has already made room for her wheelchair in the back. She's got her regular chair, knowing that the motorized one is impossible to get into a van not equipped with a lift, and Marley can hardly have arranged that. She pulls the arm off and slides herself into the backseat, lifts herself over, and calls Shark in to sit in the well under her feet. Marley figures out how to fold the chair and the driver puts it into the back.

Marley climbs in beside her, Spike at his feet, squeezing herself into a compact ball despite her size. "Off we go."

"I'm sorry that it takes so much effort."

"What do you mean? Fold a wheelchair? I know how to do that."

"It just does."

Both dogs pant, excited about the outing.

The guard at the museum doesn't even try to give them a hard time about their dogs; clearly, these aren't his first museum-going mutts. What's hard is to ask the variety of strangers to keep back, not reach out to pet the dogs, or make kissy noises to get their attention. These are dogs at work, not dogs at play.

"If they weren't so damn adorable, no one would want to pet them." Marley has disappointed a white-haired old lady intent on being the one exception to their rule. "Maybe if we put muzzles on them, they'd look scary."

"I need Shark's muzzle as a tool. And I think Spike would be crestfallen."

"We could train them to growl."

"That's an idea."

It's almost noon, and Meghan suggests lunch. It's Saturday afternoon, and, as they expected, the cafeteria is terribly crowded, but no one is lingering, so a table becomes available fairly quickly. Marley moves a chair aside so that Meghan can slide in, asks what she wants for lunch, and disappears, leaving her with both dogs obediently ensconced beneath the table.

Meghan sees the curiosity on the faces of folks not expecting to see two sizable dogs in the cafeteria, and she wonders if she should have a placard that says CLEAN DOGS, WORKING DOGS. Shark rests his chin on her foot, but she doesn't realize it until she peeks under the table. Shark is happy, but Spike is concerned and shows it with her sphinxlike pose beneath the table, her eyes on Marley in the checkout line, clearly distressed to be separated from him by even a few feet.

"Chicken Caesar salad wrap, chocolate milk." Marley sets her lunch down in front of her.

Meghan has a ten and a five in her hand. "What do I owe you?

"My treat."

"That's what you said about the Uber. And the museum tickets. Marley, this isn't . . ."

"What? A date?" He has the grace to smile.

"Well, yes. I mean, no."

"Are you saying you wouldn't date me?"

"Not at all. I mean . . ."

Marley is still smiling. "Is it 'cause I'm black?"

Meghan has too much experience sharing jibes with her troops, many of whom were brown-skinned people. "No. It's 'cause you're a marine."

"No intermilitary dating for you?"

"I'm regular army all the way, mister."

"Then give me twelve bucks."

As great as the day was, Meghan is glad to be home, cradled in her power recliner, scrolling through her Netflix choices. She hadn't invited Marley up after the Uber dropped her off. It wasn't a date, after all. Hadn't she made that clear? "See you at the dog park."

"You bet." Marley waved the Uber driver off. "It was fun. Hope you had fun, too."

"I did."

She needs someone to ask the question "Why wasn't it a date?"

Meghan hits the speed dial for Rosie.

Shark

It was the best day ever. Rides in a car, going into a place where so many people noticed him; being with his pal Spike. Everything was going along just fine, but now Meghan is in that worried funk she sometimes gets into. Sharkey pokes at her with his toys, tries to remind her that they've had a fun day. But she mutters something to him that suggests she is troubled. He hands her the *cell phone*. He's got excellent hearing and the voice coming out of the phone is his dear old friend, Rosie. He leaves off trying to jolly Meghan out of her fret. Clearly, she needs the human voice to emerge out of it. Disappointed but not discouraged, Sharkey decides on a nap.

Rosie

Another day, another discussion. Tucker has arrived. He hands me a paper cup of coffee and we head into the house to take a look at the work in the front parlor. Two hundred years of flooring modernizations have been ripped up. It's been like an archaeological dig, pulling up each generation's "improvements," from grubby worn wall-to-wall, to faded linoleum, to plywood subflooring, to the mother lode, twenty-inch-wide ship planks. "Just don't grow trees like that anymore." Tucker runs his hand along the planking, sighs with appreciation and with despair. The crew has excised the worst of the rotted planking with surgical precision, and the new planks, repurposed from a barn in New Hampshire, will be sistered in. But there has to be a reason the seaworthy original planks rotted. Somebody needs to go into the crawl space and take a look.

Frankly, I'm more interested in the plumbing project. "So, Tucker, when do you think the plumber will arrive?"

"Rosie, why don't you call him?" He says this gently, but I

get the point. This is *my* job, chasing after subcontractors—
"subs," as we call them in the business.

As if he's sorry for mentioning my job to me, Tucker adds,
"You're okay, though, right? With water?"

"I think I probably stink."

"I didn't notice."

"Really, Tucker, this constitutes cruel and unusual punishment."

"Go to my place. I'm never home during the day. I'll even
clean the bathroom for ya."

"I couldn't."

"Why not?"

I know that I must have this look on my face, a little bit
horrified, a little bit tempted. "I'll think about it."

"Just let me know. I'll give you a key."

"What about your wife? Wouldn't she be a bit surprised to
find a strange woman in her bathroom?"

"Only if she deigned to visit my apartment. We're di-
vorced."

"Sorry."

"Don't be."

The day has turned nice, warm enough the mud has already gone from black to brown; the big paw prints from
yesterday have hardened into impermanent fossils.

Last night, I thought I heard a dog bark. I am sleeping only
fitfully, still uneasy in the deep silence that surrounds this
lonely place. I woke with the same kind of startle reflex you
have when you dream of falling. I woke up listening, but I
heard nothing except the faint sound of wind through the
woods that surround this house.

Tucker catches me looking at the print. "I'll bring back a
proper composting bin when I go up the line to the Home Depot."

"'Up the line'?"

Tucker smiles, "Local expression."

Despite Tucker's offer to go to his apartment and use his bathroom—not bloody likely—I continue to rough it with water heated on the stove, and I have become proficient in the sink bath routine. I think back to the time in my life when I might have showered twice a day, lathering and rinsing with scarcely a thought for my parents' hot-water bill. And college, my first experience of high-flow showerheads and the wearing of shower shoes. Charles's South End condo had all the bells and whistles one needs when one is of pampered stock: Jacuzzi heads in the tub, a separate shower with a showerhead that made it feel as if you were in a rain forest. And, of course, the communal showering in prison. Plastic shower curtains with at least three missing rings, the ongoing combat to get into the shower before the inadequate hot water ran out. The hair pulling if you stayed too long. So, hey, maybe a quiet sink bath and an outside hose for shampooing isn't all that bad.

With only the most primitive kitchen, my kitchenware comprising two saucepans of questionable cleanliness and a slotted spoon, I opt for visiting Cape Ann's wide array of dining options. Seafood, obviously. Italian. Seafood. Pizza. Seafood. And, my favorite, Portuguese cuisine. It's at the Azorean, where I run into Tucker, also dining solo.

My instinct is to duck him, to pretend that I don't notice his presence. He's seated at a two-top table, with his back to the window, the table set for one.

"Hey, Rosie. Join me?" Without his ball cap, with a pair of reading glasses giving him a rough-hewn professorial aspect, he doesn't look quite as ursine as he does in his natural element of sawdust and debris.

"Oh, I couldn't." I'm not being polite, or coy. Whatever

would we talk about? I have no conversation that wouldn't veer off into revelations about my most recent history, which I have no desire to cop to. Besides, I can't imagine sitting down in such close proximity with any man just yet.

"Oh, come on. Unless. Are you . . . ?"

"What?"

"Expecting anyone?"

My mama told me never to lie. "No. Just me."

"We can go over some details."

Whew. A business dinner. Plenty of nice neutral subject matter. "Sure. Thanks."

The hostess quickly puts a table setting in front of me, asks after my beverage preference. I notice that Tucker has a bottle of craft beer in front of him. I order—for the first time in, oh sweet Mary Mother of God, six years!—a glass of wine. House Chardonnay. No sense getting fancy. It tastes better to me than any of Charles's high-priced, overdescribed, fancy-schmancy imported wines. I try not to guzzle it down before my Mediterranean salad arrives. Tucker has the kale soup. I have the *frango assado* and he has the grilled octopus. We talk about the project in between forkfuls. I nod and agree with much of what he's saying because, after all, I have no idea how a project of this scope is attacked. If Tucker says strip the antique shingles off and get the roof done first, then, of course, I nod in sage agreement and bring up the state of the nonfunctioning bathroom only as an aside. We agree that there must be some simultaneous inside and outside activity in order to get the place habitable by the time cold weather sets. *Habitable.* I laugh at that word. I'm living in an uninhabitable house. And that's just fine.

"I'm curious," I say, and take another bite of the amazing chicken. "What's with Dogtown?" Tucker's business name plus a couple of other Dogtown references have had me looking for wayfinders for a hidden village on this peninsula of villages. A village of dogs, maybe. A place I would feel very much at home.

"Ah, Dogtown. It's an interesting story."

"Tell me about it."

"You have to know a bit about Cape Ann history, how the first settlers came here. Out of fear of pirates and the native population, they settled away from the coast, calling the area 'The Commons.' They prospered, and every man—white man, of course—had a field and a woodlot. There were a couple of mills. A nice little village. Then, a couple of generations later, the threats were gone, and the lure of making a ton of real money on the sea had most of the well-to-do gravitating to what is now Gloucester proper. The rich people left, and the poor continued to try to eke out a living on this really rocky, de-forested land. All that it was really good for, after the trees were gone, was sheep farming, and even that was hard because of the bogs."

"The bogs?"

"Wetlands. Sheep-eaters." He paused long enough to savor the last of his dinner. "Eventually, the houses deteriorated, and today you can see the cellar holes where they once stood."

"But how did that become Dogtown?"

"Well, by the end of the Revolutionary War, pretty much the only people left in the Commons were widows, too poor or too eccentric to live elsewhere. They took in boarders, and the place ended up with an unsavory reputation. Needless to say, the women became known as one of three things: witches, cheats, or prostitutes."

"And they were called 'dogs'?"

"No, they *kept* dogs. The widows became known for keep-ing dogs as close companions—read *familiars*—and as protec-tion against, well, probably against the drunken sailors who

might prey on them. Some smart-ass probably started calling
the place 'Dogtown' and it stuck."

"Where is it?"

"Just outside your door."

I saw paw prints again this morning. I was bent from the waist,
cold water numbing my skull as I washed my hair. I saw it,
and I put my hand down next to it to get its measure. As big as
these prints looked, my hand was still larger—just.

Last night, I heard barking. I'm sure of it. Not distant barking, but close by. It woke me from a sound sleep. No, that's not
accurate; a sleep interrupted throughout the night, as most
nights, with the taint of bad dreams. I am nearly a month beyond incarceration, and still I dream of boxes and immobility.
If I am lucky, I dream of my dogs, Shark and Harry and my
unfinished Lulu. I wake wondering how they are, if they are
happy. Meghan has begun to slip away from our friendship.
She hasn't called as often, and she responds to my texts with
a new brevity. I have to keep in mind that she is now a work-
ingwoman, that her hours are filled in a way that they weren't
when we first met. And she's kind of dating. Another veteran.
I'm happy for her. I don't take it personally.

The novelty of solitude is wearing off. It's becoming plain
old loneliness.

I keep thinking about Tucker's story of Dogtown, and how
the lonely widows, or witches, if you prefer, found comfort and
companionship with their dogs. I keep thinking about what it
would be like to have a dog. One that I wouldn't have to give
up. Or one that wouldn't become the catalyst for tragedy.

"Absolutely not. We don't have the time for a dog." Charles was
never one to mince words. If he thought something was a bad
idea, then it was a bad idea, case closed.

Nonetheless, I kept persisting. "These are little dogs, nothing that's going to take up a lot of space, and, Charles, I'd love to have a companion. Something to keep me company during the day."

Charles had a way of becoming solid when he was unhappy with me. His jaw tensed; his whole body would set like concrete with the effort of containing his displeasure, as if he was holding it in, afraid of softening, of letting an issue or subject go. His eyes would go dead. Charles never touched me in anger. His violence was a withholding, the act of separating himself from me. I would find myself cajoling, then apologizing, explaining myself and my foolishness, admitting a fault I didn't necessarily believe I had, all in order to get him to soften, to accept my apology. Hours, even days later, I would wonder why I couldn't stand up to that rigidity; why it bothered me so much to be on the wrong side of that human wall.

This time, I decided that rather than chance a full-blown argument, a fait accompli was a good idea. I had the puppy already picked out, paid for, and ready to go. A Maltese-poodle cross, a designer dog. An armful of dog. "It was just a thought, Charles."

"Keep it that way." The tension loosed in his face and he smiled. "Aren't I companion enough for you?"

"Are you suggesting that you'd like to be on my leash?" I joked back.

It went on from there to a logical conclusion, and all the time I was thinking about the moment when I would bring the puppy home: *Charles, you're going to fall in love with her.* I was so certain.

I've been lucky so far; the summer warmth persists and I am comfortable in the unheated house even in the cool night, in my well-rated sleeping bag. The various interior workmen have made a little progress, at least as far as I can see. The remnants of the last occupant's twentieth-century enhancements are gone—the rugs, the linoleum, a grungy old Barcalounger. The next step in the process, according to Tucker, is to remove the battered wallboard from the interior walls. He's hopeful that doing so will expose fireplaces in both parlors. Then, once everything's stripped to the studs, the electrician will commence rewiring the whole place. In the meantime, I have electricity in the kitchen, further confining me to that space if I want to read or listen to the radio. Without a suggestion of Wi-Fi, that's my only source of entertainment unless I want to ding myself on data charges. Pete gave me the phone, yeah, but the bill is all mine.

And so it is that I am sitting under the standing lamp that I have set up in the corner of the kitchen where one of the two outlets is, rocking in the ancient rocking chair I saved from the same fate as the Barcalounger. I've got the radio on, tuned to a Boston station, but I'm barely listening. I'm deep in my book. I've been bingeing on bestsellers from the Sawyer Free Library—a name that feels apropos to a newly free woman—drunk on having a choice of current novels. One of the librarians, Shelley Brown, is getting to know my taste and has set aside some really good reads for me. No crime novels. No thrillers. Alone in my derelict house on the edge of Dogtown, it would not do to have my imagination stoked. I haven't taken Tucker's suggestion that I hike around what is now conservation land and see for myself the cellar holes and landmark boulders. I have no desire to walk alone in the woods. Some might take refreshment in being outdoors, but I am, at heart, a city girl. People get lost in the woods, and, from what Tucker mentioned oh so casually, it is a rite of passage for Gloucesterites to get lost in the Dogtown woods. No thank you.

It has begun to rain and a change of wind direction rattles the panes in the window. A whisper of colder air slips under the back door, swirls around my bare ankles. I shiver and pull them up under me. That's when I hear it, a faint scratching. "Oh, geez." All the time I've been living in the Homestead, I've worried about vermin—mice in particular. I've been diligent about food scraps, using Tucker's composting can, and keeping the rough floor as crumb-free as I can. This is not the sound of mice. Rats? My toes curl at the thought. Louder scratching. I shut off the radio. I slip my bare feet into my sneakers. Scratch. Scratch. It's not at the back door, but the one that leads to the dogtrot.

Woof. A deep, mellow request for admission. *Woof.*

Do coyotes bark?

The rain begins to pound in earnest, one of those coastal deluges that make you think of the end of days. A quieter *Woof*, as if the creature is shying away from his own request. *Please?*

I open the door.

At first, I think that maybe it *is* a coyote. It's huge, gray, and wet. It looks at me with an expression that suggests I have taken way too long to open this door. He marches in, gives a great water-laden shake, flops down on the cheap braided rug that I found at HomeGoods, and commences doing what dogs do, licking himself dry.

"Hey, who the heck are you?"

He leaves off licking his nether parts. He's one of those dogs that has what they call "furnishings," bushy eyebrows and chin hair. But he's no breed I've ever seen before. His coat is all wiry, like a wolfhound's, except that he's not quite that big. Maybe a greyhound mix, if there is such a thing. Doesn't matter; he's big and he's got to be the maker of those prints. Which makes me feel better. Not a coyote, just a big stray dog. Collarless. Friendly, because he's on his feet and greeting me in dog fashion, tail sweeping from side to side. It has a little hook in the end of it. His eyes are soulful, the little eyebrows giving him a very human expression. "Are you hungry?"

The tail swishes more dramatically. I think he must speak English.

I don't mind sharing my leftover chicken breast with him. He eats slowly, unlike my dear Shark, who inhaled food and then looked around, as if surprised it was gone. I won't make a habit of this; he'll need a proper diet for a large-breed dog. Because, of course, I'm going to keep him.

It is still deep night, but the rain has stopped; the silence is what must have awakened me. I sense the warm presence of this other living creature in the room, listen for the soft breathing. He knows that I am awake, waits for me to pat the covers and invite him to me. "Good boy," I whisper to him, which is ridiculous, because we are the only ones here. His tail wags. I am no longer alone.

Shadow

The woman invites him inside. Offers him food. She has no fear of him, no apprehension, unlike most of the humans he's met. She makes him feel like she knows him. Within moments, he allows *attachment* to settle his future. He will stay with her. He already understands that she needs him.

Meghan

One of the stranger things about independence is how quickly Meghan has gotten used to it. From complete dependence to mostly complete independence has been a long long journey, and now that she's achieved it, she's already begun to take it for granted. She equates it to when she was sixteen and champing at the bit to get her driver's license. It seemed that it would take forever, and the dream of being in the driver's seat, going when and where she wanted, was such a prize that she was certain she'd always be excited about it. But within weeks of getting the coveted prize, she was annoyed to be the designated errand runner. Within a month, driving was just something she did. The specialness of automotive freedom had subsided, turning into an ordinary activity. And now the routine of getting ready for work, waiting for the city bus with its handicap accessibility, rolling into the lobby of the building, and grabbing a coffee for the ride up in the elevator had gone from magic to mundane—except for Shark, who made this independence possible. She would never take him for granted.

"Shark, button." The dog stands on his hind legs and noses the button for her floor. When they first started this, he hit virtually every button, but now, somehow, he's refined his skill to hitting only one or two incorrect floors, and half the time he's spot-on. When others get into the elevator at the same time, she's noticed that no one reaches for the elevator buttons until Shark does; she's sure they're admiring his skills. One passenger always says, *Thanks, buddy*, when Shark happens to hit her number.

Meghan's cell phone dings with a text alert. Rosie. *Call when u get a chance. Big news,* the message says.

She taps in a quick *Will do* but doesn't send it. The elevator has reached her floor.

She's got a few minutes before her first meeting of the morning, so she thumbs Rosie's number. Rosie isn't one of those dramatic types who uses "big news" willy-nilly. If she's got news, it's got to be interesting.

Rosie answers on the first ring. "Meghan, hey. I didn't think you'd call so quick."

"I've got a minute before I have to meet with some folks, so give me the short version." She hopes that she doesn't sound rude, but Rosie is Irish enough to have the storytelling gene. No story worth telling is worth telling briefly.

"Okay. Are you ready for this?"

"What?"

"Meghan, I got a dog."

"Oh, Rosie, that's so great." If anyone deserves to have a dog of her own, it's Rosie. "What kind?"

"God only knows."

"Good breed, I hear."

"Check your texts; I just sent you a picture."

Meghan does and laughs out loud at the photo of this giant gray dog. "How many hands is he?"

"Ha-ha. Let's just say I don't have to bend over to pet him."

"Where did he come from?" She's expecting a story of a rescue, a visit to a shelter.

"He just showed up. I think he's been hanging around, because I've seen these giant paw prints, but I thought they might be a coyote's. Last night, in the middle of a rainstorm, there he was, asking to come in, like he freakin' owns the place. Plopped down on the rug in front of the woodstove and, booya, that was that. Completely at home." Rosie takes a breath. "It's like he is just meant to be with me."

"What are you calling him?"

"Shadow. Mostly because he sticks to me like my own shadow. Plus, he's grayish, so it suits him."

"I bet you're going to have a blast with him. Rosie, I couldn't be happier for you."

"Well, getting out of prison was pretty much my happiest moment, but this is a close second. He's already done two things for me."

"What's that?"

"Given me someone to talk to, and today, when the workmen arrive, I won't feel quite so vulnerable."

"You feel that way?"

"All the time."

"I didn't know."

"It's fine. Really."

"You have PTSD."

"No. I'm just a little shy. Shadow is going to help me get over myself."

A head pops into the doorway of Meghan's office; it's Bob Watson, signaling that their nine o'clock meeting is about to begin. She holds up a finger. "How's the house coming?"

"Inch by inch. Every step forward requires two steps backward. Now Tucker's insisting that the sills—you know, the timbers that the house rests on—have to be analyzed for rot. Could mean jacking the house up and having new sills installed. I don't know if I can stay in the house if that happens. It's hard enough without hot water. . . ."

"Still?"

"Yeah, don't ask. Anyway, I'm not complaining, I'm grateful to be here and not you know where."

"Me, too."

"I'd love for you to see the place. When it's done, of course."

"Can't wait. Hey, sorry, they're waving me into the meeting."

"Go. Love you."

"Me, too."

Shark

It doesn't seem silly to him that Meghan tells him things, as if he should have an opinion. Most times, he has no idea what she's talking about; he just enjoys the atmosphere of a happy, if one-sided, conversation. He utters little woofs, a yip or two, just to keep her going. This time, he recognizes the *Rosie* word and knows that something has made Meghan laugh. That's good. Because in the next minute, she holds the phone in her lap and sighs. The presence of inner trouble that rises to the surface in ways only perceptible to a perceptive dog has arrived.

Rosie

That little sign-off comes so naturally. *Love you.* It's what good friends say. And yet I can't help but feel that our friendship is suffering. Oh, we talk, but the common experience that fostered this friendship—my being a prisoner, and her being my visitor— has changed, and we haven't quite figured out the new dynamic. I vow to call less frequently. She's got a life, and I have to respect that. It isn't just the changes in my circumstances; she's moved on, too. Maybe things were fading even as she moved on to her life in the city. Maybe I just hadn't noticed it.

I hear Tucker's truck. The dog, Shadow, is on the alert; his ears are pricked forward, and his tail is stiff. As he doesn't yet have a collar, I have no way to restrain him should he take an aggressive stance with my general contractor. "He's a friend, Shadow. Be good." I know from my days of training dogs that if I'm not excited, or afraid, or concerned, if I keep my voice modulated and make no fuss, the dog will take my lead. However, I haven't trained this dog. This dog is a blank slate. I don't know what his purpose has been up to this moment. For all I

know, he's a loose guard dog. He woofs. I open the back door.
"Hey, Tucker!" I keep my voice bright.

Tucker is still in his truck when the dog paces over to it.
The dog is tall, but not quite tall enough to look in the driver's
window—that is, until he puts his feet on the running board
and lifts himself to examine Tucker through the open window.

"That's some dog."

"Yes, yes he is."

"The print maker?"

"I believe so."

"Guess you won't have to worry about coyotes anymore."

"I don't believe I will."

Tucker pops open the door and the dog stands there.

"Shadow, he's a friend." I snap my fingers. "Come."

In some kind of canine decision making, the dog accepts
my command and returns to sit by my side, letting Tucker get
out of his truck and be introduced properly. Tucker lets the dog
sniff him, puts out the back of his hand and waits patiently
while Shadow gets to know him. Satisfied, Shadow's hooked
tail is swinging. Tucker risks a pat on the dog's head, and suddenly all is well.

"I brought you these." Tucker hands me a pamphlet and
some computer printouts. "They'll give you a little more info
about Dogtown."

"Thank you. That's very thoughtful."

"Now you have a reason to go hiking. Big guy like this is
going to need exercise. Can't think of a better place than the
woods."

"I'll think about it." But already I know that I will.

I set aside the novel that Shelley Brown had recommended in
favor of studying the material that Tucker has given me. I have
a glass of wine in my hand, and nearby the soft light of a lamp

I'd found in a thrift store that I've set up on the kitchen table. As usual, by this hour, what local traffic there was along my narrow lane has stopped and only the now-familiar slap of a loose shingle inserts itself into the ultraquiet of my solitary evening. Ha, no longer solitary, but certainly quiet.

It is a strange story, the history of Dogtown. As Tucker said, the Commons, as it was originally, was a thriving eighteenth-century village, reduced in the early nineteenth century to a ghost town; in between, it became a place where the outliers of Cape Ann once lived. A place that once was the preferred location of the settlers, safe from the threat of "Barbary pirates," it had been all but abandoned in favor of a more lucrative livelihood provided by the sea. In the meantime, the place was essentially deforested for firewood. Even the pasturage was inadequate, rocky and, in places, so boggy that it swallowed livestock. By the end of the Revolution, and then the War of 1812, the only people clinging to the Commons were war widows and other outliers. It became inevitable, it seems to me, that those women, essentially indigent, would become known as witches, prostitutes, and, of course, crazies. All that is left are their names recorded in the brief histories of Dogtown: Tammy Younger, Granny Day, Easter Carter. Their names and the cellar holes.

As for the name, Dogtown, I like it. I like the idea of women keeping dogs a lot.

Guess it's a good place for me. I cannot seem to shed the feeling I do not yet belong in society. I feel like there is some kind of taint about me, a scent of injustice. I am exonerated but not whole.

I've promised, and now Shadow is anxious to get his walk started, and he nudges me with his cold black nose. The Homestead is situated a quarter mile or so from an entrance to the trailhead for Dogtown. An easy walk from our funky old house. My dog, Shadow, gambols about, puppyish as he flushes rabbits and an occasional grouse out of the thick roadside underbrush. His exuberance is uplifting, and I find myself flush with a kind of pleasure I haven't had in years. A momentary cessation of internal hostilities. I am not the child estranged from her family or the newly released prisoner blinking in the sunshine; I am just Rosie, happy to be walking down this country lane, a good dog at my side.

She was a handful of fluff, bright brown eyes in a pure white face. I didn't want to give her a common name, Molly or Maggie or Munchkin. I called her Matilda, which, of course, devolved into "Tilley" for short. The day I collected my designer dog from the breeder, I went back and forth on whether or not I should let Charles know that I was doing this, going against his express wishes regarding the puppy. I have to admit, the timing was awful, Tilley's breeder needed her to be picked up during what turned out to be the week before my father's final crisis. Would Charles have been less annoyed if I'd just waited? But how could I have known that things would go south so quickly? And there was something so comforting about having this little ball of life needing me, needing my full attention; at complete odds with the rest of my life, which had become about death.

I debated what would make Charles angrier—if I told him in advance that I'd bought the puppy or if I stuck to my original plan, which was to present this new family member as a done deal? I wavered, but then I realized that I didn't want to give him the opportunity to forbid me this indulgence. I knew that the trappings of his favorite meal, a perfectly constructed cocktail chilled and waiting for him, and me in my sexy best outfit might not be the most effective offense, but it wouldn't hurt. How can you stay angry with someone who's worked so hard to please you? How could you not fall in love with this little perky puppy face? Only a monster would be impervious to Tilley's already adorable charms. A monster indeed.

Other than my mother's telephone number, with a growing accretion of unanswered outgoing calls handily noted beside it, I have only three contacts in my phone, and so far this morning I've talked to two of them: a quick call from Meghan to get an update on Shadow, and then one from Pete Bannerman, who's doing his usual Tuesday-morning check-in. As I reach the entrance to the Dogtown trail system, it rings with the third ID: Tucker Bellingham. I almost feel popular.

"Anybody there this morning?"

"Not so far, but I've been out of the house for a while."

"Rosie, you gotta start making some phone calls. I'll text you the contact info for the plumber and for the electrician. I don't have time to ride herd on all of them. That's kind of your job."

"Okay, fine. No problem." I really don't have a clue what my job is, and Tucker hasn't been particularly forthcoming. In his view, I should *be* a project manager, not a project manager in training. He's right. "I'm happy to do what I can to get things moving."

"Start with the plumber. He's the hardest to pin down."

"You're telling me." I've got my dirty hair twisted up and I'm contemplating checking into a hotel for the night just to get a shower.

Tucker promises to text me the contact number—again—and lets me know that he'll be around sometime late this afternoon. Hopefully, I can have some evidence of success for him.

We've arrived at the trailhead, where a handy map is

posted on a wooden kiosk. A black mailbox holds copies of the Dogtown trail system. The road is crumbly tar, quickly becoming dirt and muddy truck tracks as we pass some kind of sandpit and find the path through the woods. Instantly, civilization fades and it's as if we've entered another century. The silence is deep, punctuated only by the literal *Tweet* of a persistent bird. If I listen carefully, I can hear a corresponding *Tweet* deeper in the woods. I won't lie; there is something creepy about these woods. Maybe it's knowing the history; more likely, it's the tangle of underbrush and the way the white oaks and pines creak and clack against one another in the southwest breeze. I tell myself that we don't have to go far. Certainly not so far as to get lost.

Shadow has his nose to the ground and moves deliberately, focused on whatever it is his nose is telling him. He must be tracking, because his route circles back and then he performs a perfect figure eight. He keeps looking at me, making sure that I am in his sight even as his nose preoccupies him. I keep my map handy, but I find myself trusting the dog to lead me along these, to me, confusing trails. Eventually, we come to a boulder with the word STUDY engraved on it. The Babson Boulders. In the little booklet about Dogtown that Tucker gave me is the story about Roger Babson, a somewhat eccentric quarry owner and founder of the college that bears his name, who, in the Depression, gave out-of-work Finnish stonemasons the job of carving "a sort of book" on the massive boulders that emerge from the woods. I quickly find IDEAS, INDUSTRY, and, on the verso side of a boulder the size of a house, SPIRITUAL POWER. In the deep silence of the woods, the absence of anything else of human origin, it's almost a little creepy. Text messaging from the grave.

The eastern sun has warmed the side of the massive

boulder, and I lean against it as I hit the number for the plumbing company. I put on my best project manager's voice, lowering it just a little, keeping all hints of millennial uptalk out of my tone. I'm all business. However, there's no one in the office, so I leave a detailed voice message, with only a little bit of begging leaking through.

Shadow waits, then bounds off into the underbrush, making me think that I'd better see about flea and tick protection if we're going to make hiking a regular activity. I push off from the rock and troop after him. We don't stop again until we reach a fork in the trail with a sign identifying the place as Dogtown Square. There is nothing square about it, just a random stop in the trail. I am not able to imagine this area stripped of trees, home to any kind of community. I think that I am ready to turn around and head home. Shadow keeps moving, taking the rightmost trail. I'll give our outing another few minutes; then we are definitely heading home. I don't care if there are workmen there.

Ahead of me, Shadow pauses, fixed into immobility, as if some spell has been cast on him and he's gone from flesh and blood to statuary. His folded ears prick forward like little jack-in-the-pulpits; beneath the bristly eyebrows, his eyes are intent on a pile of rocks. This place is nothing but rocks, but he's picked out this particular jumble, and I realize that we've come to one of the numbered cellar holes of Dogtown. Without the black number posted on a short granite stump, I can't think that anyone would ever take this sunken rock repository as ever having been someone's home.

Shadow sits down. He throws me a look that I can only interpret as an invitation to do the same thing. I choose a rock that hasn't sunk into the ground quite as much as the rest of the pile. If these rocks are from ancient cellars, I can't imagine that the houses were very big. The sunken areas look only about as big as a coffin. Maybe they weren't cellars—basements—as we know them, but root cellars. I hear the bird again. Overhead, leaves rustle, a breeze or maybe a squirrel.

As I sit there, the dog does something I think is curious. He moves from his place between two rocks and comes to sit beside me, uncomfortably perched on mine. He heaves a great sigh and then rests his chin on my knees. He's looking for comfort. I stroke his head, pat his ribs. Rest my head on his. I have not been a comfort to anyone for a very long time.

The branches above me sway and a single bird calls repeatedly, but I can't pick it out against the dark bark of the trees and branches; the early hint of fall shows in the faded dull look of the leaf canopy. It's hard to imagine this place naked of trees, the rocks exposed. It's amazing how thoroughly the forest will recover itself when left alone. In the distance, the sound of the high-speed train on the Boston-to-Gloucester run. Without that so very contemporary sound, it could be two hundred years ago. I keep my phone in my hand, less for convenience than as a totem. I need to keep my feet in this century.

"I called the plumber—is he really called Bob the Plumber? Anyway, we're on for first thing tomorrow."

"Good. Great. Once he's done, we can start on the walls in the bathroom." Tucker doesn't make any sort of skeptical remark about the veracity of a plumber's word, and I take that as a good sign.

"I've been upstairs. It's not pretty."

"I know. Did Pete say anything about what to do with the junk?"

"I'm supposed to start an inventory."

"Good start. Then what?"

"See what makes sense to keep and what makes sense to have appraised. My guess, nothing is worth keeping."

"A place this old, well, you've got to find something interesting. Better than two centuries of occupation, it's got to be like a midden in there—trash that tells a story."

My general contractor shifts his tool belt and says, "I want to take a hard look at the floor in the front parlor today."

We go into the house through the back door, the dog staying close behind. Tucker heads into the "best" parlor, squats down to examine the six reclaimed planks that have replaced the rotten ones. Some other builder might have opted for a plywood replacement, with a nice rug over it, but it's obvious that Tucker has no interest in shortcuts with this house. According to Pete Bannerman, the Trust hasn't squawked at the added expense of it, so Tucker takes that as a mutual desire to keep the integrity of the house as authentic as possible. He's begun to share some of his vision for the ancient house, and I find myself getting caught up in his enthusiasm. "I've been wanting to get into this house since I was a kid. It's what got me interested in architecture in the first place."

"I didn't know you were an architect."

Tucker shakes his head. "Actually, I'm not. I wanted to be, but, well, I never finished college." There is a hint of wistfulness in his tone, and I wonder what it was that kept him from his goal. He doesn't seem like a quitter.

"But you've got a great trade. A good business, right?"

"Good enough. My partner likes the modern stuff, the big additions and kitchen renos, but me, I like this, restoration, not renovation. Unfortunately, there's not enough of it. Everybody wants an antique house, but not without state-of-the-art fixtures. Can't fit most of that luxury into low-ceilinged rooms, so they end up teardowns, replaced by repros."

Shadow moves to stand over Tucker, gently sniffing the back of his neck.

"I think he likes you."

Tucker, on his knees, pats the dog, "I'm glad he does, because I sure wouldn't want to be on his bad side."

"I feel a lot safer here, with him."

"I didn't know you felt unsafe, Rosie. We can find you someplace to stay if it's your safety you're worried about."

"Not anymore. And, Tucker, who would ever take me in with a dog like that?"

Even the dog-friendliest of motels might not cotton to a pony-size dog.

His knees creak as Tucker gets out of his squat. "Man, hardly seems possible that I ever leapt after baseballs with nary a thought to the condition of these knees." Tucker goes to the interior wall, which is a cream-colored plasterboard probably installed when they first put a furnace in the house. "You think Pete would go for ripping down this board and exposing the fireplace?"

"Is that what would be considered a change order?"

"You're beginning to speak Clerk. What if I said no, that it's part of the plan?"

"It would be a cool thing to have as a focal point in this room. Would it be working?"

"I don't know. Probably not, but it would be a nice feature."

I press a palm against the rough surface of the wall. The plasterboard is so old, it bends under my hand. "Even if you didn't expose the fireplace, assuming there is one, you'd still have to do something about this wall, right?"

"Yup."

"I think I can make a case to Pete. Why don't you come up with some numbers and I'll go over the budget."

"Rosie, by George, I think you've got it."

"Don't Henry Higgins me. I've been down that path before." I don't mean to snap, but I've had enough of being someone's project. I've consciously let the down-market Boston accent I was born with creep back into my voice. I've had my hair cut to shoulder length and scraped it back into a high, tight ponytail. I've gone back to my Levi's, my cheap sneakers; I cut my fingernails with a clipper. I am slowly reverting to the self I was when I was my father's daughter.

In some ways, Gloucester reminds me of Bunker Hill, of Charlestown. Not in the architecture necessarily, but in the way the town clings to the hillside. The angle of steepness isn't quite as dramatic as those streets in my town, but steep enough. There is something, too, in the average Joe kind of guys and gals I encounter now that I'm venturing farther away from my remote, crumbling Homestead. It's late enough that the crush of summer visitors has leveled off, so the voices I hear, the remarks and complaints, are pure local. I've even gotten to the point that I no longer accidentally take the long way around, Route 127A, which skirts the shoreline. Instead, I sometimes choose that route so that I can get a glimpse, believe it or not, of Boston in the distance. I feel worlds away, and yet, there it is, skyline rising out of the sea. If I had a boat, I could sail right to my old haunts. Shadow and I get out of the car at the Bass Rocks parking lot. The air is fresh, damp, familiar. He is obedient, and I catch him before he rolls in whatever the sea has coughed up after a high tide.

Today, I'm on my way to the Sawyer Free Library, which is on Middle Street, near the town hall and up a bit from the YMCA, one street up from Main, where I've discovered a really good consignment shop. My wardrobe is limited, and purely functional. I don't have a winter coat and I'm sure,

after my foray to the library, I'll find what I want at the shop.
No one seems to mind that this giant wire-haired dog is sitting out front of the library, and he's welcomed into the shop. This place certainly seems to illustrate its Dogtown history, at least in the way dogs are welcome. All but in the Italian bakery at the other end of Main Street. Board of Health rules are adhered to in there. Maybe I should declare him my service dog and get him a vest so that he can even go in there.

I want to stay out of the house as much as possible today because the plaster walls in the parlors are coming down. Tucker has decided to do this himself, and I think he really wants me gone while he does it. He made that clear when we talked earlier this morning. "It's really going to be messy. We don't know if these walls have asbestos. . . ."

That's all he had to say to me. I knew what that meant.
"You have a mask?"
"I do."
"As project manager, should I be here?"
"Not unless you want to use a crowbar."
"Not so much."
"Thought so."

I'd already ordered a construction Dumpster so that all the debris would be contained properly. It sat outside the back door, a big blue metal box with a plastic lid flipped back. Very attractive. Shadow had marked it, claiming its presence in our yard with a degree of disdain in his eyes.

"Hey, Rosie, while you're out, would you want to stop by the Building Center and get a roll of plastic sheeting?"

This is what has become my purpose, running errands, mostly to the local lumber yard to fetch various things for Tucker. I use his contractor's account and have begun to feel a little pleased with myself for knowing where to find the circular saw blades and the drill bits. I am considering buying myself a pair of Carhartt coveralls just to look the part.

The Building Center is near the waterfront—dutifully labeled a "working waterfront" on the decorative banners and wayfinders posted along my route, as opposed, I suppose, to recreational waterfront. Indeed, the craft in the harbor aren't elegant, and neither are the stacks of lobster pots and the ropy, rank materials of the fishing business. I've seen the iconic Gloucester Fisherman statue, symbolic of Gloucester's heritage. I've eaten the fish sticks.

I get the sheeting and lock it in my car as Shadow and I continue our errands on foot. It feels good, this being outside, a to-go cup of fresh coffee in my hand and a good dog by my side, a heaven I never dreamed of a mere six weeks ago. It still feels fragile, like at any minute someone is going to grab my elbow and say, "Come with me. There's been a mistake. You're going back." I have those moments all too often, and that's when I pull my phone out of my pocket and speed-dial Meghan. She's tolerant of my insecurities. Today, she answers on the first ring. Relieved, I sit on a bench tucked a little bit out of the sea breeze. Shadow decides that it has room for him and he lounges next to me, his great head in my lap.

"Is this a bad time?" I ask out of civility.

"You caught me taking a coffee break."

"Me, too."

I don't tell her about my moment of anxiety; I don't have to.

"Tell me how the house is coming." Usually, she shies away from talk of the project, more interested in hearing about the dog, which is good, or my state of mind, which isn't always good, than the quotidian details of the renovation business. "Walls are coming down today. Tucker thinks there's treasure to be had behind them."

"Dividing walls? Like between the kitchen and parlor?" She sounds oddly distressed.

"No. Someone's idea of winterizing circa 1962." I tell her about Tucker's fireplace hopes.

"Interesting. I guess I had no idea of how old the house was. Just that it was old."

"*Is.* Is old. And bit by bit, Tucker and his minions are uncovering its origins."

"That's exciting." For the first time, she actually sounds engaged in the topic.

"Come see it. We don't have to stay there; we can stay in a motel. It would be fun to have you here."

As always, with this invitation, Meghan hesitates. I know that it's hard, maybe even impossible to get her here, but I'd love for her to say that she'd *like* to come, that she might try to figure out a way to get here.

"I'll come get you. If you can get the time off. You won't have to worry about how to get here; I'll fetch you." I say that, but the idea of driving into New York City does give me the heebie-jeebies. But for Meghan, I'd do it. For Meghan and Shark. To have a chance to see them.

"That's nice of you Rosie, but . . ."

Maybe that guy she mentions often enough that my radar is pinging, maybe he'd like to take a trip to Gloucester. I almost say something about that, but better sense takes over. "We should plan something before the weather gets bad."

I hear her breathing, and I am suddenly concerned that I've pushed a fragile friendship a little too hard. Do I sound like a begging child?

"Maybe in the spring. More of the house will be done by then and maybe I'll even have a car. I'm thinking about that, you know?"

"That would be great. But I'd still want to travel with you."
Now I know I sound like a needy friend, so I shut up.

Shadow shifts his muzzle on my legs. I pull a handful of
neck skin gently between my fingers. "I haven't asked, but
how's the dog park guy?"

"Marley. I'll send you a picture. Then you can judge for
yourself." There is a playfulness for a second, and then she
says, "I just don't know what to do. How to, I don't know, pro-
ceed."

I want to be a giver of sage advice, but I'm not. So I fall
back on the usual comforting sounds of "You'll figure it out."
Fortunately, she's a veteran of that style of advice and just
ignores me. "I don't know if I can." Silence. "You know."

Then I get it. "Oh. I see."

And at that moment, my phone beeps to tell me another
call is coming in. I glance at the screen. It's my mother.

"Meghan, I've got to answer this." I switch to the other call
even before she says good-bye. My heart is pounding, literally
banging against my ribs so hard that it hurts. Shadow sits up,
dismounts the bench, and whines, then drops a massive paw
on my leg even as I launch myself to my feet. If my mother is
calling me, it can only be bad news.

We were sitting in the chairs that flanked my father's hospital
bed, the one that was now center stage in the middle of the
dining room of my parents' Bunker Hill home. The hospice
nurse had just left after making my father as comfortable as
she could. The only sound in the room was the pop and burble of the oxygen machine. That and the wet, ugly sound of
my father's breathing. I was there, finally, and, according to
my mother, better late than never. One look at my father and I
knew that I'd come close to the never. Despite my mother's call
ten days before to say that if I wanted to see my father, I should

come, I went to Paris. A business trip for Charles, a shopping trip for me. I'd never been to Paris before.

Almost as soon as we'd gotten home, within hours, I jumped the Acela for Boston. Charles kissed me good-bye and reminded me that his offer still stood. The one that my parents had thoroughly rejected, that he—his company—would cover my father's medical expenses. This time, he added, "They should know that the offer on the house isn't going to go up; we've made the final offer." After that, it would be down the legal path of eminent domain. He gripped my elbow hard as he said this. "Make it happen, Rose."

I could hear Teddy in the kitchen, the occasional thunk of his wheelchair against the table or the counter. The teapot whistled. Even though I didn't want it, I knew better than to refuse a cup of Barry's Irish tea. It would have been tantamount to rejecting my heritage. At this point, drinking tea was about all we could do to distract ourselves from the purpose of our vigil without losing sight of it. The eternal jigsaw puzzle was gone, and only because it was playoff season was the television on, the ball game flickering behind me, the sound so low, it was pointless. Every now and then, someone would turn and notice the score and say it out loud: "Ten to five. Sixth inning. Sox up."

Four of my five brothers were in the house: Paulie, Bobbie, Frankie, and, of course, Teddy. At this point, midafternoon, my three sisters-in-law were absent, but they were expected as soon as the kids got out of school. As he had the best car, Patrick had been sent to fetch the priest. The place felt crowded to me. I wondered how it was that all of us had ever lived here, on top of one another like this, and not noticed. Add the wives and kids and I thought that the very air in here would be sucked out and we'd all suffocate. Plus a priest.

My phone dinged with a text alert—Charles wondering if I'd talked yet with my family about the offer. I thumbed a message back: *Not yet.* I thought that might be the end of it, but I got another text immediately: *Do it.*

Another woman would have shut her phone off. A stronger woman would have ignored him, secure in the fact that doing so wouldn't mean irreparable harm to her relationship with him. On my left hand glittered a two-karat diamond surrounded by another karat's worth of stones all in a platinum setting, a ring so new that I was still surprised to see it there. A Paris proposal, sophisticated and elegant and, in fact, quite unexpected. Even as he slipped the ring on my finger, I wondered how Cecily Foster would take the news that Charles's blue-collar fling was going to be her daughter-in-law. I was flattered that he had chosen me over his mother's hard opinion. That, in effect, he was defying *his* mother on *my* behalf. I felt selected, somehow. Valued.

I leaned across the gap between the chairs. "Mom, we need to talk."

I should have chosen a better time, when she and I were alone. But in that overcrowded house of vigil, there might never be such a moment. So I repeated Charles's proposal, emphasizing that it would go away and they might find themselves, living in some rental somewhere, if not homeless. We all accepted that housing values were skyrocketing in Charlestown; without fair money for their house, they might not have a hope of staying there. I spoke like a real estate agent, or a developer's fiancée. "This is a safety net, Mom. Besides, everyone else in the neighborhood has taken advantage of the offer."

She didn't look at me, her eyes fixed on the form of my father in front of us. "That's their business."

"It is your business. You can't hold out against progress. It's not like they're going to let this house sit in the middle of the project. They'll go down the path of eminent domain and you'll get less than what Charles—I mean, what Wright, Melrose & Foster is offering."

Frankie was standing in the archway between this room and the kitchen. Of all of them, he looked most like my father, and right then he wore a look that transformed him into a surrogate for the dying man. "Jesus, Rosie. This is not the time."

"It's got to be said. Do you want Mom to end up in public housing because she acted too late? And what about Teddy?"

"What about me?"

Teddy, a tea tray across his lap, rolled into the dining room. Of all of us, my father's prolonged dying had been the hardest on him. The others, myself included, had places to escape to, homes and families and other concerns to distract from the worry. Teddy had the constant presence of our mother and her worries about Dad to contend with. No relief of a day job or a kid with strep throat; or a trip to Paris. Of all of us, he looked the most like *her* and now he wore the same dark circles and paleness of bearing another person's illness on his face as she did on hers. She had shrunk; he had become bony. Fleetingly, I worried that he might actually have some infection, which he had been prone to as a kid, and that his pinched look was from actual illness and not from exhaustion. I'd always thought of him as being cared for by her, her perpetual child, but I could see that he had grown into the role of caregiver, and if she lost him, what would happen?

"With the offer, Teddy, you and Mom will have all of this medical debt gone and enough to buy a nice place with every thing you need to live well."

My mother reached over and picked up my left hand. She stared at the engagement ring, squinting as if the glare was painful. "You've been bought, Mary Rose Collins, pure and simple, and now you're spouting his evil."

"It's not evil. That's so insulting. What's evil about it?"

Paulie got into it. "You've drunk the Kool-Aid, Rosie. He's dazzling you with baubles and trips to Paris and you're doing his dirty work. I bet he dumps you if you don't talk us into this travesty."

"That's so wrong. He only wants the best for you." But the worm of doubt had been planted in my brain. Or maybe it would be more accurate to say that the doubts that were there already were given license. Of course Charles wouldn't dump me if my family snubbed his overly generous offer. He'd still marry me, but there would never be any mutual fondness between them. Of course he'd still want me.

"The best for us would be to leave us alone. Has the man no respect?" My mother stood up, busied herself straightening the sheet over my father. "And I'll take it as a kindness for you to stop talking about this in front of your father." We had been told several times, that the last faculty to go is hearing. "You're upsetting him. I don't want him to leave us worried."

I looked at the inert form of my father. Even in the few hours that I had been there, there had been a decline in the number of breaths, the timbre of his coughing. I had been so preoccupied with doing what Charles wanted that I'd lost sight of my reason for being there. "I'm sorry. We can talk about it later."

My mother left off smoothing the sheet. "There will be no later."

My text alert dinged. I saw the message: *???* Charles, of course. Impatient. His patience was fragile.

"We're not done with this conversation." My words were perceived as a threat, and a disloyalty so profound, so ill-timed that it was unforgivable. As a quiet unit, my brothers and mother faced me like a pack of Border collies, herding me away from my father's beside. No one shouted; no one spoke. My

purse was handed to me and I was pointed toward the front
door.

I fled, pushing past the priest coming up the steps to give
my father last rites.

After breaking the connection with Meghan, I grasp the skin
of my dog's neck and answer the incoming call. "Mom?" There
is no one there.

Shadow

He will defend her against any enemy, but it's not all that easy to decide who is the predator in this place. The big man, the one she calls *Tucker*, is clearly meant to be a friend. The other men who come to hammer and bang and rip and saw and stand around drinking coffee are less obviously friends, and he keeps a wary eye on them.

His new mistress has many layers. She's singing to herself, then standing still, lost in some fugue state. She has as many olfactory messages as he can interpret. Happy, relieved, sad, worried, frustrated. Mostly, lonely. He has a fix for that and he applies it every chance he gets.

Meghan

There is a new photograph on her credenza. Marley and Spike and Meghan and Shark, a foursome captured by a friendly stranger as they sat eating ice cream in Central Park. A fairly normal looking foursome if you don't consider the several disparities of height and color and scars and breeds. She and Marley are wearing sunglasses. Their smiles are a little broader than usual in the way that saying "Cheese" will do. What she likes about it, and why she got it printed in a five-by-seven size, is the way Marley's arm is casually draped over her shoulder. What it doesn't show is her hand on his thigh. Familiarity, fondness. But not yet intimacy. It's forecast but not confirmed.

She doesn't know if she can take the next step. Years ago, in a lifetime far away, Meghan fell in love in the usual way, a nice young man, worthy of being her first lover. He wasn't in the military and wasn't willing to be the spouse left at home, so they parted ways, although they kept in touch via social media until she cut off all communication with nonmilitary friends after her injury. It was too hard to be the object of un-comprehending pity. They couldn't get that she didn't regret being where she was; as much as she wished her injuries away, she'd never wish away having served.

It's why she feels close to Marley. Even though his injuries aren't physical, she doesn't have to explain to him why she gets angry or silent. He gets silent, too. And then his dog presses herself up against him and licks his nose. Meghan has such respect for him that she always turns away when he starts shaking, letting his dog do her job. Lately, though, she's put her hand on his even as she averts her eyes. He now squeezes her fingers in response. If she worries that she has no sensation where it matters, she knows that she has feelings.

Don Flint sticks his head into her doorway. "We're going in to make a decision on which case should be the next special project. You ready?"

"I am."

Shark gets to his feet as she pushes herself away from her desk. His tail wags, and he waits for some command to obey. Meghan accommodates him, "Lights, Shark." He taps the light switch down as they leave the office. She throws his ball down the hallway and he is rewarded for his work.

"So, what do you hear from Rosie?" Carol Baxter-Flint sets a glass down in front of Meghan, pours her a nice Riesling. "How's her project coming?"

Meghan's come home with the Flints for the weekend. She almost said no, but then she accepted the invitation. She's spent both days of every recent weekend with Marley and maybe it's a good idea to take a little break. "Rosie thinks it's going to cost a bit more than anticipated." She turns the stem of the wineglass, watches as the "legs" of the wine appear like ten-tacles. "You should know that."

"Is she asking for more money?"

Meghan shakes her head, "Oh, God no. She's just mentioned the contractor and his penchant for finding new problems."

Carol reaches across the counter, touches Meghan's hand. "Meghan, you haven't told her, have you?"

Meghan sips the wine, shakes her head. "No. There's no reason to." She sets the glass carefully on the granite. "It would change things if she knew."

"Between you?"

"Yes. Right now, we're pals, friends. Two damaged girls who have very little in common except that we both love this dog and that our lives have been upended by circumstance. If she knew that I had anything to do with her change of fortune, it would alter her opinion of me."

"I think you underestimate friendship."

Meghan lifts her glass, considers her answer. "It would make the friendship unequal. She might view herself as beholden, and I can't have that."

"There's a lot of strain in keeping secrets."

"Maybe so, Carol, but I'm keeping this one."

"I'll talk to the rest of the family. See if we can stretch the budget a little bit."

Shark

Shark loves being in this house, particularly the access to a couch long enough for him to stretch out on. He's nominally allowed to do so, because Meghan sits on one end of it at night when the three humans are staring at the wall. She strokes his ears. Tonight, he feels a tension in her that he hasn't before. Like the humans are not saying something important. He snuffs at her palm and the very tip of his tail taps the couch cushion as she closes a gentle fist over his snout.

Rosie

As Tucker predicted, sure enough, hidden behind the plasterboard walls that the crew has demolished today, is a shallow
fireplace with thick wood panel surrounds. Because it's not
that deep, Tucker says that it was meant more for warmth than
cooking. Even so, at some time in this house's history, this fireplace was the focal point of a parlor that probably saw very
little use. The good parlor. The one meant for receiving important guests, and for wakes. The good news is that the panels
are pristine, a little Liquid Gold and elbow grease, and the
smoke from many years of fires will give way to the soft glow
of polished oak. The mantel is gone, but that's not the end of
the world, Tucker says. He'll start looking online tonight, see
if one of the architectural-salvage places has a mantel that
would fit the era. What's even more exciting is the idea that
there's another fireplace in the second-best parlor, that maybe
the foursquare chimney has four flues and that this house will
be effectively restored to its proper number of fireplaces. Which

makes Tucker wonder if there are fireplaces upstairs, although, as he says, it's possible but not probable. Heating bedrooms wasn't a priority in the eighteenth century. That's what quilts were for. There are several trunks upstairs, all of them piled high with junk, but maybe there's a treasure trove of old quilts in one of them. It would be kind of nice to have an antique quilt restored and hung as a conversation piece.

Tucker is alone in the house, sucking up the day's debris with the work vac now.

"It's beautiful," I shout at him over the sound of the work vacuum.

Tucker hits the button to shut it off. "It is. I'm really relieved that they didn't screw around with the paneling when they mounted the plasterboard, and that it wasn't put up to hide some damage." Tucker runs a hand down the smooth wood of the raised panel to the left of the fireplace. "Such workmanship." I can hear the reverence in his voice. "All done with hand tools."

Shadow is sniffing at the right-hand panel. His little ears are cocked and he's giving it a close examination. He raises a paw and starts to scratch.

"Hey, don't do that." Tucker reaches for the dog's collar, pulls him away from damaging the panel.

"Do you think there's something behind the wall?" I'm thinking animal, not treasure.

"Oh, wait." Tucker runs a hand down the right side of the panel. Sure enough, there's evidence that the panel is hinged. "Probably a space to dry firewood." He slips a flat-head screwdriver out of his back pocket, gently fits the blade in, pulls toward himself. A narrow door opens. The centuries-old scent of dry wood drifts out.

The dog immediately pokes his head into the space, woofs.

"Shadow, what the heck has gotten into you?" I make the dog back up out of the way. It's like he wants first dibs at whatever treasures lie within.

"He probably smells old mouse droppings."

"Yuck."

"Desiccated old mouse poop—dogs love it." Tucker pulls his LED flashlight out of his other back pocket and shines it into the space. A few sticks of kindling, an empty, lidless preserve jar, and a broken candle are all that he can find. "Take a look." He hands me the flashlight so that I can get a good look at the tall, narrow space, perfect for playing hide-and-seek. Tucker starts tossing pieces of the old wallboard into the big blue barrels he's brought in.

Shadow keeps pushing his head into the narrow space; the sound of his deep olfactory exploration is almost explosive. I think about the dogs that Meghan talked about, the explosive-detection dogs, whose noses keep soldiers safe.

Following the direction of the big dog's nose, I aim the flashlight into the cupboard and see that, high up on the left-hand side, there is a narrow shelf. At first I don't see anything, but then I realize that there is an object on the shelf. I tilt the flashlight slightly and the object becomes a narrow book on its side. I reach for it. "Hey, Tucker, look at this." The dog's nose follows my hand with the book in it. The book isn't so much a book as a chunk of pages evidently torn out of a larger volume. "The pages are sewn together, repaired from their extraction from the original volume. I read the faint pencil writing on the top page. "Susannah Day, her book."

Together we go into the kitchen, where the light is better this time of day. The paper feels thick and fragile at the same time, dusty to the touch, and the pages are brown-edged, like sugar cookies left just a little too long in the oven.

I gently open it to the first page.

1st March 1832. Mr. Day at home. Set my loom with last
year's flax. Called out to attend Mrs. Tarr in Lanes
Cove. Safe delivered of daughter, her third.

4th March. Mr. Day at sea. Two yards good cloth made.
Attended Mr. Lyons for sore throat. Gave him a gargle.

"It's a diary, or journal. Susannah Day must have been a
nurse. Wonder where the rest of it is." The backmost page is
torn in half.

Tucker carefully wipes his hands on his jeans. "Can I see?"

I hand him the pages. "I wonder why it was stuck in the
wood box. Imagine that someone put that in there and it's been
there, out of sight, for decades. Forgotten."

"More than a century, if you look at the dates."

I take the book back. As gently as Tucker had, I turn another couple of pages. The writing is so thready, and, in the
inadequate kitchen light, not terribly readable.

5th March. Spun six skeins. Mrs. Pierce called. Brought
apples. ⸺

7th March. . . . brought to bed with dropsy. Will dose
with . . .

Some of the words are illegible.

"Do you know of her, this Susannah Day?" I ask.

There were Days in the area, even in Dogtown, but I have
no idea who she might be." He shrugs. "You know that I'm not
that old, right?"

"I just think of you as the local historian, you know so
much about the area."

"Thirteen generations." Some folks are satisfied with being second- or third-generation residents here on Cape Ann, and are equally as proud of their Azorean or Italian or Finnish heritage, but Tucker takes a particular satisfaction in the antiquity of his heritage—of being descended from one of the first European settlers. "It's what the ex makes such fun of, my, in her words, 'self-awarded medallion of merit based exclusively on being stuck in the same place.' But to me, it's important that my kids are fourteenth-generation Bellinghams." He pauses. "I'm glad I won't be the last."

"And your ex-wife, does she come from such old stock?"

"No. Her folks came here because her dad was hired as the hospital administrator."

I set the old pages down on the kitchen table. The dog rests his head on the table, nose inches away from the diary. He's sniffing so hard that tiny flakes of paper are breaking off the delicate edges. Tucker slides the book closer to the center of the small table and then I put it back.

"I do get attachment to place." I run a hand down the dog's back, then move to the sink, where I fill the kettle. "My family was pretty rooted to their neighborhood, even though they were only"—I emphasize the *only* kind of teasingly—"in this country for two generations. They were also in Bunker Hill for two generations."

"Where are they now?"

"My father passed a few years ago. My brothers are all over the state—Worcester, Stoughton, New Bedford; even one out in Stockbridge, trying to find his agricultural roots."

He notices that I don't mention my mother. "Your mom?"

And I burst into tears.

Tucker sets a cup of tea in front of me. I'd apologized and blushed red and then wept again. Tucker has clearly enough experience of women to recognize a crying jag that just needs to happen.

He found a box of tissues in the bathroom and quietly placed it at my elbow. The dog, for his part, keeps his big head on my lap, and in between wiping my eyes and apologizing to Tucker, I've fondled the dog's ears in the same way I used to fondle the threadbare ears of my comfort bunny when I was a little girl.

If he's got somewhere else to be, Tucker doesn't say so; he just sits and waits out the storm. Finally, it subsides with a couple of deep breaths, a self-conscious laugh, and a gathering up of the plenitude of tissues decorating the edge of the table. I excuse myself to go into the bathroom, where the gush of water makes me think of Bob the Plumber and whether or not he'll really show up tomorrow. My wits gathered and my hair combed, I go back into the kitchen.

I touch the journal with a forefinger. The dog whines. "Thank you."

Tucker takes his cup to the side of the sink. "I'll finish cleaning up that mess in there tomorrow."

"Bob the Plumber is supposed to be here tomorrow."

"You've learned to say 'supposed to be.' Good for you."

Although I can still feel the skim of moisture in my eyes, it's more a little glint of mischief when I say, "That's not all I've learned. I've become a pest. Six messages, all sweet, and then a stern one. That's when he called me back."

I follow Tucker out to his truck, the dog behind us. I've grabbed a leash from a peg, but I don't clip it to the dog's collar. It's getting dark a little earlier now. This coming weekend is Labor Day weekend.

Tucker's hand is on the door latch. In the dusk, he looks faded. "The thing is," he says, "my ex is moving the kids away. She's getting remarried to a guy in Weston."

"Why doesn't he move here? Surely the views are better."

Tucker laughs, but his face reveals the pain. "I worry that

they won't be *from* here anymore. That'll they think of themselves as kids from Weston."

I don't touch men, but I find myself reaching out, touching
his arm where he leans against the edge of the truck bed. "Nonsense. This place is in their blood. You're their blood."

"And blood is thicker than water?"

I look away, and the set of my jaw is suddenly tense. "Not
necessarily."

Shadow

The man, *Tucker*, has left them alone. The woman is sitting in the small rocking chair with her sweater drawn tightly across her chest and her feet tucked up under her. She isn't weeping anymore, and the dog takes that as a good thing. But the intensity and the unexpectedness of her outburst had startled him, and that he was powerless to halt it was his failure. He lays his head in her lap, and she halts the jagged motion of the rocking chair. There is a certain comfort in fulfilling one's purpose. This woman is much like all the others, not firmly tethered to happiness. It is pleasant to feel the warmth of her hand on his head, to discern that she takes comfort in doing so. The women he has guarded all came to depend on his presence for far more than simple protection. This one is no different. He knows that what he has to guard her from isn't outside danger, but her own thoughts.

Rosie

I am widowed. Benjamin lost at sea. I must apply to his sons. I do not think that they will have me.

Called out to attend Mrs. Lynch's lying-in. On the day that my husband is reported dead, a new life enters the world, and I am reminded to lift mine eyes to the hills, from whence shall my help come.

Mr. Baxter has already informed me that he expects me to vacate the house by month's end and is self-pleased to have given me as long as that to find new accommodations. Certainly he expects Ben's sons in Marshfield to have the keeping of me. I have heard nothing from them. A childless widow is without protection. Even one such as I, with her own way of making a living, is not to remain under her own roof alone. Unless she is one of those war widows in Dogtown.

They warned me against tending the citizens of Dogtown when I first arrived here in Gloucester twenty

*or so years ago, a new, albeit aged, bride. Dogtown is a
dangerous place. The residents will cheat you. Don't expect payment; each is a charity case. I tend them anyway. Old women, mostly. In Dogtown there are no babes
to bring into the world, just poor souls to see out of it.*

I have set aside all the other books that I have stacked up
on the kitchen table—otherwise known as my command post.
This journal is fascinating. Whoever Susannah Day was, she
reveals herself in the tiniest and most mundane of entries, and
then she drops a bomb—for example, that her husband has
died at sea. And then goes on to mention some household
accomplishment. It's taken me a few days to decipher her hand-
writing, which is at once old-fashioned and very idiosyncratic.
It isn't copperplate script, and blots and places where she's
scratched out words give the whole thing a feeling of her per-
sonality. I imagine her to be a lovely woman, if weary. I can so
picture her here in this house, maybe even using the rocking
chair that I've commandeered from the upstairs storage area.
Now that Tucker has revealed the parlor fireplace, I see her
rocking gently, staring at the fire, mourning her lost husband,
annoyed with her unfeeling stepsons. What this journal has
done for me is to imbue this old place, despite all its flaws, with
a feeling of family. Tucker has told me about "old Mrs. Baxter,"
whom he remembers from childhood, but it isn't the house's
most recent tenant who keeps me company in my imagination;
it is nineteenth-century Susannah Day. Maybe it's because
all of the twentieth-century "improvements" have been ripped
out of the house, but it is just easier to see it through the eyes of
its more distant residents. Even the attached barn means something to me now, and finding a rusted milk can forgotten in a
corner of it immediately conjures Susannah and her cow.
  Speaking of modern improvements, Bob the Plumber and

his crew have gutted the bathroom ell. I've tucked my little composting toilet in a discrete corner in the barn. I'm left with the kitchen sink as my only water source. I feel like I'm regressing into a past life. What's next? Carrying buckets from a stream? Bob the Plumber promises to be quick about it, but he's held up by the fact that we need to order fixtures. Nothing can be reused; nothing meets modern code. At some point in the house's life, the original claw-foot bathtub was replaced by a drop-in one, and that has a giant crack down the center. And the toilet is, well, let's just say it's off to Home Depot today. Oh, and that all of the pipes under the house have to be replaced. When Bob came back up from the crawl space, he looked like he'd been on an archaeological dig. "Swear those gotta be the original pipes from when they brought in indoor plumbing." Which suggests that I'm drinking water from lead pipes.

Bob had a guy with him, nameless and completely silent. They were here for two solid days and I never heard a word out of him. I wondered if he might be deaf, but I saw him with a phone to his ear; plus, Bob talks to him. As I usually do when there are men here, I made myself scarce once I knew that they didn't need anything from me. I didn't want to get in the way and I'm still not entirely comfortable around strangers. Maybe I was concerned about Silent Plumber because he reminded me of one or two of the prison guards. They were silent, too, until they weren't. Fortunately, I have Shadow, so I fear no evil.

I haven't told anyone—anyone being Meghan—about my embarrassing crying jag in front of Tucker. It was just having his innocent and natural question come so close to that call from my mother, when the line went dead, that set me off. I can't believe she'd dial and then hang up, and as hers isn't a cell phone, but an old-fashioned landline, it is crazy hurtful to think she'd do it deliberately, that it wasn't a butt dial. Maybe

she thought she could speak to me but then she lost her nerve.
I still offend her.

I fled from my parents' house knowing full well that I would
never see my father alive again. What I never imagined was
that I wouldn't ever again see the rest of my family after his
funeral. I pushed past the priest and my brother and got myself back to South Station in time for the next Acela to Penn
Station. I didn't call Charles. I didn't text. I sat in my seat, face
to the window and the ever-changing scene from urban to sub-
urban to urban, and tried not to think about my epic failure as
a daughter and as a fiancée. I had pleased no one. The one
thought that I had that comforted me was the idea that I would
swing by the dog sitter and pick up my puppy, Tilley. In the
two months since I brought her home, the poor thing had spent
more time with the dog sitter than with me. Every step forward
I had taken in her training had gone backward from my repeated absences, Paris, Long Island, Boston.

I had believed that a fait accompli was a great idea. Charles
had said no dog every time I brought the subject up. I had
pleaded, cajoled, bargained, and still he was firm in his con-
victions, which I thought of as simply the reluctance of someone who had never had a pet and didn't know how wonderful
it could be. In my naïve stubbornness, I had convinced myself
that all I had to do was bring the dog home and he would fall
in love with her. Who could resist the appeal of a tiny ball of
white fluff, big brown eyes full of charm? I'd put a deposit down
on the puppy even before she was born and was almost sick
with nervousness on the day I picked her up. I was gambling
on seeing a side of Charles that I wasn't sure even existed—
his softer side.

"What the fuck is that?" Charles dropped his expensive leather backpack to the floor.

"Our puppy. Matilda. Tilley."

"Not ours. Take it back."

"I can't." I should have said "I won't."

"Get rid of it. I said, no dogs."

"I need her, Charles. I need the company." This wasn't the way this conversation was supposed to go. He was supposed to melt. I lifted the puppy up, offering her to him. "Just touch her."

"I will not." He snatched his backpack up off the floor, and for one horrible moment I thought that he meant to swing at me. He reached into a side pocket, extracted his phone, which I hadn't heard ringing, the high hard whine of anxiety already in my ears. He left the room. I sucked in a lungful of air.

I had defied him; there was a crack in the mold into which he had poured me, that of grateful, obedient, presentable girlfriend.

Charles would have nothing to do with her, and made me keep her out of his sight, so I had to rely on a dog sitter. I'd been lucky, and found a good one, who also sat for the neighbor who had turned me on to Tilley's breeder. So now, on the train back to New York, my arms longed to hold that little white bundle of wriggle, to feel her soft pink tongue against my cheek. I needed comfort, and I was pretty sure I wasn't going to get any at home. Charles was certain to be angry at my failure to con vince my family of his well-meaning offer. What I had come to figure out was that he had a lot riding on this particular venture. The new position in New York had been predicated on his success with such a major real estate project in Boston. I didn't think he'd be sent, like a failing pitcher, back to the farm team, but Charles had made promises. As I rode that train back to New York, all I could think about was how my failure with my family meant his failure with his firm.

"Charles? Are you home?" I pushed open the apartment door, flung my overnight bag into the room, and set the puppy down on the hardwood floor. Her little legs scrambled as she scurried around the place, sniffing corners, reclaiming her stuffed mouse. I moved quickly and got her onto the training pad before her excitement caused a problem.

"Rose. You're home early. Are things better?" Charles came out of the room he used as his home office, or, as I referred to it, his "man cave." Untouched since his grandfather's time, it was done up in the style of an earlier age, the way I imagined an Edwardian-era man of the house might have kept his private space. Books on shelves, worn leather club chairs that had, indeed, belonged to his father and his father before him, as had the apartment. Buffed with the generations of male Foster backsides, they were in the center of the room, facing the tall French doors that led to a Juliet balcony and thence over a thick slice of Central Park. A glass-topped table sat between them, Charles's late-afternoon drink in its cut-glass tumbler sitting on it beside his tablet.

"No." I had no words for the story I needed to tell him. In the hours since I'd left my parents' house, it was possible that my father had passed; and I had obsessively held my phone in my hand for the entire journey.

"Don't make me ask the question, Rose." He could have meant had my father died, but I knew that what he really wanted to know was whether they would finally accept his offer.

So I gave him an answer that was true in both ways. "Not yet."

He didn't say anything. I wanted to read a little compas-

sion in his eyes, but I think that what I saw was disappointment. "I wasn't expecting you, so I made plans to have dinner
with a couple of the guys from work. Will you be all right here
on your own?"

"I will."

"I'll get you a drink." Kindness itself.

I sat in the right-hand leather club chair, slipped off my
shoes, and took in a deep breath of books and leather and whiskey. Charles handed me a tumbler with a quarter of an inch of
twelve-year-old scotch, not the good stuff, which was far more
aged and trotted out only for special—male—guests. I really
don't like hard liquor. But the bite of it and the fumes on the
back of my tongue had the effect of finally relaxing the tension I'd held on to for hours. It didn't make anything better,
but it soothed. I thought that perhaps I'd have another taste
after Charles left. I'd sit here in the coming gloom of night with
my puppy on my lap and let the whiskey work its mellowing
magic. Wouldn't everything look better if I were a little drunk?

"Are they at least thinking about it, the offer?"

"My father is past thinking. My mother is quite preoccupied."

"What about your brothers? Does any one of them speak
for your parents?"

"No." I could have added "any more than you speak for
your mother," but I didn't. I was too tired to be witty, too
whiskey-mellow to want to provoke a fight I had no energy for.
"Where's Tilley?" I just wanted her on my lap.

"Didn't you crate her?"

"Not yet. We only just got home." I meant that she needed
a little free time. I never crated her when Charles was out.

"I have to get changed." Charles swallowed the last of his
drink, dropped a kiss on my forehead, and left me to my own
ruminations. I picked up the carafe and added a touch more

whiskey to my tumbler. I forgot about the puppy's whereabouts as I studied my phone, hoping that maybe I'd missed a call or text from one of my family. I'd texted each one of my brothers to see what was going on but hadn't gotten a response from anyone. It was as if a door had been shut, a prison gate, and I was on the other side. I thought that I had been locked out, but what I had been was locked in, locked into a fate of my own making.

"Just look what this fucking dog has done!"

Charles stood in the doorway, one shoe in his left hand, the puppy in his right hand. The puppy looked pleased. The shoe, one of a pair of beyond-expensive bespoke Italian loafers, was shredded. He flung them both at me. The shoe bounced off my shoulder, but the puppy landed in my lap.

"Get rid of her, or I swear to God I will."

Late that same night, I got a phone call telling me that my father had passed. It was Brenda Brathwaite, not my own family calling. "They asked me to call, Rosie. I'm so sorry." I couldn't tell if she meant she was sorry about my father's death or about my increasing estrangement from my family.

Two days later, we drove to Boston to attend my father's funeral, where I was iced out by my family, my mother stiff-arming me as she pushed past to greet some long-lost cousin.

One of the things I like about Home Depot is the fact that Shadow can come in with me. He obviously likes the massive place, with its acres of wood and plastic and metal and porcelain, and greets everyone like he's king of the hill. He seems to know that we're not in some gigantic outdoor space with a roof and puts on his best inside manners. For the most part, I haven't had to train him. Even off-leash, he knows to heel. When on-leash, he has great manners, never pulls or decides what route we're going to take. Shadow sits, stays, and downs like a champ. Even if I leave him outside the library, I don't worry about him wandering away. I say "Stay," and he does. I am a dog trainer. It's what I expect. I believe that he has an innate sense of propriety and obedience. I don't allow myself brain space to consider that someone might actually have trained him to perfection before I came into his life. He's mine. I haven't even had to deal with bad habits. He really doesn't have any, unless you count his insistence on resting his muzzle on the kitchen table. As I use that table for everything from work to reading the newspaper to eating, it's an understandable habit. I'm thinking about going beyond basic training skills and getting into something fun, like agility. There's plenty of room on the Homestead property to build a few jumps. It would just be for our pleasure; I'm not ready to join any groups or anything. Dealing with Tucker and the various workmen is social enough for me for right now.

I've consulted with Tucker and with Pete and we've come up with a budget for the fixtures in the bathroom. I'm beginning to catch on to the whole ethos of keeping as much of the house as original as possible, and I manage to find a pedestal sink and bathtub that at least blend with the age of the house, even if they aren't exactly retro. If I really went with authenticity, I'd have to be shopping for chamber pots and a tin tub. This being without a shower has gotten very old very quickly. I talked Pete Bannerman into having the Trust buy me a membership at the YMCA, which has helped. Plus, I like the machines. I can grind out the miles on the stationary bicycles or incline and come away clean and feeling like I'm finally getting my youthful vigor back. I have my earphones and listen to audiobooks or podcasts. It's like my desiccated brain is sucking up culture and information. Both my legs and my brain are getting toned. What exercise equipment there was at Mid-State was very limited and hogged by the jocks, who liked deadlifting and giving you the dead eye at the same time.

I make quick work of the fixture purchases, which Bob the Plumber or Tucker will pick up. Then I buy a dozen of those tall, thin sticks that people use to delineate their driveways for plowing. I think that they'll make a great weave course for Shadow's agility training.

"That's some dog you got there." The middle-aged woman behind the checkout counter fishes a dog biscuit out of a plastic jug. "Can he have one?"

Who am I to say no? Shadow politely takes the treat.

"What is he?"

Ah, the most popular question, asked by many, answered by few. Each time I seem to have a different idea. "I don't know. He's a rescue." Technically speaking, I rescued him, didn't I? "Maybe part wolfhound."

Shadow has his attention focused behind me, where an older man in a tracksuit stands with his hands full of plastic plumbing parts. His tail sweeps from side to side, almost like he knows the man. He's been mostly aloof with the men who come to the Homestead. Tucker is the only one he greets, and I think that's probably because Tucker is there more consistently. I thank the woman for the treat and gather my rods.

"He's a lurcher. That's what he is." The man speaks with a decidedly British accent. Not a plummy one, more Onslow than Hyacinth.

"A lurcher?" I've never heard of it, and it sounds kind of derogatory.

"Useful farm dogs, common in England. Poachers' dogs. Deerhound mixes, whippets. Fast, skinny dogs mixed with collies or terriers."

"Not a recognized breed, then?"

"Suppose not. Good hunters. All-around dogs. Don't see many over here."

"I suppose that he's just a coincidental blend of all the right parts to come up with what you call him. Lurcher. Okay, Shadow, we'll say you're one hundred percent lurcher from now on." I thank the man, wish him success with his DIY plumbing project, and head out, my lurcher at my heels.

Goody Mallory has passed this day; more accurately, at the dark moment before dawn, before even the birds announce themselves. She was one possessed of a dog, a great gray cur of no known breed. Not shepherd, not hunting dog. Some amalgam thereof, I would have to say.

What was interesting to me—and without my Ben to listen to my whimsy, I write it here—what I observed was the way the beast nestled himself beside Goody on her corn-husk mat, and, more important, the way her crabbed hand clutched at the dog's fur, taking final comfort from the feel of it. Her other senses flown, this last sense was engaged into the harsh coat of her familiar. She smiled and gave up her last breath. The dog, for his part, remained in her dead embrace, his eyes closed, as if—no, it is a blasphemous thought—but to my eyes, it appeared as though the dog was prayerful. I could not bring myself to interrupt, as if I took him as her chief mourner, which, I suppose, he is. He did stand after a bit. Then he sat over her body and broke my heart with a single ululation. Not quite a howl, but clearly a lament.

I woke from a restless sleep and lighted my candle to add one more thought to this page. Goody Mallory was a war widow, her husband lost in the last war, her livelihood gone, her fate to scratch out an existence partly on charity, partly on fortune-telling and chicanery, but she did not die alone. I am so very alone.

I read that entry and thought about how lucky I am to have Shadow in my life. I don't know what I'd do without him by my side.

Shadow

He likes this mobility, this going out and about and not being confined to just the area he can traverse on his own four feet. No one ever before has offered him a ride. It was unnerving first, but now all she has to say is *goforaride* and he's there. He knows that he is different from others of his kind, mostly in his size and hue, and certainly in his mission. When they walk the streets of the town, he keeps close to her side. He is well aware that she appreciates his presence, especially when males approach. A creature less attuned to the language of movement wouldn't notice her subtle shrinking when men are near. He is alert to it, and keeps himself close whenever men are present, whether those working in the house or those on the street. It is his duty.

Rosie

I feel Shadow's wiry coat beneath my fingers; he rests his head in my lap as I read further in Susannah's daybook. It has evolved from a quotidian recording of accomplishments and accounting to what one might consider a proper journal, used to record thoughts and impressions, fears and hopes. When I was in the early days of my incarceration, the prison psychologist had suggested that I jot down my thoughts in a journal, telling me that it might help me figure out why I was there. Maybe even alleviate the depression. I tried for a while. It was something to do.

"Goody Mallory's dog has followed me home," Susannah wrote.

I get a little chill at those words. I put my hand on my dog's head.

I was called to attend Mrs. Dalton's lying-in. When I returned home, having not been offered the courtesy of a ride, I walked the quickest way, through Dogtown, past Goody's now-empty house. I did not see the dog, but I felt as though I was no longer alone. Seeing no one, I took it that my tiredness was playing tricks on me. Upon arrival at my own door, the cur made his presence known. I tried to chase him off, but he was obdurate. I shut my door on him, hoping that he'd haunt someone else.

Mrs. Dalton's lying-in did not go well. I am growing too old to endure the long wait for a babe to make its appearance. When her labor did not progress, Mr. Dalton sent for Dr. Bellingham. Bellingham will have my fee. I am sent home with only a meat pie as payment. Perhaps that is what attracted that beast to my door, the scent of it. I cannot pay my rent in stale meat pies. I still have no settled accommodation. I do not wish to become another widow's lodger.

I shared the meat pie with the dog. He was very grateful. I will allow him to stay.

I love that she's kept him. I read between the lines and see that her dog, like mine, is filling an empty space.

I bump into Tucker again, this time at a place in Rockport, Roy Moore's Fish Shack. It is jammed, and I am waiting for a table when Tucker walks in. Seems like the right thing to do, so I ask him to join me. Funny, it's quicker to get a table for two than a single. Fish cakes and beans. Yum. We share an appetizer of fried calamari. Naturally, the talk centers on our common project, the Homestead, which leads me to bring up the journal we found. "I've been curious about something. Susannah mentioned a Dr. Bellingham. Any relation?"

"Our most illustrious ancestor. Elijah Bellingham. His father was a fisherman, but he inculcated a love of learning in his one and only son. Sent him to Harvard. Couldn't keep him off the Cape, though, and he came back to practice medicine."

"That's cool. And you're a direct descendant?"

"He was my fifth-great-grandfather. My dad was named Elijah. Fortunately, they went with a different tradition when they named me and my brother."

"What was that?"

Tucker points to himself. "Mother's maiden name, also a longtime Cape Ann family, and my brother was given her favorite boy's name, Steve. Stephen."

"Are you the elder?"

"I was."

I note the past tense. I wonder if I should ask about it, but our desserts have arrived.

Tucker licks the last of his blueberry pie off the end of his fork. "So, what did this Susannah woman say about my ancestor?"

Dr. Bellingham's name had come up in several entries, always in relation to a patient she either was attending or thought she would attend. Apparently, from what I can gather from the arcane style of her writing, women, mothers-to-be especially, were turning more and more often to the doctor instead of to Susannah, who had been a local midwife. I tell Tucker this, then add, "I think she was in trouble. She asked this Baxter guy if she could stay on, but he wouldn't barter anymore. He wanted cash and she was cash-poor."

"Because this Doc Bellingham was horning in on her territory?"

"Maybe." I push the remainder of my pie aside. "Do you think she ended up in Dogtown?"

"I suppose so. Although I think that Dogtown was pretty much defunct by her time."

I start rooting around in my purse for my wallet. "You know, she had a dog." I pull out my share of the tab. "She wrote that he followed her home as she walked through Dogtown. She said that he belonged to one of the old ladies—somebody she called Goody Mallory."

"You seem to have gotten really caught up in Susannah's story."

"Do I?" I laugh. "Well, I have gotten kind of attached to her. Imagine, here's somebody who lived in the same house I'm in. Who had a good life, and then trouble, and, well, then a dog."

"Like you?"

For the first time I wonder what, if anything, Tucker has been told about me.

"Yeah. Like me."

I thought that the only thing that might mitigate Charles's anger at me and Tilley was to act on his wishes about my parents' house, now just my mother's house. I would become complicit with Charles in persuading my grieving mother that she had no choice but to give up the house where she and my father had lived for forty years, where she'd raised her six children. Where she had lodged memories in every nook and cranny. Yes, I chose the wrong battle. I knew that I couldn't talk to her, so I approached it in another way. I went to Paulie.

On the face of it, what Wright, Melrose & Foster was doing wasn't altogether unreasonable. One last house on a block destined for improvement was an obstacle but not terminal to the project.

"Paulie, they'll get it in the end. You have to help her see that she can get so much more if she just asks for it." I was in Charles's study, a place that felt more appropriate to this conversation. Tilley played at my feet. I wanted to make this call when he wasn't around, to talk without being cued as to what to say. To do this in my own way. I picked the puppy up and put her in my lap, fully aware that what I was doing was bargaining for her continued presence in my life.

"It'll kill Teddy."

"Paul. Teddy is a grown man. He won't die from leaving his childhood home. He might even benefit from it." I believed my own rhetoric. I felt like I'd stumbled upon a truth, and I pressed the issue. "Isn't it just possible that Mom has, well, *enabled* Teddy?"

"Enabled, how? By caring for him? How do you enable someone so physically *disabled*? You make it sound like he had a choice."

The cell phone in my hand began to feel hot to the touch. Tilley was still on my lap and I realized that I was clutching her neck skin in my fingers to the point where she wriggled to get free of me. "That's not what I mean. I mean that if he had a place to live where he could be better accommodated, he might develop some independence. She might get a break." I put the puppy down.

"Rosie. Isn't it enough that she's lost her husband? Does she have to lose her home, too?" Paulie sounded tired, weary of my badgering. "I swear to you, if your boyfriend's company pulls this eviction off, we will never forgive you."

"It's eminent domain, not eviction. They will pay fair-market once. If she negotiates with them now, she'll get a better deal."

"Listen very carefully, Mary Rose Collins. You will never be forgiven. You will have chosen the wrong side. Are you willing to chance that? Do we mean so much less to you than

Pretty Boy? You like the money; you like the high living. We represent your upbringing, Rosie. And that's why you're on his side, pretending to be something you're not."

I was shocked, to say the least, that my eldest brother, the most adult of all of us, could resort to this kind of threat. "I'm just trying to get Mom the best option. I'm looking out for her, and you all have your heads in the sand. You can't prevent it. Don't you get that?"

"Perhaps not. But that still puts you on the wrong side. That still makes you a traitor."

"That's harsh, Paulie. For just wanting to do the right thing."

"That ship sailed, Rosie. The right thing would have been to keep your mouth shut when you were here, when Mom was so vulnerable and we had more important things on our minds." I heard my brother suck in a deep breath and I thought that he was trying to calm himself down. "Your moral compass is screwed up, Rosie. Frankie was right, you've swallowed whatever high-priced Kool-Aid that bastard is feeding you. You ran away that day. Don't you get it? You should have come back. You should have shut your trap and sat there like a good daughter and been with us when Dad passed. Not run back to your cushy life in New York, showing up at the funeral all decked out in fancy high-priced clothes, never letting go of that man's arm for fear you'd show some freakin' emotion."

I was beyond words. So much hate spewing from my eldest brother's mouth.

"Do you all feel this way?"

"Yes."

I flung my phone across the room. It landed softly on the Aubusson carpet.

I left the study to throw myself down across our bed in a fit of weeping. Charles wasn't home, and for all the fantasy about greeting him with good news from my conversation with Paulie, I was about to fail in his eyes once again. Maybe it was grief, maybe frustration, maybe fear, but the tears flowed until I was gasping for breath and crumpled up on the floor. How could my eldest brother, almost a surrogate father to me when I was growing up, talk to me like he had? Where was the love, the kindness, the care that had informed our relationship from the time I was born? By the time it was over, tears had gone from hurt to anger. And then I realized that Charles was home and Tilley was, once again, loose in the house.

I scrambled to my feet. Charles had come in and gone straight to his study, which usually suggested that he wasn't in a good mood. I heard the tink of decanter against glass and I knew right then that my failure to convince Paulie to help would be incendiary. I washed my face, reapplied foundation and blush, and ran a hand through my hair. Shoulders straight, chin up. I was going to pretend that I hadn't made that call. I went into the kitchen, made it look like I'd thought about dinner.

"Rose." Charles's voice was flat.

"In the kitchen." Mine was cheery. "Do you want to order out or shall I pull out steaks?"

"Get in here." Beyond flat now, his voice was steely, and I almost knew without seeing that Tilley's latest infraction was the worst yet.

The puppy had, in the short time I'd been wailing into my hands, taken her tiny needle-sharp teeth to the corner of Charles's revered grandfather's leather club chair, chewing off a great strip of leather, peeling it away from the frame, leaving a gaping hole and masticated ancient leather. "Oh my God, Charles, I am so sorry."

Fury had drained all the color out of his face. His mouth was fixed, a fleck of spittle in one corner. His eyes narrowed and his fists clenched. His body was rigid and I was helpless to soften it. I was afraid for myself in that moment. I had no idea of the kind of violence he was capable of.

"Where is Tilley?"

Shadow, who has been waiting patiently for me in the car, nudges me from the backseat. These memories rise from time to time, like a recurring illness. I don't go so much into submission against these thoughts, as I have learned to push them away when they come. But, sometimes, I haven't the strength. I fit the key into the ignition.

Meghan

Shark trots along at Meghan's side as she motors herself down the block. They've got some quick errands to do before work—a stop at the bodega for a sandwich, another at the dry cleaner's to pick up her dress. She hopes that they've been able to get the grease stain out of the jersey fabric. It's her go-to dress for those increasingly frequent casual occasions when Marley swings by and says "Let's go to the" and then fills in the blank with anything from getting ice cream to barbecue (hence the stain) to a stroll, or "roll," as he calls it, to a gallery opening or an afternoon in Central Park. The one place he hasn't taken her is to his own home, a fifth-floor walk-up.

Since her last weekend with the Flints, Meghan has stopped worrying about spending too much time with Marley. Although Carol had dropped the topic of telling Rosie the truth, she hadn't been able to keep herself from suggesting that dating was a nice step forward and Meghan should stop saying that what she was doing with Marley wasn't dating.

They still haven't taken the next step. In the solitude of her own bedroom, the ambient light filtering between the drawn curtains, she thinks about it and tells herself that there is nothing to be afraid of, this final frontier of recovery. And in the broad light of day, she studies her scars and pinches the insensate skin of her legs and wonders that she can even think about enjoying a physical intimacy. She sees a vague image of herself, an unmoving lumplike thing. Marley deserves better.

Errands completed—success with the stain removal—Shark points the way toward the office. It's such a nice early-fall day that Meghan decides to forgo the bus and go the ten blocks under her own power. Shark absorbs all the looks from strangers; he is the attractive distraction from her unique occupation of the sidewalk. People see him and smile, and then see her, and if those smiles sometimes soften into dismay, or embarrassment, she's learned to smile back and nod in that way of New Yorkers, acknowledging without acknowledging. He also makes it clear who needs to give way when they hit those complicated spots in the route, places where construction and open grates and sandwich boards constrict the easy flow of foot traffic. He clears the way at the curb cuts, nosing foolish upright beings out of the way when they don't sense her behind them. They make almost as good time as if she'd taken a car; they've miraculously gotten all the walk lights in their favor. Her mother is still horrified at the idea of her handicapped daughter at large in this city. She has no idea how comfortable it has become.

"Come see, Mom. Come stay with me."

"Oh, I don't know. Your father . . ." Meghan wonders that her mother, who once lived all over the world, has settled so firmly into her little retirement home.

"Then come alone." She says that and can picture her mother's face, a mask of fear and horror at the idea of flying alone to a strange city. Before Evelyn can begin the litany of obstacles to what is actually a fairly common adventure, Meghan says, "I'll send a car to pick you up."

Evelyn parries the idea by saying, "You must have some time coming. Why don't you fly down?" Meghan takes a little satisfaction in the fact that her mother, who expresses such concern over her living in New York, credits her with the ability to get to Florida without trouble, a sort of diametrically opposed set of ideas.

"Not yet." She doesn't mean that she doesn't have time coming; she does. But tucked into the very back of her mind, Meghan holds a vague notion that she will use that time when she finally gives in and goes to Rosie. She hasn't allowed herself to articulate that notion, but it's there all the same.

Shark rises up on hind legs and punches the steel plate in the wall. The glass door slowly opens and Meghan and Shark go through. Don Flint is in the lobby. "Good morning, Don."

"Hey, kiddo." He pats Shark with the hand not holding his travel mug. "Who's a good boy?" Both Don and Meghan know that patting a service dog is considered bad manners, but Don is family and the rules don't apply.

Shark wags his tail and gives Don's hand a quick lick. Shark isn't one of those reserved dogs who tolerate adoration from outsiders. He pretty much sucks it up.

"You going up?" Don leads the way to the rank of elevators. A covey of young law clerks stand silently, studying their phones. Meghan smiles at Don's eye roll. "Carol's wondering when you might grace us with another weekend visit. It's been a while."

Marley and she have had plans for so many late-summer weekends that she knows she's been neglecting her only family. Before she can say anything, Don says, "Bring your friend. We'd love to meet him."

"I might just do that. But he's kind of shy."

"We deal with all kinds. We'll make him feel comfortable, I promise." The elevator doors gasp open. Without so much as raising their eyes from their screens, the covey of clerks, noting Don's rank and Meghan's chair, stand back to let them on.

As they enter their floor, Don puts his hand on Meghan's shoulder. "After you get settled in, come on down to my office."

Shark leads the way to Don's office, tail active behind, hopeful that there might be a treat in there for him. It's not without precedent. Don has been known to keep a stash of Wheat Thins in his desk drawer, and Shark snaps them up as if they were meant for canine consumption. Meghan chooses to ignore this training sin. As long as Don doesn't make Wheat Thins a prize for a trick, she figures the dog knows the subtle difference between a treat and a reward.

She parks her chair in front of Don's big desk, where he keeps an empty place just for her visits. He comes around from behind his desk and sits in the guest chair beside her. For some reason, Meghan starts to worry that he's got bad news for her. "How's your friend Rosie doing?"

"Rosie? I think she's doing just fine." Meghan gently scratches the knob at the top of Shark's skull. "She has this dog now, and I think that's been good for her."

"You should go see her," Don says, and Meghan hears his office voice, the one he gives orders with so gently that most folks don't realize they've been told, not asked.

"Don, it's not that easy."

"I think it is. We'll take you, if you want."

"I can get there; it's not that. Marley would be happy to get me there. It's just that . . ."

"Look, I know that you think telling her that you had something to do with her release is going to change the dynamic between you. But, don't you see, *not* telling her has already done that."

He's right, of course. She has begun ducking Rosie, and the absence of her friend's voice and counsel is painful. But she just can't keep pretending.

Shark lifts his head to encourage Meghan to keep scratching his occipital bump. Then he drops his head in her lap, sighs.

"Besides, we'd love a report on the house. A firsthand report. Something we can put in the family newsletter."

Meghan doesn't mistake an order for a wish. She gives Don a smile. "Let's give it another month; then there will be more to report on. Maybe in another month, I'll be able to get inside it and really see what's going on. At least on the first floor."

"Okay. Another month it is."

Meghan knows that there is something unreasonable about this stubborn refusal to solve Rosie's central mystery. It isn't like she didn't have moments during their conversations when she wasn't tempted, but there is no way, to her thinking, that admitting that she put Rosie up for acceptance by the Advocacy for Justice isn't going to be a bit awkward. It isn't just that; it's also having orchestrated the further benefit to Rosie of having the Homestead project given to her, a place where she can regroup, build up her reserves, and then make her own decision about what's next in her life. That's all that Meghan wished for Rosie. But, having done it, she worries now that Rosie will resent the intrusion. The presumption. Meghan knows firsthand that it can be galling to be grateful.

Those first weeks after she had been returned stateside to undergo the surgeries that weren't life-saving, but those intended to make her life endurable, any act of kindness was enough to make her feel vulnerable to a complete loss of self. An orderly would pick up the dropped magazine off the floor and silently hand it back to her, a thin smile on his lips; a nurse would pat her hand even as she changed out the IV. She was perceived as someone needing comfort, kindness, tenderness, and the feeling was as painful as the persistent ache in her spine, the exquisite pain as her skin sloughed. The numbness of skin not her own. As wounded as she was, she resented being reminded of it by these thoughtless acts of kindness.

Shark presses himself against her, his thick-skulled head in her lap. Meghan strokes his head, puts her cheek against his muzzle. "What would I do without you?" He hunn-hunns. His rudder tail swings. "I'm so glad I have you." Maybe Don is right; maybe it is time to get over this need to keep Rosie in the dark about her hand in the events that have changed Rosie's life. For someone who saw some pretty horrible sights in-country, Meghan finds herself squeamish at the thought of having a conversation that begins with "Oh, by the way, I'm the one who put your name in at the Advocacy for Justice. I'm the one who suggested that you go to Dogtown." The first thing Rosie will want to know is why. Why keep *that* secret? And that has no answer.

When Meghan gets to the dog park after work, Marley is already there. Spike is flopped down on the ground, exhausted from chasing the ball. Shark goes up and nudges her with his nose and her tail twitches in a halfhearted doggy hello. Marley gives her a similar greeting. "Hey."

"Hey yourself." She maneuvers her chair to the bench where he sits and sends Shark off to chase his ball. "You're here early."

"Been here pretty much all day." He looks ashy, and she can see a slight tremble in his hand. A bad day. Meghan and Marley have known each other long enough now that she recognizes the signs. Despite Spike's best efforts, Marley is in his dark place.

She knows better than to ask what has triggered the mood; she understands better than most that talking about it doesn't necessarily help. So Meghan takes the hand that trembles and holds it in her lap, which has no feeling, and they sit quietly as their dogs come back to sit with them, tennis balls left on the ground.

The sun is setting, so the light between buildings blooms into a gorgeous orange glow and then fades. And still they sit there, although Marley has put a long arm around her against the evening chill. The dogs wait, heads on the laps of their respective people. Other dog walkers have come and gone and now the place is theirs alone. It feels like they are in a cocoon of their own making. No, not a cocoon; that would suggest that they were somehow transforming, growing, and would be released into a glorious freedom. More a cave or a den. A place to hibernate, to lick wounds.

Suddenly, Shark jumps to his feet, shakes, and slams a heavy paw down on their conjoined hands. He woofs.

"I think its dinnertime." Meghan says.

"Past time."

"Come up. Stay with me."

Marley takes back the arm over her shoulders and the hand she's grasping. "Not if I can't stay in the way that I wish you wanted me to."

"I want you not to be alone."

"I want you to want something more than mollycoddling me, treating me like a . . ."

"How? How do I treat you?"

"Like a friend. Like you got my six." He pushes himself to his full height. "I want you to treat me like a lover, not a fellow fallen soldier."

"I can't give you what you want." Meghan grabs for his hand, but he pulls it back. Spike is on her feet, and pushes her way between them, a little confused, her training preparing her for defusing conflict, but this conflict is beyond her ken.

"It ain't the sex, Meghan. I hope you know that. I love you."

"I love you, too." Even to her own ears, it sounds tepid, devoid of the kind of feeling he deserves.

Marley snaps the leash on Spike's collar. "When you can let yourself get to the point where you can accept someone's true feelings, you'll have finally recovered. In the meantime, I'll find another dog park."

"Marley, no. Please. Come home with me."

He stands there in front of her, a tall, handsome black man, slightly balding. The trauma of war exposed by the tremor in his hand and the way the curly-coated dog presses herself against him. The disappointment of rejection, for that's what she has done, writ large on his face.

Shark

At home, Shark presses his stuffed bear into Meghan's lap, but she ignores the plea for a quick game. She is immobile, more than usual. He play bows and wags his tail, but it's like she doesn't see him. Finally, he flops down on the floor in front of her chair and sighs. Sometimes humans are confounding. A nap may help.

Rosie

Tucker Bellingham reminds me of a Russian circus bear. When he gets to his feet after examining some low-slung repair, it's like watching an ursine performer rise to his full height. "That joist is going to have to be sistered," he'll say, or something equally as arcane and mystical to my ears. Of all the men who come into this house to effect some repair or renovation or contemplation over a problem, Tucker is the only one Shadow seems to like. It's not that the dog is openly hostile to anyone, but Tucker is the only one he greets with a tail wag. Since the night of my epic breakdown, Tucker has taken on a somewhat paternal air with me. He hasn't gone so far as to try to put an arm around me—maybe he instinctively knows that I'd flinch—but he shows up with fresh vegetables he claims he was given too many of, or a heavier-weight sleeping bag that he says his boy never used. It is October, and I still have no heat except for the woodstove sticking out of the old kitchen hearth. Tucker gave me a tutorial on making fires. I think he considers me a city kid. Guess maybe he's right. My only experience of lighting fires was when our family would make its annual trek up to Maine, but even then, the campfire was my father's responsibility. And the fireplaces in our New York apartment were conveniently rigged for gas.

I wonder sometimes how much of my story Tucker knows. He seems to be an incurious man, but, that could simply be shyness. That makes two of us.

Today, I've been taking Shadow for a long, meandering walk that has fetched us up at a cemetery. As we stroll among the oldest headstones, I can't help but notice the names inscribed there are those that Susannah mentioned in her journal. Fitzwarren, Dalton, Pearson. It's like seeing a familiar face; or maybe like meeting a Facebook "friend" in person. You don't really know them, but you know that they like puppy videos. I am studying headstones in a graveyard of strangers, but these people lived, grew old, or died young and feel very familiar to me from simply having read their names and, in some cases, their ailments in Susannah's book. Shadow sniffs along the stones but is respectful.

Then comes a large plot of Bellinghams. Lots of them. The oldest stones are slate, and if they weren't in close proximity to the cenotaph towering over the plot, they would be anonymous, the fine writing washed off by centuries of acid rain. As Tucker says, there have been Bellinghams on Cape Ann since time immemorial. The stones evolve from slate to marble and then to granite, harvested in the nearby quarry, no doubt. As befits a prominent doctor, Susannah's nemesis turned sort of colleague, Elijah Bellingham, is closest to the cenotaph.

In the northeast corner of the plot lie Bellinghams who are not so long dead. *Elijah "Bud" Bellingham 1940–1988. His Wife, Helen Tucker 1943–1988. Their Son Stephen Andrew 1972–1988.* This has to be Tucker's family. What terrible thing had to have happened that all three were gone in the same year? For all my estrangement from my family, at least I know that they are alive.

"I've got a pot on. Want a cup?"

Tucker is sitting at my little kitchen table, making notations on a schematic. "Huh? Oh, yeah. That'd be nice. Black."

I carry over mugs for both of us. Shadow rests his chin on the table briefly, just making sure there is nothing on there he should be interested in. I shoo the big dog over to his memory-foam bed beside the crackling woodstove. Beside my elbow on the table sits Susannah Day's journal, encased now in a proper archival-quality box.

Tucker taps the box with a knuckle. "You should do something with this. It's local history."

"I will. I just want to finish reading it first." I set my cup down on the table. "Susannah lived in this house; I'm certain of it. She refers to it as the 'Baxter house,' and she and her husband rented it from . . ."

"Jacob Baxter."

"So, you know this?"

"I've devoted a lot of my life to local history."

"She had a dog, you know. Like this one."

"So you mentioned the other night." He scratches Shadow behind the ears as he asks, "What do you mean by 'like this one'?"

"What I mean to say is, she had a dog that came into her life just as she was widowed. To help in her loneliness." Even to my ears, it sounds kind of woo-woo. I hadn't meant to become all mystical, but I finish the thought. "Because Shadow also just showed up. When I needed him."

Shadow, as if alert to being the subject of my words, shakes himself thoroughly. Just like the dogs that I had the privilege of training, he presses himself against me to stanch the sudden onset of hard thoughts.

"And he helps with your loneliness?" Tucker betrays a sensitivity that one would not expect in a big, somewhat rough-edged man.

"He does. It's okay, Tucker. I'm fine. I don't mean to get melodramatic."

I think of the three headstones I encountered in the cemetery and find that I am burning with curiosity, but I don't know how to ask the question without seeming callous. I could have looked it up online, checked into deaths in 1988 in Gloucester, but that seemed intrusive, or just nosy. It's really something I want him to tell me, not something I want to know without his being aware that I do. "Um, I took a walk in that cemetery off of Washington Street the other day."

"Did you? It's a very nice spot to walk."

Shadow's chin drifts from my knee to Tucker's.

"I noticed the Bellingham plot."

Tucker finishes the last of his coffee, makes to rise, then stops. "When I was a junior in college my family died in a house fire. My parents and my younger brother."

"Oh my God, Tucker, that's so sad."

"That remains an unfillable void in my life."

"I can imagine."

"My point isn't to make you feel sorry for me. My point is that you still have a family, Rosie. You still have one."

The women in the correctional facility came from as many different family configurations as is possible to imagine, but so many of them came from matriarchal families, where a single mom had raised her kids and then raised theirs. Aunties and grammas. Sisters raising nieces and nephews. Only the few, mostly those who had committed so-called white-collar crimes, seemed to have come from intact families. Or had them. I was different in that I had come from a patriarchal paradigm. My father was benevolent overlord of the family Collins. And during the days of my father's illness, Paulie had easily stepped into the role of family head. Which brings me to the conclusion that Paulie, not my mother, is instigating this nuclear winter toward me. He always had her ear. She depended upon him as the eldest to be the enforcer as the rest of us grew up and grew louder and grew unmanageable. And when Teddy was shot, that role was made manifest by the way she deferred to Paulie, granting him almost parental rights over the rest of us. Dominion over me.

So, in some ways, it made sense that Paulie, and the others, despised Charles. Charles also wanted dominion over me. Had dominion.

"Tucker, I don't think the rift between me and my family is ever going away. I made a couple of bad decisions. . . ." Even I grimace at my weak vocabulary. "And I made my own bed." My mother's parting words to me, by the way.

"I can't believe that."

"Did Pete Bannerman tell you anything about me?" I have lost a certain reticence. My deepest desire to keep my most recent history a mystery to everyone is more fragile than I thought.

"No. Only that you needed a place to . . ."

"Hide?"

"Heal."

"And he didn't tell you from what?"

"I think it's something to do with your family."

"I suppose that's one way of looking at it." I don't know why I'm suddenly feeling this urge to blurt out my shame, but there is something about Tucker's big bearlike presence that changes the air in my lungs from pent-up to expressive. But I don't say anything. There are no words to start that conversation.

Tucker cradles his coffee mug in his big hands, takes it over to the sink, where the breakfast dishes are still stacked. Oh for a dishwasher. I stay where I am and watch as his shoulders, already downward-cast, grow more slumped. I think about what he's just told me. His whole family, gone. Not simply living apart from him but gone. Then, like the bear he is, he pulls himself up to his full height and turns to smile at me. To carry the bear analogy further, I notice that, surrounded by the shaggy goatee, his teeth, very white, also have pronounced canines. "I think that you need to reach out to your family." Even before I can protest, he holds up one finger. "And don't take no for an answer."

Shadow sits beside me as I read deeper into Susannah's diary. "Attended Son Haslet for sore throat. Six others have same ailment. Dr. Bellingham mentioned to me that he has seen more than eleven himself. We concur on treatment and admit concern over possible epidemic. Although he is my chief rival for work, the doctor welcomes my assistance and we have come to an accommodation of sorts." My heart breaks when I read in Susannah's book how she has no one to ask for help. Her family seems to have forgotten her, and her husband's children are unwelcoming in the extreme. She soldiers on, though. Selling off what she must, bartering for services. Finding herself called less and less often to the bedsides of the women who are ill or pregnant. Her pal Dr. Bellingham seems oblivious that he's taking Susannah's livelihood from her. I have walked those woods so often that I can picture exactly how isolated she must have been. How desperate.

It's been interesting, how her perfunctory recording of daily life in 1832 has evolved into something far more confessional: from an account book, essentially a ledger, to an account in and of itself of a difficult time in her life. My hand finds the soft ears of my dog and I read how she accepted this orphaned dog into her house. I look up from the pages and think that, now that Tucker and his crew have revealed the older house beneath the mid-century "improvements," I am looking at what Susannah looked at. The beams above my head in the low-ceilinged kitchen would have had hanging bunches of herbs but are bare now. Blank out the woodstove, and the kitchen hearth must look much as it did in her time. There is a mantel above it, and I bet she kept her salt there, maybe used it as a convenient place to rest a cup of tea as she stirred the pot hanging on its pot hook. Susannah has become my invisible companion in the house where she once lived, her voice becoming more and more distinct as I read her words. I sometimes find myself wondering if she would like the improvements slowly accreting to the Homestead.

It's grown chilly in here, and I open the door of the woodstove and slip in another split. I poke it a bit and am pleased with myself for stirring the fire into life. Tucker has shown me how to bank it for the night, but it's far too early to go to bed, although my rhythms have become more like those of the mid-nineteenth century, up at dawn and exhausted by dusk. Exhausted by inertia more than action. Shadow monitors my movements. His tail thumps a little, then gains momentum as I approach the refrigerator. I know he hopes for a treat, but I am not convinced he needs one for simply being in the same room with me. I grab a slice of cheese and go back to reading. "Tomorrow I must leave this house. I have sold my goods except for what is absolutely necessary in my new home. Two pots. My good tick and three coverlets. I have done what I can to make Goody Mallory's hovel clean and comfortable."

She's moving to Dogtown.

I've got the radio on, and the voices of WGBH natter on about important things, although I haven't been paying attention; I just like having the sound of other voices in the room. It's loud enough that I don't realize my phone is ringing until it quits. I look at the log. I've missed a call from Pete. It's unusual for him to call so late, after business hours. I call him back and he answers on the first ring.

"How're you doing, Rosie?"

"Fine. Things are coming along." I'm wondering if he's lost track of time and is choosing eight o'clock on a Wednesday night to check in on things here at the Homestead. "They've got all the old wallboard removed and the chimney guy is going to be here—"

"Mrs. Foster's legal team contacted me."

I sit down.

"She's thinking about filing a civil suit. Wrongful death."

"What can she get from me? I have nothing."

"That's the point I made to them."

I am speechless. What can I say? That I'm surprised? The truth is, I've almost been expecting this, or something like it. She was never going to go gently into that good night.

There is a beat or two before he continues. "I tried to suggest that raking all this up again, especially in a courtroom, would serve no purpose and that only we, the lawyers, would benefit."

Now I wait a beat or two. "Should I assume that the Advocacy wouldn't be taking this on, if she carries out her threat?"

"Correct. They got your sentence vacated; that's what they do. You'd have to fight your own civil battle."

"Pete, what could she possibly gain from this?"

"In a word? Revenge."

"It wasn't enough that I served time? I'll never get those years back. My life was derailed."

I hear him take a deep breath, let it out slowly. "So was hers."

We sat in that courtroom, she and I, never looking at each other. She sat in a seat behind the prosecutor's desk, and I, of course, was seated at the public defender's table. Out of the corner of my eye, all I could see was black, a dark presence in my periphery. I wore that orange jumpsuit of the as-yet-to-be convicted prisoner. I couldn't make bail. I'd watched too much *Law & Order* and thus expected my time on the stand. I had my words all rehearsed. *I never saw him. He stepped behind the car. I didn't see him. I was crying. Upset, blinded by tears.* But I was never called to the stand to defend myself. My PD had wrangled what she thought was a good deal. A plea bargain. The judge hammered down the deal like an auctioneer, and Mrs. Foster rose to her feet. That was the first time I'd looked her straight in the face, and what was looking back at me was raw emotion. Raw fury. She thought that I had gotten the better deal. That my punishment for the death of her heinous son was somehow a benefit to me. That I'd gotten away with it.

"She wasn't happy that I got twenty years. She wanted life without chance of parole. She'd have been thrilled with a death sentence." Shadow presses his head into my belly, then sniffs my face. "I can imagine that finding out I'm exonerated must be killing her."

"Rosie, your verdict was vacated. You weren't properly defended, and the investigation of the accident was flawed. So, *exonerated* is a bit of a misnomer."

Sometimes I forget that I actually did run Charles over with his own car.

Shadow

He does his best to get Rosie to pay attention to him, to get her to sit up straight and tell him that he's a good boy, say his name, *Shadow.* He loves the sound of that soft sibilant expression. He pokes at her with his nose and then his forepaw. He stands over his bowl and pretends that he hasn't already eaten. He leans his chin on the table and breathes in the scent of the old book, the one that reminds him of another time, another woman. Another solitary. Finally through the hand on his back, he feels the agitation begin to ebb.

Meghan

Meghan pulls her mind out of its funk, and Shark is instantly on his feet. Evening comes on so quickly and it's already dark in her apartment. She gives the command and Shark flips the light switch in the kitchen, turns in clear expectation of his reward. With a vehemence she doesn't usually exert, Meghan throws his stuffie across the room. It smacks the opposite wall, and the one decorative touch she's added to the blank walls of her apartment, a generic but pretty landscape, tilts. She doesn't know how she'll get Shark to push it back into line. Marley was the one who hung it there, showing an unexpectedly good eye.

How could he? How dare he? Doesn't he know how she feels? Doesn't he care? He's not the only one with needs. So what if his are invisible to the naked eye? Doesn't he know how incredibly hard it is to be visibly damaged? He can hide his flaws. She cannot.

Meghan forces herself to open a can of soup for dinner. Shark gets his kibble, which he inhales, and then acts like he hasn't just had dinner. With every action, opening the can, dumping the soup, adding the water, putting the pot on the burner, she chews on Marley's words. And then on Don's not so subtle directive that she confess to Rosie. And then on Rosie and how she actually hasn't heard from her in a while, which makes her feel all the more guilty. It's so hard to keep a balance between being a friend and being a liar. Well, not a liar per se, but whatever withholding the truth constitutes as a flaw.

Hey, are you mad at me? A text from Rosie. Meghan had been slow to answer texts; worse, she has merely replied with emojis.

No, why? Texting has the benefit of disguising a guilt-strained voice.

I dunno. We haven't spoken in a while. What Rosie doesn't say is that Meghan's phone goes right to voice mail when she calls. Does she know that Meghan has hit DECLINE CALL?

I've been so busy, sorry.

No response.

I'll call tomorrow. A smiley face. A broken promise.

Rosie hasn't communicated since that bitter little exchange. What do they all want from her?

Shark shoves his stuffie into her lap. *Play with me. Play with me.* "At least you're easy to figure out." They play a little gentle tug-of-war while the soup heats. The dog pins his red-rimmed eyes on her; his lips scroll back, revealing his white teeth. He looks like he's working hard at trying to get the toy out of her hand, but she knows that he judges her strength precisely and never exceeds her ability to hold on. She's seen him with Spike, and how his shoulder muscles bulge against the torque; how he's literally dragged the other dog into the dirt. Spike. Oh dear, Shark is going to miss Spike.

The soup is tasteless and Meghan leaves the bowl on the table, wheels herself out of the kitchen. She's left her phone on the table. "Shark, phone." The dog has no trouble finding the instrument and mouths it as he might have retrieved a duck for a different kind of owner. He delicately hoists his forepaws to the table surface and, with a desirous glance at the cool soup sitting within reach, he grabs the phone and drops to the floor. He puts the phone in her lap. "Good boy." His reward, another round of tug-of-war. He is so easy to keep happy. Why can't other people be as satisfied with simple rewards? Why did they need to have more from her? Love. Friendship. Trust.

"Okay, settle." Shark, dismissed, finds his bed and performs his circle ritual. Meghan slides from chair to recliner, picks up the remote, then puts it down. Picks up her phone, then puts it down. Picks it up. Texts *Got time to talk?* and in a moment her phone rings.

"Rosie? I've totally screwed up."

To her credit, Rosie Collins doesn't do a "This is what you should do." Instead, she listens, and Meghan can picture her nodding. When Meghan finally comes to the end of her diatribe-cum-vent-cum-self-serving whinge, Rosie takes a breath and then says, "Better?"

"Yeah, a little. I don't usually do this, you know, talk."

"I was aware. It's really hard for you because I think you spent a lot of years keeping stuff inside. Letting things out only on a need-to-know basis."

Meghan is the one nodding now, and she reaches for a tissue. "You get it, don't you? You get me."

"Don't we sound like a rom-com chick flick?"

"No. Well, maybe." Meghan laughs.

"Meghan, there's nothing wrong with feeling things."

"I wish I could, I mean, where it counts."

"You think that Marley doesn't understand that? Do you

really think that he doesn't care that it might not work for you? Or do you think he is convinced that he can *make* it work for you?"

Meghan hesitates. "I don't know. Maybe both. No. He's too much of a gentleman; he's not selfish."

There is a pause. Meghan can hear Rosie's dog in the background; a door opens and shuts.

"Meghan. Don't you like him enough to want to give it a try?"

"I'm afraid."

"I know. Life is scary. I'm scared all the time."

"I've been in the killing fields and I was never this afraid."

"That's because you were trained; you were doing what you had been prepared for. No one is prepared for love."

"What about you?"

"I'm not in love with anyone. Except Shadow, of course."

"They really are enough, aren't they? Who needs men?"

"Well, let's not get weird here."

Meghan laughs again. Rosie, whose life is so upended, can always make her laugh. "Do you think you'll ever do it again? Love, I mean."

"No."

"I think that you will. The right man, a kind, giving man, will show up someday and treat you the way you should be treated."

"I'm pretty happy right now. It's not perfect, but I am happy enough. I don't think I'm lacking anything. Maybe I'm even happier than the happiest day I had with Charles. With him, there was always this balancing act, this need to keep things steady."

"It's what you sacrificed your family for, always having to pour oil on his emotional waters."

"Yes."

"Still no contact?"

"No. Tucker is on my case now, so you don't have to be."

"I won't. So, nice segue. What's new in the house?"

As Rosie details the current goings-on in the house, Meghan tests herself. Is it possible for her to stop Rosie mid-description and blurt out, "I put your name in for the Advocacy. I suggested the Baxters give you a chance"? They sit there, the words, filling Meghan's mouth. But they will not come out. She just can't imagine that Rosie won't question her prolonged silence, consider it a hostile act. Maybe not hostile, but certainly inexplicable. Even Meghan knows that her keeping her own kind act a secret is inexplicable.

"Well, it sounds like things are going well."

"There is one thing."

"Oh?"

"Mrs. Foster, Charles's mother, is filing a civil suit."

"Shit."

"Exactly."

As soon as their call ends, Meghan hits the speed dial for Carol and Don.

Shark

Shark performs all of his tasks joyfully, and is rewarded with Meghan's approval and a round of the tug-of-war game. But he knows that her heart isn't in it, and very quickly the game is over. Today she and Spike's person spoke words that put both dogs on alert. There was a sharpness, a blade's width of anger in their voices, although they spoke softly, privately, in that place. Even Shark could smell the disarray in Marley. Respectfully, he let Spike do her job, just as he did his with Meghan. When they parted, it did not feel right. And now, curled into a ball at Meghan's feet, Shark concentrates his whole being on Meghan's soft sighs.

Rosie

In order to distract myself, I take Shadow to the beach. Otherwise, I would be chewing my nails over Cecily Foster's machinations and drinking too much coffee. Pete has promised to do what he can to stop it. But, I wonder, can he? Who am I kidding? I may be out and about and picking up random bits of shoreline detritus, but I am sick with worry. Almost as soon as I let my thoughts drift to the problem, Shadow is there, grabbing my unfocussed gaze into his brown eyes. *Woof.* It is an uncanny echo of something that Susannah writes: "The dog holds his eyes upon my own as a sheepdog will eye his charges into motion."

"Are you a sheepdog?" I ask.

Shadow shakes himself from nose to tail and then play bows to me, clearly hoping I'll throw this nice piece of driftwood for him.

My only consolation against Cecily's threat is that she doesn't know where I am. Pete has promised me that all contact will be through him. I picture him, this little man dressed in suits made for boys, standing up to the legal giants of the Foster family's firm. His fists are balled, his chin is lifted, and he has a pugnacious look on his beardless face as the giants aim their lances at his chest and run him through.

I shake my head, much like my dog shaking his to clear his thoughts. No. Pete may be small, but he's big enough to give the Foster's firm a run for their money. This I have to believe, and then wonder how I'll be able to afford him; there has been no suggestion of any more pro bono for Rosie Collins.

The day has grown chilly, the October sun giving way to an early dusk. Daylight saving time will be ending before long. I'll be going to bed at six-thirty if I'm not careful. Shadow and I head back to the house.

There is a car in the yard. I don't recognize it, a black Lexus with Connecticut plates. No one is in the car. Shadow is on the alert, his smallish ears at attention, his whippy tail straight out, slightly elevated. He lowers his head but doesn't growl, withholding judgment.

The grass muffles our footsteps as we go around the side of the house to the back. There is a woman standing there, her back to us as we approach. She's staring up at the house, her fingers just touching her mouth, as if hiding a reaction.

I let the fear-inspired tension go, giving space for curiosity. "Hello?"

I've startled her. She's a slender woman, dressed in good jeans and a pair of really nice boots. "I'm Carol. Carol Baxter."

I notice that my dog's tail is beating a happy rhythm. "Rosie Collins." And, because it seems appropriate, I add, "Project manager."

"And who's this?" She's clearly not put off by a big wire-haired mutt who is giving her the canine once-over. She bends at the waist and gives him a good thumping pat.

"Shadow."

She straightens. "After my grandfather passed, my grandmother got a dog kind of like this one."

Baxter. I get it. "You must be from the Homestead Trust."

"I am. I'm sorry for dropping in like this, I should have given you warning. But would it be possible for me to take a look inside?"

The flippant side of me might have said: "It's your house," but I have nothing to be flippant about. I smile and gesture toward the back door. "Right this way." And, like any tenant, I hope that I've left the place in good order. Which, of course, it isn't. A lot of it is under plastic while the second-best parlor's ceiling is being pulled down. "It is a bit of a hard hat area, so watch your step." I lead her inside; all the while my mind is spinning. Have I just met my mysterious benefactor? Do I have the guts to ask?

Happily enough, my kitchen, the only room under my control, is tidy and the woodstove is still warm to the touch, lending it a cozy feel. Carol stands in the middle of the room, then steps to the table, touches the surface, and points to the standing lamp that I've placed beside it. "My grandmother's lamp. I remember it so well. I knocked it over once and let my brother take the blame."

"Mrs. Baxter?"

"Gramma to me, but yes. Henrietta Fitzwarren Baxter. The last of the family to live here. Can you imagine?" Carol runs a hand over the mantel, where I've set a collection of crocks that Tucker pulled from the crawl space beneath the kitchen ell. I've placed them in descending order of size. "Can you imagine all these Baxters in an unbroken chain being born, growing up, and dying here?"

"It's an old house."

She moves toward the first parlor. "Can I go in here?"

"Just watch your step. The workmen aren't very good at picking up their toys."

We spend half an hour touring the house and inspecting the work. I assume that's why she's here, to see if the bills are in line with the progress being made. I've tried hard to keep it that way.

We venture up the stairs to the two bedrooms, both of which are packed with the detritus of generations of Baxters. I don't know why, but I apologize. "I'll be doing an inventory in the next few weeks."

"I used to sleep up here. Spent the nights worrying about mice crawling into bed with me. I was such a city kid."

"They're persistent, but we've pretty much conquered them."

Back downstairs, I offer Carol a cup of something, tea or coffee. I want to ask her one important question: *Why me?* Why did the Homestead Trust take on an ex-con as a project manager? More to the point, what's the connection between the Homestead Trust—the Baxter family—and the Advocacy for Justice? Is there any?

Carol accepts a cup of tea and we go outside with our cups to sit on the stone bench. A nor'easter has been predicted for three days, and I can feel the moisture in the breeze as we go out. The sky above us is a grim gray color, streaked by the contrails of jets leaving Logan. The brand-new cedar shingles on the back of the house seem to glow against the scrim of gray.

Carol sighs. "Wow. A lot has changed, what with the restoration. But, you know, there's still enough of what I remember to get me all sentimental. Like this bench. And that gnarly apple tree. I used to climb it."

"Did you live here? With your grandmother?"

"We came every summer for two weeks up until I was in college. Then, well, once Gramma passed, no one had the time or interest in the house. But no one wanted to sell it, either. So it just sat, and we, the children and grandchildren, put together a family trust to keep the house in good-enough repair and pay the taxes and insurance all these years. We're all finally at a point where we can get the old place in good repair and begin to use it again."

My tea is cold. I set my cup on the edge of the granite bench. Carol is looking out over the yard, which I have brought back under control with the help of a good mow crew. The breeze ripples through the trimmed rye grass. The stone with *Boy* painted on it is prominent, and Carol touches it with a toe. "Gramma's dog."

Shadow, who's been lying quietly, shifts and rests his chin on my feet. I ask my question. "Why me?"

She doesn't do the "What do you mean?" dodge. "You were recommended to us."

"By whom?"

I have spent enough time with evasive women, women who keep their secrets closely held. There is a shuttering of the face. Eyes dart to the side; hands touch lips. *No, I didn't take your shampoo; no, I didn't touch your stuff.*

Carol drops her eyes to the ground, digs a little rut into the soft dirt with the toe of her boot. "A friend."

"Yours, or mine?"

Carol takes a deep breath and my heart beats in dread and joy. She touches my knee. "You ever take a pinkie pledge?"

"Uh, yeah, when I was a kid."

"Well, I took one and I have to keep it."

Shadow leaps to his feet as I burst into laughter.

Shadow

The nor'easter that had been making him restless has finally abated, the wind gusting only now and then and the rain pushed well offshore. He doesn't think these things, but senses them, feeling the breeze lift his fur, breathing in a less salt-tangy air. After a night of heavy rain and blasting wind, the dawn is sparkling with welcome sunlight, dappling the grass beneath their feet. Crows in the boughs above carry out a call and response, three caws made, three caws answered. He barks at them, sitting so boldly in the apple tree. They ignore him and he accepts their disrespect.

A truck pulls into the yard. Shadow eyes it, sniffs. Wood, with a hint of machine oil. Another truck wheels in. The day is beginning. Shadow trots into the attached barn and lets himself in through the dogtrot. It's his newest trick, letting himself in and out now that someone—he doesn't know who—has made a swinging flap in the lower half of the door.

His person is also aware of the arrivals. She's dressed and

sipping from a mug "Got to do a supply run," she says. He doesn't understand the words, but he absolutely understands the meaning. He swings his tail. A car ride!

She talks to him the whole ride and he comprehends only that she's in a mood of some anxiety. Of some turmoil. As she often does when her mood thickens, she grasps the skin of his neck and holds on. He keeps his big head thrust between the two front seats so that she can touch him when she needs to. They made the usual rounds, three places he must wait in the car and two places where he is welcomed. Finally, they stop at the big building where she'll let him out to sleep under a grand tree. She pulls out a canvas bag filled with those objects she stares at for hours at a time. They all smell like other people's touches.

Meghan

Meghan hears Carol come into the room. "Out here." She's sitting on the patio outside of their hotel room. The view of Good Harbor beach is stretched out in front of her, down the hill from their delightfully old-fashioned and dog-friendly hotel. Not that she has to worry about dog-friendly, not with a legitimate service dog by her side, albeit a snoring one right now.

Carol drops into the plastic chair beside Meghan. Hands her a glass of wine.

"So? How was it?"

"It sure doesn't look like Gramma's house anymore."

"That's not what I meant, and you know it."

"I like her. I like her dog. He reminds me of the dog Gramma had, the one she had after Grampa died. Boy."

For a brief moment, Meghan is hopeful that Carol is not going to bring up the subject, but then she says, "Meghan, I'd really like to drive you over there."

Meghan sets her glass down on the little plastic table between them, zips up her jacket. The setting sun has left them in the shadow of the building. In the distance, the water has turned dark, and lights are coming on in the homes at the foot of the hill. In another half hour, the sea and the shore will blend into a blank space, punctuated only by the occasional bright spot of some vessel's running lights. "Did you tell her?"

"No."

"Thank you."

"But I did invite her to dinner tomorrow night. She suggested a place called the Azorean."

Meghan faces Carol. "Well, have a good time."

"Don't be a child, Meghan. This has gone on long enough. She has another battle to fight. She should have all the information she needs, even if that means your having to give up this false modesty of yours."

"False modesty? You think that's what this is? Humblebrag?"

"Maybe. Self-indulgent anyway. She helped you gain your independence; you've helped her gain hers. Let her know. What's the worst that can happen? She feels grateful? It's not like that Chinese proverb that if you save a man's life, he owns you."

"I think it's that you own him."

"Whatever. The point is, isn't it time you let Rosie decide for herself whether or not being done a kindness is a relationship killer? If feeling gratitude is a bad thing."

Meghan is silent for a time, long enough that Shark gets to his feet and shoves his nose under her hand.

Meghan had arrived on that last training day with Rosie, the sense of hope and joy so enormous that she could barely speak; her gratitude over what Rosie had done for her had effectively rendered Meghan speechless. She had applied herself to the work so hard, as she had always undertaken training. Meghan had never entered into anything without applying her entire being into accomplishing the task, whether it was on the obstacle course or the rifle range. And so it was with learning how to work with Shark. And that ethic had given their official work together a seriousness, a life-and-death aura. But at the end of their sessions, in those few minutes when the work was done, Shark was resting from his labors, and they had time to just be two young women waiting for Meghan's escort to arrive, they'd entered into a friendship that had seemed so likely, so normal. On that last training day, even as Rosie got a little weepy, Meghan found herself too burdened by respect and an overwhelming sense of indebtedness for what Rosie had done for her to utter a word of thanks. Rosie was an inmate, and they were not allowed to hug good-bye. Sitting here on the cement patio of the hotel, looking out over a darkening sea, Meghan knew that if they had been allowed to touch, she would have wept along with Rosie, and said thank you.

"I put her name in to the Advocacy because I knew that she was deserving of a second chance. I didn't do it to be thanked."

"Again: Why don't you let her decide that?"

At the Azorean, Meghan and Carol are already seated, Carol in the booth, Meghan's chair positioned at the end, when Rosie arrives. They see her before she sees them. They watch as Rosie speaks to the hostess and then falls in behind her, being led to where they wait. Where Meghan waits, feeling as if this is a surprise party and they are the only guests. Which, looking at the expression on Rosie's face, it is.

"Oh my God! Meghan!"

That hug that they weren't allowed to have when Rosie was an inmate finally happens.

Rosie

It takes me a moment to wrap my head around the fact that Carol Baxter is the cousin Carol whom Meghan lived with while training with Shark, which means that she, Meghan, is part of the extended Baxter family of the Homestead Trust. It takes another moment to figure out that there are no coincidences in life. The look on Meghan's face compels me to ask my question again, only this time as a statement. "You're my benefactor."

Meghan's expression could be best described as caught between shame and relief.

"And the Advocacy? That, too? Getting my release, that was you?"

"Not exactly. Don Flint, Carol's husband, listened to your story. He's on the Advocacy board."

"Okay, that's one degree of separation. But who suggested me?"

"Well, I did."

I look around, "Where's Sharkey?"

"Home. I mean at the hotel. I've got Carol, so I gave him the night off."

I won't lie; I'm disappointed. I sit down, sliding into the booth opposite Meghan's cousin. To say that my brain is spinning is an understatement, and I am relieved when the server comes by with our drinks. I open the extensive menu but can't read a word. I close it. "Why didn't you tell me?"

It's as if Carol has vanished. I don't see her; I see only Meghan's pained look.

"Why didn't you tell me?" I say it more gently this time, but she doesn't answer.

Carol edges her way out of the booth. "I'm going to the ladies'." Belying that, she takes her drink with her.

"No, don't. Stay." Meghan reaches out with her damaged right hand,

In a perfect imitation of Mike Meyers's "Coffee Talk" character, Carol says, "Rosie did something good for you; you did something good for Rosie. Discuss." And she walks off.

Simultaneously, Meghan and I take long swallows of our drinks. I reach for her hand, take it. She lets me. "So, thank you. For all of it. However it happened. I'm beholden to you."

She flares up, those silvery patches on her face intensify as the living skin around them darkens. "That's exactly what I didn't want. For you to feel beholden."

"Not *beholden* in the sense of peasant to king. Grateful. Is that a better word?"

"I just wanted you to have the same freedom as you gave me."

We dive into another gulp of drink. Flag the server. Another round. Meghan has a Moscow Mule; I've got a Lemon Drop.

"Okay, so maybe we've achieved quid pro quo?"

Meghan nods.

I think about it for a moment. "Except for one thing."

"What's that?"

"Why didn't you, or the Advocacy, or Carol, for that matter, tell me that I had a chance, or even that the Advocacy was working for me? Why keep me in the dark?"

"No one—okay, *I* didn't want to give you false hope."

"Wasn't I entitled to know?" There is something unintentionally demeaning in this. If she were a man, I would call it being patronizing. "I am not a child."

"Of course not. But I didn't want to get your hopes up and then fail in the mission."

"Did you think I couldn't handle the disappointment?"

Meghan has no answer for this.

Fail in the mission.

"I wasn't a mission, Meghan. You could never have failed me."

Carol slides back into her seat. She picks up her menu and we follow suit.

Shadow

He likes it when she's happy. Tonight, she told him to stay and watch the property and then left in her car. His heart broke at the sound of the car driving off, but then he remembered his orders and got to work patrolling, sniffing, woofing, marking, and otherwise recalling how it felt to be a watchdog. She would return to a place made secure by his attention to detail. He waited patiently, a sentry by the driveway. Occasionally, he would sit up and yawn, listen for the sound of her particular car coming along the lane.

The night was overcast, but the moon broke through the clouds. He worried then that she would be the one who didn't return. And then she came back. And, for the first time, he knew her to be completely happy. She bore the scent of someone else, someone she had touched long enough that skin cells had sloughed off and attached themselves to Rosie's hands. She grinned and snapped her fingers. "Let's go for a walk."

Rosie

I am equally worn to a nub and energized, or, more accurately, buzzed with the combination of good food, possibly one too many Lemon Drops, and the relief of finally having the central mystery of my recent life solved. I've been so in my own head that I probably could have figured this out on my own if I'd just picked a little at the clues that were there.

Shadow is ecstatic to see me. His tail thrashes and he play bows and hunh-hunns. "Let's go."

It's not that late, but the darkness around this lonesome stretch of back road is thick, punctuated only here and there with determined stars. Not a house light in sight. After last night's storm, it's rained on and off today, and everything is wet. The moon is waning, but bright enough as it breaks through the cloud cover to suddenly shed some light on the path that leads to Dogtown. I've acquired a pair of Hunter Wellington boots, so the wet grass is not a problem. Skunks are, but we are lucky as Shadow and I head to the old Dogtown road. Dogtown in the daytime is unsettling enough, but at night it takes on a whole different eeriness. One's imagination runs to werewolves and witches. The uniquely weird sound of a screech owl sends shivers down my spine.

Shadow does what he does best, sticks close by and leads me to his favorite spot, the cellar hole I have come to decide must be where Susannah ended up. Maybe it's my propensity for romantic notion, my idea that this dog has somehow identified the presence of a woman gone more than 150 years, but I don't think that's such a far-fetched idea. I don't think it unreasonable to believe that my dog might be a descendant of the unnamed dog that attended Susannah. Any more than it is unreasonable that my fairy godmother has turned out to be Meghan. Or that someday my phone will ring and it will be one of my brothers or even my mother calling to see how I am.

Yesterday, I talked to Shelley Brown about the journal. As casually as I could, I mentioned how it was found, and what I've read in it. As I feared, she immediately suggested that the book needed to go somewhere appropriate, either the library's history collection or the historical society's. I argued back, right off the top of my head, that the book really belonged to the Baxter descendants. She agreed, and asked if I'd be willing to address the issue with them.

Them, as I thought at the time, was Carol. Now I know that it's Carol and Meghan and Don Flint and a host of others. And, truthfully, I completely forgot about the journal, about Susannah, caught up as I was in the excitement of the moment at the Azorean.

Shadow has led me to the cellar hole, and, as is his habit, he circled and settled in the depression. I shut off my phone's flashlight and sit on a remnant cellar stone, fondle his ears. I can't give up that daybook until I find out what happened, if Susannah ever made it to safer shores than this desolate and lonely place. If she and her dog were rescued.

A glance at my phone and I see that there is a voice message from Pete, no doubt about Cecily Foster. But I'm going to let that one wait till tomorrow. Right now, I want to enjoy this quiet outing with my dog and let the pleasure of knowing that someone has loved me enough to do what Meghan set in motion on my behalf. I have not felt beloved in a very long time.

Meghan

It's really hard to be quiet when you have to get yourself from bed to chair to bathroom, then back to chair, but Meghan tries as hard as she can not to wake Carol up. Or maybe Carol just has the good grace to pretend that she's still asleep. Shark, on the other hand, is right there, ready to work. He closes the bathroom door, then opens it when she's ready. The room itself is retrofitted to ADA accommodation specs, but pretty awkward for all that, and the dog is almost more in the way than not. They head outside so that the dog can use his own bathroom facilities, a neat fenced-in area of grass.

The breakfast room in this hillside hotel is beneath the main building, and Meghan takes the path slowly as it curls around and down. Despite the chill in the air, she sits on the terrace with her coffee and homemade blueberry coffee cake— still warm from the oven—after all, she feels the cold only in her upper body. The rest is just blank space. She realizes that she's forgotten to put anything on her feet, but it's not so cold that she should worry about frostbite. It's that lack of sensation that has become central to her identity, to her idea of self.

Carol doesn't know that she and Marley have broken up. Meghan expects that, like Rosie, Carol will lobby on behalf of Marley's integrity. She just can't handle any more drama. Last night was painful, and ultimately releasing, and she wishes that she didn't have the "Marley situation," as she thinks of it, and could just be glad that the weight of keeping secrets from a good friend is gone. Today, Carol is taking her to the house so that she can see for herself the work being done and spend a little more time with Rosie before they have to head back. It occurs to Meghan that Rosie might say something about Marley, about their breakup, in front of Carol, in which case she can look forward to being counseled on the long drive home. Shark senses her distress and pokes his nose into the hand that has drifted away from the coffee cake. He licks it and she laughs. "Hoping for crumbs?"

He wags his tail.

"I should have renamed you Goofy."

He wags it harder, engaging his whole back end. Happy to have prompted his person out of her funk.

"That looks good." Carol drops her handbag onto a seat.

"It is. Still warm from the oven."

Even with the overcast sky, the view of the choppy sea stretched out before them in shades of pewter is stunning. The sand of Good Harbor beach gleams white against the gray, and even from where they sit, they can see that the parking lot is virtually empty. Carol comes back with her breakfast, slides a paper napkin onto her lap. "Not a beach day."

"No, but it's a good day to take a ride around. Rosie said we should visit Rockport."

"She's settled in, I think."

"She has."

Carol takes a bite of coffee cake, makes yummy noises, sips her coffee. "How are you?"

She doesn't look directly at Meghan, giving her the opportunity to be as casual about the answer as she wants to be.

It makes Meghan think back to adolescence, to when her mother would prove to be right about something and want Meghan to admit it. It was killer, giving her mother her due, letting her know that she'd been right. Right about a poorly chosen friend. Right about getting caught skipping school. Right about the appropriateness of getting a service dog. Has she told her mother yet that she was so very right about that?

Has this been the right thing, coming clean with Rosie? Is the burden lifted? "I'm good. About telling Rosie, yes. I'm okay."

"And your friendship? How do you feel about that?"

Meghan didn't answer right away, feeling around for the answer. "There's a nick in it, but it's whole otherwise. It'll heal."

"Good." Carol takes a last bite of the cake. "Now, tell me about this business with Marley."

"How did you find out?" Had Rosie said something? Meghan thinks that now she and Rosie are truly quid pro quo if she did spill the beans to Carol.

"You haven't mentioned his name all weekend."

"That doesn't mean anything."

"Not in and of itself, but you just confirmed what I was worried about. How did I find out? You just told me."

"It's no big deal. People break up all the time."

"I know. I'm just sorry. We liked him. We think he's a nice man." Carol wipes her lips with her napkin. "Isn't he?"

"Yes. He's very nice."

"It was hard, wasn't it, being with someone suffering from PTSD?"

"No, that wasn't it." Meghan feels herself sliding into Carol's trap. "It's mostly fine, and when it's not, we cope." She isn't aware of using the present tense until Carol gives her a soft smile. Meghan has witnessed interviews conducted by professional interrogators with lots less skill than this mother of grown children.

Rosie comes out through the back door of the Homestead, her welcoming grin not for the humans in the Lexus, but for the chocolate Lab that comes bounding out of the backseat of the car. He looks to Meghan for permission before throwing himself into Rosie's arms. "Go say hi."

Rosie drops to her knees and the dog throws himself into her open arms. He wriggles and she hugs. He does the unthinkable, and showers her with doggy kisses, which she doesn't discourage. She plants kisses all over his blocky head. She's laughing and weeping, and the dog is ecstatic to see her, to feel her touch, to be reunited with his first person.

Meghan's grin reveals she is just as pleased. One of the stranger things about seeing Rosie again was her worry about this shared history with Shark—the ember of jealousy that might spark. She is relieved that it doesn't. Just to be sure that it doesn't, she finds herself referring to his former trainer as "Auntie Rose."

A burly guy in a pair of sagging Levi's and work boots comes out of the house. Tucker Bellingham. Handshakes all around and then Carol stands back and says, "I think I remember you from years ago."

"I think you do. We came over here a couple of times while you were visiting. My dad took care of your grandmother's plumbing, so if I could, I'd tag along, because she made the best cookies."

"Oatmeal chocolate-chip raisin."

"Oh yeah. With walnuts."

There is a moment of silence as Carol and Tucker bow their heads in memory of Gramma Baxter's baking skills.

Rosie breaks up the moment. "Let's go in. I want you to meet my dog."

"Hang on a minute." Tucker pulls out a measuring tape. "I think that this isn't going to work." The back door is not only too narrow to accommodate Meghan's standard chair, the sill is six inches off the ground. Even the door in the dogtrot won't allow the chair to go through. The three of them stand pondering the problem until Tucker comes to the only reasonable solution. "Not to worry. I can lift you."

Meghan is caught in that oh-too-familiar junction of annoyance at the person offering and the resentment that she needs help in the first place. She hates this. She hates the dependence upon others to accomplish such a simple feat. Shark can help her in so many ways, but until he can carry her on his back, she's too often confronted—ADA regs notwithstanding—with these situations.

Both Carol and Rosie sense Meghan's thinking and simultaneously chorus, "Go ahead, Meghan, let Tucker do it."

Rosie and Shark lead them in. Carol follows with the folded wheelchair.

Standing in the middle of the braided rug positioned in front of the warm woodstove where Rosie ordered him to "stay" is a dog, a tall, gray, wiry-haired beast of no recognizable breed. Meghan whistles under her breath. "Holy mackerel. That's Shadow?" His pictures have not done justice to his actual size.

"It is."

Shark is at Meghan's left and she can feel his quiver of excitement at seeing this new dog. "Is he going to be okay with Shark?"

"I think so."

And both women wait to see how their dogs will react to each other.

As the host, Shadow makes the first gesture, stalking over on stiff legs to Shark, who is obediently sitting beside his person. His head is up, then down as he makes contact, nose-to-nose. Rosie steps closer to Shadow, within reach should the bigger dog take a dislike to this jolly interloper. With interrogatory sniffs, Shadow takes Shark's measure. No one is saying anything, caught up in the canine version of meet and greet. Meghan thinks that maybe this introduction should have taken place outside, in a less territorial place, but then Shadow sits, raises a paw, and gently places it on Shark's shoulders, looking for all the world like a guy saying hi to a buddy. Except, and Meghan knows it, this is a gesture of dominance. Shadow is making sure that Shark, although welcome in his home, knows that he, Shadow, is the boss.

Rosie recognizes the gesture, as well. "Shadow, be nice."

Dogs have their own language of hierarchy, and Shark is well versed. As the guest, the interloper, he responds to Shadow's dominance by flopping onto the wide plank floor and showing his belly. *Nothing to fear here,* he says. *I'm not a challenger.*

With that, both dogs start playing; their mouths half open, they are mock biting. They get rolling around, and finally the humans make them go outside to play.

He misses Spike, Meghan thinks. Or maybe she says it, because she sees the glance Rosie and Carol share. "What?" Rosie says.

"Nothing. Show me the house."

Rosie grabs the handles of Meghan's chair to get her close enough to the entryway that she can see through to the best parlor. While the dogs were getting acquainted, Tucker pulled away all the plastic sheeting. An industrial vacuum sits in the middle of the room. Once they've had their tour, one of the guys on Tucker's crew will finish sucking up all the debris from the job, and, Rosie tells her, by tomorrow, this room will be as close to its original condition as it can be made to look. The wide plank floorboards have been sanded; the plasterboard walls and ceiling are gone, exposing the original beams and the hand-hewn gunstock joists in each corner of the room. The fireplace surround has been cleaned and the newly exposed cherry paneling polished. To see the rest of the house, Meghan sits in her chair, FaceTiming with Carol as she retraces her tour of the day before.

Back in the kitchen Rosie asks, "So, as far as you can remember, there's always been plasterboard on the parlor walls?"

"Yeah, with old-lady wallpaper on it." Carol laughs. "Sprigs and ivy, as I recall. I remember her television, a little black-and-white set that no one could ever tune in. Dad was constantly fiddling with the antennae; rabbit ears. No cable. No dish. And Gramma only had a rotary-dial phone, too."

"When Tucker pulled down the wallboard, we found a cubby next to the fireplace. A wood box. In it was this." Rosie has an ecru-colored box in her hands, the corners reinforced with metal. She places it on the kitchen table and pulls out a tattered book.

Shark

Rosie Rosie Rosie Rosie. She was there, and it was as if they had never been parted. Until the other dog reminded Shark that he was the new dog in Rosie's life and that he, Shark, belonged to Meghan. That was a fact that Sharkey hadn't forgotten, even in the exuberance of seeing his first remembered human being. Meghan was his always, but Rosie was his past.

Rosie

I hand the daybook to Carol. "This is what we found."

"Actually, the dog found it." Tucker is behind me, stirring sugar into his coffee. "I don't think anyone would have spotted it otherwise. It's a pretty cool object."

Carol gently opens the book. "Imagine this being tucked away like that for all these years."

"And you've read it?" Meghan takes the book from Carol, looks at me.

"I have, a lot of it." I tell them as much as I know about Susannah from her book—about her having been a tenant in this house, a healer and widow. I open the journal to my favorite passages, pointing out the methodical way Susannah recorded the quotidian and the remarkable. And I read them this:

"'Today I have encountered Doctor Bellingham along the Commons road. He is kind enough to have offered me a lift. And appalled when I gave him my new address.'"

Carol asks, "What was her 'new address'? I thought she lived here."

Now I feel like a storyteller winding up to the climax and I give in to a perverse need to keep them waiting. "Anyone want more coffee?"

"Just tell us." Meghan holds her mug up for another splash.

I set the carafe on the table. "Jacob Baxter has evicted her because she can't pay the rent. She's in Dogtown." I hear the present tense in my statement. Susannah is, for me, very much in the present.

The cousins suddenly wear the same expression of dismay, and for the first time, I can see that they share blood.

"He threw her out? A widow?" Meghan sits back in her chair, slaps the table. "What kind of a man was he?"

"It was more gentle than that, if you read her writing. From the get-go, once her husband was gone, she knew she couldn't stay here. She wrote that it was a place meant for a family, and she had none. Baxter had five kids."

"But Dogtown? That was considered a place of ill repute, wasn't it?" Carol looks at Tucker as the historian in the room. "You know, witches and prostitutes?"

Meghan sniffs. "What else do you call an old impoverished woman but a witch or a whore?"

Tucker shakes his head. "No. By her time, the area was pretty much abandoned, so she must have holed up in one of the last houses standing."

"She did, Goody Mallory's place. Which is interesting, because she says the dog, the one that followed her home, belonged to Goody."

"Was the cottage nice at least?" Carol looks embarrassed on her Baxter ancestor's account and it's painful to tell her that it wasn't a "cottage," but a hovel.

"She wrote that it stank. She called the stench a 'miasma' that penetrated everything. Even her clothes."

"This Baxter sounds like a jerk." Meghan tips the last of the coffee into her mug.

Our historian chimes in. "It was the way things were done. Most widows would have gone to live with one of their children, but I guess, from what you've told us, Rosie, she had no one."

"She mentioned that her husband, Ben, had two sons from his first marriage, but neither of them offered to take her in. Besides, I think she was attached to Gloucester, to Cape Ann. She didn't want to go back to Marshfield. She had a life here."

Tucker walks his mug over to the sink. "Except that my ancestor, Doc Bellingham, was making it hard for her, horning in on her livelihood."

I remember something from my last reading. "Tucker, I haven't told you, but I found an entry where she wrote that Dr. Bellingham had asked her to help him with a case."

"That's good. Maybe he helped her out. But still. Ending up in Dogtown."

I gently close the daybook and put it back in its archival box, close the cover, tie the black string that holds it shut in a neat bow. "She was a strong, independent woman who got treated pretty shabbily. She went from happily married to homeless, an outcast in her own town." I'm looking at Meghan. I want my friend of the here and now to understand that this long-ago woman and I have certain things in common. "It may sound weird, but I relate to Susannah. We both have a solitary existence, a lack of accepting family. We are both victims of circumstances beyond our control. We both have a companion dog for comfort." I stop before I get weepy. Shadow is back in the house and has dropped his chin onto my lap. I scratch behind his ears. I notice that Shark is getting the same treatment from Meghan. "But, you know, maybe Susannah found some solace. I mean, I'm in Dogtown, too, and"—I smile at Meghan, still amazed that she's been my secret benefactor all this time—"it's been really good for me."

Meghan nods, puts her scarred hand on mine. "I was hoping that it would be."

"And, in some ways, maybe there is something of Susannah in you, Meghan."

"What?"

"Her strength in the face of adversity."

There seems nothing left to do but go out and get lunch before Carol and Meghan have to head back to Connecticut. Meghan rides with me, Carol following so that they can get on the road right after.

"So, what do I do with it? The diary. Does the family want it?"

"Carol will survey the rest of them, but my guess is that we might want a copy of it, and the original can go to the library or the historical society."

"I keep feeling like there must be another piece of it out there somewhere. I'd love to find it. Find out how the story ends."

It's a ten-minute ride to the Lobsta Land Restaurant, but I take my time around Grant Circle, never comfortable with rotaries at the best of times. It's started raining in earnest now and I must need new wiper blades, because my windshield is all blurry. I have only minutes to ask Meghan my nosiest question. "What's up with you and Marley?"

Meghan

"How're things with your family?" Meghan snaps back.

"Okay, off-limits topics. I get it."

"I'm sorry. I've just been badgered by Carol over it; I'm a little fragile."

Rosie laughs. "I don't think so. You're about the least fragile person I know." She signals for their exit. "The answer is, I haven't broken through their radio silence yet."

"And I haven't talked to him in a week and a half. We didn't leave it very comfortably."

Rosie doesn't say anything, but Meghan feels Rosie's hand on her own.

Meghan rides in with Don the next morning, having spent the night with Carol and Don at their home in Fairfield. Shark likes the backseat of Don's Mercedes-Benz, stretching out on the leather seat like a pasha. Over dinner last night, she and Carol filled Don in on the good work being done at the Homestead, and the sidebar of Susannah Day's extraordinary diary.

Don gives Meghan a side glance. "So, how was it? 'Fessing up to being nice?"

"I won't lie. It feels pretty good."

"Dare I say a relief?"

"You might. It is a weight lifted, for sure. I had no idea being so guarded with a secret could be so wearing."

"How'd she take it?"

"Kind of pissed initially. But she's not the kind of person to stay that way, and she's so happy. Don, she's really in a good place."

Don spends most of the rest of the drive into the city on the phone, while Meghan's thoughts drift. Thinking about Rosie, Meghan feels very relaxed, maybe for the first time since she put Rosie's name into consideration by the Advocacy. It's true what they say about the weight of a lie. Not a lie per se, but a withholding. An omission. It's like being released. She extricates her phone from her bag, sends off a quick text to Rosie: *It was great to see you. Hope to see you again soon. xxoo.* She's never done that before, add those little letters *x* and *o* like some kind of schoolgirl. Next she'll be drawing hearts over her *i*'s. In an instant, her phone chimes. *xo to you.*

Meghan is unaccountably pleased. It's good to have a friend. At least one that she hasn't alienated. She was rude to Rosie about Marley but was forgiven. She was pretty cold to Marley, but she doesn't expect to be forgiven about that. Another ding. *Will call tonight to talk about the M situation.* From what she's been told, it's always good to have someone to talk to about hard topics. Not so much a shoulder to cry on as a fresh perspective. Fresher certainly than Carol's. Rosie doesn't know firsthand how sweet Marley can be.

Her phone chimes again, but this time it isn't Rosie. It's Marley. It's like she's conjured him with her thoughts. Meghan doesn't open the text, just sits with the phone in her lap, staring down at the screen. They've entered the city and Don is waiting his turn to drive into the parking garage. Shark sits up and pushes his nose over the seat, pokes her cheek with it. She reaches back to pet him. The dog, being an equal-opportunity lover, bumps Don's cheek, as well. Meghan sees Don's smile. Sometimes the best part of your day is getting dog kisses.

The parking garage leads right into their building, and as they pass into the atrium-style lobby, Shark's tail begins to wag with a vigor that can only mean he sees someone he loves. He softly woofs as he spots his pal Spike and her person, Marley.

Suddenly, Don is six strides ahead of Meghan. "Hey, Marley, nice to see you." He shakes the other man's hand and then fairly leaps aboard an open elevator.

Meghan wonders if Marley is going to block her way to the rank of elevators and then wonders at her own cowardice. This from a woman who performed sweeps of potentially booby-trapped buildings or ones harboring snipers.

Spike has her own agenda, and she and Shark are quickly nose-to-nose, and other important areas, tails whipping from side to side. Spike breaks off from Shark long enough to greet Meghan. Because of their history, because of their former relationship, Meghan has no compunction against petting this working therapy dog. She runs her hand through the curly top-knot on the dog's head. Spike meets her eye like an equal and Meghan has a fleeting moment of whimsy that the dog is asking her to please give Marley another chance. Meghan shakes the impression off. In the next moment, Shark and Spike have flopped down on the cool, shiny floor of the lobby, directly in front of her wheels. Evidently, it won't be Marley blocking her way.

"Hi."

"Hi yourself." Marley snaps his fingers and Spike goes to his side. "Got a minute?"

She could plead an important meeting. She could say no. She is looking up at Marley, and he seems taller than ever. She gestures toward a bench. She doesn't want to be forced to have a conversation with her head tilted—a position of vulnerability.

Marley sits on the edge of the bench and she pulls her chair up to be beside him. She doesn't want to be facing him. It's easier to talk if she doesn't have to look at him, at his eyes. Marley very gently, very respectfully takes her hand in his, her more damaged hand. "When I first came home from Iraq, I pretended that everything was fine, normal. That I was fine, normal. I wasn't. So I turned, like so many of us do, to drugs. They helped on the surface, making it easier for me to deny what had happened. No, that's not right. They were supposed to help me to deny that what had happened had affected me. But, of course, they were false gods. I wasn't any stronger for taking them. The images and the fear and the nightmares were only blunted, not faced, not cured. And then I got Spike, and some of that I was able to put away. Not the fear, but the drugs. Not the nightmares. But the consolation of having this dog with me has helped. I am coping. Understand? Coping. That's all we get, you and I. The ability to cope. We aren't ever going to be perfect."

"Why are you telling me this?"

"Because I think that you *can* cope with life going on. You have. And unless you really don't have feelings for me, I think that you can cope very well with having me be a real part of your whole life, not just a compartmentalized section of it."

Meghan is aware that Shark's fairly climbing into her lap, a sure sign that she isn't coping.

"The question I'm asking, Meghan, is, are you happier with me outside of your life, or in it with you?"

It's been only ten or twelve days, but despite the distraction of going to Gloucester, these have been the emptiest of days for Meghan. Even having Rosie fully back as a friend has been bittersweet, because all she could think of was that she didn't have Marley.

"Stay with me. Be in my life fully." Meghan puts her good hand over Marley's.

Shark eases himself off Meghan's lap, shakes, and flops down at her feet. Spike, already at Marley's feet, drops her head on Shark's rump and sighs.

"Marley, I'm not sure I can do more than just be a friend."

"Then I won't ask you for anything more."

But in the next moment, he's kissing her, and it feels awfully good. "But you can always ask me for more."

Shark

Spike! Life is good. The heavy feeling that he last detected between Meghan and Marley is lighter, if not entirely gone.
Spike and he both keep their attention on their people, but then
they do that mouthy submission thing that people do and he
knows that it's okay to start playing.

Rosie

I've been holding the inventorying of the upstairs rooms at arm's length as long as I can. The late summer and early fall made prolonged periods in a dusty, musty attic seem very unattractive, more the kind of task one would undertake during the worst of the winter. However, the men are going to need to get up there sooner rather than later, so it's upstairs I go, brand-new tablet in hand. I'll record the items, snap a picture of each, and save the whole thing on the device to share electronically with the Homestead Trust, aka Meghan and Carol et al., and Tucker. I don't think anyone believes that the key to buried treasure is up here, but who knows. Gramma Baxter was a pack rat.

Chairs piled on chests. Bedsteads dismantled and leaning up against walls. A layer of gray dust coats everything, and I wonder if I should wear a mask. Carol said that they, the kids, slept in these rooms, and I imagine that in high summer it was an oven up here. There is no ceiling, no insulation, just rafters and roof boards. There's a tiny bit of light like a star, and I realize that despite the fairly recent roofing job, there are problems. Indeed, beneath that glint is a crumbling cardboard box that has clearly suffered repeated wettings. Another job to add to Dogtown Construction Company's ever growing list.

I can't imagine what it was like back in the day. There is no sign of a fireplace in either of the two upstairs rooms. Whichever people lived in this house after Susannah, they must have bundled together like puppies in their rope beds, the only heat up here body heat. Even today, a fairly mild October Thursday, I wear a fleece vest against the chill in these rooms.

Shadow sits outside the bedroom door, which is a good thing, since he can only be in the way as I start to shift things around. I tally the big things: four beds—one iron, one spool, two very much 1950s-style rock maple. Most of the slats for this collection of beds are missing. In this room, no sign of a rope bed, which would have been interesting. I list the beds with their styles and move the headboards to snap photos of them.

Next, I deal with the sheet-covered pier glass—nice, maybe worth something, except that the silver backing is worn and the mirror barely gives back my image, which I count as a blessing. It has been so long since I've had a good look at myself, I've been able to convince myself that I look just fine, not in desperate need of highlights, a manicure. A fresh look. I'm still pretty much rocking the jeans-and-T-shirt look of prison life.

The chairs I lift and examine one by one, all very ordinary, all very broken. There's a rolled-up braided rug similar to the modern one I put downstairs, except that this one's colors are muted into a uniform color of highway slush, and the threads holding it together are frayed. It uncoils as I lay it out for its picture. Still, I think, it could be professionally restored. Maybe salvageable.

So it goes for a couple of hours, and I'm surprised to find that I've gotten through room number one so quickly. I was imagining that this would be a weeks-long effort, and then I worry about what I'll have to keep me occupied, keep me from thinking about the rest of what's going on in my life. By which I mean this civil suit. Pete has tried to keep me off the ledge emotionally, with assurances that it won't go anywhere, but I still fear Cecily Foster's tentacles.

"It was a horrible accident." I kept saying those words over and over as the too-young cop pulled out his Breathalyzer device.

"Just puff into this."

Why did I feel like I was doing something obscene?

It had been Charles who had been drunk, not me.

We were in Connecticut, at the extravagantly tasteful wedding of the daughter of one of Charles's late father's business partners, who also happened to be Charles's godfather. Tatiana Bigelow and Charles had been destined for each other since the cradle. Until I came along, of course. So she'd found herself a consolation prize in the son of a well-placed political family. When his name was spoken, it was with the hushed reverence due a rising star, a future senator or even a president. Plus, they were richer than Croesus.

I was not speaking to Charles and had no intention of going to the wedding. How could I bear the long ride to Litchfield side by side with someone who could prove himself so cruel? His abhorrent act should have been enough to send me out the door of his well-appointed luxury apartment, but I couldn't think of anywhere to go. I had no friends in the city. Charles kept the credit cards, and I didn't have enough money in my own checking account to get a hotel room or even a train ticket as far as Providence. I told myself that I was biding my time, that as soon as I heard from Paulie or from my mother, I could bolt. I was willing to suffer the "I told you so" that either or both would pummel me with. I was so broken. Even my angry family would have to see that I couldn't stay with a man so vile and would take me back. I was willing to take my lumps.

"You will go." That's what he said. That's what his mother said. "You will not embarrass me." That's what they both said. I guess it was far better for Charles to show up with me on his arm as his certified fiancée than have Tatiana entertain second thoughts even as she glided down the aisle. Her missed opportunity. No one had ever told me why they broke up, but I bet now I could figure it out. Either she had more backbone than I did or she, too, saw the cruel side of Charles Foster.

I sat in the backseat of the car, Charles's favorite indulgence, his 1968 Chevy Camaro. Cecily was up front with Charles. I said not a word. They chatted about "dear people" they would soon see. It mystified me, how Charles went on as if he hadn't done the thing he had, as if he had no moral compass. I realized then that he really *didn't* have one; that his interaction with my own family proved that he had nothing more than ice water in those patrician veins. All the way to Connecticut my mind replayed what had happened to Tilley.

"Where's Tilley?" Charles said nothing. A knock on our door. A flicker of reaction from him. Doris from next door: "I'm so sorry; I think that your dog fell from your balcony. You'd better come." Silence. A knowing silence. The crushed body of my little dog. What did you do?

Charles remained silent, sitting in the damaged club chair, stroking the ruined leather as if it were a living thing. "What did you do?" The answer, a bald-faced lie: "I didn't touch her.

She must have squeezed through the rails." Except that I had stretched wire cloth across the rails to prevent just such an accident. If he had just pretended to be shocked and sad, I might have bought his innocence.

Ice water might have filled his veins, but molten lava was building in mine.

I sat in my seat at the wedding reception and drank one glass of champagne. Every other glass of wine poured for me over the several courses of dinner I slid over to Charles. I stubbornly refused to dance with him, not caring what the others at our table thought. Cecily happily took my place. She was one of those middle-aged women who keep themselves in such good shape that they don't look ridiculous on the dance floor, and Cecily had moves like a much younger version of herself. Every now and then she'd throw a glance my way, a self-satisfied look on her face. I think she saw the end of my relationship with Charles, and that suited her just fine.

It was, of course, a perfect midsummer evening, and the wedding reception took place under a grand marquee on the sweeping lawn of the massive faux Newport manse that was the Bigelow family home in Connecticut. By the time the wedding party had performed all the obligatory elements—the toasts, the first dance, yada, yada—I was bored and so weary with the anguish of what had happened, not just Tilley's brutal end but all of it, my father's prolonged dying, the alienation from my family, which seemed permanent. I was enveloped in a miasma of grief and with it came this curious inertia. I knew that I had to get out. I just didn't know how. Somewhere along the line, I'd become emotionally disabled.

I left our table and skirted around the dance floor until I was out on the lawn and heading toward the house. I wanted a private place to make yet another call for help. I had left so many messages on Paulie's phone, I was pretty sure I'd broken it. And then I had a flash: There were other people besides family I could call. I thumbed my contacts until I found my old friend Brenda Brathwaite. Okay, maybe it had been a year or more since I'd done more than hit "Like" on one of her Face-book posts, but a friend was a friend, right?

When she answered on the first ring, I burst into tears.

"Rosie? What happened? What's wrong?"

At the sound of her voice, I melted into a warm puddle. I don't actually recall my words; I only have the impression that I was blathering, incomprehensible, and it took her a few tries before I settled down enough to ask her to come get me.

"Where are you?"

"Litchfield, at a wedding."

"It's after nine now. Are you at a hotel?"

The devil is in the details, they say, and the fact was that this wedding would be long over by the time Brenda could drive all the way from Boston, and there was no place I could wait for her. I didn't imagine that these perfect strangers were going to let me sit on their steps deep into the night. "No. We're in the middle of nowhere."

"Okay." The good news was that Brenda was clearheaded and not suffering the surfeit of emotion that was clouding my brain. "Can you go home with him? Get back to the city? Then get out, go to a hotel?"

"I don't have any money." How mortifying it was to say that.

"Go to the train station. I'll buy you a ticket and you can pick it up."

"Okay."

"Be smart, Rosie. Don't let him know what you're going to do." The implication was that my grand boyfriend, for whom I had sacrificed my family, was dangerous.

After calling Brenda, I spent a few minutes in the powder room, freshening up. I had to repair the smudged mascara and hope that the redness of my eyes wouldn't be obvious in the soft lantern light of the marquee. I ran a brush through my hair. As I walked out of the small room, there was Cecily Foster. It looked a bit like she'd been waiting for me.

"Rose, Charles is looking for you. Where have you been?"

The flip answer would, of course, have been "The bathroom, obviously." Instead, I kept my mouth shut and waved her toward the open door of the powder room. Instead of going into the little half bath, she grasped my upper arm in a clench. "Charles hasn't appreciated your behavior today. You would have been wiser to behave like a loving girlfriend instead of a child in a snit. What do you suppose the Bigelows are thinking? What is wrong with you?"

Cecily had imbibed enough that her reserve was slipping; she fairly hissed, and clearly didn't realize exactly how loud that hiss was. I was embarrassed for her, and furious. "Did Charles happen to mention why I might be angry with him?"

"Something about your dog, your foolish insistence on getting a destructive dog. Those chairs are family heirlooms."

"Did he tell you that he threw her off the balcony?" I wasn't even trying to keep my voice down. "That he killed her?"

Cecily blinked. Her mouth went hard. "I doubt that very much." Ice water in the veins indeed. She looked at me with utter contempt.

At that moment, a cluster of bridesmaids appeared, heading for the powder room. There we stood, Cecily Foster and Charles Foster's fiancée. I'm sure we looked like we were about to spit in each other's faces. If there was one thing I'd heard over and over all the way from the city to the Litchfield Hills, it was how wonderful Tatiana Bigelow was, how beautiful, charming, and, oh, gosh, suitable. The gaggle of pink-flounced bridesmaids would surely communicate to the lucky bride that her ex's fiancée was an out-of-control head case.

My heart was beating so hard, as if I'd been running a marathon. I jerked my arm out of Cecily's grasp.

I had the last lick. As I passed the cluster of women, I rolled my eyes, suggesting that Mrs. Foster was the one not quite in control.

The reception had wound down to just a few stragglers when Charles came up behind my chair and put his hands on my shoulders. "Time to go. Where's Mother?"

I shrugged. I wasn't going to break my silence. I watched as he went off in search of Cecily, and noted that he was swaying, a gentle side-to-side movement that suggested he was pretty drunk. Charles wasn't a man to overindulge, but this wedding—that of his could-have-been wife—coupled with my sliding my wine to him throughout the evening, had broken through his reserve. I saw him slap an old classmate on the back, and literally guffaw in the man's face. Oh, yes, Charles was in no condition to drive the two-plus hours home. But I needed to get back to the city. My salvation was waiting at Penn Station in the form of a prepaid ticket.

Charles had his mother by the arm and the two of them were making their way slowly toward the circular driveway of the house. I'd spoken to the valet, and the car was sitting there, idling in neutral. I decided that it would be best if I drove us home. Charles never let me drive if he was in the car, but I was certain that this time he'd see the wisdom of my being the designated driver. I slid into the driver's seat, began adjusting the rearview mirror, the seat, the seat back. Charles handed his mother into the backseat, an awkward maneuver in the low-slung two-door muscle car. I waited for him to get into the front passenger seat, but instead, Charles's face appeared at the driver's window, startling me. He rapped on it. "Get out."

I rolled down the window."No. You've had too much to drink and I'm the DD."

"You can't drive a stick." He was derisive, but it didn't deter me.

"I certainly can." Not entirely true, but not untrue, either. My father had taught me years ago on his old Bronco.

I just needed a minute or two to get used to the car. I knew I'd probably strip the gears and that would set Charles off, but it was better than his driving us off the road. But this was a vintage Camaro with a heavy-duty clutch and a hair-trigger transmission. Not my father's Bronco.

Charles leaned his hands on the roof of the low car and leaned closer to me. I could smell the whiskey he'd had as a nightcap with that fraternity brother. He swayed a little.

The valet came over. "Sir, let her drive. You don't want to wreck this car."

Charles shot him a look. "Fine."

The valets were lining up cars in that circular drive and there was now an Escalade ahead of me. It was clear that the driver wanted to get going, and I needed to back up to let him out. I put the clutch in, feeling that tension of the heavy-duty mechanism fight against my left foot in its five-inch heel. I ground the stick shift into reverse. I knew that I would stall if I didn't get the gas-to-clutch ratio right, so I hit the gas at the same time I let go of the clutch and the car flew backward. I heard the thud, felt the Camaro roll over something. Then my world closed down around me.

It was a terrible accident. But Cecily Foster had powerful friends. And she believed that I had motive to want to kill her beloved son.

For some reason, I am sitting on the floor of the landing between the two upstairs rooms in the Homestead with a large gray dog on my lap. Shadow literally holds me between his paws and rests his big head on my shoulder as I am overwhelmed by memories. I served my time for a sin I didn't mean to commit, and now Cecily Foster is going to rake me over the coals again, punish me further. What will become of Shadow if I get carted off to prison again?

Shadow

She is surrounded by things and he has to climb over them to get into her lap. Something has frightened her and he can't figure out what it is. He has sniffed every corner, listened hard, and nothing external seems to be amiss. It is inside of her, this thing that has caused her to breathe as if she's been running, this thing that has produced streaks of wet down her cheeks. Once again, he feels as though he needs a human tongue to make this outburst stop. He has only his dog tongue and he uses it lavishly to stanch the panic.

Rosie

Meghan says that I should just focus on the here and now and not worry about the future. She means I should stop dwelling on the threats and just look to the things I have some control over, like doing my job. Which, today, is to sit down with the invoices and write some checks. Shadow throws me a plaintive look, sort of an *Aww shucks. Can't we play a little hooky first?* I tell him no. We must persevere. I promise him that a good long walk through Dogtown is in order afterward. I've gotten quite comfortable in those woods now, and they no longer give me the creeps. I can find my way to the reservoir and back along two different trails without feeling like I'm on the verge of being lost. Most of that is because Shadow leads the way. I fear nothing. Not even the gunfire from the firing range abutting the trailhead off Cherry Street. The first time I heard it, I nearly dived for cover; but now I know it's just target practice at the Cape Ann Sportsmen's Club. Still, I always hurry by.

Now that I've inventoried and pretty much cleared out the

generational detritus from upstairs, the most recent project for Tucker's crew is to install Sheetrock and insulation in those bedrooms. There was some talk of simply leaving the lathe and plaster, but in the end the family decided that they shouldn't err on the side of keeping it authentic and expect humans to be comfortable in here year-round. Tucker and his team will begin the painstaking installation of Sheetrock so that the beams will remain exposed but the humans won't freeze to death. The *pop pop pop* of nail guns is augmented by the on/off/on roar of the compressor that runs them. Then there is the *scritch scritch* whir of drills. I realize that my teeth are on edge and my dog has abandoned me for the great outdoors.

Gathering the envelopes and pulling on a jacket, I head out to join him. I've grown complacent living out here in isolation, and my keys are in the car, along with my wallet and, I notice with a little chagrin, my phone. There are no text messages, but the log indicates that Pete Bannerman has called three times, twice from the office and once from his cell phone. Shoot. So much for Meghan's advice. I tap Pete's name. Shadow stands between my knees as I sit on the granite bench.

"Hey, Rosie, I was getting worried."

"Sorry, I left my phone in the car and I just saw that you'd called." I feel this weird little sense of pleasure in hearing Pete say he was worried about me. He's such a nice guy.

"I met with Mrs. Foster's lawyers yesterday. I want to bring you up to speed."

I always assumed that the expression "heavy heart" was a metaphor, but as he enumerates the many ways that Cecily Foster won't give up on punishing me, my heart does indeed feel like it's taking on ballast. I always thought you couldn't be tried for the same crime twice; although there had been no trial per se, just a plea bargain excruciatingly extracted out of my confusion and my PD's reckless disregard for the truth. As the

Advocacy challenged in its brief, there really had been no crime. What happened was an unfortunate accident. Except— and this was Cecily's cudgel—I had motive. According to her, I was exacting revenge for my poor dead dog. As painful as it is, I understand her logic, but I know, as angry as I was with Charles that night, I didn't intentionally kill him. *But there was one brief moment when I wasn't sorry.*

"I think we're going to have to prove that you were in fear for your life." I'm brought out of my thoughts by Pete's comment.

"I was; it's hard to live with a man with such cruel tendencies."

"And it's commonly thought that animal cruelty leads to domestic abuse."

"Yes. Charles separated me from everyone I loved. Isn't that also indicative of domestic abuse?"

"It is."

I see where Pete is going with this. I have had plenty of time to look back over my time with Charles and come to the same conclusion. For six years, I lived with women who had endured unspeakable domestic situations. Mine was a paler version, but I related to their entrapment in households of fear. I hadn't been screamed at or punched, but Charles's silences were surely a form of abuse; the way he was able to cow me with a look. Even his generosity became a form of control, a way of turning me into his paper doll. I slide my ponytail through my fingers, look down at my sturdy cheap sneakers. I have a mystery stain above the left knee of my Levi's. I am comfortable with all of it. I never expect to walk down Newbury Street again, and I don't care. I had my Cinderella moment, and those glass slippers were painful.

"We need to set up a time for depositions."

"What, take a day off from my exacting job?"

"Half a day. Next week. Tuesday."

"Of course." We sign off and I am no lighter of heart than
before. A deposition, where I will be effectively grilled by a
friendly lawyer and an unfriendly one. And I have nothing to
wear.

My phone rings again; it's Pete.

"Rosie, I don't want you to worry. You're not being defended by a hack this time. You've got me."

"Oh, Pete, I know that. Thank you." I smile down at my
feet. He's right. This time I have a real advocate.

"We're in this together. I won't let you down."

"I know that you won't. I trust you."

"So, no bad thoughts. Just good ones. Promise?"

"I do." And I don't.

Saturday morning and I'm in my car, heading toward the massive Burlington Mall to find something appropriate to wear to
the deposition. I'd poked around in the Main Street shops of
Gloucester and had then gone over to Rockport to poke around
in its boutiques, but I'd found nothing that seemed just right.
I don't know what I have in mind, but I just know even my
favorite consignment shop didn't have it. Maybe it was just that
I was ready for a foray into a larger environment than I had
been comfortably inhabiting these many weeks. I remember
thinking when Meghan and Carol were here that it was time
for bright lights, and now I'm going to them. I hope that I won't
be dazzled and run for the comfort of my dimly lit temporary
home. Shadow lounges, if that is a good description of a dog
who is longer than the backseat of my car, behind me. His long
legs hang off the seat. He's got his head propped on the arm-
rest of the back door. I can't say that he looks comfortable, but
he seems okay with it. The temperature has dropped into the
mid-forties, so he'll be fine in the car while I do my thing in

the mall. I won't linger. Even as I find a parking place, I can feel my urge to do this fade. I haven't been in a crowd for a very long time. I haven't been in a mall for even longer. I sit, gathering my resources, and watch families go by, young couples holding hands and an older couple, she with her arm through his. I'm here all by myself. Solitary shopping. Pairs of teenage girls reinforce my sense of solitude. Shopping should be shared. How will I judge what I try on? I wish that I had the guts to claim Shadow as an emotional support dog. But I won't.

Meghan and Marley are back together and she sounds as happy as I have ever heard her. Marley's dog, Spike, features prominently in her conversation, as if she and Marley now have stepchildren of whom they are fond. Spike is Marley's emotional support dog, and I know from my time training dogs in prison that all dogs can be labeled as such, but those for whom that is their singular role are so deeply embedded in the psyche of their guardians that it is impossible not to see the difference. I glance back at the recumbent Shadow and acknowledge, not for the first time, that he performs that role for me perfectly. I don't know what I'd do without him, and I will insist that he accompany me to the deposition. So there. Even if I have to buy him a fake red vest.

Okay, time to fish or cut bait. I crack the windows and give my dog a kiss on the nose. "I won't be long." He doesn't look like he's worried.

I have some money to spend, given that I have been paid biweekly and have virtually no expenses except those of my phone and food. And Shadow, of course. I can visit the better stores, or I can go to my old standbys from the days prior to my conversion as a fashion plate. I choose the latter, skipping Nordstrom and Michael Kors. Macy's is more my speed these days, or the Gap if necessary.

It really doesn't take that long to pick out a skirt suit, navy blue, white piping, above the knee, and a simple silk blouse to go under the jacket. Blah. But it makes the point that I am a reliable, rational, unemotional woman. No frills, no fakery. I look like an airline hostess or whatever it is that they call them these days. I put them back. I move on to the dresses. I've lost the prison weight and I like what I see, but these dresses are meant for happy occasions, dinners out or going to a show, not depositions. I really don't want to invest in a dress that I will associate only with unhappiness and probably never wear again. In the end, I select two pairs of nice tailored trousers and three pretty, but not too pretty, blouses to go with them. I add a black blazer and there you go. Done. Except that I need footwear.

All in all, it takes an hour and a half to shop. It feels like a lot longer, and I worry about the dog in my car. I pass Cinnabon as I head toward the exit, but I do not want to jeopardize my body, newly restored to its original shape, with an ill-considered fling with sticky dough.

"Rosie? Rosie Collins?"

My hand is on the exit door, but I turn toward a very familiar voice. "Brenda!"

It takes a few moments, but soon enough the surprise falls away and we are once again two girls on a bench in the mall.

Of all the people I should have called upon my unforeseen release, Brenda was, except for my family, at the top of the list; but I hadn't. I had gotten so stuck on my mother's silence and my brothers—all of them—ignoring me that I assumed everyone from my former life would do the same. It was a surfeit of embarrassment and the fear of further rejection that kept me from calling Brenda Brathwaite. And that's what I babble to her now.

To her credit, Brenda doesn't seem insulted. "So, you're in Gloucester to regroup?"

"Essentially, yes." It would be a much longer conversation to explain about the Advocacy and the Homestead Trust and Meghan and the rest of it. I've condensed it down into a flat miracle. "I got out and they gave me this odd little job and here I am. At least for a while."

"Gosh, your mother must be so happy."

What do I say to that? Brenda has known me a long time, has known about my estrangement, so I can give her an honest answer. "No. She still won't talk to me. I haven't seen or heard from her since I was released. She wouldn't let me visit her."

"That's just crazy talk."

"Well, I think so." I crack a smile. Brenda has never been one to mince words. I suggest lunch, anything to prolong this unexpected reunion.

She shakes her head. "I'm meeting some, um, colleagues for lunch at the Cheesecake Factory. Practically a business lunch."

I get it. How would she ever explain me to a nice group of friends? I give her my blessing. "Yeah, and, really, I don't have time. My dog is in the car."

"It's so good to see you."

"I'm so glad to see you, too." I get up. "I should go."

"Rosie?" Brenda Brathwaite, the boon companion of my youth, has changed. She's a grown-up woman. While I lingered in the rarified atmosphere of my gilded cage, and then lived out the monotony of prison, I failed to mature. I feel stunted. "Give me your number."

I give it to her, momentarily cheered by her request, the suggestion that she will stay in touch with me.

We hug.

"Rosie, you should go see your mother."

"She doesn't want to see me."

"And that stops you, how?" As I said, Brenda never minces words.

Rosie

Go see your mother. But how can I? The dog puts his head over the seat back and pokes my neck. It's as if he's saying, *Put the key in the ignition, point the car south on 95, and just go.* So I do. I tell myself that if traffic is bad, I'll get off and turn around. But it's Saturday afternoon and for some reason only a reasonable amount of highway traffic is heading toward Boston.

There is a point on the highway when the road turns just so and the skyline of Boston is revealed. I feel the urge to sing the Boston anthem, "Muddy Water." It's either that or "Sweet Caroline." Or both. I've missed that view. I get off before the Zakim Bridge and wend my way through the familiar streets until I am in Charlestown. In my Bunker Hill neighborhood, I notice that my family home is still intact. Having carefully set the hand brake against gravity on this steep street, I get out of the car. The dog follows. He sniffs a telephone pole and promptly leaves a canine calling card against it. From somewhere up the street, a little dog barks. Shadow cocks his head but doesn't attempt to leave my side, despite the fact that I haven't leashed him. He thrusts his head under my hand, and I press on him to maintain my equilibrium. I realize that I am shaking as hard as I did that long-ago day when I was escorted into the Mid-State Women's Correctional Facility.

I have not laid eyes on my only parent since before that day. She never came to Connecticut to be by my side during the lead-up to my plea bargain. She said she couldn't leave Teddy. At the time, I felt as if she'd chosen him over me, that her physically wounded son was more fragile than her emotionally crippled daughter. I called her. I begged her to please just come be with me, let one of the others take care of Teddy for a day or so. I was so afraid. I had no one.

I stand on the sidewalk where I once chalked hopscotch frames. Where Brenda and I met up for our walk to school. Where I waited for boys to pick me up for dates. I look up at the house and notice for the first time that the windows are without curtains, that there is a blankness to the face of the house; no one is home. No one is living there. I don't know why I've fetched up here. Of course they wouldn't be here.

"Is that you, Rosie?" I hear a familiar voice and turn to see my old crush from junior high school, Ryan Dean.

"Oh my God, Ryan. How are you?" I rein in my gush. He's still cute, even with his ring finger adorned with a wide gold band. I wonder if he's married a Charlestown girl or ventured farther afield.

We chat, not exactly catching up—that would be too hard—but certainly tossing out a nice array of pleasantries: "You look great." "How've you been?" "What're you up to?" This last from my mouth, not his. He certainly has to know what I've been up to. And, as if he just remembered this, he takes a step back. At first, I think he's suddenly shy of chatting up an ex-con on his street, but then I realize that Shadow has approached him, and, let's face it, Shadow can look a little malevolent with those bushy eyebrows and his height. "That's just my dog. He's friendly."

"He's kind of unusual, isn't he?"

"You have no idea." I rub the dog's ears. "Maybe you can shed some light on this." I gesture toward the empty house. "Do you know where they've moved?"

As if he's not surprised that a daughter might not know where her parent lives, Ryan simply shrugs. "I don't actually live in the neighborhood anymore. My mom still does, though. She'll know." He takes out his phone. I prefer to assume this is more efficient than his taking me to his family home half a block away. I am not going to let myself get paranoid at this late date.

A moment later, he hands me his phone. "Mrs. Dean, how are you?" I'm not sure I can do much more chitchat. My impulse to confront my mother is waning. I'm hungry and I want to flee back to my Dogtown bolt-hole.

"They've been gone for years. Why don't you know where?" Unlike her son, Mrs. Dean is bluntly curious.

I'll be blunt, too. "We're estranged. But I want to see her. And Teddy."

"Well, she's living with one of your brothers, I think."

"And Teddy? Is he there, too?"

"I don't know. I don't think so. I think he's in some kind of facility."

"Wait, Teddy's in a nursing home, you mean?"

"I guess so. Something like that. I really don't know."

"Do you remember which brother my mother's with? Paulie? Patrick? Frankie?" I enumerate the brothers, but she can't remember which one. Bobby? But, of course, I don't list Teddy.

I am on a fool's errand.

The dog sits at my side, his head at my waist, and I keep a

hand on his head. Ryan says good-bye and good luck and I am left standing alone in front of my abandoned childhood home. Abandoned because the firm of my erstwhile and deceased boyfriend bought them out and then, in cosmic irony, never built the project. I begin to see the neglect, the peeling paint and the cracked front window. The screen door is leaning on its hinges. The shrubs are out of control, and the euonymus vine has climbed to the roof. I go up the steps and straighten the screen door. I lift a chip of paint off the trim and wish that I had a scraper. I tug at the vine, but it refuses to let go of the siding. I could fix this. I've learned a great deal from watching the various workmen who have inhabited my world for the past months. If the roof is good and the foundation solid, this old place could be rehabbed. I almost call Tucker Bellingham.

Then it hits me: Brenda will know where they are.

Thinking she might still be with her friends, um, colleagues, I text the question to her. I get a ding almost immediately. Mom's with Paulie's family in Stoughton. Teddy is in Randolph. She's kindly added the address of Teddy's place. It sounds benign, High View Estates. It doesn't have the ring of a "facility," but then these places sometimes go out of their way to seem homey. I'll go see him first. I open the back door of the car and Shadow jumps in, taking his position in the dead center of the seat. "Let's go introduce you to Teddy." Shadow *hun-hunns* his approval. Firing up my trusty Waze, I work my way back to the highway and keep tracking south.

At about the Braintree split, my phone sings out. I punch the Bluetooth without looking to see who it is.

"Rosie Collins? This is Shelley Brown, at the Sawyer Library."

Ruh-roh. I haven't gotten back to her yet on the family's decision about the journal pages.

"I have some really extraordinary news."

I wish that I wasn't on my way to a date with destiny—I mean my surprise call on my estranged brother—but Shelley's excitement is enough to distract me from my growing dread.

"I found the rest of the journal."

This is unbelievable, and I hear my voice pitch up to preteen level. "Oh my God, where?"

"In the historical society's archives. I stopped in this morning, just on a whim, and, lo and behold, there it was. They are really interested in what the family wants to do with those pages you have. Do you know yet what they plan on doing with them?"

"I told them about it, but I haven't heard yet what they want to do with them." Close enough. "Except that they might want a copy."

"As I'm sure they don't mean running these fragile pages through a copier, you have to know that digitizing is expensive and probably not in the budget."

"Let me talk to them. See if we can work something out."

"Good. I'll hear from you soon." A statement, not a question.

This is unbelievable. There's more to Susannah's story. I am so freaking excited! Maybe this is how fans of *Twin Peaks* felt when they announced that the series would continue. I know that I am conflating my renewed friendship with Meghan with learning that there is more to Susannah's story, but it feels remarkably the same—like I am about to be reunited with an old friend. Just as I am about to be reunited with my brother. I am either going to be made whole or shattered utterly.

I take my exit. I'm not going to call the Trust—Meghan or Carol—just yet. That will have to wait. Right now, I'm listening to my Waze voice direct me to where I will see the brother I have always considered my friend, my ally, my competitor. I haven't seen Teddy since my father's funeral, when he sat in his chair, a borrowed black overcoat awkwardly tucked behind him. I had offered to push him back to the waiting limousine, but he'd rejected my help. "I don't need your help, Rosie. Not anymore."

Stung, I reached out to take Charles's hand. He gripped mine and drew me close to his side. I felt the soft merino of his overcoat against my cheek. Among the mourners, a wide-ranging group of family, friends, neighbors, and coworkers, we stood out. Not because I was the only daughter of the deceased, but because we looked like peacocks in a gathering of pigeons. Even in black, the cut and material of our clothes defined us as *other*. I might have come from here, but I had been transformed. My clothes, my accent, my cross-fit body proclaimed me to be capable of selling out my family. Everyone by this time knew that Wright, Melrose & Foster had bought out the neighborhood. And that I had done nothing to prevent it. Little could anyone, even my family, know there was nothing I could do to dissuade Charles from anything he set his sights on. I was not an influence on him; he was an influence on me. But there we were, his arm through mine, holding me close. I stumbled a bit on my six-inch Louboutins and worried that the hard ground of the cemetery would wreck them.

Your destination is on the right says my AI companion. It's a boxy apartment building making up the short end in a rect-angle of buildings just like it. According to Brenda's text, Ted-dy's building is number 4, and it only briefly crosses my mind to wonder how she knows this. Could my dear friend have been keeping track of my family in their diaspora from Bunker Hill?

I pull into the only parking space not designated HANDICAP. There are two other vehicles, both the kind of vans that easily transport wheelchairs. I shut off the car. Shadow nuzzles my ear, telling me that he's got my back. But I don't get out of the car. Not just yet. I watch as very ordinary sorts of people, men and women, pretty much all twentysomethings, all attached to their devices, come and go from the other buildings. It must be that number 4 is a group residence and the rest of the apartment buildings are habitation for the millennial population of Corolla-driving postcollege residents dreaming bigger dreams.

Good for Teddy. He's no longer stuck in the narrow confines of our family home, watching as everyone else of his generation moved on. Then I think of Meghan and how she broke out of her dependence with Shark, and I decide right then and there a group home is okay, but I want to get Teddy independent. And I know exactly how to do that.

I suck in a big breath of air. Shadow breathes it in as I exhale. "Let's go."

I should have brought a present, I think as I enter the small lobby of the building. I'm dropping in empty-handed. A six-pack. A pizza. I almost turn around and bolt for the nearest Dunkin' Donuts for a box of twelve.

"Can I help you?" A woman is seated behind a small desk tucked into an alcove to the left of me. She smiles, but it is the smile of a prison guard, more a warning than a measure of good intentions. She has a mane of reddish blond hair loosely braided. She's one of those women who don't use eye makeup correctly, ending with a squinty look instead of enhancement. I dislike her on sight.

"I'm looking for Teddy Collins? I believe that he lives here?" I'm nervous and the uptalk reveals it. "I'm his sister." And then I wonder if that is a stupid admission. If this guard—I mean receptionist—knows anything meaningful about Teddy, maybe she knows about me, too. And what of it? I think. So what? I'm a free woman. I have to keep reminding myself of that. I do not wear a sandwich board announcing my former status as inmate. And yet, as this redheaded guardian of the gate to my brother's abode stares me down, that's exactly how I feel.

Shadow is standing precisely at my side. He lifts his nose

and points it directly at her. She stares right back at him, then looks up at me. "Only service dogs are allowed here."

"Yes. That's right. A service dog." Shadow is performing a service right now—I can feel his rough fur under the tips of my fingers where they graze his skull.

"Then where's his vest?"

"At the dry cleaner's. Now, which is my brother's apartment?"

"Is he expecting you?"

I almost go Monty Python on her—"No one expects the Spanish Inquisition"—but I don't, pretty certain she wouldn't get it. I almost lie and say yes. In the end, I go with the truth. "No. I'm surprising him." Understate much?

She gives me that guardish smile, but I no longer feel intimidated. Enough of being a wimp. "Which apartment is his?"

"First floor, four-oh-one. On your right."

There is one of those decorative wreathes hanging on a picture hook on the door, encircling the apartment number, complete with a cutesy plaque that says WIPE YOUR FEET. Indeed, there is a thin doormat, also requesting that I wipe my feet. I do. Clearly, my mother is still in charge. Shadow sits, but I can see his nostrils pulse with an investigative intake. His tail moves, but it's not quite wagging.

Shadow

This is new for him, being in a building like this. The ride here has been long and he's been alert for Rosie's distress, but she exudes only a sense of determination, which is new for her. There are nerves, yes, but there is something else that keeps them in check. That, and his sturdy presence at her side.

The sounds from behind the door are different, too. He doesn't know why Rosie doesn't just open the door, but people have odd customs. He thinks he might bark, as he would to be let into their house, but something tells him not to. He, like Rosie, waits outside the closed door. Unlike Rosie, he can hear the carpet-dulled approach of rubber wheels.

Rosie

Teddy's apartment doesn't have a doorbell, so I knock. Even I can tell that my initial knock is tentative, as if I am reluctant to impose myself, afraid of disturbing him. I am, I suppose. I am struck with bashfulness, or its more insidious relative, cowardice. *He'll be surprised to see you. He won't want to see you. He'll be angry. He'll be glad. He'll welcome you with open arms. He will slam this door in your face.* My inner dialogue is a rant of incoherence.

Shadow stands beside me, his expression suggesting that he doesn't understand how I'm not using my magic hands and just opening up the door. I knock again, this time with a little more emphasis. Not so much that it would sound like I was a bill collector on the stoop, rather than a friend. Do people ever arrive unannounced anymore, what with the ability to drop a warning text? I don't even have Teddy's number. Until an hour ago, I didn't even know that he was living here.

Maybe he's not home. Maybe that's better. I'll write to him.

Give him some warning. Maybe he knows I'm here and is hiding.

When we were little, before his injury, hide-and-seek was one of our favorite games. Teddy was good at it, managing to hold his breath even as I got so close that I could smell him. This thought makes me realize that my dog absolutely knows that someone is behind that door. I can tell by the way his head is cocked, the way he's capable of hearing even a held breath.

Shadow pushes his head against my hip, as if pushing me to knock again. So I do. The dog pumps his front feet up and down, his signature move for when he is impatient. Obviously, there are no conflicting emotions for him; he fully expects the door to be opened.

Then I hear him, his voice as he calls out, "Who is it?"

I don't have an answer. "Um, me?"

A solid pause.

"Who?"

"Teddy, can you open the door?" Have I been gone so long that he doesn't recognize my voice? His only sister's voice? I think that the answer is yes. I haven't spoken to Teddy in more than six years. Could anyone hold the memory of a voice for that long? "It's Rosie, Teddy."

The extra-wide front door opens and my brother and I face each other across the threshold. Is the look on my face as astonished as his is? I'm surprised at how grown-up he is; how tall, despite the chair, or maybe he looks taller because the chair he sits in is one of those high-tech ultralight chairs that the para-athletes use. No longer sunk in a sling of a seat, he is upright and looking altogether handsome. The last time I saw him, he was hunched, as well as angry and weeping; wearing borrowed funeral clothes. Today, he stares at me and I see a grown man dressed in a tidy polo shirt and jeans. What he sees, I don't dare guess. An older version of my former self? Someone for whom the sparkle had long since flattened out?

"Rosie? What are you doing here?" His eyes dart to look behind me, as if he thinks I am a fugitive and the cops are on my tail. "How did you get here?

"Brenda told me where you were living."

"Brenda?"

"Brathwaite."

"I know who Brenda is. I just meant. I just meant that I am surprised . . ."

"That she told me? That she speaks to me?"

I'm still standing in the hallway. A door down the hall opens, shuts. "Can I come in?"

He makes room for me to enter his apartment, and Shadow and I follow as Teddy rolls his chair into the comfortably large space of his uncluttered living room. All has not changed with my brother; I spot an unfinished jigsaw puzzle on his dining-area table. A big flat-screen television is on one wall. No coffee table, no obstacles in that room. A two-cushion couch in masculine brown and a plaid armchair are the only pieces of furniture, both neatly pushed to the opposite wall, leaving a wide swath of oatmeal-colored wall-to-wall industrial carpet. A picture window with drapes pushed to either side looks out onto the courtyard central to all four buildings. I see my mother's influence in the way the drapes are held back with tasseled tiebacks—her signature decorating touch.

I haven't rehearsed this reunion. I have no preconceived notions about how it might go, and so I stand, then sit, then stand. Neither one of us speaks for the longest time—long enough that the dog finally takes charge. He stalks over to Teddy to sit in front of him, then drops one paw into my brother's lap, for all

the world like a guy putting out a hand in friendship. Teddy
stares at the thing in his lap, then says, "Heck of a dog." He puts
a hand out for Shadow to sniff, then ruffles Shadow's neck fur.
The look on Teddy's face is so plainly distressed.

"I shouldn't have come, I shouldn't have surprised you like
this. It wasn't fair."

"No, it's okay, Rosie. I'm just stunned, that's all."

I lean down and hug my brother.

For half an hour, we babble and cry and babble some more,
until finally my story is more or less told. Over a cup of Barry's
Irish tea, I begin to get a sense of his life. This place is designed
for people like my brother, all handicap-accessible and with on-
call help available. A medi-lift to pick him up to take him to
his job delivering interoffice mail at a corporate office park. A
medi-lift to bring him back home. This program at the mercy
of a successful annual fund-raising campaign by the nonprofit
that runs it. Teddy is not quite independent, but better than he
might otherwise be.

For a moment it seems like everything that happened to
me will somehow be worth it if I can help my brother.

"You should have a dog. A service dog."

"Is that what he is?" He gestures toward Shadow, who is
sound asleep at my feet, stretched out so that he is an obstacle
to both of us, or a perimeter.

"No." For the first time, I admit to myself what Shadow is.
"He's more of a therapy dog. It's what I did—I trained them,
Teddy. Service dogs."

"When?"

"In prison. It was—is a program. It works. You'd have
someone to pick up what you drop, shut off the lights."

"I can clap for that. And I have a grabber stick."

"Shark, my first dog, has made it possible for his person,

who is now maybe my best friend, to live alone and have a job. She lives in New York City."

"I live alone. I have a job."

"You live in a group home."

"That's not how I describe it." There's the old Teddy, the one with the scowl. The one mad at the world.

"I'm sorry. I'm a little sensitive about living in an institutional setting. This is certainly better than that."

The scowl doesn't lighten. It intensifies, as if he's just realized the elephant is in the room. "What happened, Rosie? Why did you leave us?"

Is this the party line? I left them? That I wasn't pushed out because I was making a life for myself? I almost say this, but then hold my tongue. "How's Mom? Is she all right? Brenda said I should go see her, and I got the impression that something was the matter."

Teddy manipulates himself away from the table, around Shadow, to stare out the picture window. I can tell that his low-set view can't give him anything but a look at the collection of stunted trees that form the landscaping of the courtyard. Maybe the heads of people walking by. Limited.

"Teddy? Is there something you don't want to tell me?"

He shrugs, always an awkward gesture, since he can barely lift his left arm. "How can I know what I do or do not want to tell you? You are a stranger to me. How long has it been? Six years? More if you count those months you left us to work out Dad's terminal illness and how to defend our home against eminent domain." He puts one palm on the windowpane. I can almost hear Mom yelling at him not to touch her clean window. "You were gone from us even before that. You couldn't wait to leave, and getting into that fancy college just started the transition from our sister, their daughter, to a stranger who looked down on us."

"That is so not true!" We could be our elementary school selves.

"Isn't it? Do you remember how you kept correcting my grammar?"

"I did that?"

"You did."

"I didn't want you to be handicapped. I mean . . ."

We both heard what I'd said and spontaneously laugh.

"Did you think perfect grammar would make anything better for me?"

"It couldn't hurt." Shadow is no longer recumbent, but sitting up, his eyes following the conversation, his ears at the alert. "So, you still haven't told me what's going on with Mom."

Teddy rolls himself away from the window, turns his chair to face me. "There's nothing wrong with her that getting a life for herself wouldn't cure. She's being passed around from Paulie to Frankie to Pat. Bobby's the only one who won't take her, because he lives in a place not a lot different from this one. Too small."

"Is she depressed?"

"Probably."

"Is she getting help?"

"No. Not that I know of."

I sit down on the couch. Shadow rests his head in my lap and I stroke his ears. I feel a wash of guilt. I should have pushed harder to break through her silence. What kind of daughter am I, what kind of woman, to give up so easily?

"How long has she been like this?"

"Since Dad died."

"So why hasn't anyone told me? If not Paulie, you, Teddy. I feel like I was shunned. And I don't know why."

"Mom is a very powerful woman and she forbade us to."

"And you grown men kowtowed to her?"

He has the good grace to blush. Shadow leaves me and waltzes over to Teddy. Again, he drops his big head into someone's lap and gets an ear scratching as a reward. Teddy looks up at me. "Tell me more about service dogs."

"I can introduce you to one," I say.

Meghan

The text from Rosie reads *When can I give you a call?* This is followed by six happy faces, which should drive Meghan into hitting the call button to find out what is going on, but she doesn't. This is not a good time at all. *Will call you when I can,* she replies, and leaves the phone on the table. She simply doesn't have the strength to fake happy.

Meghan pulls away from the kitchen area and motors into the living area. Marley sits on the couch, his dog at his feet, or more accurately, *on* his feet. He stares straight ahead at the television. He is very upright, very stiff, as he has been ever since the most recent mass shooting. He doesn't have the sound on; he uses the closed captioning instead of having to hear the continual replay of video from phones recording the mayhem, the barrage, broadcast over the networks. His big hands haven't stopped shaking. Spike has done her best, pressing herself into him, resting her head on his feet, nosing his hands until he grabs her fur. Meghan has done the best she can. He won't stop watching, and he won't talk. She has seen only mild episodes of his PTSD; this shooting has caused Marley to spiral into a full-blown panic attack. He cries and makes no apology for it. She can't get him to eat; she can't get him to rest. She has called in sick because he can't bear to let her leave the apartment.

To be fair, Marley had warned her. When she cried to him about her own fears, he warned her that his were a bigger issue in terms of their relationship. She might be afraid of intimacy, he said, but he was just simply afraid. Most days, he told her, he could pretend he wasn't. Spike helped normalize his world. Having Meghan in his life made him feel good. But on days like this, when the sound and fury of senseless violence made this country look like the worst of Afghanistan, then there was nothing he or anyone could do to mitigate his panic.

"Can you call Dr. Markowsky?"

"He'll only tell me to come in. I can't. Not yet."

"Would he prescribe anything?"

"Maybe."

"Do you want me to call him?"

Marley takes her damaged hand in his. "Do you have any oxy left?"

Meghan hasn't used her painkillers with any frequency in months, but she keeps a prescription for emergencies. She remembers how close she came to dependency on those little white pills, and her other hand goes out to touch Shark's back. "Yes. But they're meant for pain."

Marley lifts his chin to look into her eyes. His are bloodshot. "Ain't that what I'm going through?"

"You're safe. You don't have to worry." She knows he's not in a place where he can take in her words; she's uttering the same kind of babble a mommy offers an inconsolable child. But it's all she's got.

"Isn't that what all those people thought, too? Going to

have some fun. Less safe than I was in Afghanistan, walking down the street in full body armor."

"I was there, too, Marley. You forget that sometimes. I wore the armor; I commanded a platoon; I sent people just like you into buildings. I was blown up. So, yeah, I get your fear. I recognize it and honor it. But I'm not going to let some crazy asshole take my freedom from me out of fear. I'm going to keep on living the best life I can. The fullest."

Shark is on his feet; Spike, too.

Tenderly, Marley takes her face in his hands and kisses her. "Then let me touch you."

In Iraq, in Afghanistan, Meghan's troops needed her; they needed her orders, her direction. They needed to know that she was there, that she was in charge, and that she could be trusted with their lives. She reveled in that responsibility. She was content in it, comfortable being their leader. Marley Tallman needs her now. It is a far more harrowing responsibility, being someone's comfort.

She shuts off the incessant television coverage of the latest shooting, then moves herself from her chair to Marley's side on the couch, where he wraps her in his long arms. He whispers in her ear, her good one, "Sometimes I envy you."

"Why?"

"Because people can see your damage."

She has no answer for that. She certainly doesn't envy him, with his unpredictable and uncontrollable reactions to sound and circumstance. And then she thinks that not all of her damage is visible, and he certainly can't envy her that. "Touch me."

For a long time, the world condenses into the feel of his skin against her living skin, his touch, his slow kindness. For her, there is no magical release, no well-what-do-you-know moment, but there is a soft transition. She sighs and he kisses her fingertips.

Afterward, she invites both dogs onto the couch with them, and there they are, the foursome, holding and stroking, huddled together against the frightening things.

Meghan's stomach rumbles and she thinks that at least she's got feeling there. "I'm going to make lunch."

Marley shifts. "No, let me."

She stays put as he eases himself out from under the dogs and heads into the kitchen area. This is good, she thinks. He hasn't eaten in days. She watches him from the couch, making sure that he is moving, is really foraging for sandwich makings. She's drained, exhausted. It's harder sometimes to cope with his emotional pain than with her own physical pain. And yet she is undeniably content.

"Grilled cheese?"

"That would be lovely. And can you toss me my phone?"

Marley walks it to her.

"Rosie called. I've got to call her back."

"Tell her hi from me." Marley bends and kisses Meghan.

A sense of relief washes through Meghan. He's through the worst. And maybe she is, too.

Rosie wants Meghan to show her brother Teddy what a service dog can do.

Shark

He is exhausted. Spike is, too. They spoon together in the larger of the three dog beds in the apartment. The storm of emotion from their people has become a distant rumble. Their people have weathered it and now both dogs fall into a well-earned and deep sleep.

Rosie

It should be enough, this reunion with my youngest older brother, but it isn't. My original purpose in making the journey away from the solitary comfort of Dogtown was to see my mother. The urge to bail, to call it a day, is strong, but my spine has stiffened over the course of the past few years. "Where's your phone?" He tells me and I hand Teddy his phone. "Tell her whatever you want, but don't let her say no."

"Call her yourself."

"She won't answer me if she sees my number."

"I can dial, and you speak."

"She hangs up on me."

Teddy can't look at me. "Really?"

"I'm not going to demonstrate it for you. Just ask if she can drop by."

Teddy has told me that she makes a habit of dropping in, taking care of his laundry, making sure he has food in the fridge. For all his vaunted independence, he's still letting his clinically depressed mother take care of him. He says it makes her feel better. I think that it's part of her problem, having these chronically dependent children. She babysits her grandkids for the rest of them; for Teddy, she babies him.

"Hey, Mom. I'm good. Just wondering . . ." Teddy stares at me as he speaks to our mother. Just like in a dime-store novel, the look is daggers.

I flash back to our youth. Teddy in his chair, me dancing around him, wearing a towel as a cape and holding a Barbie doll in one hand, flying it past his face as if she were Wonder Woman, as if I were Wonder Woman. I see Teddy getting mad, yelling for Mom to make me stop. Defenseless against me and my mobility. My lack of deference toward his immobility.

I put my hands on his shoulders as he asks our mother to drop what she's doing and come see him. He doesn't have to work hard. As always, Teddy asks and Mom does.

I have paced and sat and paced and helped myself to a bottle of water uninvited, drinking it all in one long swallow, and still my mouth is dry. Teddy has said nothing. He's set the stage and now he has left me to act out the story. He wheels himself into his bedroom, shuts the door. Stoughton and Randolph share a border, and within fifteen minutes I hear the key in the lock. My mother has her own key to Teddy's apartment. Why am I not surprised?

Shadow is beside me, his head lowered and his ears pricked at the sound of the knob turning. I grasp a handful of his neck skin, balance my weight against him, so, so grateful to have the bulwark of his presence as I face my mother.

She is nothing like the image I carry in my mind. The last time I saw her, my mother was a new widow, bent under the weight of having cared for a terminally ill husband for the better part of a year. A year that saw repeated hospitalizations and then permanent residence in the dining room, the room she had been so proud of as a young mother. The room where she had once been matriarch over joyful family gatherings, not death. She'd looked bruised and old in her belted trench coat and Naturalizer pumps, leaning first against Paulie and then Bobby as the priest intoned the words of the committal service over the casket.

This woman is straight and slender and dressed in Ann Taylor slacks. Only the Naturalizers on her feet resemble what I remember of my mother's sartorial habits, and even those are pretty trendy-looking. I realize that my father has been gone for almost seven years. I have been gone. It all seems to blend, one thing into another—my father's death, Tilley's death, Charles's death, my deathlike existence in prison. But months, even a year or more, had transpired between each of these events. Still, it is a blur, and as I look at my mother, I realize for the first time that the bulk of my twenties were spent in separation from her, from my family. I will be thirty-one this next birthday, and no longer a girl. I wonder if she will see that.

"Rosie." She says it almost as if she's not surprised to see me. Almost as if she's been waiting. I half-expect her to add "Took you long enough."

"Mom. I'm here."

"I can see that. Where's Teddy?"

"In his room. He's giving us a few minutes."

My mother starts down the short hall to the bedroom.

"Mom. Wait."

She rests one hand against the wall. Unlike me, she doesn't have a giant dog to support her. I leave Shadow with a quick *stay* gesture and reach out to touch her.

Most people will say that their mothers have shrunk, but mine seems taller, firmer, and far more rigid. "Don't."

"Mom. Don't keep pushing me away. I don't know why you hate me so much." I drop my hand, step back. Then I do as any good Irish woman would. I put the kettle back on the electric stove and heat water for tea. I grab three bags out of the Barry's box and a fresh cup for her; my used mug is still on the table beside Teddy's. I plop the bags into the cups, retrieve the milk from the fridge, and send Shadow to scratch on Teddy's bedroom door, pointing and saying, "Go get Teddy."

The dog does. His comprehension amazes me.

"Sit down, Mom."

To my relief, she does.

Teddy rolls back into the kitchen area. "I've got cookies."

I think that only the Mad Hatter's tea party could be any weirder.

With tea bags dunked and cookies shared, milk poured, sugar asked for and received, we finally face one another across the table. And say nothing. So I break the ice. "When I was in prison, the only tea you could get from the commissary was Salada. You remember Salada? The boxes used to come with those little ceramic animals. You had a collection of them, didn't you, Mom? Don't I remember a tiny horse and a goat?" Okay, I've used the *p* word. *Prison*. Let's get this party started.

"Where did you get the dog?" My mother asks this just as Shadow has nuzzled up to her, his expressive brown eyes beneath the bushy eyebrows seemingly beseeching a cookie from her, so it's not that much of a non sequitur.

"He showed up, where I live. Just sort of joined me."

"And where do you live?"

"On the edges of a place called Dogtown. In Gloucester. I'm the project manager for a family foundation renovating an antique house. For now, I'm living in it."

Okay, so the conversation is like one that any two strangers might have. It's a start. She hasn't left the building yet. Teddy dunks his Chips Ahoy.

"I trained dogs in prison." Again I use the word *prison*. Do

I detect a flinch in my mother? "I told Teddy he should look into acquiring a service dog. They can be such a help. And company, too."

"Can you imagine my shame?" Ah, now we're getting somewhere.

"Yes. But you have to remember that I was failed by my defense."

"I mean how you treated us. Throwing your family over for a rich snob."

"I killed that rich snob." I am not sorry for the words I've blurted, but I am a little shocked at them. "By accident, but I was leaving him. I was trying to get home that night. Brenda Brathwaite was coming for me."

"You were our only daughter; your duty was with us during that time. You chose Europe and diamonds and the glitter of New York over being a good daughter, helping me with your father. And with Teddy."

Teddy sits up straighter in his chair. "Leave me out of this."

"I came. I helped."

"Not enough. Swanning in every couple of weeks to spend half a day, that's not helping. And then threatening our very home? Siding with that man?"

"I have told you over and over, there was nothing I could do."

"Because he was your sugar daddy, your puppet master."

I won't lie; I was half-expecting this characterization of Charles. She's not wrong, not really. I *was* Eliza to his Henry Higgins. He not only dressed me; he chiseled away at my flaws—as he perceived them. Duty to family. Filial love. All eyes must be on him at all times. All his needs met in exchange for the trips, the rings, the clothes, the expensive haircuts. Loyalty to him. No distractions. "You're right. And I

was very young. I've learned a few things since then. You have
to give me a chance to mend things."

"Your father was very hurt."

I get up from the table. Shadow watches me but stays beside Teddy. I dump out the dregs of my tea into the sink, which
is filled with dirty dishes. There is no dishwasher in this starter
apartment. I grab a sponge and turn the water on full blast. I
don't want her to see me cry. I don't want her to know that
she's gotten to me.

"Mom, that's not a fair statement." This from Teddy. "He
didn't know she wasn't there. Not at the end."

If Teddy intends this to help, it doesn't. It just serves to
hammer home the fact that I was absent when he passed and
that is something no one, not even I, has forgiven me for. So I
say so. "I wasn't there, and not a day goes by that I don't feel
terrible about it." I turn away from the sink. "But"—I point my
soapy finger—"you were the one to throw me out."

"I didn't."

"No, Paulie was the one to shut the door. But you never
stopped him."

Our voices are starting to rise, and I hope that the neighbors are all out on Saturday errands. I hope that the receptionist in the foyer doesn't start to worry, or, worse, call for help.
But at the same time, it feels *good*. Not so much the argument,
but the fact that we are in the same room, facing each other. I
have been so very alone. For some reason, Susannah comes to
mind. She was very alone, too, except for her dog. As I have
been except for mine. She'd accepted what life had thrown at
her, moving into that hovel in Dogtown, making her house
calls, keeping body and soul together with whatever she could
find to earn or barter for. I shrug on a little of her courage and
walk over to my mother, who has her teacup clenched between

her hands. I set my hands on her shoulders. "Mom, I love you. It's okay if you don't love me, but you're not going to lose my love."

Teddy very quietly, for a man in a wheelchair, leaves the table and opens the front door. He snaps his fingers at Shadow, who follows him without my say-so.

My mother and I are in the room alone together. I have so few memories of its ever being this way; there was always someone else in the room, in the house. Teddy primarily. A constant presence. We were never the mother/daughter pair to go shopping together or cook together or share girlie chat. Although I was assured I was the longed-for daughter, now I wonder. Maybe I was just a mistake.

My mother lets go of her grip on the cup. She takes her right hand and touches mine, which is resting on her shoulder. Pats it. Her hand is very warm, very soft. I can smell the Herbal Essence in her hair—the same fragrance I remember from my youth. "Where did you get that awful dog?" We're back at the beginning.

"He came to me."

"And you say that you train dogs?"

"I did. It was a program that paired puppies to be trained as service dogs with prisoners, and, Mom, it made all the difference in my life."

"Would Teddy really benefit?"

"Yes."

"Will you help us look into it?"

"Gladly." I gently squeeze her shoulders.

As I drive away, Shadow once again recumbent on the backseat, I call Meghan again. This time, she answers and I win this round of telephone tag. I quickly fill her in on Teddy and my suggestion that she come demonstrate Shark for him. "Your brother?" Meghan knows all about my family dynamics.

"Yeah." I am filled with a happiness I haven't had in many a year. "My brother."

Traffic through the tunnel is thick, but I don't care. Maybe it isn't that I'm *filled* with happiness; maybe it's closer to say that I've been emptied. The weight of my estrangement from my family is gone. We will never be perfect, but at least we can be together. Grievances will no longer be a wall between us. Of course, this assumes that Paulie and the rest of them will be persuaded to come around to accepting me back in the fold. By the strength of the hug that my mother gave me when we parted, I think she'll make that happen.

Shadow

He is very happy to be back in the car, heading north. The swirl of emotion that he's observed coming from Rosie has his nerves on edge. The man and the other woman were so hard to befriend, and yet he has the sense that they are very well known to Rosie. It wasn't just the touching at the end of the visit, something that he's begun to expect from her; it was the way they all handled their mugs, and some of the expressions on their faces were so like Rosie's, even the timbre of their voices. When he and Rosie left, he had the distinct impression that this would not be the last time they saw these people.

As she drives, Rosie is making conversation, and although he can't understand all of her words, or those of the voice coming out of the ceiling, he does pick up on the general tenor of happiness Rosie is exuding. He's never sensed this much of it in her before, and it makes him think that something is changing.

Rosie

11th December 1832. Have bidden Goody Mallory's shack good-bye. With relief, I have accepted Dr. Bellingham's invitation to board with him. In exchange, I will attend those cases not requiring his particular attention. He has kindly allowed me the dog. He says that his son will benefit from the dog's companionship.

*   –Susannah Day's journal.*

I am sitting in the historical society's reading room. Shelley Brown is opposite me. Beside me, in its archival box, is the portion of the journal that has been in my possession. Shelley has had the society's librarian bring out the remainder of the journal, and we wear white cotton gloves to look at it. "She's saved."

"Saved?"

"From Dogtown. Dr. Bellingham has offered her a place to

live." I feel tears prick. I take a big breath. "The Homestead Trust will pay to have it digitized."

Shelley gives me a wondrous smile. "That is really good news." She accepts the box from me with as much dignity as if I had been handing her the Host. "Would the family spring for getting the whole journal done? Access for everyone."

"I don't see why not, but maybe we'd better have a cost estimate done before I ask." I'm getting better at the project manager mentality. Cost, cost, cost.

It feels a little bit like I'm sending a favorite aunt to a nursing home, this giving up of Susannah's journal. She has kept me company through many a long, dark night in my secluded old house. Her voice has kept me from feeling completely devoid of human contact. I can almost hear her speaking voice. I think she would be an alto. Her voice never pitches up; she never whines. Her lines are declarations, not complaints. She cares about her neighbors even as they show little care for her. See how I've put her in the present?

After I leave Shelley and the journal, I take a detour that leads me to one of the older cemeteries, the one with the Bellingham cenotaph. Tucker's family's graves have recently been groomed, mums in fall red and gold have been planted. When I told him that I'd been to see my mother and brother, he gave me this look of surprised satisfaction and then put his arm around me. "Good. Good." And then he went back to filling nail holes in the Sheetrock. I stand here at his family plot and see how he is more alone than I am. He's got his work and he's got his weekend visits from his kids, but he's also got time to take care of this sad place. I never hear him speak of a date, or a lady friend. Any number of times now we've shared a restaurant meal, coincidentally having chosen the same place at the same time. He and his business partner, who was also his best childhood friend, bowl once a week and sometimes grab beers after work, but I've come to the conclusion that maybe that's the sum total of Tucker Bellingham's social life. I would think that every middle-aged divorcée in Gloucester would be after him. He's attractive, if in a bearish way.

I move on from Tucker's family plot, studying each gravestone along the way to see if I can answer the question that is dangling in front of me. If Susannah ended up essentially Edward Bellingham's nurse/housekeeper, did she stay there for the rest of her life, or did she end up going back to Marshfield? The very last entry in the pages that I have been reading of her journal mention a letter from a nephew with an invitation to come to Marshfield, to help his new wife with their baby. Women were indeed chattel. Come not because you need a home with family, but because you will be useful. I secretly hope that she told him to kiss off; where was he when she was living in Dogtown?

Shadow is sniffing all around the most ancient of the collection of gravestones, almost as if he's able to identify the tenants below us, who are, of course, no longer so much as dust. I linger, reading the epitaphs, the remarkable and the unremarkable notations, all that is left of these people; no one is alive who can remember who they were, whether they were kind or mean, fun-loving or dour. Here and there, a familiar name from Susannah's diary. This Alma Pierce, could this be Susannah's gossipy neighbor? Here is a Richard Daltry. I recall the Daltry name from her list of patients. There, his wife, Anna. I get this weird little thrill to recognize names. It's a little bit like finding Jane Eyre's grave. Names in a book become names on a gravestone that I can touch. I begin to leave pebbles on the stones. *You are never dead until no one remembers you.*

Shadow has come to a stone across the lane behind the Bellingham cenotaph. It's a granite stone, no doubt quarried at Halibut Point, in Rockport. He has his nose deep in the thin grass. He throws me a look and I get my answer. The dog has found it for me; this is Susannah Day's resting place. I bend and scrape off lichen that obscures the lettering. I'm hoping, I guess, that these words will tell me everything I want to know about her last days. At the very least, I know that she did live out her days here in Gloucester.

Benjamin Day, lost at sea 1832; Susannah, his wife, died 1834. Healer. Friend.

Someone cared enough that she isn't totally alone in death; now she is with Benjamin. But it's the two little descriptive words, *Healer* and *Friend* that move me to tears.

I wake up in the middle of the night with the dog draped across my middle. He's nuzzling me, and for a nanosecond, I dream that I am being made love to. What I have been dreaming is far from that of being loved. I have been dreaming of Charles. It isn't an exaggeration to say that I haven't dreamed of him in a very long time, but this new threat from his mother has re-ignited the long-suppressed fears. Before I was sent to prison, I dreamed of him every time I closed my eyes. As much as he filled my thoughts in the day, he expanded his presence into my nightmares, appearing most often as a heavy weight crushing me beneath it. Sometimes the weight was a bar of iron; other times, it was a giant bell, and I was under it. But I always knew that it was Charles in his metaphorical guise. I would wake up gasping, sucking in air, as if I were being suffocated. Once I was in prison, the dreams of suffocation, the bearing of a great weight devolved into being caged, and no waking ever helped dispel that. My waking and my dreaming were one and the same. Until Shark, until the program that moved me from cornered to capable.

Shadow licks my cheek, dismounts. This time, I really do have to suck in a lungful of air; my dog isn't light. I sit up.

Dawn is graying the sky, the first intimation of the new day. It's late enough in the fall that I know it's already close to six-thirty. Hardly early for someone having to make the trek to Connecticut and get there by one o'clock. I'm still sleeping in the kitchen, even though the two upstairs rooms are now empty and insulated, although not yet painted. Maybe when they are, I'll move up. But for now, the kitchen is cozy with the wood-stove, and certainly convenient should I have to get up in the night, as the only functioning bathroom is still the one off of it. However, the upstairs rooms, with their six-over-six windows, do afford a nice view of the trees, full green pine and denuded oaks. It's not the view that Susannah and Benjamin would have had—that would have looked out over stony fields—but the regrowth is pretty in its own way. I've gotten used to the clack and squeak of windblown limbs. They no longer frighten me. Not as much as the day's agenda of deposition and the unnerving sense that I might lay eyes on Mrs. Foster.

One thing is certain: Although Tucker has offered to keep an eye on Shadow, that dog is going with me.

Rosie

I dress in my new trousers, slip into the luxury of my new silk blouse. It needs a little something, but I no longer have a box full of nice jewelry. I insert my only pair of earrings into my earlobes; after so long with not so much as a stud, the plain gold hoops were my first out-of-prison purchase. I have no idea what's become of the two years' worth of presents that Charles bestowed upon me. The clothes, the jewels, the really nice coats, the shoes. I walked into Mid-State Women's Correctional Facility in my plain black skirt and blue blouse and walked out of it six years later in the same outfit. It begs the question of what can Mrs. Foster possibly think suing me will get her other than me back in her life, live and in living color. Sitting across from her in some courtroom, going over the tragedy of her only son's death in minute detail yet again? Revenge is such an out-dated motivation, good only for television productions and romance novels.

My calendar's notification alert reminds me that I'm due in Connecticut at one. Even if the traffic sucks, I've got plenty of time. It's only seven-fifteen. Shadow stares at his still-empty bowl. In the dim light of the west-facing kitchen, his gray is pronounced. Susannah never referred to the dog who followed her around by any name. Did he outlive her? Did he meld back into the woods of Dogtown whence he'd come? Whence I really believe my dog came? This place, isolated on its narrow road, edging against the haunted precincts of Dogtown, still sets me off on flights of fancy despite the physical improvements. For the first time, I wonder what I will do when this project is completed. Where will I go? I feel the first glimmerings of nostalgia for this kitchen. It has been a sanctuary without doubt, albeit one with challenges. Shadow nudges his bowl with his nose. Looks back at me. Who's trained whom? I think.

I've put the black-and-white photograph of Grandmother Baxter with her dog, Boy, on the mantel above the kitchen fireplace. If there is one nice thing about this trek to Connecticut for the deposition, it's that I'll be staying with Carol tonight. Needless to say, I'm hoping that Meghan and her beau will be there. I have yet to meet Marley, and I'm excited about the prospect. Anyone who is important to Meghan is important to me.

I dump kibble into Shadow's bowl and debate making coffee or just heading out and grabbing some on the way. I hear a truck horn. It's early, but Tucker often catches me in my pajamas. Well, he won't today. We have spent too much time together in this house to stand on ceremony, and he comes in without knocking, trusting that his horn will have alerted me.

"Here." He hands me a paper cup of coffee, sets a white bag from the Stop & Shop bakery on my table. "You need your strength for the journey."

"Funny." I pop the lid off, add sugar and a dash of milk. Hand Tucker the carton.

"You look, um, nice."

"You mean dressed like a grown-up?"

"Hmm." He sips his coffee, then opens the bakery bag and extracts a sticky bun.

"So, what's your plan for the day?" Don't I sound all clerky?

"I got a guy coming to estimate the paint job."

That sounds like something I should be present for, and I say so.

"I'd say yes, but he's only got today to come by. Didn't you say that you can't get out of this trip?"

"I did." Needless to say, I haven't apprised Tucker of what this Tuesday trip to Connecticut is all about. As far as he knows, it's Homestead Trust business and Pete Bannerman is simply the Trust's lawyer.

"You want to pick out the colors?" Tucker lays a trifold sheet of sample colors, all from the Williamsburg Collection.

I shrug. "Whatever is authentic."

He gives me a pleased smile. As if Tucker Bellingham would tolerate a shade of cream that wasn't period-correct.

I go to the fridge and pull out a yogurt. No sticky buns for me, thank you very much. "I found Susannah Day's gravestone yesterday. She's behind the Bellingham plot. Close but not in it." I show Tucker the picture of the headstone on my phone. *Friend. Healer.*

"That's really nice." He hands me back my phone and then sits, stroking his goatee for a meditative moment. "I hope that my ancestor was good to her."

"I think he was. I think that he respected her." I sit down at the table. "She never said a bad thing about him in her journal. I mean other than noting that he was horning in on her practice."

"That's a Bellingham. Kind of oblivious."

Oblivious. I wonder.

Maybe it's time for Tucker to know a little bit more about me than that I'm the project manager foisted on him by the

Homestead Trust. "Tucker, I think there's something you should know about me."

And so I tell him that I spent almost six years behind bars for an accident. That I was advocated for on the recommendation of Meghan Custer; that I was subsequently employed by the Homestead Trust. I don't look at him while I give him the thumbnail version; it's the first time I've rehearsed this particular phase of my life and I'm a little wobbly in my delivery. In some ways, Tucker is the perfect audience. I don't actually work for him, so he can't fire me. He's not a boyfriend, so he can't dump me. He's not a relative, so he can't shun me or deny me. He's a guy who is a workplace friend, and if he pulls his friendship, I'll be sad, although maybe not devastated.

"So, there you have it." I begin to bustle around the kitchen, tying up the half-empty trash bag, running water to rinse out the sink. I realize that I've been sweating a little as I've told Tucker my story and now I'm chilled in my thin blouse. I haven't stirred up the woodstove this morning, so I pop open the firebox, poke the embers, and add a few pieces of kindling. He'll be warm while he waits for the painter.

"Let me do that. You don't want to put a hole in that nice blouse." Tucker moves me aside, sets two pieces of cordwood into the firebox, closes the door. "You should get on the road; traffic is going to be a bear up the line."

"I know."

"I'll text you the estimate if he gets it to me before you get home tomorrow."

"Sounds good."

Shadow precedes me out the back door. I snap the handle of my wheelie suitcase up. Tucker takes it out of my hand. He follows me out to where Shadow waits to be let into the car. I pop the hatch; Tucker sets the bag inside.

"Okay, then. I'll see you soon."

Tucker shakes his shaggy head. "Thanks. For telling me."

"I had to."

A slow grin comes to his face, and he strokes his goatee. "You know, I already knew. But I'm glad you wanted to tell me."

"All this time?"

"Pretty much. Pete called me the second day you were here."

"Jeez." I start to laugh and open my arms to give him a hug. Just to continue with the bear analogy, it really is like being bear-hugged to receive Tucker's embrace in return.

Tucker was right. I had completely underestimated, and the traffic was horrible. I barely make it to my destination in time. Rather than having a little breathing space so that I could take Shadow for a walk, collect my thoughts, and power through this, I am still shaking from the intensity of having to speed the last hour and the two near misses that I'd dodged along the way. And I have to pee.

Pete Bannerman's vintage Oldsmobile is parked in the lot beside the courthouse. I slide my car in next to it, take a deep breath, and climb out, opening the back door for Shadow.

"Rosie! We were getting worried." Pete appears from across the parking lot. It is only the second time I've seen him in the flesh, and once again I am struck by his jockeylike build. This time, he's in a charcoal gray suit with a crisp white shirt and a blue-and-red-striped rep tie. I can't help but imagine that he was the butt of many a frat house prank. It makes me like him even more.

"Traffic was horrible. I thought I'd allowed plenty of time."

"No matter." He spots Shadow, who is lifting his leg against a handy signpost. "Whoa. Are you going to tell me this is a service dog?"

"What, and start the day off with perjury?"

"He's going to have to wait in the car."

"Then I'm not going in. I need him."

"Then I guess he's a service dog. What do they call them? Emotional support?"

"Well, that's exactly what he is. His name is Shadow and he's my emotional support dog." I snap a leash to Shadow's collar. "Don't forget, that's what I did in prison, trained dogs."

"So he'll be on his best behavior."

"I guarantee it."

"Shall we?" Pete gestures toward the steps leading into the courthouse. I swallow hard. The last time I saw those steps, I was being escorted in. I wore orange; my hands were manacled. The truth is, I didn't go up those steps that time; I was led in through a discrete back door, made to wait in a cell, and then taken into the courtroom. Despite that, I truly believed that I would be set free that day, that I would walk down those steps. I sat where defendants sit; my feckless public defender was glancing at her phone, texting back and forth to someone who was far more interesting than I. I looked out at the few people in the courtroom, Cecily Foster and her legal team, Charles's cousin, and a couple of friends there for support. For me, no one. No one.

The deposition will not take place in a courtroom, but in a small room down the long, cold hallway.

"Pete, can I have a minute? I've got to . . ."

He nods. "I'll let them know that you're here."

I ask Shadow to sit and stay and then push open the heavy oaken door to the ladies' room. And there is Cecily Foster.

What's interesting is that she doesn't seem to recognize me. Dressed as I am, in the plebeian attire of an average woman of little means, I have a split second of leisure to study her, to see for myself that she actually doesn't have horns. She's wearing a

silver gray suit made of some shiny material that absorbs the
faintly pink glow of sunshine coming through the frosted
window. She's carefully drying her hands with a rough brown
paper towel. The knuckles on her left hand bear the weight of
thousands of dollars' worth of diamonds—her engagement
ring, an anniversary ring, and, on her pinkie, the ring that, if
I am not mistaken, Charles had given me.

I had been assured that I would not see Cecily Foster during this part of the process. Somebody had gotten that wrong.

I enter the nearest stall, fairly confident that she hasn't
recognized me and that maybe she'll be in the deposition room
before I finish. I wait, rip off a handful of toilet paper. Wait
some more, but there is no sound of heels heading for the door,
clicking against the white honeycomb-shaped ceramic tile.
There is no sound except the slow wiping of hands with harsh
brown paper towel. I realize that she's waiting for me.

I can sit here like a coward until Pete gets so nervous he
comes banging on the door. Or I can tidy myself up and stalk
out of this stall, wash my hands, and leave with my dignity
intact.

This woman has intimidated me for the last time. I have
been among women for whom intimidation is an Olympic
sport. Giving it and taking it. I have been surrounded by men
who were even better at it, adding the threat—and sometimes
action—of sexual predation to the mix. What more can Cecily
Foster do to me that her son hadn't already done? Kicked my
self-esteem to the curb. Went beyond cruel to punish me. She
wants to sue me for wrongful death? I should countersue for
mental cruelty.

"Rose?" Her voice has changed. It sounds reedy. Or maybe
she's as nervous at seeing me as I am at seeing her.

I flush the toilet, pull myself together, and exit the stall.

"Hello, Cecily." I won't further infantilize myself by call-

ing her Mrs. Foster. I wash my hands, running the water hard,
hitting the soap dispenser three times. Scrub, scrub, scrub. I
look at my image in the spotty mirror over the sink and wish
that I'd done better than just pulling my plain brown hair into
a loose bun; that I'd put on lipstick instead of ChapStick. I can
see her behind me. As usual, she is immaculately put together,
but there is something different about her, and then I realize
that during the intervening six years since I last saw her, she's
aged beyond where Botox allows the impression of youthful-
ness. She looks like she's wearing a mask, a Cecily Foster
mask. I think she's had a face-lift, and instead of bestowing a
Fountain of Youth rejuvenation, it's turned her into her own
caricature.

"I didn't think that I would see you here." Her voice is
whispery, and I wonder if there is something wrong with her
vocal cords.

For some reason, the last time this woman and I met in a
bathroom comes to mind. The night of Charles's unfortunate
accident. How she admonished me about my "behavior."
This time, I turn and look right at her. "Neither did I. I really
didn't think that I would ever have to see you, or hear you,
or think about you again. I've been punished enough, don't
you think?"

"If I did, we wouldn't be here now. You plea-bargained your
way to a twenty-year slap on the wrist that, somehow, you've
managed to get out of. Rose, you killed my only child."

I can't dispute that. The facts stand for themselves. "And
you and I both know that it was an accident. Wrongful? Perhaps he shouldn't have walked around behind the car. Perhaps
he shouldn't have gotten drunk and been incapable of driving home. Perhaps he—"

"Stop."

I hear this faint scratching at the ladies' room door. It's

Shadow. His acute hearing has picked up on the scene behind that door. I glance at the door but don't open it. Cecily and I face each other over that honeycomb tiled floor. I haven't shut the faucet off tightly enough, and there is a slow drip coming from it. It plinks into the sink. I lean back and tighten the faucet but don't take my gaze off Cecily. Is it snakes you have to keep your eyes on, or lions, to make sure they don't strike? With her artificially wide-open eyes, it is the cobra I imagine, hooded, angry, ready to bite. Until, to my utter shock, tears start to flow from her wide eyes, and her immobile face struggles with the emotion behind the mask.

I pull a few tissues from the box on the counter, hand them to her. She dabs her eyes, then buries her face into the wad. Her shoulders shake, and I do the only thing possible: I touch her. I have never touched her before. She has never embraced me, not even after two years of my being Charles's girlfriend. I put my arm around her shoulders, shocked at how bony she is beneath the shantung silk of her suit. She is half a head shorter than I am, another shock. To me, she had always seemed towering. What is even more shocking is that she lets me. Indeed, she presses her head into my shoulder. What else can I say? "Go ahead, let it out."

The storm is over in less than two minutes and she swiftly collects herself. "Oh dear. I look horrible. I can't . . ."

"Cecily?" I pull a towel out of the dispenser and wet it. "I'm sorry. I'm really sorry."

And I am. I have never told her that. "I *am* sorry, not just because this horrible mistake changed my life forever but also because it changed yours. I understand. Charles was your son and you loved him and he was all you had. I get that. I never intended for what happened to happen, despite how angry I was. How unhappy." There, it's out. The words that I have withheld from her for so long. Words that, maybe, I've owed her. "I'm so sorry."

Shadow woofs softly at the ladies' room door. Pete will be charging in here any minute to see what's keeping me. I wait for her to say something. Anything. She pats beneath her eyes with the wet paper towel. Plucks a dry one from the dispenser. Pulls open her handbag and roots around, extracting an old-fashioned compact. She leans over the sink, and I realize that we're done here. I'm dismissed.

"Good-bye Cecily."

"Rose. Thank you." She keeps her gaze on her own image as she says this, but there is a faint smile, a release.

Shadow greets me as I exit the restroom, acting as if I have been gone forever.

Shadow

This place is so beyond his experience that he nearly misbehaves when Rosie closes the heavy door between them. He wants to call to her, to bark, to let her know that she shouldn't walk away from him. That man, the small one, keeps a careful hand on Shadow's collar, but the dog figures that if he jumped up and tugged, the man would let go. It's only that because he can smell Rosie behind that door, and hear her voice, that he remains fixed in place.

The words are indistinct, Rosie's and another woman's, but the pain is not.

Epilogue

I stand at the second-story window, looking out over the back-yard, and spot two deer munching on the lilies I planted in the fall. Why the dog doesn't chase them off, I cannot say. He seems to have a détente with them, as much as he'd assault any pred-ator that should wander into the yard. Not that any ever have. I have a dog.

Today is my last day in the Homestead. I'll miss this view and the easy access to Dogtown, but I'm excited to finally have a place of my own, one with all the amenities a modern apart-ment can offer, including, thank God, a dishwasher. I've de-cided to stay in Gloucester; it's been a refuge and a place of healing, and although I could, maybe should, go back to the Boston area, Cape Ann is close enough to my family that we can see one another anytime we so desire. Besides, Tucker of-fered me a job as his office manager. He's never had one before, and I can't wait to get started whipping his business into ad-ministrative shape. I'll be the voice of Dogtown Construction.

The Baxter family will be arriving in dribs and drabs for

the dedication ceremony Carol has invented. There are trestle tables set up already and a bunch of rented folding chairs. Rather than have everyone struggle to come up with a pot-luck item and then have to travel some distance, they had me hire a caterer. I had carte blanche and have organized a traditional New England lobster boil. The weather gods have graced us with a perfect July day, not too hot, and only a little overcast, with an onshore breeze.

Meghan and Marley will come with Don and Carol. Meghan's mom and dad are scheduled to fly into Boston and drive up by noon. The rest of the far-flung clan have either already arrived in the area or will be here soon. My mom and Teddy are coming. After meeting Meghan and Sharkey, Teddy has decided to pursue getting a service dog of his own. He's applied to the prison program I was involved with, and I'm not sure how I feel about that.

Pete Bannerman is coming from Connecticut. Even though Cecily Foster dropped the suit against me, and the house is done, he's become a friend, and I'm looking forward to seeing him today.

The house has the feel of an empty stage just waiting for the actors to appear. I think back at how different it was a mere ten months ago, a tumble-down wreck of an old woman's neglected home. Its renaissance as the summer home of a flock of that old woman's descendants has been astounding, and I have to credit Tucker Bellingham with being stubborn and exacting.

I walk through the rooms, admire the way the wide plank floors gleam with Butcher's wax, the way the Delft tiles surrounding the two parlor fireplaces draw the eye. I've put the antique candlesticks that I discovered upstairs on the marble mantels that Tucker found on eBay. In the bright summer sunlight coming through the six-over-six restored windows, the polished paneling that flanks the "good" parlor fireplace fairly glows. The new but authentic wrought-iron latch reveals the hidden wood box.

I feel Susannah's presence.

I have so little to pack that I haven't done more than stow the folding cot, my sleeping bag, and my few dishes in the back of my car. Somehow, the act of moving my things has upset Shadow, and he's been pacing and whining every time I take an armload out to the car. "It's okay, Shadow. We're going to be very happy in our new place. You'll love it." It wasn't all that easy to find a pet-friendly rental, especially with the size of my pet, but I did. There was no way I was going to leave Shadow behind. He has been my rock. With him by my side, I fear no man.

The Dog

The air is warm and carries upon it the scent of roasting meats and baking pies, the pungent scent of boiled vegetables, and the oceanic scent of lobster. I lick my lips, shake my head, the better to taste the scent in the air. From a safe distance, I watch this gathering of disparate humans—a few children in constant motion, some men, mainly women. From these last will I choose the next woman to serve. I will choose from those who sit on the outside of the circle. I know already that someone needs me. For her, I will walk out of the shadows. I am a watcher. I am a guardian.

Acknowledgments

This was a complicated book and I was pulled to safety several times by my incredible agents, Annelise Robey and Andrea Cirillo. Thanks also to the whole team at the Jane Rotrosen Agency—Chris Prestia, Danielle Sickles, Donald Cleary, Julianne Tinari, Michael Conroy, Sabrina Prestia, Hannah Rody-Wright, Ellen Tischler, and Gena Louque.

To Jennifer Enderlin, queen of editors, who guided me toward the best version of this story with patience and vision, to you my constant gratitude.

Thanks to the excellent team at St. Martin's Press, especially Rachel Diebel, who so ably makes things happen. And to Lisa Senz, Young Lim, Jordan Hanley, Brant Janeway, Lisa Davis, Clare Maurer, and Matie Argiropoulos.

To Carol Edwards, copy editor par excellence, who, as always, saves me from embarrassing myself. Thank you.

Tom Dresser introduced me to Dogtown and this book would never have been conceived without his history, *Dogtown: A Village Lost in Time*. Kathy Schad of Gloucester was incredibly helpful with getting a flavor of life on Cape Ann. Dagmar Lewis gave me some insights on the puppy training program in New York prisons. Thank you all.

I am deeply indebted to the Rev. Cristina Rathbone, who provided me with a view into the lives of women in prison. Any veracity in this book I owe to her.

Lastly, thank you Shelley Brown, Brenda and Leon Brathwaite for lending me your names.

This book has lived large in my imagination for a long time, and it is exactly that, a work of my imagination. Whereas I wanted to create a believable universe, it may be somewhat flawed. That's the joy of writing fiction.

Resources

Dogtown: A Village Lost in Time. Dresser Thomas. 1995, revised 2008.

A World Apart: Women, Prison and Life Behind Bars. Rathbone Cristina, Random House, 2005.

A Midwife's Tale. The Life of Martha Ballard, Based on Her Diary, 1785–1812. Ulrich, Laurel Thatcher. Vintage Books, 1990.